Cycle of Ages Saga:

Sands of Sorrow

Cycle of Ages Saga:

Sands of Sorrow

by

Jeremy Hicks & Barry Hayes

To Summer,
Enjoy your trip across the Sands of Sorrow.
Jeremy Hicks

Cycle of Ages Saga:

Sands of Sorrow

Copyright © 2015 Jeremy Hicks & Barry Hayes
Print ISBN: 978-0692540435
eBook ASIN: B015XYM7CQ

All rights reserved. No part of this book may be reproduced, duplicated, copied, or transmitted in any form or by any means without the express written consent and permission of the author.

This is a work of fiction. The names, characters, places, and incidents are fictitious or are used fictitiously. Any resemblance to any person or persons, living or dead, is purely coincidental.

Published by Broke Guys Productions

Cover Art by Rob E. Brown
Cover Design by Kevin 'Fritz' Fotovich
Interior by D. Alan Lewis

Dedication

We can never thank our family, friends, and fans enough for their love and support, especially those who enjoyed the tall tales and role-playing games that provided an outlet for our imaginations until we had the confidence to put it in writing.

More than anything, the Cycle of Ages Saga is for you.

With all our love,

J. Jeremy Hicks *Barry A. Hayes*

P.S. To the Mayan people, thank you for providing inspiration for our elven cultures, religion, languages, and more. You were always one of the more fascinating subjects in my anthropology classes. And I hope to visit your homeland one day soon. To the divine spirit of the ancient poet Ah Bam and his translator, John Curl, thanks for providing the basis for "Dor's Song" with "The Mourning Song of the Poor, Motherless Orphan" from The Songs of Dzitbalche. -- J.J.H.

FALTYR

N
Baraviel Sea
Sea Of Fallen Dragons
General Brack
West Brack
East Brack
Broken Lands
Tuk
Saj Confederacy
Maru
Northern Wastes
Ugra
Gulf Of Shang'ete
T'or Binel (Silent Brook)
The Spire
Crescent Bay
Zailya
Tumblerun
Empire Of Chi'kakal
Crimson Phoenix
Fransemouth
Barto
Yu
Xine
Nargavale
Norchgate
Thonesh
Ror
Pelican Gulf
Siobhan
Hermopolis
Arpichius
Grymsburg
Mok'Drular
The Jade Sea
Arpichia
Enech
Skyoonta
Kingdom Of Oparre
Uchenia
Mollinar
Sands Of Sorrow
Eastgate
Minoras
Asterion
Baax Sea
Laeg
Impurnim
Panglov
Nubari Sea
Zugura
Ar Islands
Logus
Aremychias
Xoc'ne
Gulf Of Oparre
Corr Deyratre
O'nal
Kingsport
Kolomat
Ch'ab
Moor'Dru
Qua
Myth
Sibal
Ireri Ocean
Porobal
K'akla Sea
Frolov Keep
Sea Of Moor'Dru

Chapter 1

Three shrouded figures padded across the terracotta roof of the Drunken Djinn Inn, and Kaladimus Dor followed. The stubble from his beard rubbed against the fabric concealing his narrow face. Tugging at the bothersome balaclava, Dor failed to see one of his confederates sidestep a loose piece of tile. Unaccustomed to footwear, much less crossing rooftops, he slipped when unfamiliar soles met unreliable shingle.

Dor's balance evaporated as quickly as his enthusiasm for their mission to recover a missing piece of the *Seadragon*, the Hallowed Vessel. He pitched sideways, only to be seized by an unseen hand. The Protectorate Mage found he could not breathe as the taut garment constricted around his throat. He gasped for air while his savior reeled him in like a floundering fish on a line.

The pressure eased before his consciousness fled completely. His dizziness increased as his unseen savior spun him like a top. When he came to a stop, he faced the stern, disapproving gaze of the hulking company captain. Dor smiled sheepishly. He recalled another occasion on which Breuxias had throttled him, only then he would have sworn the Brute had meant to take his life.

From strangler to savior.

And to think, Braigen had said he wasn't a people person. If only his master could see him now, prowling about on rooftops on a moonless night with not one but an entire company of companions, plotting the theft of an object of great power, ultimately for a greater good.

Dor hoped that last part was true. For all his friend's bluster and bravado, he had yet to be fully convinced that the Brute was the hero type. The mercenary still seemed disinterested in all but the most profitable pursuits, like their present caper. After all, he'd led them to the remote desert city of Eastgate to recover the *Seadragon*'s true figurehead, an enchanted bust of an aquatic wyrm taller and heavier than Breuxias.

For the foreseeable, Dor's true mission remained on hold. To be honest, he didn't know if he had a mission anymore, only a burden. The weight of the metal chest, secreted within the woven pack carried on his back, served as a constant reminder. With Salaac dead and Braigen missing, who knew what in the Nine Hells he was supposed to do with the damned thing. Dor's primary objectives had been to find it and deliver it to them in Moor'Dru. In the process, he was not to let it fall into the hands of the seditious Proleus faction or their powerful allies, such as King Orson's Mage Army and the Cult of Darconius.

"Much obliged," Dor offered.

Breuxias shushed him, adding in a whisper, "Damn fool wizard."

His footing restored, Dor crept along behind the taller man, until they reached the position of the other two robed figures. One wearing a dun-colored kaftan worked to remove terracotta tiles while another dressed in black used long, clawed fingers to unwind a coil of rope from around his waist.

Breuxias joined Katar, the dun-wearing junior guildsman, in the task of dismantling a section of shingling. As they labored, they produced a dark rectangular opening in the inn's roof. They stopped soon afterward, shifting only enough tiles to allow the largest of them to slip into the room beneath them.

Dor crouched beside Yax'Kaqix, his black-robed confederate, and watched as the elf performed his familiar rope trick. Yax wiggled his fingers with the practiced ease of a puppeteer. The coil came alive, snaked around the beam supporting the roof, and tied itself into place.

With the rope secured, the elf descended into the inn. Katar went next, followed by the Brute. Dor waited long enough to scan the sleeping city around him, listening for any tell-tale sign their nocturnal activities had been betrayed.

Dor's attention shifted to the colorful display beyond the high walls of Eastgate. The aurora danced and played over the desert sands to the north and west of the border city. Known as the Sands of Sorrow, the desolate area between Eastgate and the broken profile of the Meshkenet Mountains was a byproduct of the Cataclysm, the final apocalyptic battle between Artemis and Ra'Tallah. Dor shivered as he recalled his previous visit to that terrifying, twisted wasteland.

His allies' grumbling pulled Dor from his horrific reverie. With some considerable effort, he tore his lingering gaze from the hypnotic patterns swirling in the haunted desert's glowing skies. He took hold of the rope and lowered himself into the inn. The weight of the chest shifted within his pack, causing him to swing toward the wall. Luckily, the rope stopped short of sending him face first into the wall. Sighing with relief, he clung to the line and waited for it to cease swaying.

That blasted chest, it'll be the death of me yet.

Fortunately, the mage landed with more grace than he descended. He crept across the dusty floorboards to join the others by the door of the unoccupied room. They'd ensured its vacancy earlier by paying a beggar to rent it but stay elsewhere.

As Dor approached them, Yax whispered, "Sure you've got this?"

"Not a problem. They'll never know what hit 'em."

The elf nodded, turned to Katar, and said, "You take the door. I'll keep watch on the hallway."

The junior guildsman removed a small metal vial from his belt. Uncorking it, he administered the bulk of its contents to the door's iron hinges before applying the remainder to its brassy knob. Finished with his handiwork, he stowed the empty vial and edged the door inward. Without so much as a squeak or creak, the portal opened inch by inch. He stopped it once he'd provided enough clearance for the mage and his cumbersome backpack.

Katar closed the door behind him once the wizard was in the hallway. Bending down, Dor removed his head wrap and stuffed it under the lip of the entryway to form a seal. Straightening up, he allowed himself a moment to relax. He focused on the variety of soft sounds permeating the inn. Snores, sniffles, groans, and even a few moans floated to his attentive ears. The welcomed sounds of sleep and sensation would better facilitate his spell, one that would put those in range into a deep, blissful slumber.

Dor raised his arms as if prepared to conduct a symphony. Closing his eyes, he hummed softly through his thin lips. The melody of his lullaby rose and fell as his limbs moved with an ease and grace not typically seen from the clumsy young wizard. His open palms revolved around each other, never touching, as if circling some invisible sphere. Between them, particles of light danced and shimmered like micaceous glitter in the sun. When his humming stopped, his hands ceased to spin. The sparkling cloud of enchanted dust hung suspended within the invisible sphere of Aethyr energies channeled by the magician's weave.

He exhaled through pursed lips.

The particles in the cloud bloomed outward to fill the entirety of the corridor. The fae dust curled under doors where it sought out anyone within range of the spell. It snaked into noses, clogged eyes with sleep, and painted the victims' dreams with tranquil images meant to lull them into an ever deeper, more restful slumber. A collective yawn signaled their surrender to the weave.

Dor waited for the dust to dissipate before retrieving his balaclava. He tapped on the door to signal the rest of his team.

Team, he thought, relishing the sound of it. *Team* made him feel part of something greater than himself. And he hadn't felt that way in a long time. He'd always felt like an outcast, even among his peers on the island of Moor'Dru. He'd longed for something different.

Who knew I would find it among a company of thieves and mercenaries?

Despite the head coverings masking their faces, the human members of Finders Keepers yawned as they entered the hallway. For a fearful moment, Dor worried they might succumb to the spell's lingering effects, but they remained conscious.

Yax'Kaqix didn't blink much less yawn as he passed by Dor.

His voice barely above a whisper, Yax asked, "Did it work?"

"They're asleep. Well, asleeper, more asleep. Whatever."

"Is that everyone?"

Dor replied, "All except for the sentry downstairs."

"For your sake, I hope so," Breuxias added menacingly.

Yax made no noise as he padded toward the stairs at the end of the hall. Katar crept after him while Breuxias lingered at the junction. Dor waited until Yax and Katar descended the stairs before he moved away from the door to their escape route.

Reaching the end of the corridor, Dor hesitated as his eyes adjusted to the dimness of the stairwell. As the Brute caught up to him, the magician made his way from the first step to the second.

So far, so good, he thought.

CREAK!

Dor winced as the third step protested under his weight.

Breuxias jabbed him in the back and hissed, "Damn--"

"Fool wizard," Dor finished the curse for him. "I got it."

Dor cast his eyes about to make sure no one had been alerted to their presence. Instead, he saw Yax lower the stunned sentry to the floor while Katar stood watch at the front door of the inn.

Dor sighed with relief, finishing his descent with extra care.

"The street is clear," Katar said, turning back to them.

The junior guildsman removed the covering from his face to reveal a wide grin framed by a well-groomed moustache and goatee. His dark wooly hair, olive skin, and cosmopolitan tastes betrayed his Baax ancestry. A splintered form of the Baax Empire survived the Cataclysm, but its eastern remnant couldn't hold out against the onslaught of Gre barbarians from the north. The descendants of those redheaded invaders sat the thrones of Ror and the Crimson Phoenix as well as this evil land, the Kingdom of Oparre.

The very idea of being in Oparre again sickened Dor. He wanted to be well away from here before the sanguine war sweeping the main continent drew them into its maw, or the authorities here threw them into a prison to await trial. Upon conviction, they would either be burned alive or, if fortunate, extended the King's Mercy, the amputation of tongue and both hands. No human who wielded magic openly in Oparre escaped these fates for long, unless they bore the tattoo of the Royal Mage Army, the only magic-users trusted by King Orson.

A similar fate awaited Yax if caught. Orson had decreed that any elf, gnome, or other fae creature caught within Oparre's boundaries or any land claimed by its crown should be arrested, tried, and then executed as enemies of the state. Neither mercy nor quarter would be shown to those of the fae races, ancient allies of the dragonic god-kings that had once ruled Faltyr.

The genocidal king's decree had led to the Blood War. The crown of Oparre contested the border of the Nargawald and Silent

Brook forests, established by treaty centuries ago. The Winaq'che elves of Silent Brook did not respond lightly to invasion and genocide. Neither did their human allies in Ror or the Crimson Phoenix. The Brack Union and the faraway Empire of Chi'kakal had issued statements warning Orson that his expansionist policies could lead the entire continent of Ny into a world war. For now, the conflict spread east and north instead.

Flaunting the bloody decree, Yax'Kaqix pulled back the hood of his cloak, revealing his pronounced ears. Long and pointed, they were secured by a leather thong tied through his bone ear plugs.

His inhuman eyes flashed red in the dimness of the hearth light, their normal blue hue obfuscated by his large, dark pupils. Suddenly, they fixed on an object at the back of the expansive barroom.

Yax whistled lowly, almost inaudibly, drawing Dor's attention beyond the sea of tables and chairs. The longest bar in Eastgate stretched along the back wall of the Drunken Djinn Inn. Shiny brass and polished wood glowed in the firelight cast by the room's single giant hearth.

Impressive, but far eclipsed by the figure hanging above it.

The massive bust of a dragon, with scales shaped like fish, dangled from a thick iron chain. The height of a troll and the girth of horse, the piece had been carved from a single block of ironwood, the same species of tree used in the construction of the *Seadragon.* Judging by the Aethyr energies the item harbored inside it, it had to be the Hallowed Vessel's true figurehead.

The wondrous item practically crackled with arcane energy. How had the poor fools in this town never noticed? Or had they? Did the locals treat it like something sacred, some great god of horseplay, and come here to pay it homage with drink and reverie?

Dor doubted it.

Although Aethyr energies filled the universe, the vast majority of people lived and died without ever knowing it, much less experiencing, channeling, or transmuting them. Elves and other fae races brought to Faltyr by the Cosmic Dragon were natural conduits for these energies, but over the ensuing eons humans and others had evolved to draw upon them to alter the fundamental nature of reality around them too.

"Is that it?" Katar asked Yax. "It's a real beaut. Should look nice back on the *Seadragon*."

"Without a doubt," Yax replied, licking his lips.

Oh hells, Dor thought. He knew that look.

The wondrous item had enthralled the elf already. The Wand Bearer possessed an unnatural curiosity for Aethyr devices and other forms of magic. This propensity, this greed for power and knowledge, had gotten him into trouble countless times during six centuries of travel and adventure.

Yax would want to test the limits of the object's power as soon as they returned to the ship. The elf's unhealthy curiosity with all things magical, coupled with his combative nature, would demand it. But its creators had disassembled the *Seadragon* and hidden its vital components away for a reason.

With its scattered parts reassembled, the Hallowed Vessel would become an awesome tool or a terrible weapon. The ship's nature depended on the agenda of whoever commanded it. And right now, Kaladimus Dor stood as its captain. And responsibility for any destruction the *Seadragon* caused would fall on his narrow shoulders.

Approaching the figurehead, Breuxias asked Dor, "Think you can shrink it?"

"Like I said before, I don't see why not," Dor answered after a moment, his nagging doubt evident in his wavering voice.

"Wait. You said it wouldn't be a problem."

"I said I didn't foresee it being a problem."

Yax interjected, "Couldn't we have argued about this before the actual burglary?"

Katar added, "Yeah, let's get this thing and get out of here. I have the death sentence if I'm caught in Oparre."

"You're not the only one," Yax reminded him.

"All right," Dor relented. "I'll try it, but I'm not promising anything. This is an object of spectacular power. I'm not sure if it's mutable, even by magical means."

"Stop talking and get to it then," Breuxias said.

Dor huffed, rolled up his sleeves, and positioned himself under the figurehead. He drew a series of symbols in the air as he spoke in a guttural, alien tongue. As he finished the weave, the Protectorate

Mage extended one open palm toward the massive object suspended above him. Visible Aethyr energy flowed from Dor to the artifact, but failed to have any effect on it.

Disappointment colored the faces surrounding him.

Dor tried once more to shrink the enchanted item, but its size remained fixed. He did, however, manage to shrink the glasses and mugs in a rack behind the bar.

"I'll be damned," he cried. "Won't shrink."

"Didn't foresee a problem, huh," Breuxias muttered.

"I'm not a diviner; I'm an invoker. It's not my job to foresee things."

"Damn fool wizard," mage and mercenary repeated at the same time.

They smiled in spite of themselves.

Katar interjected, "Then let's get out of here before we hang for nothing."

Dor said, "For theft? Here? We should be so lucky. In Oparre, they hack your hands off."

"That supposed to be reassuring?"

"No. Not at all."

Katar pleaded, "What do we do? They won't sleep all night."

"I beg to differ." Dor corrected him. "They'll sleep until the cock's first crow, quite soundly too."

Breuxias interrupted their banter with a suggestion.

"Using my belt, I can carry it out of here. But how in the Nine Hells do we get it out of the city?"

Dor's eyes narrowed as the eye-shaped gem inset into Breuxias's magic belt flared with fiery light. The aptly named belt provided its wearer with titanic strength and endurance.

Not all hope is lost, Dor thought.

Yax responded to the question first. "There's always Plan B."

Groaning, the Brute said, "Not Plan B. Anything but Plan B."

"Come on," Yax prodded, grinning toothily. "You like to juggle."

Breuxias fixed Yax and Dor with an icy stare.

"You bastards."

Chapter 2

Yax'Kaqix dipped his head lower as Faltyr's lone sun rose over the thick sandstone walls protecting Eastgate. He found the first rays of the day to be uncomfortable as his eyes readjusted to the visible light spectrum. While his vision cleared, the elf shifted his attention toward the shadowy alleys of the old city.

Various shades of undesirables--thieves and fences, harlots and johns, drunks and junkies--plied their illegal trades or indulged in their various vices. Not one of them looked happy to see the cacophonous caravan of wagons winding its way through the narrow streets. The old city's winding streets yielded to the broad, well-planned avenues of the merchant quarter. Town guards mingled with tradesmen and travelers stopping along the Long Road, the ancient overland trade network that linked the nations of eastern Ny with the distant Empire of Chi'kakal, the homeland of the Chi 'Zhan peoples.

Yax rode beside Katar in the rear wagon, its open bed dominated by the *Seadragon's* figurehead, disguised as a gaudy parade float. Wreaths of desert roses and strings of cheap glass beads served as its primary means of decoration…and camouflage. Barrels filled with water, mead, and wine kept the object of power upright and the revelers around them properly lubricated.

Since his party couldn't avoid attracting attention while transporting something the size of the figurehead, an impromptu parade honoring Paneasta--god of celebrations, frolic, and virility--seemed to provide the best cover. Like any market city situated at a crossroads, the dizzying array of shrines, temples, and bazaars contributed to a confusing assortment of holy days and festivals. If their luck held, they would be outside the city walls before the theft was discovered.

As soon as he faced forward, awkward circumstances forced Yax to divert his gaze once more. In the back of the lead wagon, a veiled belly dancer undulated in a sensual, snake-like fashion. The satiny material clinging to her glistening ebony skin did little to hide the skilled performer's substantial curves.

While Yax admitted to a certain proclivity for human women, the elf did not consider the dancer, Tameri, to be a woman. Despite her risqué costume and statuesque build, he saw her as the curious girl who'd laid eyes on her first elf the day Breuxias had brought him into her mother's shop. Though he'd known the Brute had family, including at least one former wife and a few scattered children, the reality of Breuxias the Father had not materialized for Yax until after meeting Tameri and her mother.

Judging by the sullen, disapproving expression on his face, her father did not like seeing his daughter on display any more than Yax. What father would, even if it was for a greater good?

The elf recalled a similar situation when he had married his own daughter, Lian Ba'n, to a prominent merchant-prince in Uthenea. On the day of their nuptials, before the entire capital of the republic, Lian had shined like a jewel fit for any sovereign's crown. But despite her apparent happiness, Yax worried so much he didn't sleep the entire fortnight the couple honeymooned.

After escaping Frolov Keep, he had spent a number of sleepless nights wondering how his half-elf daughter managed to survive in the growing atmosphere of intolerance sweeping the continent. Some nights, he wondered *if* she had survived it.

Shivering despite the heat of the desert morning, Yax'Kaqix drew the voluminous cloak tighter around the robe concealing his armor. The world-worn warrior focused on the exchange developing between father and daughter rather than his own brooding inner monologue.

Breuxias sat astride a prancing horse, juggling his flashing knives expertly. Using his knees, he steered the dappled steed through the sea of half-drunken, off-key merrymakers. As he approached the lead wagon, Tameri raised a single eyebrow, a mirror of her father's signature look of disapproval.

A thousand pairs of hungry eyes watched her shaking hips and jiggling breasts, but only Breuxias's seemed to make her uncomfortable. His hawkish eyes flitted warily over the crowd gathering at the perimeter of the street performers--jugglers, dancers, minstrels, and acrobats--paid to provide cover for their processional until it cleared the gates of the city.

"Did you hire every performer in this miserable city?" her father asked, spitting onto the sandy avenue.

"Just most of them," Tameri said. "I think the rest decided to tag along for fun."

"And do you have to dance so…" Breuxias blustered, "…so provocatively? Wherever did you learn such a thing?"

Tameri suspended her hypnotic dance for only a moment, enough time to cut her eyes and respond, "My mother. Your former wife."

"I should've remembered," Breuxias said with a grin.

She returned to her dance with renewed vigor. Her eyes were like two abyssal pools, as dark and full of danger as any deep in the hollows of the Underworld. Again, they mirrored her father's as closely as her sardonic mannerisms and fierce temperament.

Yax'Kaqix chuckled to himself. In the past, he had remarked on the number of similarities between father and daughter, usually as a reluctant peacemaker caught in the middle of one of their frequent heated arguments. Inevitably, he would catch hell from both sides. Yax had learned to fight his natural tendency to meddle and remain neutral during their times of conflict.

Dor and Leishan, the lead wagon's driver, laughed at the acerbic exchange between Breuxias and Tameri. They looked away before their eyes lingered too long on her tantalizing dance. Clearly, neither the awkward magician nor the almond-eyed, golden-skinned guildsman from the Säj, a vast highland plateau on the western coast of Ny, wanted to anger the infuriated father further. They had been present when Breuxias threatened every guildsman's manhood over her honor and chastity.

Yax's attention drifted toward the olive-skinned man seated in the wagon beside him. A rookie prospect from the Baax Coast region, Katar remained unproven in the old warrior's eyes; but their sagacious patron had vouched for the brash Baax rogue and his skills as an acquirer of things lost and arcane.

Crinkling his nose under his cowl, Katar looked to be offended by the acrid white smoke rising from the thurible swaying in Yax's hands. The elf had all but forgotten about the smoking censer, despite being its sole source of heat. The Wand Bearer was such an expert Aethyr magician that he channeled the requisite energies for the familiar ritual without even focusing.

"What in the Nine are you burning? It's stinging my eyes!"

"Stop your whining," Yax cautioned Katar. "It's only copal."

"What's that mean? Elven for 'noxious vapor'?"

"That's the human word. It's a tree resin. Very cleansing."

"By cleansing, do you mean: makes you want to vomit?"

"Quite the opposite. It keeps me from puking as we pass through this pit of sand and shit."

"How're you heating that thing? There's no flame, no fire."

Yax's inhuman face contorted into a wide grin. "Practice."

"Practice? You were a monk?"

"Sort of. Once upon a time anyway."

"Really?" Katar asked, sounding incredulous.

"Would I lie to you, my son?"

The elf's face contorted when he said the word "son". He pronounced the word as if it caused him physical pain. Forcing himself to focus on the present, Yax banished memories of his dark past, of losing Kan Balam, his only begotten son, to the minions of the Underworld.

One called a child who had lost a parent an orphan. But Yax knew of no word in any elf or human tongue for one who had lost a child. The pain and anguish associated with such a hellish, unnatural experience defied something as simple, as concrete as a label.

For Yax, the loss of his son defied acceptance, even now, more than a decadus after the fact. He feared no amount of time would heal that particular wound.

Katar studied the elf's face before answering. Finally, the rogue smiled slyly and said, "Probably."

Despite the painful flashback, Yax provided a cheeky response. "Probably why I made a lousy monk."

He trailed off, his attention wandering once more as the city's north gate came into view. Yax expected it to be guarded, but the arrival of a heavily armed convoy served to further complicate their most expedient means of egress.

The caravan entering the city included a caged wagon full of robed-and-hooded slaves or prisoners; having been both in his lifetime, the elf saw little difference in the two states of captivity. Its substantial escort included a trio of shining knights and their men-at-arms, all mounted on horses equipped for the open desert.

"Oparre regulars," Katar said, steering their wagon toward the far side of the avenue to make room for the military wagons. "Looks like they're escorting prisoners," he added as they drew closer to the caged wagon and the array of horsemen.

Yax spat between the two caravans and said, "If there was any justice, someone would wipe this shit-pit off the map."

"Why don't you pray for it?" Katar prodded.

"Be careful. I might just do that."

Despite his better judgment, he did. When the universe responded to his prayers moments later, Yax didn't realize he'd go to his grave without deciding if it had been worth it. The events his divine appeal appeared to set into motion would haunt him the rest of his days. And his destiny, like that of Kaladimus Dor, would become tied to the Sands of Sorrow forever.

As the prison wagon drew near, Yax's eyes fell upon those of the captives. Their inhuman nature spoke volumes to the elf. After all, he might as well have been looking into his own. They held a soulful sadness few humans suffered long enough to attain.

Elves! Every last one of them, Yax realized. *They aren't slaves. And they aren't just prisoners. They're prisoners-of-war. A result of King Orson's Blood War no doubt*, he thought, seething with anger.

Memories flooded back to him. He recalled being led into an I-shaped coliseum, paraded in chains before a crowd howling for his blood. He had suffered the fate of all captives among the Unen'ek, the elves of the Southern Isles: trial-by-combat to determine a prisoner-of-war's worth to its captors. If a captive survived three matches, he signed a blood oath to serve his new masters for a term of seven cycles before being paroled.

For the Unen'ek, a person was only as good as their word. Oath-breakers had no honor. As a result, the elves of the South Isles did not make promises lightly. And they preferred to have them signed and sealed in blood.

In fact, the royal status of the color purple on Faltyr could be traced back to ancient pacts signed in human and elf blood, red and blue mixing to make the deep purple used to pen the earliest treaties between their peoples. And now, more than a dozen millennia later, a sovereign swathed in purple threatened to drown the main continent in red and blue again. Current events forced Yax to recall a prophecy in the Scrolls of Time, one of the apocalyptic auguries regarding the end of each cycle of ages, about periods of violence when rivers would run violet.

The rustling of wings drew his attention to the top of the cage. After the horrors experienced while acquiring the Hallowed Vessel, Yax would not have been surprised to see the undead wyvern stalking them once again. Instead, he saw a fresh horror, a phantasmal seraph perched like a vulture on the side of the prison wagon.

Peering through the smoke wafting from the censer, Yax recognized the bearded visage looking back at him. Sir Caayl's accusatory eyes bored into his soul. The elf had never felt so exposed, so judged in all his days.

When the apparition spoke, it said, "Make me a promise."

Chapter 3

The ghostly words of Sir Caayl reminded Yax'Kaqix of his duty, of his promise. If the knight failed to complete his quest and expose the dark forces behind the Blood War, Yax swore to pick up the gauntlet, carry on the crusade, and do what he could to bring the genocidal conflict to an end.

In seeking the scattered parts of the *Seadragon*, he figured assembling such a potent weapon of war took precedence over immediate action. But it seemed the restless soul of the fallen knight cried out for direct intervention.

Yax tore his eyes from the black-winged seraph and said, "Change of plans."

As the elf rose from his seat, Katar asked, "Where in the Nine are you going?"

"Don't worry about me. I'll race you to the gate."

Yax turned back toward the wagon full of elves. The anthropomorphized image of Sir Caayl no longer perched on the top of its cage. Even without its spectral presence, the elf still he knew what he had to do…but not for the dead; for the living.

Yax judged the distance between his wagon and the prison transport traveling toward him. And then he leapt. Crossing the gap in a single bound, the elf raised the red hot censer high above his head. As he landed, he swung the heavy end of the thurible at the teamster's head. The human's turbaned helmet crumpled under the force of the elf's blow, crushing the man's skull and killing him instantly.

Confusion swept both caravans as the hooded elf hijacked the prison wagon in broad daylight. Taking advantage of the chaos he created, Yax worked to turn the caged wagon around in the busy street. He whipped the horses into a frantic state that caused the performers, merchants, and bystanders to scatter. He'd never liked the foul-smelling, often unreliable beasts, so he felt no compunction about forcefully lashing them to get clear of the crowd and the cavalrymen.

Katar accelerated wildly and steered the wagon with the artifact through the confused masses and around the lead wagon. Behind him, the relic shook and jumped with each sharp jolt along the avenue. Yax followed his trajectory toward the gate.

“Which plan is this?” Dor asked no one in particular.

“The one where we get the hells out of here!” Breuxias answered, slapping their wagon’s lead horse across its broad ass.

The horses raced toward the gate so rapidly that Leishan had to tighten his grip on the reigns. The moon-faced guildsman settled into his seat, ducking low to avoid the crossbow bolts fired by guards along the crenellated wall. The lighter wagon overtook the heavier prison wagon, but not Katar’s.

As Katar and Leishan closed on the yawning gate, the guards scattered like gnomish bowling pins before their thunderous approach. Tons of wood, iron, and horseflesh barreled over those who failed to move fast enough. Katar’s wagon caught air as it rolled over one unfortunate guard and then another. It hit the ground with a jolt.

One of the braver guards called, “Close the gate! Close it now!”

Tameri silenced him with a single arrow through his windpipe. She notched another arrow from the quiver at her feet.

The bearded guard at the dead man’s side reached for the gate controls, but someone else had him in their sights. Dor directed a blast of flash frozen air at him, and literally froze the guard in his tracks. The icy weave’s effect on the panicked crowd was immediate.

Someone screamed from the crowd, “It’s a wizard! Run!”

And run they did. All but the stoutest of heart fled for their lives. The crowd stampeded through the stalls and booths of the marketplace like so many frightened sheep. Cries of “wizardry” and “witchcraft” arose from all quarters.

On the other side of the coin, the guards and cavalrymen seemed to be invigorated by the presence of a hated adversary, a spell-caster. The crossbowmen targeted Dor’s wagon with a hail of missiles, but didn’t hit anyone with their first volley.

Their second volley missed Breuxias as he spurred his horse to intercept the three knights charging toward the captured wagon. His horse thundered past the caged wagon at a full gallop.

Yax watched as his friend slid effortlessly from the steed's back. The speeding horse rushed between two of the knights, forcing them from their mounts. The third knight avoided the collision by reigning in his charger. The warhorse reared on him, but the skillful cavalier remained in the saddle.

Sparing no time, Breuxias grabbed the prison wagon's bars, hauled himself onto its side, and climbed onto the top of the wagon. In doing so, he dodged crossbow bolts fired by guards stationed along the wall.

The Brute dropped onto the seat beside Yax. He didn't look at all amused by his friend's abrupt, spiritually-inspired change of plans. The elf knew enough to leave out the bit about the ghost. The human didn't doubt the existence of spirits. He acknowledged their existence and hated all dealings involving them. As a result, his bullish attitude tended to get him into trouble with spirits rather than currying their favor.

"What're you doing? Besides trying to get us killed!" Breuxias shouted over the din of the chaos around them.

"Improvising," Yax replied tersely.

The ring of steel on iron arrested both mercenaries' attentions. The lone knight still on horseback had caught up to them as the wagon careened toward the gate. His swing had missed Breuxias's neck by mere inches, glancing off the bars of the heavy duty cage.

Wasting no time, the Knight of Oparre stabbed across his body at the mercenary. As the Brute scrambled backwards, Yax slid toward the far side of the wagon. The elf braced his feet against the floorboard and held tight to the reigns to avoid bouncing out onto the avenue. Sparks flew as the blade ground against the wagon's bars.

"Hells no, you don't!" Breuxias cried.

Ducking another powerful swing by the persistent cavalier, Breuxias activated his Belt of Titan Strength.

Grabbing the wagon's cage with his right hand, he used it as an anchor as well as for momentum. Unable to reach the knight himself, Breuxias swung out with a wide haymaker. The effect was devastating.

The empowered warrior made contact with the side of the horse's barded head with the force of an ogre's club. Its neck snapped sickeningly as its head twisted away from its body at an obscene angle. The horse's front legs collapsed, catapulting its rider from the saddle. The Knight of Oparre crashed to the sandy stone of the avenue and tumbled to a stop. Alive or dead, they had one less pursuer for now.

Amidst another hail of crossbow bolts, the three wagons burst forth from the gate in a scene of unmitigated chaos. Katar's wagon had a slim lead on the one ferrying Leishan, Dor, and Tameri; but the prison transport gained ground on them. Judging by the panicked way they ran, Yax reckoned his team of horses would be as happy to escape their merciless elven taskmaster and his horse-slaying companion as they would the crossbowmen and cavalrymen lobbing missiles at their exposed flanks.

Whatever works to get the captives to safety, Yax thought.

If such a thing as a safe place for his kind existed in Ny anymore. He doubted any of the Winaq'che elves would submit to leaving the main continent; much less accept refuge amongst his tribe, the Unen'ek. The Schism between their tribes seemed insurmountable.

The sundering of the elven Jade Throne had occurred eons before the most recent cataclysm, one of many since his people had descended from the stars to join the Eternal War for the fate of Faltyr. But with their long-time ally, humanity, turning against them, these elves of Silver Brook--the adopted homeland of the Winaq'che--might prefer their estranged cousins of the Southern Isles to the races of men.

For now, the survival of the elves in the cage depended on the caravan's ability to flee far and fast from Eastgate, preferably without anyone in pursuit. His Aethyr magic could shield them from crossbow bolts, but outrunning Oparre cavalry with a team of wagons seemed improbable. *But not impossible*, he reminded himself. Not for the wily old Wand Bearer anyway.

Yax'Kaqix whipped the horses to a near frenzied state in an effort to catch Leishan's wagon. Breuxias clung onto the bars of the cage to prevent being jarred from the wagon's seat. His stare bored into his elven companion.

Finally, Breuxias exclaimed, "We'll never make it at this rate. One of those crossbowmen is going to get lucky sooner or later."

Yax replied, "Don't worry. I've got an idea."

"For the record," the Brute said, "I don't like the ideas you're having today. *Hate* may be a better word for it."

Yax grinned and then quipped, "Oh, you'll love this!"

Breuxias shook his head as he took cover behind the cage.

"Dor!" Yax shouted. "Throw up a firewall!"

That should stop crossbowmen and cavalry alike.

The elf pictured their panic as a towering inferno arose between the enemy and the escapees. A perverse sense of joy filled his warrior's heart.

Maybe they'll all burn.

Cupping his ear, Dor nodded in the affirmative. The magician dug around in his seemingly bottomless pouch before extracting his familiar black staff. Dor flipped the potent Aethyr device over his shoulder and aimed the gnarled end at the city gate.

"One fireball coming right up," he mouthed.

"No, I said--"

The roar of the ball of fire drowned out the rest of Yax's sentence. The fiery projectile sped from Dor's staff toward the city at spectacular speed. It struck the tower west of the gate.

The guard tower exploded as if it had been struck by dragon fire and spewed flaming shrapnel in all directions. Dense, dark smoke boiled from the burning structure. As guards staggered away from the conflagration, they slapped at their bodies to try and stop the spread of the flames. Despite the smoke and heat, the soldiers in the opposite tower continued to empty their repeating crossbows at the trio of wagons leaving the city.

Yax shouted, "A wall of fire! Not a ball of fire, you idiot!"

"Oh!" Dor managed, mesmerized by the level of devastation wrought by the staff. In his defense, he added, "Well, why didn't you say so?"

Tugging at the sleeve of his robe, Tameri urged, "You've got to put it out. That fire is liable to spread to the whole city."

Dor sighed and put away the staff. He stood, on the toe board below the seat, as bolts from enemy crossbowmen struck around him. He pushed up the sleeves on his over-sized robes, a look of determination fixed on his face.

"What in Kahl's name is he doing now?" Breuxias asked.

"Oh no! He's trying to fix it."

Yax didn't know if he could stop the Master-of-Disaster, but he had to try. The city itself contained a fair number of innocents who lived somewhere along the twisting streets leading to its rotten core. But Dor reached the apex of his spell-casting before Yax could hand the reigns to his friend. The localized buildup of Aethyr energies caused the wizard's hands to glow brightly. As he prepared to unleash the weave upon the city, an iron bolt struck him under the collarbone.

Dor stumbled, but Leishan seized the wizard by one sleeve and hauled him back onto the seat. Yax marveled at the strength of the stoutly built Säj mercenary as he controlled the wagon's team with one hand and saved the mage with the other.

When Dor's cupped hands came apart, the ball of Aethyr energy shot upward before dissipating into the partly cloudy morning sky. As Tameri and Leishan maneuvered the wounded, semi-conscious magician into the back of the speeding wagon, the clouds multiplied rapidly, growing darker. The unnatural, Aethyr-charged cloudbank blossomed into a rotating storm front.

Over his shoulder, Yax saw a twister half-a-league across descend from the swirling sky. Like the finger of an angry god, the vortex touched down near the burning tower. The flames scattered to the four corners, along with that section of the city wall, peppering the merchant quarter with more shrapnel.

"Holy Hells!" Breuxias exclaimed. "What's Dor done now?"

Unable to process the scene of devastation before him in any other context, Yax muttered, "I'll be more careful about what I pray for in the future."

"What do you mean?" Breuxias asked.

"Nevermind. Let's get out of here."

The last sight the elf beheld as the ragtag caravan fled over the sandy rise was the sickening, yet satisfying, sight of the tornado devastating Eastgate, punishing the wicked city full of slavers and soldiers dedicated to King Orson's evil agenda. He was not without sympathy though; he hoped as few innocents as possible felt the storm's wrath. But he doubted it. Whenever Yax'Kaqix took an active hand in events, there was always collateral damage. His heart as heavy as the overloaded prison wagon, he recalled a familiar elven proverb: Be careful what you pray for; you just might get it.

Chapter 4

Months before he laid waste to Eastgate, Kaladimus Dor laid eyes on the scenic port of Fraustmauth from the deck of the *Seadragon*. At the time, the errant Mage of Moor'Dru didn't realize the sprawling capital of the Crimson Phoenix would become his home away from home. Or that his association with the mages and mercenaries of Finders Keepers would only grow by the day, until their adventures became the stuff of myth and legend.

Dor had visited Fraustmauth once before, and on that occasion, the fabled city had lived up to its name. Damarra's morning rays had set the ice and snow ablaze with scintillating colors. Dazzled by its light, the young magician understood why the city had been nicknamed the Jewel of the North.

Snow blanketed the entire city, including the mountains and rocky shoals beyond its impressive walls. Their glistening granite blocks were quarried from manmade passes constructed through the rocky range leading north into the Broken Lands, the ancient homeland of the Gre.

After migrating south, these enterprising barbarians had cast off the weak, scattered remnants of the Baax Empire and united the region under the banner of the Crimson Phoenix. The deep water port of Fraustmauth became the center of a new hybrid culture born of the bastard get of the Gre conquerors and their more cosmopolitan Baax subjects.

On Dor's previous voyage, spires of ice had choked the city's expansive harbor and left it impassable without the aid of a specialized watercraft and a reliable sea witch. However, Braigen had contracted a masterful captain and crew to ensure his apprentice's safe arrival despite the treacherous conditions.

Understandably, trade trickled to a halt during those wintery months. As a result, Dor's previous visit had not prepared him for the dizzying array of traffic present during the warmer seasons. Standing on the aft castle of the *Seadragon*, he surveyed the dizzying number of craft maneuvering around him.

Though the Hallowed Vessel obeyed his mental commands readily enough, Dor still hadn't mastered navigating a vessel of this size in tight quarters. As its de facto captain, he'd given Breuxias permission to recruit additional hands--a couple of members of the mercenary's own family--to handle normal day-to-day operations on the *Seadragon*. Dor preferred the company of Tameri, Breuxias's willowy daughter, to the Brute's adopted brother any day. Maczitalius and Breuxias proved a caustic comedic combination. Wise-cracking Macz wore on Dor's nerves after less than a fortnight aboard the Hallowed Vessel.

Since Finders Keepers's headquarters was located in Fraustmauth, they intended on staffing the rest of the crew roster with fellow guildsmen. Despite his reservations about a prolonged association with these sellswords, Dor comforted himself with the knowledge that a proper crew would draw less attention than a lone mage piloting a ghost ship. And a loyal crew would provide extra security against the myriad perils of sailing Faltyr's seas. He would act as both captain and seawitch though, which worked for him. He did not relish the idea of trusting another Aethyr user with the *Seadragon*'s safety.

Dor understood the concept of safety in numbers, though he loathed embracing it except in the direst of circumstances. Yet he'd relied on members of Finders Keepers to help him on his quest with the chest in the Sands of Sorrow. And he'd chosen them as allies again after shipwrecking the *Nightsfall*'s survivors on that godforsaken island, home of long dead Frolov Keep and its undead residents. With enemies beyond measure and his allies dwindling, Dor chose to trust the guildsmen employed by its patron, a sagacious wizard named Caleb.

The humbly named mage awaited their arrival without pomp, standing at the end of an ancient stone pier situated at the base of his granite tower. Caleb's tower doubled as one of the city's lighthouses. Its powerful beam, visible despite the gray light of day, marked the location of the rocky western shoals of the harbor channel, an area best avoided by any ship with a draft too deep to navigate upriver.

Dor's heart thudded in his ears as he drank in the familiar sight of the bookish blonde woman standing by Caleb's side. Though he hated to admit missing anyone, even his own master, Dor realized at that moment how much he'd longed to see Keera's smiling face once more. During his previous visit, the sage's youngest daughter had spoken to him with greater kindness and treated him with more tenderness than anyone he'd ever known. Now he'd returned to her, drawn by the hand of fate back into her arms. Or so he hoped.

As the *Seadragon* edged closer to the pier, Dor felt the icy, irrational shadow of doubt pass across his warm, reassuring thoughts. He'd traveled nigh on ten thousand leagues in between trips to Fraustmauth, and the young mage had lost count of how many times he'd killed or nearly been killed since she'd last looked into his eyes. Would Keera see the darkness, doubt, and pain there? If she did, would she reject him or hold him closer to her heart? Would he know what to do with her if she did?

In his heart of hearts, Dor knew the answers, yet he wouldn't admit it. Why? Because he wasn't comfortable with people praising him or providing him with positive attention. Most of his life had involved training, drilling, serving, and, of course, screwing up. He had become to consider himself an expert at the latter. So he was used to receiving more criticism than praise.

In a mental fog, Dor watched the others cross the gangplank to Caleb's private dock. He lingered at the back of the pack, pretending to check the damaged lock on the chest while he exchanged nervous glances with the sage's daughter.

Caleb advanced on those who'd disembarked from the *Seadragon*, but the ship had his full attention. The old sage gawked at the Hallowed Vessel, pie-eyed as a fat kid sitting down to his first Midwinter Feast. He whistled through the thick, white whiskers around his thin lips, drawing Dor's attention.

Approaching Yax'Kaqix, Caleb remarked, "She's more beautiful than your messages indicated, Old Man."

"More than mere words can describe," Yax replied.

Dor's gaze settled on Keera's smiling face once more. The mage muttered, louder than intended, "You can say that again."

His bold words hung between them for a brief moment, until Caleb's disapproving eyes fell on him. The sage smiled at Dor, but drew his daughter closer to his side. Keera giggled.

Seems like she missed me too, Dor thought.

"Hurry up and come inside, my happy band of reprobates," Caleb said, breaking the tension. "I want to hear all about it, the island, the beasties, and the boat. But I don't want to get soaked to the bone in the process."

Gesturing to the intimidating array of storm clouds gathering to the south and west, Caleb added, "According to the almanac, storm fronts will become more frequent, more intense in the foreseeable future. Perhaps they echo the chaos of our times."

Or maybe it's my fault for coming here at all, Dor worried. *Problems, much like storms, do tend to follow me.*

❧❧

Later that evening, as the tempest roiled and rumbled, Kaladimus Dor sat in the cozy confines of Caleb's study alongside Breuxias and Yax'Kaqix. The old sage, accompanied by one of his many loyal retainers, joined them. Caleb took his customary seat at the head of the table while the pear-shaped woman served the tray of beverages.

Thunder boomed as Dor accepted the steaming mug of hard cider from the serving woman. He leapt from the chair, startling her worse than the storm. They jostled the mug between them like two guilty siblings trying to pass the blame. Dor ended up on the losing side, fumbling the container and covering himself in hot, sticky cider.

"Sonuva--" Dor started.

"Language, boyo!" the matronly retainer reminded him, waving a meaty finger in his scruffy face.

As proper friends always would, Breuxias and Yax chuckled at the mage's misfortune. After the tragic events on the island, many a direct result of his own actions, laughter was a welcome sound to his ears. Before Dor realized it, he'd joined them. Despite the soggy robe and scalded flesh, he felt better than he had since leaving Myth.

Caleb called them to order and then ordered the serving woman to depart. She left Dor with a hand towel, a dirty look, and an empty mug when she exited the room a moment later. He grinned in an attempt to salvage another failed first impression, but still felt a fool.

Perhaps Keera was right after all; maybe I don't have charm or charisma. But if that's the case, why did she look so happy to see me?

Caleb's voice brought Dor out of his head when he asked, "How did you come across the *Seadragon* exactly? Your message was short on details."

"Ask that damn fool wizard," Breuxias replied, gesturing to Dor.

"I couldn't put much into a note carried by bird," Dor explained.

"Guess it depends on the species of bird," Yax commented.

"Yeah," Breuxias added, "You could have chosen something bigger than a canary."

"Any of the larger birds I could have summoned off the coast of Moor'Dru would have been spotted flying over the island. And I don't think any of us wanted that message falling into the hands of the Proleus faction. We were lucky enough to sail away from those waters with our lives."

"No thanks to you," Breuxias said. "If you'd listened when we warned you the usurper on the High Council had seized power. Hells bells, did you need to see Salaac's corpse or duel with old schoolmates to be sure? Because we did both."

"Ease up on Calamity's Door here and let him explain," Caleb said, wagging a finger to admonish the Brute's abusive behavior. "His presence does explain quite a bit though."

"Calamity's Door," Dor said, repeating the familiar moniker. "Braigen called me that. Old Salaac preferred Master-of-Disaster. I hated them both. The monikers, not the men."

"Speaking of Braigen," Caleb said, "he called on me three or four moons ago."

"My master yet lives?!" Dor inquired, leaping from his seat for the second time in as many minutes. "We heard rumors to the contrary when we made landfall on Moor'Dru. I couldn't confirm it though."

Shaking his head, Yax said, "I cautioned you against believing idle peasant gossip."

"Aye. I would not think one of the High Three so easily slain. By the looks of it, they had to use a small army to get Salaac,"

Breuxias added with a chuckle. "Same way I hope to go out someday." The Brute pounded his palm with a fist for emphasis.

"Makes two of us," the smiling elf said, relishing the idea.

As Dor settled back into his seat, Caleb said, "Getting back to the matter at hand, I can attest to Braigen living and breathing before he left for the Dragonvale. Now, I have no clue to his whereabouts. He's gone far beyond my ability to see."

"And where is that?" Dor asked.

"Through the looking glass," Caleb replied, gesturing not to a mirror but to a star chart on the wall of his study.

Confusion and fear clouded Dor's mind, dulling his reason.

"Why?"

"Seeking our salvation," the sage said, clearing up nothing.

"Salvation." The word rolled off Dor's tongue, leaving a bitter aftertaste. It seemed a better word for clergymen than men of magic.

"Perhaps 'hope' is a better translation." Caleb said.

The benefactor, and brains, behind Finders Keepers moved his crooked finger from the astronomical chart tacked to the wall to the scorched chest situated on the table.

As Dor's gaze settled on the accursed box, Caleb said, "You may have the key to this mess, but without Braigen's sacrifice, all of this is for naught."

The heavy metal lockbox was the unspoken albatross in the room, radiating an aura of dread so palpable that even someone as bullish as the Brute could not ignore it. The specially prepared, enchanted container harbored as many secrets as the magician who recovered its sinister contents. The lightning-scarred chest had seen better days since Braigen had saddled him with it less than a year ago.

The empty strongbox had seemed an innocent enough item. But his master had been teaching him a valuable lesson that day. Looks could be deceiving. And too often were. Contents were what mattered. It was a lesson Dor had yet to take to heart, much to his chagrin.

"How do you know about that?" Dor asked.

"Who do you think made that chest?" Caleb asked. The rhetorical nature of the question was obvious from the sage's sardonic tone. He added, "Braigen may be a capable wizard, but he's no artificer."

"I'll be damned," Dor replied as the pieces fell into place. It certainly explained the connection between Caleb and Braigen. After all, if his master had trusted the sage enough to involve him in one part of their plot, perhaps he'd trusted him with the rest.

Unless Caleb had been the real mastermind all along.

Dor shuddered at the implications of being a pawn in an even grander scheme. He didn't mind his role, or his burden, as long as he felt like he had some measure of control over the situation.

Then again, aren't we all puppets? Isn't that our purpose in this life, to play our role upon the stage and then make our exit?

Breuxias interrupted the mage's musings on the wise words of a long dead bard when he said, "I'll be damned if I hear another word about that chest without a proper explanation."

Caleb looked surprised. He said, "Dor hasn't explained its purpose or its contents?"

"Neither," Yax said, shaking his head. The elf eyed Dor across the table. "He's been tighter about that subject than your hands on your purse strings."

Dor saw the disappointment coloring their faces. He'd let them down by abusing their trust and endangering their lives. He wondered what had jeopardized more relationships in his life: his secretive demeanor or destructive nature. But to be fair, Dor had his reasons, even if they seemed like rather foolish ones at times.

"There's a lot at stake," Dor explained. "You have no idea. I couldn't trust just anyone."

Breuxias said, "We help you kill a Wyvern…twice, escape from an island you stranded us on, and you don't trust us?"

"But I was sworn to secrecy?"

"If your master felt comfortable enough discussing this with our patron," Yax replied, "you should trust us enough to come clean."

Breuxias added, "Especially if you want us to help you."

"Help him again you mean," Caleb muttered.

"Again?"

Before Dor had a chance to silence the sage, Caleb explained, "Much like his master, Dor was willing to accept help from our company in recovering the chest's contents. In fact, two guildsmen made the trek to Oparre last season for that purpose."

"You didn't mention any of this," Breuxias cried as he sprang from his chair. "I told you what would happen if you lied again."

The last time the Brute had been this upset Dor had barely escaped with his life. And he had no intention of becoming prey to anyone, especially a so-called friend and ally. Dor raised his hands defensively, his fingertips crackling with electricity. Lightning flashed anew and thunder rattled the windowpanes.

Breuxias halted his advance but continued to glare.

"Sit down!" Caleb ordered. "I'll have none of this. No one attacks anyone in my home."

Dor lowered his hands before something bad happened, like turning the lighthouse into a lightning rod.

"Don't blame Dor," Yax interjected. "It's Caleb's fault too. Nothing in the message he sent to us on Corr Deyraire mentioned the chest, its contents, or any previous dealings with our new friend here. We were told to escort Gneut to his destination and help him find his prize. But I have a feeling we were there keeping an eye on Dor too."

"Some friend," Breuxias muttered before sitting back down. "That goes for both of you. Not sure who lies more, wenches or wizards."

Smiling, Caleb replied, "How was I supposed to know a former client booked passage on Gneut's ship months beforehand? I'm a sage, not a swami. I translate and collate other people's prophecies; I don't make them."

"No," Yax said, "but you do have a network of spies and informants that would make the Emperor of Chi'kakal envious. So don't play coy with me."

Caleb chuckled again but offered no further explanation. He shifted his mischievous eyes in Dor's direction. But his gaze had migrated to a masterfully detailed map of Faltyr on the wall. Dor's tired eyes settled on a region in southeastern Ny on the border of Oparre and Panglov, a sprawling desert with a most unnatural origin.

"All right," he relented. "I'll tell you the whole story. The chest means nothing without knowing why it was constructed. Or what it was meant to hold. It all starts with the Sands of Sorrow."

Chapter 5

Breuxias listened with growing interest as Dor came clean about the dirty job he'd been sent by Braigen and Salaac to perform. The aptly nicknamed Master-of-Disaster had been entrusted with a mission of critical importance to the future of Faltyr's peoples, especially if one put stock in prophecies.

There's always a prophecy somewhere in the mix.

A notable exception among the mercenaries roaming the wilds of Faltyr, Breuxias was not only literate but well-read. If he couldn't solve a problem with the appropriate application of brute force, he prided himself on the fact he could think his way out of a jam. Yet matters of divination, prognostication, and prophecy irritated him to no end.

He had a difficult time believing that the ravings of a cloistered religious zealot, probably one stoned out of his gourd on some hallucinogen, foreshadowed the course of world events. Any wily zealot or charlatan could use astronomical charts forecasting celestial events and then pair any sort of apocalyptic rubbish alongside it. After all, it had been done countless times before and after the only real cataclysm in modern memory, the one initiated by a pair of feuding lovers.

In fact, he thought it a masterful touch that the prophecy Dor and Caleb discussed with Yax and he involved this very cataclysm. Or rather a re-creation of it in the near future, one triggered by the return of the warring deities who'd initiated the fiery end of Faltyr's cycle of ages through their pawns, Artemis and Ra'Tallah.

To Breuxias, this so-called prophecy sounded more like well-established history:

When the stars are right, two gods chosen by death and bound by a servant of fire shall stand together at the end of a cycle of ages. However, should one fall under the sway of the Awakener of the

Dead, Faltyr will endure a cycle of chaos and destruction unseen since dragons ruled the sky and titans walked the earth.

"Rubbish," he muttered, louder than he intended.

All three mages turned his way and stared at him gravely. He was used to it from Yax and Caleb, but not Dor. Despite his years of learning and exploration, he felt like the town fool in the presence of more learned men. He lapsed into silence and listened rather than commented.

What the mercenary heard, if it were to be believed, alarmed him. Though it did help him empathize with Dor's plight. After all, his daughter Tameri had been sixteen summers old when she'd saved her city from an invading army. Her actions could have easily gotten her tied to a stake and set aflame, but she had used whatever means were at her disposal to save Istara.

These troubling times put unusual demands on the young. Too often youth and innocence are casualties here on Faltyr.

He recalled his own violent upbringing, first among ogres and then among mercenary companies. He had bathed in the blood of countless "enemies" before he had been old enough to understand the difference between friend and foe.

Despite his growing sense of dread, Breuxias waited quietly while Dor summed up his mission to the sunken remnants of Laeg, an abandoned Ireti city on the western edge of the Sands of Sorrow. It had been inundated by floodwaters in the wake of the Cataclysm. Shortly thereafter, Laeg had been overrun by an army of Sobeki lizardmen intent on occupation instead of invasion. Though ostensibly part of the Kingdom of Oparre, the entire area was rumored to be controlled by the scaly bastards now.

Breuxias developed a newfound sense of respect for the young Protectorate Mage once he realized that Dor had survived a quest into the heart of the ruined city. Even the crusaders in mighty Oparre gave that region a wide berth. Too bad it sounded like the two members of Finders Keepers who'd accompanied the Master-of-Disaster hadn't been so fortunate. But he wasn't ready to give them up for dead just yet.

"What about Bishop and Uruk?" he inquired.

"We split up after I recovered the chest's contents and escaped the temple," Dor explained. "It was too dangerous for the three of us to travel back through the heart of Oparre. I had to take the most direct route available. They're not on a time table."

"Are you still on a time table?" Breuxias asked.

"Of sorts."

"Something to do with 'when the stars are right' I'll wager."

Dor snapped his fingers and replied, "Exactly! Now if I just knew what stars and when they'll be right, I'd know my deadline."

"It's not that simple," Caleb said.

"It rarely is," Yax said, "especially in regards to prophecies."

"That's my problem with this whole deal. It's predicated on the dubious power of prophesy," the Brute retorted. "How do we know it's not bullshit? This whole thing could be some fiction perpetrated for unsavory purposes. For all we know, it could have been fabricated by a cult as a way to control its followers."

"Isn't that the purpose of every religion?" Yax quipped. "Scaring people into behaving better than their nature."

Breuxias was in no mood to be assuaged much less amused.

"No wonder you were a lousy monk."

Yax shrugged in response, refusing to rise to his friend's bait.

"With all these tangents," Caleb interjected, "It's a darn good thing my body went before my mind did. You'd consternate the senile, Breuxias. Let the poor boy finish his story before he gets worked up and calls down a bolt of lightning on all our heads."

"Again, you mean," Breuxias said.

"I'm not that bad," Dor said. "Am I?"

Hardly," Yax replied. "I've travelled with worse."

Finally grinning, Breuxias joked, "Hey! I resemble that remark."

The guildsmen's nervous laughter echoed within the stone walls of the study. As it faded, everyone but the Protectorate Mage lapsed into silence.

Dor talked and talked, telling them about the half-submerged Temple of Darconius, the female Naga guarding the object of his quest, and their desperate fight in the watery confines of the demon serpent's lair. Breuxias listened intently as the mage reached the heart of the matter, the chest's mysterious contents.

"As I pulled the horrid item from its resting place, I heard it whisper to me; I felt it reach out to my mind. Its voices were legion, for they were many. But one rose above the others. It wailed in my head before speaking to me, directly to me. As it spoke, I felt its hypnotic voice reverberate in my soul, much like tapping a tuning fork against stone."

Dor gulped visibly before he continued his tale of terror.

"It said: I have waited a long time for you, Kaladimus Dor. Though I have slumbered, I am not dead. I yet dream. And I have dreamed of you often."

A tear ran down the mage's cheek and his voice shook.

"So I asked it: How is this possible? How do you know me?"

Breuxias stared wide-eyed at Dor. The wizard had grown paler, trembling as he reached the climax of his story. He asked the shaken sorcerer, "And what did it say?"

Dor wiped the tears from his eyes before replying. "It said four words: You are my salvation."

"Sonuvabitch," the Brute managed.

"What does that even mean?" Yax asked.

"It means there's another prophecy," Caleb interjected.

"Of course, when one bloody prophecy isn't enough, add another to the mix," Breuxias lamented.

Caleb placed one small wrinkled hand on the tall man's broad forearm and whispered, "Do you want to hear it or would you rather listen to yourself talk?"

Breuxias slunk down in his chair, feeling embarrassed again, like he'd been slapped across the face by the old sage. He cut his eyes toward Yax as the elf stifled a laugh. Even Dor chuckled despite his teary eyes and sorry disposition.

No sympathy for this old devil here.

Breuxias prodded Caleb, "Well, go on then, before I'm as gray as you."

The sage looked over his thick glasses and down his nose. It was his customary expression of displeasure. Clearing his throat, Caleb recited, "As the cycle of ages spins round again, a Dweller in Darkness shall rise from the ranks of the Light. A promise broken by a Son of the Servant of the Storm will ensure it."

"I don't get it," Breuxias said, scratching his bald pate with a jagged, chewed fingernail. "How does that relate to Dor or the chest?"

"To start with," Yax began, "the closest translation for *Maelanfaidh*, the elven term for Dor's peculiar nature, is 'Son of the Servant of the Storm.' It refers to magic-using scions descended from the line of Taranis, the God of Storms, Chaos, and Destruction."

"Are you shitting me?" Breuxias exclaimed. "Dor's a demigod!"

"Not quite," Yax cautioned.

"Exactly," Caleb said. "He's far enough removed from divinity that the only vestige of his legacy is the instinctive way he casts spells, much like elves and other fae creatures. It allows him to cast faster, more powerful spells than most humans or elves but at greater risk to himself and others."

"So he's more like a semigod," Breuxias commented.

"Something like that," Caleb replied.

Dor sat quietly as he waited for the sage to finish his explanation. None of this information seemed to come as a surprise to him.

Breuxias asked, "So what in the Nine does Dor being a semigod have to do with that infernal chest?"

"It's the contents that matter," Caleb said.

"Whatever. Chest. Contents. Just tell me."

"It's not my place to say," the sage teased.

"Godsdammit! Will someone just tell me?"

"It contains a phylactery, all right!" Dor shouted. "It's an object of immense power, and Ra'Tallah's soul is bound into it."

Yax cursed under his breath.

"That bad, huh?" the Brute asked the elf.

"Worse. The only powerful object that Ireti devil had in his possession when his body died was on loan from the Underworld."

"You don't mean a copy of the *Liber Inferum*?" Breuxias said, the sinister implications finally becoming clear.

"Not a copy. *The* Book of the Underworld," Dor interjected.

"Holy hells!"

Eyeing the chest warily, Dor said, "More like unholy hells."

The downtrodden wizard sat for a few minutes without speaking. The flickering firelight made Dor appear older than his twenty-odd years. Or perhaps it was the spiritual weight of his unwanted burden that cast him in such a light.

After a pause too long to be considered dramatic, Dor said, "I reckon that about covers it. During my escape from Oparre, I made a deal with Gneut for passage from Kingsport to Myth, a map for a trip home. It seemed like a good deal at the time. But that's when everything went to pot."

Yax cursed in his native tongue again and then said, "We've been travelling with that thing amongst us the entire time."

The elf eyed the chest in a new light. Breuxias recognized the glint in his friend's eyes. Yax harbored an unhealthy obsession with all things magical, especially items dealing with the dead. Surely, he knew better than to mess with the *Liber Inferum*.

"And it will be until Braigen or I can find a way to destroy it," Dor corrected the elf.

"Braigen is in no position to help at this point," Caleb reminded the Protectorate Mage.

"Then I'll succeed on my own if I have to," Dor said, "at whatever cost."

Caleb urged, "You don't have to handle this alone. You're one of us now. Finders Keepers can help. I can help. The bulk of my library is here, housed in the lighthouse and the vaults below it. If you stay, my resources, as well as my guild, are at your disposal."

"Would certainly make things easier," Dor admitted. "I can't go back to Moor'Dru while the Proleus faction is in control. Not with the chest anyway. I can't let that book fall into the wrong hands. It's dangerous enough on its own. But if someone were to bind Ra'Tallah's spirit into a living vessel, it would be cataclysmic…again. I don't know what Braigen or Salaac intended on doing with the book though, much less where to hide or dispose of it."

Yax said nothing. His gaze fixated on the chest, his mind likely remained on the book. With the elf's lingering interest, Breuxias was not sure what worried him more, that awful book's presence, the prideful devil bound into it, or his friend's riveted interest in them. The Wand Bearer possessed extensive knowledge of the necromantic arts and had used them to terrible effect, but usually for the best reasons. However, power tempted the elf, and often it cost him. More often than not, it cost him someone he loved, as it had done on Minotas.

Bringing the conversation back around to their original topic, Breuxias said, "That would give us time to find the other parts."

Caleb asked, "The other parts? You mean to the *Seadragon*?"

"Yeah, the figurehead, anchor, and sails," Yax said. "Gneut had maps for them, but he hadn't decoded them. And I couldn't."

"Mind if I take a look?"

"Here you go," Breuxias said, passing the map case to Caleb.

The sage dumped the maps onto the table unceremoniously. After sorting through them, grunting occasionally, he said, "This is highly encrypted. It'll take me some time with each one to unravel its weave. For now, all I can tell you is which map leads to which missing piece."

"How long before you unravel the rest?"

"A single lunare or more per map, give or take a fortnight."

Breuxias sighed. Patience was not one of his virtues.

Caleb ignored him and asked the elf, "Any preference, Old Man?"

"What preference?"

"Which piece do you wanna go after first?"

"Good question," Breuxias offered, anxious to get started on another adventure, especially one involving objects of great power. Though ignorant of its functions, he hoped their first quest would lead them to the ship's figurehead, for the sake of aesthetics if nothing else.

Yax said simply, "Let fate decide."

Closing his eyes, the elf selected one of the maps at random.

Caleb examined the map and declared, "Figurehead it is."

Despite gloomy news concerning doomsday prophecies and demonic souls trapped in otherworldly tomes, Breuxias grinned. Perhaps the Fates were on his side after all.

Chapter 6

Tameri awoke from an uneasy slumber. Beads of perspiration stood out against the skin of her furrowed brow. She blinked away the horrific, recurring images burned onto the insides of her eyelids. Memories of the war, the siege of Istara, and the dark days of occupation plagued her nights as well as her days. They made sleep nigh on impossible.

Normally, she didn't dream of the traumatic circumstances that led to her ill-deserved nickname, The Savior of Istara. Her sleeping mind refused to return to that unfortunate series of events despite her waking mind's inability to think of little else. Until the day she'd met Kaladimus Dor, her father's new associate, Mage of Moor'Dru, and captain of the Hallowed Vessel. Now the disheveled, socially inept wizard haunted her nights, accompanying her on one hellish replay after another of the events leading up to the liberation of her home city.

But why Dor? What about him triggered memories of those dark, lonesome nights deep within the labyrinthine catacombs beneath Istara?

Tameri stole from the borrowed bed, an overstuffed canopy situated in the far corner of the guest room provided by Caleb. She wore nothing but the diaphanous silk sheet. It clung to her nubile body like the togas still popular among the Baax peoples to the south.

Her bare feet padded noiselessly across the stone floor of the chamber as she moved toward the southron window. Bittersweet thoughts of home caused her to pause before its leaded glass pane. Despite the thick banks of rain-swollen clouds, Tameri imagined that she could see all the way home.

She couldn't help but feel like she'd made a mistake by leaving Istara. On the other hand, Tameri knew that she could not stay, could not live the same lie each and every day. She had been unable to return to the cemetery or the catacombs since that last fateful night before the liberation of her besieged city by crusaders from the Church of Shamash (or Damarra as Mother Sun was called in the North).

Tameri hadn't found a way to tell her Mother either. How was she supposed to tell the woman who showed more pride in her than anyone else in the wide world that she was worse than a liar and a fraud? She might have saved her mother and the rest of Istara, but she'd damned herself in the process. Tears mixed with beads of sweat as she recalled her reasons for leaving her home and family behind. Despite the events that had transpired in Istara, she missed them both…ached for them.

She cursed herself. And her father, the big oaf. She didn't know why she thought it'd be different this time. He was likeable, even loveable, but he had always been a failure as a father. Now she'd come to him, baptized by blood, sweat, and the fires of the Nine Hells, asking for nothing more than a chance to travel with him, to get to know him after long years of separation.

Was it so wrong for a girl to need her daddy, even if she was a grown woman and he was a stubborn, self-interested shithead?

But what had it gotten her? He'd lured her north, to the barbarian kingdom of the Crimson Phoenix. And now he wanted to lock her away in a white-haired wizard's tower until she'd mastered her control over the Aethyreal arts. After the events surrounding the liberation of Istara, Tameri didn't want anything to do with magic, crypts, or even books.

She'd witnessed her true potential one stormy night in the catacombs below the city cemetery. It terrified her. And it might have cost Tameri her soul.

She shivered despite the stuffy confines of the bedchamber. Sighing, she took one last mournful look south, towards home. Then she decided to do what came natural. Fight.

Tameri decided to ambush her father and verbally browbeat him into joining the expedition to recover the *Seadragon's* figurehead. But he would be reluctant, if not downright ornery. Tameri would need an ally on her side, a powerful, preferably elven one.

ଔ৪ଊଔ৪ଊ

Tameri followed Yax'Kaqix as he ascended the main stairwell of the *Seadragon.* She continued her attack despite his repeated rebuttals. She hoped the elf's defenses caved before she succumbed to the fumes created by the moldering supplies carried on their backs.

Yax set the bag down with a thud. Despite the overwhelming odor of mold and decay, he replied to her request without missing a breath.

"Not 'no' but 'Hells no!'"

The willowy built elf grunted, shouldered the sack again, and practically raced up the stairwell onto the deck of the *Seadragon.*

"Buh, but," Tameri stuttered, struggling up the stairs.

"No, buts," Yax commanded decisively. Tameri couldn't decide if he sounded more like the general of old or the frazzled father figure. He had been both in his centuries on Faltyr.

Continuing in his autocratic tone, he stated, "My job is to offload tons of spoiled supplies and then refill the ridiculous holds of this peculiar vessel before the week's out. I am neither the captain of this ship nor this company. And I am not your father. Decision's not mine to make. You'll have to talk to him."

"You know how he'll react," Tameri said, slamming down her bag of ruined grain on the discard cart. "He's thick-skulled and iron-willed."

Her heated words with the elf drew glances from Breuxias and her Uncle Macz. She hated to admit how much her father's furrowed brow matched her own. Perhaps they were too much alike to ever get along.

Yax waved his hands dismissively and said, "I don't want any involvement. It's a bad idea."

"A bad idea. But you said?"

Tameri's father approached her and the irritated elf. Looking concerned, he asked, "What's a bad idea?"

Yax shook his head dismissively and then busied himself with a fresh bag of grain from the other cart.

Seeing her battle going badly, Tameri decided to regroup. Seizing a sack from the wagon, she ignored her father.

"What's a bad idea?" he repeated with an edge to his voice.

Shifting tactics, Tameri went on the offensive and locked eyes with her father. His wide inky orbs were identical to hers.

"Accompanying you to Oparre."

Breuxias boomed, "Absolutely out of the question!" But then, in a grave tone, he added, "I brought you here to learn from the greatest sage of our age, not to join our ranks."

Tameri recognized the concern on her father's face. She'd seen it every time he'd left them behind. Only she hadn't realized the emotion behind the expression until now. She softened her approach but continued to press her advantage.

"But you're taking Macz. He's not part of Finders Keepers."

"No, but your uncle's a skilled sailor and navigator," he retorted. "Plus, he's good in a fight. He'll stand as second mate and join the company inside of a season, two at most."

The foundation for her father's argument was shaky at best. Judging by his expression, he knew he'd made a mistake with his reasoning. She could read a map better than him or Macz.

Tameri moved in for the kill. She strode forward, carrying the hefty sack of grain with little effort. She refused to capitulate without getting her way. Sounding more like a viper than a daughter, she talked as she walked.

"So you take me away from my mother, bring me all the way here, to do what? Abandon me again? Imprison me in some old wizard's tower, call it an education, and forget about me? Well, I won't do it! I'm a grown ass woman, not Daddy's little girl anymore! So you can either take me with you or take me home!"

Tameri did not stop walking until she finished her tirade. Without realizing it, her father had ceded most of the dock to her. He'd backed to the edge of the pier during her rant. She'd trapped him between her fiery resolve and the frigid waters of the sea.

Yax had escaped, slipping downstairs while she was distracted. Her uncle had been trapped between his warring relatives and a cart full of molded grain. But Macz could barely restrain his laughter. Her fiery nature amused him to no end.

Once again, she'd won a major victory against an overwhelming foe. Dropping the sack at his feet, Tameri said, "I'll get my things."

cs so cs so

Tameri didn't take long to pack the few possessions she'd brought from home. After all, it was not as though she intended on staying in this stuffy tower with a bunch of strangers from the North. When she left Istara, she had planned on adventuring with her father all along. And after arguing him into a corner, she'd won the right to join his crew.

Tameri knew better than to give him time to change his mind or devise a strategy to sail away from Fraustmauth before she made it back to the *Seadragon*. She wouldn't put it past him. He'd done it to her mother before. Though to be fair, he had left her with a fortune, enough to build and stock the finest bookstore and scrivener on the Pelican Coast.

A lifetime ago, Tameri had thought this was what she wanted: a tower full of books, mystical arts to master, and a renowned sage to teach her. But that was before the foul invaders had defiled her homeland and burned her family's business to the ground. Ultimately, they'd forced her to commit mortal sins to free her city from their viselike grip. She credited her father for remembering her childhood dream, but her inner child had been one of the many casualties during the siege of Istara.

Tameri belted on her slender dueling blade and shouldered her oiled canvas duffel. Last but not least, she retrieved her unstrung composite bow and quiver full of steel-tipped arrows from the corner. Her prized weapon, a present not from her father but her uncle, had been by her side since before the siege.

Breuxias was the better marksman, but Macz was the better father figure in her experience. Her real father had taught her how to be a masterful archer, but Macz had taught her when it was appropriate to disable, maim, or even kill. On the other hand, her father had taught her stubborn, selfish adherence to personal goals. Her goals at the moment included making it to the *Seadragon* before she ended up marooned in a strange city amongst even stranger folk.

As Tameri wound her way around the guest level of the lighthouse, she found herself in front of Kaladimus Dor's chambers. She had passed his closed door on her way to the stairs several times, but now the portal stood slightly ajar. She could hear voices inside his room, one of them belonged to a woman.

Tameri had inherited another trait from her father, insatiable curiosity, and it drew her toward the door. She leaned in to listen.

"Why can't you leave it here? It'll be safe," the unseen female entreated her conversational partner. Unless Tameri was mistaken, the singsong voice belonged to Caleb's daughter, Keera. "My father and I will make sure of it," followed her initial statement, confirming the identity of the speaker for Tameri.

"I can't do that," Dor said. "It's not your burden to bear. It's mine and mine alone, especially if Braigen is truly gone from the face of Faltyr."

"Why, Kal? Why? You're not alone."

"I told you not to call me that."

"Fine. Dor. Stupid name for a stupid, stubborn man."

Don't trust her, Tameri thought.

Pet names, sweet words, and playful jests meant Keera had an agenda. It might be innocent enough. But with her father being the most powerful wizard in the North, Dor couldn't afford to be too careful, especially if he was protecting something of note.

"It's trouble. Like me. Nothing but trouble. I can't risk making you or your father, much less all of Fraustmauth, a target."

Such a noble, selfless soul. But what was his burden?

"A target for whom?" Keera asked in an exasperated fashion, displaying the fiery nature usually hidden by her bookish demeanor. "What's so damn special about this box?"

"It's not the chest, rather what it contains."

Intriguing, very intriguing.

Keera asked, "What in the Nine do you have in there anyway?"

What indeed, Tameri echoed, hoping to sneak a peek.

"Trouble. Deadly serious trouble," the mage answered.

Keera laughed and then said, "You're a strange man, Kaladimus Dor. Damn peculiar, in fact."

"Part of my charm."

"You have charm. Hmph. Hadn't noticed."

"Not even a little bit."

"Nope. Not the slightest. Good day to you, sir."

Tameri sighed. The conversation had devolved to flirtations and pleasantries. She wasn't likely to get anymore answers eavesdropping outside of her new captain's door, at least not this time. However, she was likely to be discovered if she lingered too long. Taking her leave lightly, she headed for the stairs, the ship, and the sea.

Chapter 7

In the wake of their stormy escape from Eastgate, Yax'Kaqix became the silent taskmaster of his sanguine yesteryears as he guided the prison wagon into the desert. He relied on his commanding presence and sheer taciturn determination to persuade the others to follow his lead without having to issue a single verbal instruction.

Not wanting to repeat himself, Yax refused to explain his rash actions to anyone, including Breuxias, until they reached a safe distance from the epicenter of Dor's botched weave. The Aethyr-fueled twister in the distance presented a looming threat to their exposed party, especially if it decided follow the fool who'd summoned it.

The teams of horses struggled through the desolate wastes that formed the bulk of the weird, wild region known as the Sands of Sorrow. Yax struggled to imagine the area as it had been in the time of his great-great-grandfather, before the apocalyptic end of the war between rival lovers, Artemis and Ra'Tallah, laid waste to it. In those days before the Cataclysm, countless towns and cities had dotted the rivers and streams that flowed forth from the resource rich Meshkenet Mountains.

However, the explosive climax of the lovers' feud sundered the mountains and buried the entire region in a thick layer of ash, dust, and sand. In the process, it had warped the fundamental nature of reality in the area. Now, the unnatural desert took a toll on anyone using the Aethyr to fuel magical effects and abilities.

If exposed to the draining, disruptive energies of the sprawling desert for an extended period of time, items of minor enchantment such as poisons, potions, and poultices would either spoil completely or transmute into a wholly different substance. Fortunately, powerful relics such as Demon Queller and Starkiller were all but immune to these corrupting effects.

Spotting a ravine snaking its way through the desert floor, Yax steered the wagon in its direction. Their circuitous route occupied most of the day but allowed them to find refuge in a dry gorge carved deep into the red rock by a fast-moving waterway in the days before humans or elves called Faltyr home. He didn't stop until the wagon train reached the inkiest pool of shadows cast by the steep-sided drainage. Hopefully, the combination of distance and darkness would keep them from being seen from the rim of the ravine.

Regardless, Yax knew their party could not remain in one place for long. As soon as the storm dissipated, riders from Oparre would be out in force looking for them, especially the precious cargo in the prison wagon and the elf and wizard who liberated them. He had to free the prisoners, listen to their story, and then decide on a plan of action. Somewhere in there, he had to make sure Dor didn't bleed to death from the crossbow bolt protruding from his torso.

Katar dismounted as soon as he parked his wagon in front of the one carrying the hooded prisoners. He rushed toward Yax as if he had something to say. Without hesitation, the elf leaped to the ground and drew Demon Queller, causing the ancient blade to ring menacingly.

Yax smiled toothily as the whelp skidded to a halt. Katar detoured toward where Tameri and Leishan aided the ailing magician. Dor had a length of cold iron through him, but he had looked worse when he'd washed ashore after the sinking of the *Nightsfall*. Judging by the placement of the bolt, Yax wagered the mage had awhile before the wound became critical.

First things first, he thought as curiosity overcame concern.

As Breuxias approached, ignoring the brandished blade, Yax sliced clean through the heavy lock on the cage door. Demon Queller rang happily, satisfied with another victory of elven steel over wrought iron. With the lock defeated, the elf sheathed the blade and turned to his comrade.

"What in the Nine Hells is going on here?" Breuxias asked. "You risked the mission, risked our lives, for what? To rescue some common criminals? To sign our names to a death warrant?"

With the Brute leading the attack on Yax, Katar worked up the nerve to add, "King Orson will have our heads for this! If his knights don't get us first!"

Breuxias and Yax yelled at the same time, "Keep out of this!"

The quarreling mercenaries smiled despite the tension.

Dor screams drew their attention from the prisoners. Tameri crouched over him in the back of the wagon. She applied direct pressure to his wound with her blood-covered hands.

As Leishan tossed the crossbow bolt over his shoulder, Tameri said, "Can we focus on one thing at a time? Dor is bleeding to death."

"He'll live awhile yet," Yax corrected her. "Unless you want to patch him up instead?"

The Savior of Istara looked away and returned to her mundane ministrations. She had the ability to heal the magician but refused to call upon the same eldritch powers that had aided her in liberating her homeland. Breuxias hoped Caleb's tutelage would help his daughter find another way to utilize the Aethyr. Yax, however, felt her destiny lay upon the dangerous path she'd started walking in Istara.

"Answer me, godsdammit!" Breuxias boomed. "And with none of the wizard riddles. I'd like a real explanation for once."

Ignoring their intrusions, Yax opened the cage door of the wagon before responding. He loathed admitting it, but he had a flair for the dramatic. He'd developed it during his days fighting in the city arena to repay a debt to his father, a ransom paid to free the noble son from an Arpithian prison.

As the hooded figures emerged from the cage, Yax said, "They aren't criminals! They're prisoners. Prisoners of war."

"War? Hold on a minute! We're not involved in any war."

Looking around the Brute's sizeable biceps, Katar interjected, "If we weren't before, we are now. Thanks!"

"Shut it!" Breuxias and Yax shouted again.

Katar plopped down in the sand to sulk. Yax understood that the man's regional expertise and particular skill-set had been necessary for recovering the figurehead. But the junior guildsman needed to learn his place at the bottom of the organizational pyramid.

Finders Keepers was no idyllic Baax democracy where one man's opinion carried as much weight as another. Finders Keepers was an adventuring company, and Yax was a major stakeholder in its profitable past as well as its promising future. So Katar's opinion carried about as much weight with him as gnat shit on a dragon's wing.

Half dozen robed figures crept from the prison wagon. Three of them ignored their saviors, staggering in the direction of the closest water barrel. Two others assisted the remaining prisoner's gingerly descent from the bed of the wagon onto the dry riverbed.

Once their companion was safely on the sand, the taller of the two prisoners removed its hood, revealing a full-blood elven woman. Her smallish, unadorned ears marked her as one of the Winaq'che, the Elves of Silent Brook.

Despite obvious malnourishment and lingering signs of torture and abuse, Yax found her to be an elf of uncommon beauty with an almost regal bearing. Judging by her posture, she had to be high born, military trained, or possibly both, like him. He stood there dumbly, transfixed by her intense blue eyes, a mirror of his own.

"I am Zoltana," the vision spoke, stirring Yax from his reverie, "and my eternal gratitude is yours. This is my sister, Zarena. And her midwife, Xotl. The guys drinking like horses from a trough are Shell Horse, Yellow Ant, and Yawning Deer."

Zoltana gestured one-by-one to the other prisoners. As they removed their hoods, Yax noticed that she already had a mirror image, an identical twin to be precise. *Well, not exactly identical*, he told himself, noticing Zarena's swollen belly.

Adding to Yax's surprise, the pregnant woman's midwife turned out to be a half-elven woman. No self-respecting Unen'ek woman would allow herself to be attended by a half-breed. But then again, Yax was a failed monk and errant Choj'Ahaw turned adventurer who'd had his own half-elven children once upon a time. So he wasn't exactly the type to stand on tradition.

"I am Yax'Kaqix of the Unen'ek," he replied formally. "And this man is my friend, my brother, Breuxias." Yax bowed his head respectfully but never lowered his eyes.

Breuxias nodded curtly as he surveyed the assortment of elves, but his eyes softened to their plight. Judging by his expression, the sinister implications of the situation burdened his mind and weighed on his heartstrings. He wouldn't dare admit it, but he became softer of heart as the weight of his years weathered him like a pebble in a raging torrent.

Yax lamented that humans, much like canines and cattle, rarely survived long enough to come to acceptance with themselves, much less the awful grandeur of the universe. Yet Breuxias had seen more than most in his forty odd years wandering Faltyr.

Catching him lost in thought, the Brute beat Yax to interrogating the prisoners. But it was a good sign. If his friend displayed an interest in their fate, the masterful Choj'Ahaw could exploit it to get his way in whatever future decision had to be made regarding them.

"How did you come to be this far from Silent Brook?" Breuxias asked. "There are no forts north of Eastgate, just desert until you hit the mountains."

"There is now," Zoltana answered. "Oparre has seized the ruins of Mok'Drular. It is both fortress and prison."

"And was almost our grave," Zarena added, holding her belly.

"As it has been for so many."

"Too many."

As the twins explained the particulars of their people's grim situation, the mercenaries looked at each other intently. In a single determined glance, their path became clear. It looked like Finders Keepers was going to war after all. And for once, Yax didn't care if it was good for business. He'd made a promise.

On the night Sir Caayl died, the noble Knight of Ishta'Kahl had confessed the truth of his involvement in a plot against his liege. Consumed with hatred for all things elf and fae, King Orson flew into a rage when told his heir, the crown prince, had a secret liaison with Lady Shy'elle, the current Queen of Silent Brook, during her captivity.

But the mad king's mood turned murderous when the prince confessed his love and told his father that the elf queen was with child. In his naivety, the well-meaning son hoped to save his father, end the war, and unite their kingdoms with his particular brand of bedroom negotiations. But he underestimated the darkness growing within the aging king. And the prince paid for it with his life.

Even as senior Knights of Damarra, led by Sir Frederick, carried out the death sentence, Sir Caayl and several of his order conspired to smuggle the elven queen to safety. A knight named Sir Ausic headed north with Shy'elle while Caayl fled south with a decoy, one of her bodyguards.

Separated during the relentless pursuit, Caayl made his way to Kingsport. He ran into his childhood love, an employee of the *Nightsfall's* captain, and took it as a sign to sail with them to Moor'Dru. The valiant knight hoped to uncover the truth behind what had turned his king to evil and stop his genocidal war before it drowned the main continent in blood. But he never made it.

Instead, Caayl had dumped his quest squarely on the shoulders of the closest elf. Then he let himself be killed by a child turned into a vampire in hopes of joining his love in the Underworld. Now, Yax endangered his friends and their mission for an oath pledged to a dead man. Once more, fate proved herself to be bitch god who worked in mysterious ways. Some days he loved her. Most he hated her.

Though he loathed doing it, Yax outlined a two-pronged plan to divide their meager forces to accomplish separate objectives. Zoltana and the two younger elves would guide Yax, Breuxias, and Leishan over the remnants of the mountains to the ruinous ogre city of Mok'Drular. There they would devise a plan and create whatever distraction necessary to liberate the thousands of elven prisoners taken from Silent Brook.

Dor, Tameri, and Katar would guide the others south to the coast, rendezvous with the *Seadragon*, and then sail it round the Horn of Panglov. Their mission would be to patrol the coastline north of the terminus of the Meshkenet Mountains for any prisoners who survived their rescue attempt at Mok'Drular.

Having freed Tameri's mother from slavery, Breuxias showed unusual empathy for the plight of the elves, siding with his longtime friend on the issue. Having survived one ordeal in the Sands of Sorrow, Dor preferred to keep the item he'd obtained there as far as possible from the desert's strange weft and weave. Katar proved to have less backbone than a Baraviel Seajelly; he supported any idea that would get him out of Oparre alive.

The sole source of opposition on the matter came from Tameri; she'd been left behind by her father when he went to war too many times. Even as the other two wagons left the heavy prison conveyance behind in the riverbed, Tameri and her father lingered to discuss their issues. From what he overheard, Yax realized that Tameri understood the importance of the mission but not her father's motives.

As a father, Yax knew the Brute's simple motivation: to protect his daughter. Tameri would be safer back on the ship with her uncle rather than taking on a suicide mission. He'd allowed his only begotten son, Kan'Balam, to accompany him and Breuxias on one, and it had ended in tragedy. Yax would never forgive himself. It didn't matter if a thousand years passed between now and when the reaper's blade finally took him home.

As they exited the ravine, the Brute joined him in the wagon full of supplies. Breuxias grimaced when his daughter waved at him before climbing into the back of the other wagon alongside the figurehead. If possible, his countenance grew a few shades darker than normal.

Yax didn't know what to say to comfort his friend. So he did what came natural. He said nothing.

Chapter 8

Sir Frederick awoke among chaos and carnage. Unsure as to what had happened or how long he had been unconscious, he raised his aching head and looked around. Flames leapt wildly about him. The smell of burning timber and flesh flooded his nostrils.

Searing pain shot through his leg. The knight rolled over and sat up to examine the extent of his injury. The impact of his fall had driven the blade of his dagger through its leather sheath and into his left calf. He wrapped his wounded leg and tried to clear his head.

The Knight of Oparre, King Orson's Executioner, rose to one knee and drew in a labored breath before pushing himself fully erect. His heavy plate armor made the task difficult. Despite the enchantments woven into it, it had been a poor choice for crossing a desert. The suit was not only a gift from his king but worth a fortune. So he would not leave it behind at Mok'Drular.

Sir Frederick stood battered and bleeding, but not broken. His dark blue eyes peered through the smoke-filled streets around him. Bodies were strewn throughout the street, some twisted into impossible angles. The wind whipped smoke, ash, and his long blonde hair about his face. Through squinted eyes, he saw where the twister had spread flames from a ruined tower across the city.

Soldiers farther down the street battled the massive infernos while the citizens of Eastgate fled toward the heart of the city. Some stopped to help others on their way out, but most fled clutching whatever possessions they could carry.

A murderous expression crossed his blood and ash smeared face as he drank in the scene before him. Eventually, Sir Frederick's gaze fell upon his fallen steed. Jorva'Kar lay twisted grotesquely not far from him. The horse's head was completely hidden beneath its body.

"Gods damn those who did this!"

"Sir Frederick! My lord!" a voice called from behind. Galil, his squire, rushed to his side.

"Are you alright, my lord? You're bleeding!" Galil exclaimed as he tried to determine the extent of the knight's injury. "It's close to the wound Sir Ausic left during his escape. It's a deep puncture and is going to need..."

Galil stopped talking when Sir Frederick smacked his hand away, but the squire's observation was accurate. Aided by several confederates, Sir Ausic had wounded him and escaped with Lady Shy'Elle and her two captains. The dutiful knight had chased the fugitives all the way to Ror, eluded capture, and stolen Shy'Elle out from under Ausic and his allies. Now, if Frederick could just *recapture* her. Putting aside his thirst for vengeance, he forced himself to focus on the matters at hand, like the missing wagon full of prisoners.

"What happened?" Sir Frederick asked.

"A wizard, my lord, a wizard did all this. He made a real mess of the place."

"I need a horse!" the knight shouted.

"I'll go find you one, your lordship, but we must first get you to safety. The fires are out of control and there is only one secured passage out of here," Galil said. Placing an arm around the knight's waist, he added, "Hold onto me, my lord. I'll lead you to safety."

"Damn it, boy!" Sir Frederick shoved his squire away from him with enough force to set the younger man on his butt. "If I need your assistance, I'll ask for it. What I need is a horse, so I can catch those responsible for this outrage."

Sir Frederick turned at the sound of a horseman approaching and stepped in front of his steed. He waved his arms and startled the horse. The beast stopped, reared onto its hind legs, and spilled its rider onto the ground. The knight stepped over the groaning man lying in the street and seized the bewildered beast's reigns.

"This one will do," he said. "Pay the man, Galil."

Refusing his squire's assistance, the knight hoisted himself into the saddle stiffly. He grunted away the pain and jerked the reins on the horse hard. Sir Frederick rode away, on his appropriated mount, disappearing into a cloud of smoke and ash. As usual, Galil was left to make apologies and occasional reparations for his lord's crimes in the name of the crown.

ꕥ

Sir Frederick rode through his company's encampment, located at an oasis north of Eastgate. The bulk of his men had camped here while he had ridden ahead to escort the prisoners to a secure holding facility in the city. Judging by a cursory inspection, most had remained in camp despite the inferno raging in the merchant quarter of the nearby city. Fighting fires fell well within their duties as soldiers. After all, fire could be a tool, a weapon, or the enemy.

The Knight of Oparre's mood darkened further by the time he arrived at the command tent. When he dismounted, he didn't even bother to tether the steed. A nearby soldier grabbed its reins and steadied the animal. He nodded to the enlisted man and brushed by him.

The senior knight pointed to two other soldiers loitering outside of his tent and barked the command, "Follow me!"

Sir Frederick swiped open the tent flap and stepped inside. The soldiers followed him. His subordinate knights sat on the opposite side of a large table. Sir Balmoor choked on his ale when he laid eyes on his superior, and Sir Stogal stood so rapidly that he almost flipped the folding table onto its side. Clearly, they'd thought him dead. Judging by the number of mugs tumbling to the sand, the bastards had been celebrating.

A petite elven slave woman stopped in her tracks and clutched at the silver platter holding bread and cheese. She curtsied to Sir Frederick as he entered, but he did not return her courtesy. Instead, he strode toward both the knights seated at the table. As he drew his sword, Lightbringer, from its jeweled scabbard, the elven woman yelped in fear and dropped the platter of meat and cheese. Sir Frederick's blade sliced through the air and cleaved the table in twain, causing her to seek refuge behind one of the other soldiers.

His actions shocked Sirs Balmoor and Stogal too. They leapt away from the ruined table. Their hands shook as badly as the slave, yet neither one of them dared to draw steel on their superior.

Too bad. I'd have respected them more if they'd provoked me to kill them where they stand.

"What in the Nine is this?!" Frederick boomed. "Two Knights of Damarra who've sworn oaths of fealty to my king sitting on their asses and swilling ale while one of His Majesty's cities burn!"

"You're alive?" Sir Balmoor exclaimed, looking as surprised as his companion.

Balmoor had his stringy, black hair pulled into a braided ponytail, a common enough style among the helmeted Knights of Oparre. Streaks of gray hinted at his true age. His round belly spoke to his passions for carousing and comfort, and he stood a full head shorter than his companion.

They were celebrating my demise. Treacherous bastards.

"Of course I'm alive! And likely to stay that way, unlike the two of you. If I were to report to King Orson how you sat by idly, while one of his cities was devastated, he'd have your heads on pikes!"

Sir Balmoor chimed in again, "I beg your pardon! We sent troops to battle the blaze and help the people out."

"You sent troops? From what I saw, most are still in this encampment, while those fighting fires are struggling."

"Frederick, we were discussing what direction the elves and those who helped them escape may be heading, the Sands of Sorrow are vast," Sir Stogal interjected.

Excuses and diversions. Always the way with these eastern knights. A few months on the front would toughen them right up.

In a swifter motion than earlier, Frederick brought the tip of his blade to the base of Stogal's unshaven chin. For a brief moment, the intrusive knight remained silent.

"We swore fealty to Orson, but our fates are in your hands. I'm sorry for not doing more." Stogal pleaded, "And beg your forgiveness."

The tall knight's thick black hair clung to his forehead and beads of sweat rolled down the sides of his head. A long, deep scar ran across Stogal's chin and down his neck. He stood straight before his superior in spite of having his life threatened.

Spineless too it seems.

Sir Frederick glanced over his shoulder as the tent flap parted and Galil stepped inside. The knight turned his eyes back to his apologetic, if unreliable subordinates.

"Meditate on your failures to the Crown. I will be sure to elaborate on them to him when we return to Grymsburg," Frederick replied. "Between now and then, I'm sure you can come up with a reason why he shouldn't have your heads. For now, gather your best riders! We will find those responsible for this outrage and make them pay with their lives. You have your orders; now get out of my sight!"

After Balmoor and Stogal beat a hasty retreat from the tent, Frederick rounded on the terrified elven woman and said, "That goes for you too, my pet. Leave the mess; I'll have Galil clean it up later." Gesturing to the soldiers he'd summoned earlier, he added, "Guards, seize this woman and put her back in her cage. We don't want this one to get away as well."

As the guards secured the iron manacles around her wrists, Sir Frederick lifted the woman's chin with his finger and stared deep into her eyes. He could see how frightened of him she was, and he enjoyed watching her anticipate his unjust wrath and his unwelcomed affections.

"You are a pretty one. Not as lovely as your queen, but in her absence, I may have a use for you when I return," he said, letting his finger trail from her chin to the exposed top of her pale bosom. He smiled at her as he sheathed his blade, imagining him as blade and her as sheath. To the guards, he grinned and added, "Don't ride her too many miles, boys. I'll expect her to be fresh for later."

The two soldiers exchanged awkward looks and then escorted the prisoner out. The perverse knight cared little for their opinions. He doubted she would be the first elf they'd ravage. And if they didn't enjoy that perk of the job, they were fools. It's not like elves had any rights in Oparre anymore. They were either pets, prisoners, or fuel for a pyre. Many had become all three.

"Get your horse, Galil; you're coming with me. As you've yet to fail me, you're more trustworthy than anyone else at my command. And one of the few fools with any sense in the East."

The squire beamed at him and said, "Thank you, sire."

"Don't get emotional on me, boy. You're supposed to be a knight-in-training. Time to sack up and start acting the part."

Exiting the tent, Frederick thought, *he's as loyal as a dog and twice as loving. Like Ausic and Caayl, that'll be his downfall. Unless I can beat it out of him first.*

As the squire readied his steed, Sir Frederick stared down the soldiers lingering around him, going about their assigned tasks with the enthusiasm of boulders. He lamented the sorry discipline of these eastern levies. Even the knights proved unable to be trusted, but he would have to make do with them.

After all, it was his duty to recapture the prisoners, especially the Queen of Silent Brook, the woman he coveted more than any other. He could see what the prince had seen in her, which made it easy enough to end her human lover's life when the execution order came down.

"All of you there," Sir Frederick called, "stop what you're doing and listen up. Today, you have failed me, and in turn you have failed your country. A band of rogues has taken it upon themselves to make a mockery of the King's troops, of my troops." Very few of them could hold his gaze as he continued to admonish them. Shame could be a powerful motivator. So could fear. Fortunately, he was good at instilling both. "But these criminals will not go unpunished. We will capture them and show them what happens to those who defy Oparre. Let me remind you, you have a sworn duty to serve King Orson and, by extension, to serve me. I expect results. So, if any of you fail me again, I will send you screaming into the Nine myself!"

As night approached, Sir Frederick swung himself into the saddle of a fresh mount and rode out of the encampment. Though he hadn't ordered them to do it, his men broke camp hastily and followed him back into the Sands of Sorrow. His reputation served him well. They feared the King's Executioner more than any haunted desert or renegade wizard.

❧❧

The fading light of day colored the horizon behind Sir Frederick and the score of armored riders at his command. His charred riding cloak flapped in the wind behind him. Balmoor and Stogal rode behind their commander. He could feel their eyes on his back, but he saw himself as robust, merciless as a dragon.

What do dragons care of the opinion of sheep? They don't.

They continued to ride through the early evening, using the light from the eerie aurora over the Sands of Sorrow to follow the wagon tracks. Sir Frederick maintained eye contact with the tracker riding ahead of him, yet his thoughts wandered elsewhere. Familiar pain wracked his wound, reminding him of the fight between himself and Ausic.

Frederick remembered walking in on the traitorous Knights of Ishta'Kahl as they escorted the elven queen from her cell. Sir Ausic had lunged at him and attacked before the dangerous Knight of Damarra could draw his sword. Nimble Ausic had spun around him like a dancer, sliced open Frederick's calf, and then toppled him to the ground. The weight of their betrayal registered with him right before Sir Caayl's boot kicked him in the face, the surprising blow that had rendered him unconscious.

The Executioner urged his steed faster, not to run away from his past but to catch up with the tracker. The man had dismounted and appeared to be inspecting something. As he drew his horse alongside his scout, the knight noticed the abandoned prison wagon concealed under a rocky outcropping.

"They've lightened their load," the tracker explained.

While Galil held aloft a lantern, the soldiers examined the prison wagon. Satisfied with their discovery, Sir Frederick remained silent in his saddle for a moment. He drummed his fingers on the new metal dagger sheath Galil had secured from the company quartermaster.

"Continue tracking them; we'll catch up," he ordered.

The local man nodded his assent to Frederick and disappeared into the darkness to pursue his quarry once again. As he drank from his waterskin, the knight lamented not having more men under his command like the laconic tracker. *If only all these Ireti peoples had his work ethic.* After returning the waterskin to its place on his saddle, he stared down the retinue of sorry soldiery around him.

Avoiding his gaze, Balmoor asked, "Are you all right?"

"I couldn't be better," the senior knight answered, sarcasm coloring his voice. "I enjoy chasing escaped prisoners, and the wizard who freed them, into the same bloody desert we just crossed. At least, it's a lovely night for tracking fugitives, wouldn't you agree?"

Balmoor grunted a noncommittal response.

"A valuable contribution as always," Frederick gibed. "Now that we've had this heart-to-heart, let's continue our pursuit."

Several of the men in the troop chuckled at his comment as they galloped after him. Balmoor's men kept quiet, however, either out of loyalty to their commander or fear of raising his ire.

They rode through the ravine for what seemed like hours before finally coming upon the tracker once more. Holding his horse by the reigns, he knelt beside two sets of wagon tracks.

Speaking through the shemagh protecting his face from the blustery desert winds, the tracker reported, "The wagons split up here, your lordship. The heavier of the two has gone south toward the coast; the other is headed north, toward the mountains."

Sir Frederick asked, "Is there anything else to report?"

Pointing to blood-stained rags tangled in a sage bush a few feet from the southbound tracks, the tracker said, "I can't be certain, my lord, but I'd say the one bound for the coast is carrying wounded."

"It's a reasonable assumption," the King's Executioner replied. Turning to his troops, he directed, "Stogal, Balmoor, take four riders each. Scout ahead and report back."

The two knights and their selected riders left their superior and then rode off in different directions. Once they were out of earshot, Frederick turned his attention Galil and the tracker.

The tracker asked, "What about me, sir?"

"What's your name, my good man? You've done His Majesty a valuable service this night. I want to see you are rewarded for it."

"Tokeyet. And you do an old man proud with your words."

"Just see that you do not fail me, Tokeyet. Galil can tell you that I am a generous benefactor but an implacable enemy. This next task I have for you is a vital one."

"Your orders, my lord?" the squire questioned his superior.

"Find our surest, swiftest horse. Then send Tokeyet here back to Eastgate to locate Marduk. I'd rather not be tracking a wizard without one at my side."

"Yes, your lordship," Galil replied. "What about the troops?"

"We will camp here until Marduk arrives, or we receive word from Balmoor or Stogal," Frederick stated as he dismounted the tired and sweat drenched steed.

Frederick disliked wizards, but he seemed to have no alternative than to call in one to assist them. Instead of risking his life foolishly confronting the renegade mage on his own, he would wait for someone to even the odds. He had learned one caveat during his service to King Orson: Like power, never underestimate magic or those who wielded it.

Chapter 9

Kaladimus Dor climbed as if his life depended on it, because at the time it did. Jagged rocks cut into his fingers and toes as he scrambled down the slippery slope toward the raging black river far below him. A relentless deluge of cold rain and vicious little hailstones threatened to dislodge him. The icy barrage pelted his back, shoulders, and his tender ears. Hot blood flowed from one.

And yet he descended from the treacherous heights of his mountaintop home as if demons from the Nine Hells chased after him. Instead, it was the uniformed men of Guvmint. Unable to understand his destructive nature, the superstitious fools saw him as the devil. Now they had come to take him from his family.

Though they said it was for his own protection, Dor knew they lied. His uncles had told him all Guvmint men lie to get their way, the way of their faceless masters. So he'd run. And he'd keep on running. As a country boy running the ridges with his outlaw kin, he'd accepted the provincial caveat: Liberty or Death.

Every muscle in his young body ached when he finally reached the bottom of the ravine. If he stopped moving for long, he feared they'd cramp and he'd fall. If he didn't die, he'd certainly be caught. Even now, he heard the braying of the Guvmint men's hounds between booms of thunder. They came from the path winding down the far side of the ridge, so he had little time to spare.

Dor ran for the river, known to the fae natives as Moratuc, the River of Death, for its unpredictable, oft devastating floods. Through the deluge, he spied his only means of escape from the hypothetical horrors awaiting him at the puritanical hands of Guvmint. He slogged through the mud toward his uncles' secluded campsite, their tiny dock, and the riverboat beside it.

He dodged around the fire pit and sidestepped a series of copper vats and pipes before stumbling over a crate of ceramic jugs. He landed face down in the muck, smacking his head hard enough on a rock to jar his senses. The mad, muddy world at the bottom of the ravine swam before him.

Lightning flashed again followed by rolling thunder.

Dor rose to his feet like a fawn standing for the first time. He mopped mud and blood from his eyes with the sleeve of his ruined smock but only created more of a mess. He staggered toward the rushing water as the baying hounds drew close enough to see the dancing beams of light cast by the Aethyr-powered wands carried by their handlers.

Dor stopped short of pitching off the side of the rocking pier. The fast-moving water threatened to tear it and the boat from its moorings. He moved quickly rather than gracefully, diving into the craft. Working as fast as possible with his numbed, bloody fingers, he cast off the lines and then held on for dear life.

The river sucked the rudderless craft downstream at breakneck speed. At every turn, he expected to be tossed from the boat or pulverized against one of the myriad stones protruding from its treacherous waters. But fate had others things in store for him.

As the out-of-control craft rounded a wide bend, Dor spied the distinctive arch of a steel-and-stone bridge ahead. The span crossed the river along the military road built long ago by the men of Guvmint to aid in their conquest of the rebellious clans and their fae allies hiding out in the hills. He told himself he'd find a new home, far from the intrusive nature of Guvmint and its minions if he made it past the bridge. Then he'd be safe.

He saw the enemy stationed upon high, huddled along the metal railing of the imposing structure. Beams bright as lightning bolts lanced out from their wands, darting along the river and its banks, searching for any sign of him. He had to do something before they spotted him.

Hesitantly, his eyes rose to the stormy sky. He would turn out the lights, just the lights. *Destroy their wands but leave them be*, Dor instructed the dangerous elements at his disposal before raising his hands to the heavens.

Did the universe listen? Always. But not very well.

His hair stood on end as a shower of sparks flew skyward from his fingertips. Lightning flashed and thunder rolled as the tiny boat shot toward the archway beneath the bridge. Shock and awe filled Dor when a magnificent bolt of pure energy streaked down from the sky. The lightning bolt exploded in a spectacle of pyrotechnics atop the bridge. Its energy coursed through the structure and electrified everything in its path as the bolt sought the swollen river below. And the boy who'd cried out to it.

Dor screamed as he careened toward the crackling wall of energy. Pain filled his body. A dazzling array of colors exploded and faded away before his eyes, forcing him to shut them tight.

When he opened them again, they beheld the swirling aurora over the Sands of Sorrow rather than the storm swollen skies over his old dominion. Despite the violent rocking motion of his conveyance, the startled magician sat up abruptly. Familiar faces mixed with unfamiliar ones as he stared wild-eyed around him, blinking away the dream.

Dor, however, knew it to be more than a dream. It was a memory. One he preferred to keep buried away, repressed along with much of his past. He couldn't bear the pain of facing his origins beyond the Veil. So he ignored it once more, embracing the immediate pain of his wound.

Zarena's midwife, Xotl, made it easy for him when she extracted a splinter from deep within the puncture. Her tapered nails substituted for tweezers and worked as skillfully as any chirurgeon's. Tameri assisted her, hovering over him like an exquisite ebony image of Eresh, Goddess of Death. With her chiseled features and leonine musculature, she looked as much a goddess as any woman he'd ever met.

Captivated but confused, Dor raised one pale hand and caressed her cheek with his fingertips. Reflexively, she nuzzled his hand and smiled sweetly. The feverish young mage felt the broad grin spread across his stubbly cheeks. Self-consciousness overrode their lonely hearts as the elves in the back of the wagon stared at them curiously.

The unspoken spell between them lingered. They stared into each other's eyes for a long moment without speaking. Dor saw so much pain and loss in hers that he almost mistook them for the reflection of his own. The radiant Savior of Istara, liberator of an entire city, shined so much on the outside. But the darkness inside threatened to consume her.

How did Dor know? He'd long grown accustomed to that look in his eyes, a look he'd come to identify with the tortured and the damned.

Dor found he could no longer hold her gaze. Her pain was simply too much for him to bear in his present state. Writhing, he yelped when Xotl removed another fragment left over from the crossbow bolt.

The midwife said to Tameri, "Hold him still."

The human woman pressed down on his bare, bloody chest, using her weight and leverage to keep him from thrashing around too much. Her hot hands burned against his cold flesh, yet the midwife's felt even hotter. White light and intense heat blinded his senses, causing him to squirm like a fat tomato worm.

Dor wailed as the healing energies flooded through him. They worked to stitch the ruined flesh penetrated by the discarded missile. The diminishing wound burned as much as it itched, causing him to struggle against the women pinning him down. As the light and heat receded so did the pain, leaving the calamitous mage with naught but a star-shaped scar and ample soreness.

Tameri wiped the sweat from his brow with a cool, damp cloth. Dor smiled again and she returned the gesture. Finally, she said, "I've seen worse. You'll live. And you'll even have a neat, new scar to impress your lady with back in Fraustmauth."

Blushing, Dor looked away before answering. "I don't have a lady. But I appreciate the gesture. You're very skilled at this."

"Too much time in the trenches stitching men back together."

"You and me both," Xotl remarked, a faraway look in the half-elf woman's pale eyes. "If you'll excuse me, I have to attend to m'lady."

Smiling at her, Dor said, "Thank you for your kindness."

Fortune had blessed him with not one but two healers to care for him. Maybe someone upstairs was finally getting the message. Dor was as dangerous to himself as others. Either way, in uncharacteristic fashion, he thanked the gods and goddesses of Faltyr for sending him such tender angels of mercy. Thanks to Tameri and Xotl, he might live through his second harrowing expedition to this desert after all.

Dor lay in the back of the wagon. Tameri held him close to her, like a babe in her arms. Though she was little more than a stranger to him, he relished her warmth. He shivered in the cold desert air despite the heat provided by his friend's caring, curvaceous daughter. Shock and blood loss had taken its toll.

The swirling aurora in the sky above him caused him no small amount of distress. He remembered those same sinister skies over the ruinous Temple of Darconius on the night the Sandy Sea of Laeg had claimed it for its own, with a little help from the Master-of-Disaster. He looked away lest she see the dark inner recesses of his mind, his secret sins.

Tameri broke the silence between them when she asked, "How'd a Protectorate Mage of Moor'Dru end up travelling with my father? He seemed hesitant to discuss the particulars of your capers together."

"He was unfortunate, I suppose."

"As are we all," the snarky voice of Katar interjected.

Dor wagered Tameri's grimace mirrored his own. Neither of them seemed to like the mouthy rogue. Yet another thing they had in common.

Could they build something lasting based on shared affection for one person and shared enmity for another?

Why not? After all, the peoples of Faltyr have been doing it since the dawn of recorded time.

"He's a good man, your father," Dor began. "He's hardheaded though. You've got that in common." He smiled sheepishly. "But you don't look anything like him. You must take after your mother."

"Is that a compliment?"

Dor shifted his gaze to avoid her dark quizzical eyes. He put more weight on the backpack lying beside him rather than the lovely woman crammed into the crowded wagon with him. Leaning back, he narrowed his eyes, smiling slyly instead of answering Tameri. With her taut body and smoldering heat by his side, Dor imagined he could sleep better than in the arms of Lady Death Herself.

Soon enough he did. He slept deeply but not soundly. This time he dreamed of his mother and their single tragic night together. A score of winters had passed since he'd killed her, and by circumstance his father, in one fiery stroke summoned from the heavens. Still he wasn't sure which had been the real tragedy, his birth or their deaths.

Dor awoke to the lilting voice of an elf. Though he had not yet opened his tired eyes, he knew it to be the velvety voice of the minstrel. As Yawning Deer sang in his native dialect, the mage's mind translated it with ease while it reeled at its mournful yet mocking content.

I was just a lad when mum died,
when dad died too.
Hey-ya Hey-ya Hi-yo!
Raised by fiends as well as friends,
I got no family in this godsforsaken land.
Hey-ya Hey-ya Hi-yo!

Many moons ago my friends did go
across the mirrored Veil,
to a windy city as violent as a jail.
Hey-ya Hey-ya Hi-ya-yo!

One day I awoke alone,
a stranger in a strange land,
one where angels fear to tread
and good men fear to take a stand.
Hey-ya Hey-ya Hi-yo!

Much evil holds sway here
on faraway Faltyr. So much
I think the tears won't stop
till I drown in beer.
Hey-ya Hey-ya Hi-yo!

Alone, alone I walk,
crying day and night.
Only cries console my soul
under evil so severe
here on faraway Faltyr.
Hey-ya Hey-ya Hi-yo!

Take pity on me, sweet Eresh,
put an end to my suffering.
Bring me my death, Milady Death,
and set my soul free!
Hey-ya Hey-ya Hi-ya-yo!

Poor, poor Dor
alone in an alien land,
pleading, insecure, lonely,
and venturing door to door.
I ask every person I see to forgive me,
I who have no faith, no hope, no home.
Hey-ya Hey-ya Hi-yo, Death, take me on!

If not, take pity on my poor soul
and give me the strength to endure
my hellish life on faraway Faltyr.
Hey-ya Hey-ya Hi-yo!

As Yawning Deer's voice faded with the final syllable of his song, Dor wiped his eyes. He had to find out how in the Nine Hells the minstrel had come to know so many private details about his life.

Before he could ask, Tameri said, "That's a beautiful song."

"Yeah, it ain't half bad," Katar added. "For an elf anyway."

Yawning Deer puffed up like a proud peacock at their compliments. The venerable elf's countenance glowed as much as his eyes; a mercurial smile touched the corners of his thin lips as his gaze settled on Dor.

Yawning Deer said, "Nonsense. My voice sounds like a dying cat dragged across hot coals. I haven't been allowed to sing in so long I almost forgot how."

"Still better than most humans can manage on their best days," Tameri reminded him.

From the front seat of the wagon, Katar complained, "I might like it better if I knew what in the Nine it was about."

"It's an ancient tune, even for elves." Yawning Deer lied. At least Dor hoped it was a lie. The other alternative on his mind was maddening. "Has to do with storms gathering on the horizon."

"Are we talking literal, figurative, or metaphorical?" Tameri asked, causing Dor to admire her all the more. He loved smart women. And in the mage's mind, one couldn't get more intelligent than a former bookseller and scrivener who knew her literary devices.

"Why don't you judge for yourself?" Yawning Deer gestured toward the horizon where an expansive cloud of dust and sand swirled darkly in the distance.

"A sandstorm!" Katar shouted, stating the obvious.

"Guess you meant it literally," Tameri replied.

"Guess again," Yawning Deer quipped and pointed below the clouds.

Though Dor could not see over the lip of the wagon, he understood the dire implications of Tameri's warning. She cried, "Knights of Oparre! We're being followed. So the song did have a double meaning, you sly old devil."

As the wagon accelerated from a trot to a gallop, Dor searched the old elf's face for answers. The mage realized the song held more than one meaning. In fact, its contents didn't have a double meaning; it featured a triple entendre, the coveted poetic provenance of riddle makers and religious writers.

But how had the minstrel known so much about him? Dor had struggled with dark, depressing thoughts most of his life. He'd lost track of how often he'd thought of taking his own life because of the blood on his hands. Strange occurrences like these didn't help.

He hoped Yawning Deer's song had been inspired by his turbulent, talkative slumber, a byproduct of shock and blood loss. After all, Dor didn't relish wasting his remaining time of Faltyr on the vicissitudes of another doomsday prophecy. So he ignored it, focusing on the glint of steel on the distant horizon instead. Like the late first mate of the *Nightsfall*, Dor had come to fear live steel and the zealots wielding it more than vague prophecies.

As a result, he'd grown lax in his stewardship of the sinister thing he'd been sent to retrieve from the western edge of this very desert. He focused on the known threat rather than the unknown. And it cost him. In the end, it'd cost all of Faltyr.

Chapter 10

While they waited for Leishan to feed and water the horses, Yax and Breuxias surveyed the area from atop the highest dune. They had found it necessary to keep the supply-laden wagon in the swales between the dunes, so they had climbed one to plot the route ahead of them. Their party needed a way across the Sands of Sorrow that would be expedient but survivable. Yax knew it would be a tough task to accomplish in an area named for the misery it brought to those foolhardy enough to try and cross it without proper preparations.

To the west, the dune sea stretched to the horizon. Fortunately, the proximity of the Meshkenet Mountains made the northern route easier. However, if they strayed too far west, they'd likely exhaust their water supply before reaching the oases at the base of the mountains. Channeling the Aethyr to assist him, Yax sketched a mental map in his mind's eye and then imprinted it for easy recall. The handy ability, acquired over centuries of travel across the known world, made for a better memory but not necessarily a happier life.

As far as survivability, Yax recalled a dozen ways to find water in a desert, but few allowed them to move rapidly over the terrain. To provide for such a sizeable party and a team of horses, he'd have to locate an artesian well, dig to the bedrock, and then drill with Starkiller until he struck water. That would consume precious time and energy.

Though preoccupied with land navigation and logistics, Yax did not fail to notice Breuxias's fixation on the southern horizon. Once he turned his attention to the south, concern colored Yax's face as well. An expansive cloud of sand and dust dominated the skyline southeast of their position, likely the remnants of the freak storm conjured by the calamitous mage of Myth.

But what is the other, smaller plume of dust? Cavalry?

"Riders!" The Brute cried, confirming the elf's suspicions.

"A score or more I'll wager," Yax said.

"Can you tell which way they're headed?"

"West for now. But they are liable to turn north or south at any moment. We'll have to start covering our tracks better."

"I knew better than to get my daughter involved."

"She'll be fine," Yax said. "Dor will take care of her."

With a snort, Breuxias retorted, "Are you kidding me? He's out of control, a walking calamity. The fool's as likely to kill himself or someone else while trying to wipe his own arse. I never should have allowed her to come with us.

"But what was I supposed to do? She already hates me. And worst of all she's right. She's not a child. She's the Savior of Istara. A warrior in her own right. I can't wall her away in a tower and pretend that awful business never happened."

"No, but you can prevent her from going down the same bloody road as us," Yax said. "That's what you should have done in Fraustmauth." The elf wished he could take back his hasty words, but the glowering expression on his friend's face showed him the damage had been done. He braced himself for the impending, explosive reaction.

With an edge sharper than elven steel, Breuxias asked, "Could you? If you could go back right now, could you stop Kan from fighting by your side, dying by your side. Would you?"

Breuxias had hit him below the figurative belt when he'd used his dead son to make a point. The elf's long fingers tapped the wand stuck in his real belt. He debated drawing it and blasting a hole through his friend. After all, when push came to shove, he had killed people he'd known a lot longer than the mouthy human. But Yax swallowed his pride and his pain, more for the sake of the mission than the safety of his friend.

Biting back the bile and rage, Yax said, "Is that really where you want to steer this conversation? Because the last thing I want to hear is parental advice from someone younger than my grandchildren."

The human softened his tone, but not his expression.

"Kan'Balam was my friend." Breuxias said. "I know he was your son, your only son, but he was my friend. And you know what? He died happy. He died doing what he thought was right, fighting alongside his old man. Who am I to deny my daughter the same right?"

Apparently drawn by their verbal tirade, Zoltana placed a calming hand on the agitated men's shoulders. She smiled warmly despite the recent tortures she'd endured and would likely endure again to free her people. With her honeyed voice, she asked the squabbling friends, "How about we focus less on dying and more on living?"

Returning her smile, the Brute replied, "Now that's a sentiment I think Yax and I can agree upon."

Unable to stay angry with his friend for long, especially in the presence of such an enchanting woman, Yax grinned and said, "Exactly. The dead don't get paid, right?"

"Right," Breuxias echoed.

But the specter of death loomed on the distant horizon beyond the Sands of Sorrow. Yax felt it even now, watching and waiting for them. When it descended upon the canyon concealing Mok'Drular, he hoped it didn't come for anyone in their midst, especially his dear friend. Despite their occasional duels and disagreements, Yax considered him to be the closest thing to a son he had left on Faltyr.

☙❧☙❧

Breuxias found the night sky over the Sands of Sorrow a wonder to behold. The stars danced as they drifted across the void beyond the aurora shimmering in the sky over their makeshift camp. The shifting display of Aethyr energies over the magically-created desert made for one fantastic lightshow. However, it distorted the night sky enough to prevent them from navigating by the stars.

Time to settle in for a long, cold night.

Leishan crouched beside him, tending a portable camp stove. It contained a small foul-smelling fire fueled mostly by manure. The Brute thought he'd never meet anyone with more empathy for the four-legged beasts than the former Rider of the Säj stoking the cook fire. That is until he met the comely Lady Zoltana, one of the Rangers of the North.

As she fed the horses by hand, she whispered lovingly to them in her native tongue. The ranger seemed pained by their exhaustion.

Her alabaster skin glowed under the luminous skies of the Sands of Sorrow, but her eyes remained their natural blue rather than bright red. Enough ambient light radiated from above to spoil her ability to see in the dark.

If that were true, Yax had lied to him earlier when he'd slipped into the darkness to scout their back trail. That meant his infuriating friend wandered the sandy wastes without the benefit of his dark vision. Sometimes Breuxias felt like he was surrounded by nothing by fools, stubborn fools. At other times, he felt like he was the biggest fool of them all.

He shivered as a series of cold gusts of wind blew through the campsite. Sand swirled about him and sought his eyes, nose, and throat. The frequency and intensity of those gusts had only increased since nightfall. Though he couldn't see the horizon beyond the dunes, the rising winds led him to believe that the storm tracked north.

But what about the riders? Who were they? And where were they headed? If they head south, they'll likely overtake the wagon carrying Tameri.

Sure he had other daughters, but she was his favorite. And there wasn't a damn thing he could do for her now but sulk and worry. He loathed doing either but was quite adept at both.

A familiar curse in a foreign tongue stirred him from his dour introspection. He watched as Shell Horse tossed the hand axe he'd been sharpening onto the sand. The irate elf spat in an exaggerated fashion, as if to make a point. Breuxias had heard Yax curse often enough in the both elven dialects for him to recognize the inflection. However, he had never convinced his friend to teach him anything but their trade tongue.

Turning to Yellow Ant, who actually spoke the Common language, Breuxias asked, "What's he so fired up about?"

Grinning broadly, Yellow Ant replied, "He thinks your weapons are shit."

"At least they're steel."

Shell Horse jabbered at both Breuxias and Yellow Ant.

"Barely," Yellow Ant translated. "He says he was forging better steel before your grandfather gave up his mother's teat."

"Hey, I don't make 'em," Breuxias clarified. "I kill people with 'em. Is he any good at that or just running his mouth in the absence of a forge?"

Shell Horse launched into his retort but halted suddenly as Yax'Kaqix slipped from the dark of night into the firelight. His abrupt return kept the human from getting a translation. Absent his usual grace, Yax plopped to the ground with his back to the wagon wheel. He yawned as he wiped sand from the corners of his eyes.

Zoltana asked him, "Any sign of tracks?"

"None but ours," Yax replied. "And I took care of those. I don't think we were followed though. I'd have heard them by now."

"Sonuvabitch!" Breuxias exclaimed. "That means those knights went after the other wagon. We have to go back!"

Yax shook his head and said, "We've already travelled a half day in the opposite direction. No way to catch up to them in time."

That blasted elf sure likes talking with his boot in his mouth.

"In time?" Breuxias asked accusingly. "Do you mean before they reach the ship or their pursuers reach them?"

"Either."

"I knew this would happen. Less than a day into this damn fool excursion, and I'm already saying I told you so."

"You are quite adept at that," Yax replied.

Breuxias willed the magic belt around his waist to answer his command. Despite the effects of the Sands of Sorrow, the Belt of Titans responded to his mental command, its eye-shaped gem flaring to life. It would govern his herculean strength at a reasonable level rather than let it run wild. He snatched one of the steel swords from the sharpening pile.

Addressing the elves, he said, "If my daughter dies because of a promise to a dead man, this is what awaits all of you."

The empowered Brute bent and twisted the weapon like it was putty in his hands. He tied it into a bow, tossed it onto the ground, and then looked around at the elves. His dark flashing eyes settled on Yax'Kaqix, a so-called friend who manipulated his associates as easily as Breuxias did steel.

He had accepted Yax and his duplicitous nature because any warrior worth his salt played at deception as often as they practiced swordplay. Even knowing this, he had trusted the elf with his life on more than one occasion. But there was a line.

Yax had crossed it when he'd endangered Tameri by hijacking a prison wagon in broad daylight. Had the elf thought with his head instead of his heart, he would have formulated a more cautious plan. They could have escaped with the figurehead and then returned after nightfall to rescue the elves. Instead, Yax had taken one look into the elf woman's eyes and risked all their lives for the freedom of others. Breuxias didn't know whether to admire his friend or hate him for it. Probably both, he decided.

Unfazed by his display, Zoltana walked toward him. Her large blue eyes held his gaze. He found it hard to think clearly as she continued to stare. She smiled sadly, and Breuxias knew she felt his pain. Truly felt it.

When she finally looked away, Zoltana said, "I share your concerns. Believe me. Likely, my sister and her unborn child are the only family I have left on Faltyr. Thousands of my people are suffering at Mok'Drular though.

"Do you know what that's like? Your daughter does. Even in far off Silent Brook, we have heard of the Savior of Istara, a woman-child who saved her city from armies of the living and dead. She is marked for great things, as is her father. Let her fly to her destiny as we rush to meet ours."

Breuxias accepted the prudence of the elf woman's words. But her statement about his daughter worried him to no end, mainly because he knew the terrible truth about Tameri's role in the liberation of Istara.

A role made possible by her unfortunate parentage. Though Breuxias did not know his birth father, he knew his mother's people. His first adopted father had read the signs on him and prepared him for his role in this world. As a result, the Brute worried about the descendants of Eresh's bloodline, scions of Death Herself, remaining in close proximity to the object of the Underworld concealed within Dor's chest; his stomach churned at the sinister implications. No wonder Breuxias had been drawn to Dor when he'd met the mage on the *Nightsfall*.

Did the influence of the Liber Inferum bring us together? Is that why Dor trusted me enough to carry the chest?

He worried his daughter would be drawn to the mage and his burden too. If Tameri discovered the nature of the chest's contents would the temptation prove too much for her again? The version she'd come across in the catacombs beneath Istara had been a church copy, an incomplete version of the Book of the Dead used by the living priests of Eresh. What damage could she cause with the master copy?

For now all Breuxias could do was worry and wonder, two of the most frequent, torturous aspects of being a parent. Regardless of whether or not he liked it, fate continued to lead him and his daughter down separate paths. He hoped they didn't converge in one of the Nine Hells, at least not before they'd lived long lives and died noble deaths.

Chapter 11

The cloud of sand and dust created by the wagon and its team proved impenetrable to Tameri. The daughter of Breuxias could no longer tell if they were being followed by the riders of Oparre, but she doubted they'd give up their pursuit now. More likely than not, she and the others had spotted the scouts for a larger contingent. Even if they managed to elude those particular troops, how many more would await them in the port city of Imputnim at the southern terminus of the road to the coast?

As if reading her mind, Dor turned to her and said, "We'll never make it to the port. And even if we did, more of Orson's men will be waiting." Gesturing to the giant wooden figure in the back of the wagon, he added, "We're sure to be seen."

"My thoughts exactly, so stop reading them. You won't like what you find lurking there."

The mage shrugged his shoulders and then winced in pain. "What can I say other than cliché? Great minds and all that rot."

"Dangerous minds perhaps."

Dor's bright eyes bored into her. "Of that I have no doubt."

"Is there another place Uncle Macz can meet us?"

Despite being jostled by Katar's reckless driving, he managed to extract one of the maps from the scroll case he carried. After examining it, he replied, "There is, but it's likely a rougher ride."

Tameri glanced at the elves seated across from them. Pain stitched Zarena's face while Xotl and Yawning Deer chanted a soothing song in the dialect of the Winaq'che.

Turning back to the handsome but haggard Protectorate Mage, Tameri said, "We've got no other alternative then. We're all dead if those bastards catch us before we make it to the *Seadragon*. But how do you plan on getting a message through to Macz?"

Dor held one finger aloft and then slipped the same hand into the pouch at his side. He extracted a grey-speckled carrier pigeon. Although ruffled and alarmed, the bird appeared no worse for wear despite being in the enchanted container for Eresh knows how long. The mage stroked a finger across its back and cooed in its fluff-covered ears.

Dor offered the pigeon to Tameri who took it with reluctance. The bird nestled against her as he scribbled a note and then attached it to the leg of the animal. Taking the pigeon from her, he stared into its black eyes and whispered to it again. After he released it, the pigeon circled the moving wagon once and then twice before darting off in the direction of the coast at an improbable rate of speed.

"Fly swiftly, my friend," Dor cooed after the bird.

"Useful pouch you have there," Tameri commented.

"It pays to have a bag of tricks if you plan on living long as a wizard, especially in these troubling times."

"If you say so," she said and then patted the elegant sword in the sheath hanging from her belt. "But I prefer a couple of feet of cold steel myself." She thought of something else that made her feel safe, involving plays on "pouch" and "sword", but left it unspoken.

With the enchanted bird out of sight, Tameri's dark eyes lingered on the narrow face of the mage. Even with his shadow of a beard and crazy hair, Dor had a certain charm about him. And despite his lack of grace, he acted with coolness under fire, as if his entire life had been one series of thrilling adventures or possibly harrowing misadventures.

Could explain the hair, she thought and suppressed a giggle. She could relate to bad hair days and bad days in general.

Her own misadventures during the siege of Istara had left her a changed woman. And with no further signs from Eresh, she wrestled everyday to come to terms with what that meant. Tameri had yet to tell anyone the whole truth behind the liberation of her home city, about the temple, the book, and Lady Death's intervention on her behalf.

Her father knew more of the story than anyone. Despite his obvious failings as a parent, his knowledge of the Aethyr and the Underworld surpassed that of her mother, a former slave and dancer turned stationer and scrivener.

Tameri turned from Dor to the dusty road behind them.

"See anything?" the mage asked after a moment.

"Nothing, but they may still be leagues behind us."

"I hope so," Katar interjected from the front of the wagon. "The horses are going to need a break soon. That's the last thing we need: a wagon without any horses."

"We can't stop now," Tameri cautioned. "No telling how far behind the scouts the main contingent could be."

"We'll make it." Zarena assured them. "We have to."

"I'm glad someone thinks so," Dor said.

Placing a slender hand on her swollen belly, Zarena added, "I can't allow myself to think any other way."

Though she had no children, Tameri understood what the elven woman meant and respected her conviction. The Savior of Istara vowed then and there to go screaming into the Nine before she'd allow the men of Oparre to put their filthy, murdering hands on the lovely, loving mother-to-be. If it meant calling upon Eresh to destroy them all, so be it. Though her own soul was damned, Tameri could not sit back and let evil befall a mother and her unborn child.

After fiery Shamash set below the western horizon, the road to the coast went from being treacherous to downright dangerous for the exhausted team of horses pulling the wagon containing Tameri and her party of fugitives. In the absence of Mother Sun's warmth, the foam-covered, four-legged animals shivered in the cold desert air.

"Katar, ease up on the horses," Tameri said, neither asking nor commanding. "But keep them walking until I find a suitable place for us to camp. I don't want their legs to cramp."

"It's about time," he replied in contemptuous tone.

"Why is it that three women, one of them pregnant, bitch less than you?"

Everyone in the wagon inhaled sharply, and Katar flinched as if she'd slapped him across his mustachioed mouth. But she didn't give much of a damn what any of them thought at the moment. She'd had enough of the mouthy coward's negativity and nay saying for a life time. Shooting her a poisonous look, he jerked the reigns, halting the wagon.

"I said," Tameri spat, "keep them moving. If the horses cramp, your stupid ass is pulling the wagon *and* the team all the way to Imputnim."

"You can't--" Katar sputtered.

"I can and will talk to you however I damn well please." She grabbed him by his curly mane and snapped his head back as if they were the reigns clutched in his hands. "And if we don't make it to the coast because of you, I'll kill you myself." The tip of the dagger pressed into his back punctuated her point perfectly. "Got it?"

Katar shook his head and snapped the reigns. As the horses plodded forward, she released the handful of curls and sat back. The others broke their curious stares as she turned back toward them.

Only Dor met her gaze. He even held it and smiled. The mage asked, "Where are we going to camp?"

"Not sure yet. We can't stay on the road, but we can't risk wandering too far and getting stuck in loose sand."

"Perhaps on the other side of that low rocky knoll," Yawning Deer suggested. The minstrel pointed toward an indistinct lump on the horizon illumed dimly by the swirling aurora visible in the night sky over the Sands of Sorrow.

"Want me to accompany you?" Dor asked.

"Nonsense. You need rest," Tameri replied. Leaning in close, she whispered, "But keep an eye on Katar. I don't trust him."

As she pulled away, her lips almost brushed his own. She felt her heart skip a beat. But she wasn't sure if it was exhilaration or terror. After all, the last lips she'd kissed belonged to a dead girl.

"I'll accompany you," Yawning Deer offered. "My old elven eyes should be better suited to nocturnal capers than yours."

"You'd be surprised," Tameri responded, grinning at him.

"Quite possibly," Yawning Deer said with a mercurial smile.

ঔৣ☬ঔৣ

Thanks to her new way of viewing the world, a side effect of Eresh's dark investiture that started with her tumble down a flight of stone stairs into the land of the dead, Tameri observed countless spirits, shades, and other specters as she passed through the haunted desert. The population living in the shadow of the Meshkenet

Mountains rivaled the heartlands of the Ireti Empire in the days before the Cataclysm.

If the scrolls of history were to be believed, the armies that fought in the shadow of those doomed peaks numbered in excess of a million humans, elves, gnomes, ogres, and a smattering of a half dozen other races. They all died in a single moment of catastrophic devastation brought about by two warring lovers who almost dragged Faltyr screaming into the Nine with them.

Artemis and Ra'Tallah ended humanity's Golden Age, but every cycle of ages ends. We'll see the end of another soon, once the stars are right.

Avoiding the restless dead in the Sands of Sorrow was almost impossible, myriad souls of infinite shades wandered the wastes. When one camped in this desert, one made camp as far away from them as possible. And if one had to share their bed with the dead, it was best to make sure that they were inoffensive and incorporeal. A wandering, wailing specter was noisome, but a ghoul or wraith would consider her party a feast sent by the Lords of the Underworld. A brief stroll around the stone strewn hilltop led the young priestess to proclaim it safe enough to steal a few hours of respite before merciless Shamash and the riders of Oparre tried to kill them all.

Returning from the knoll, Tameri and Yawning Deer caught up the wagon as the horses picked their way along the rut-filled road. She took the animal on the left by its bridle and led it into a wide turn. She and the elven minstrel walked ahead of the horses to ensure a path free of hazards. From quicksand to deadly burrowing creatures, the Sands of Sorrow had earned its name honestly enough.

As they reached the base of the rocky rise, Tameri called out to the others, "We'll camp here for the night."

As Xotl assisted Zarena in exiting the wagon, the midwife asked, "Are you sure it's safe? Aren't we exposed here?"

"It's the lesser of the many evils surrounding us in this strange land," Tameri explained. "I don't think those horsemen will risk the road at night. It invites catastrophe for a column of mounted troops. Let's not take chances though. We'll leave before first light."

Xotl replied, "Good a plan as any at the moment I suppose."

As Tameri watched, the midwife seated Zarena on a table-like slab of sandstone. She fancied it had been an altar used by the sun-worshipping Ireti in days past. Waving the human woman away, Xotl helped Dor out of the wagon next. Once the magician was safely on the sands, she returned to her primary charge. Tameri took a seat near the two women.

Dor removed the infamous black staff from his pouch. Putting most of his weight on it, the awkward mage looked for a suitable place to sit. He selected a concave stone beside Tameri and sat down with a grunt.

He pulled a briar pipe from his robes, packed it to the brim with a stinky herb, and then lit it with his fingertip. The pungent blend of burning organic matter stung her nostrils, but its aroma reminded Tameri of her mother's apothecary, a side venture almost as profitable as their bookstore and print shop in Istara.

"Nice trick," Katar said as he removed gear from the wagon.

Tameri ignored the rogue's presence, but Dor stared at him without speaking. The mage puffed at his pipe, its light casting an eerie pall on his grime-and-stubble-covered face. He offered the pipe to Katar, but the troublesome guildsman waved it away.

"No, thanks." Katar replied, holding up his hands. "Need to keep my wits about me. Never know what's lurking out there."

Dor smiled at him. "I know exactly what's out there."

"Death and the dead," Tameri added, leering at Katar.

Instead of replying, the rogue went back to shuffling equipment.

Zarena urged, "We can't do anything about the dead, so why don't we concentrate on the living and those soon to join our ranks."

"How are you feeling, Lady Zarena?" Tameri asked.

Rubbing her belly, the elf said, "I don't know if the child is moving or if I'm still feeling the effects of that so-called road."

"Probably both." Xotl quipped. "My butt is sore."

"At least you have one to be sore," Yawning Deer quipped. "Mine's as bony as a troll's den."

"This mode of transport isn't ideal, but I'm sure the ride will be smoother now," Tameri responded with a mischievous grin. *Now that we've sanded down the rough edges of our teamster.*

Tameri refused to put Katar in the same category as famous mercenaries like her father or her adopted uncle, Yax'Kaqix. In her opinion, the spineless rogue didn't deserve to drive a wagon for them, much less call himself a member of Finders Keepers.

Katar broke her relentless gaze and asked Dor, "You think Maczi Boy got your note?"

Between puffs and yawns, Dor said, "We'll find out soon enough."

Placing her hand on the mage's arm, Zarena said, "Thank you for helping us out back there."

"The rescue wasn't part of the plan. Not all of us are in the savior business, but you're welcome nonetheless."

Unsure if Dor was making fun of her unwanted moniker, Tameri went to check on the horses. She didn't know whether or not to be hurt by his flippant statement; after all, he seemed as awkward socially as he was physically. She focused on the horses instead.

Tameri watered the exhausted animals and then strapped feed bags onto their damp muzzles. She leaned in to whisper a "thank you" to the wagon team. But a commotion behind her drew her attention.

"Set my pack down," Dor ordered. "It stays in the wagon."

"What's in this thing?" Katar asked, shaking one of several woven basket backpacks. "Something breakable? Valuable?"

"I said leave it!" the Protectorate Mage shouted, rising to his feet. He thumped the gnarled staff on the stone at his feet. Cracks radiated outward across its rocky surface. Thunder rolled louder than his officious, out-of-character tone.

Here is a lion, not a mouse.

Katar released the pack's strap and said, "You got it, boss."

"That's Captain to you," Dor reminded him.

As the other man retreated from the wagon, the mage took a seat on the edge of it. Reaching into his magical pouch, he extracted bread, cheese, and fresh fruits.

Tameri interpreted his action as a peace offering to the group when he said, "Is anyone hungry?"

"Yes!" Zarena cried as loudly as the stormy mage.

Dor distributed the food before taking a seat alongside the pack Katar and he had quarreled over. Tameri knew it contained the chest. *What does that strongbox conceal from the eyes of the uninitiated?*

She dreamed about it as much as she dreamed of Dor. She couldn't stand Katar, but she understood his curiosity.

"Are you not eating?" Tameri asked the guarded magician.

"I'd rather sleep if I can. The pain's still pretty bad."

"You rest then," she said. "I'll take first watch."

As Dor reclined in the back of the wagon, Tameri watched an object dart out of the darkness and light on the sideboard. The pigeon cooed as it tried to roust its master. She stood and moved to examine it closer. She attempted to remove the message, but the bird's eyes flared red. It hissed and nipped at her finger.

"Wake up and deal with this damn fool bird!"

Blinking sleep from his eyes, Dor rolled over and said, "Now you're starting to sound like your father."

She glared at the irksome mage as he checked the note. Tameri debated on whether she should poke him in the kidney with her dagger too. She chose to hear what he had to say instead.

"Macz got the message," he proclaimed.

"Obviously," she ventured with a slight grin.

Dor returned her mirthful expression in his own exhausted fashion and said, "We're to leave the main road when it turns toward Imputnim and then head due south. He'll be waiting just off the coast."

"Anything else?"

"Yes." Dor yawned, "And this is the vital part. It's naptime."

And he was serious. She heard him snoring as soon as his head hit the floorboards of the wagon. This time Tameri let him sleep. After all, if he hadn't earned it yet, he would after they raced toward the coast with a contingent of cavalry in pursuit.

Chapter 12

The sun crested the horizon, and with Mother Sun's appearance, the sickly greenish aurora over the Sands of Sorrow receded to the edge of human perception. The red and orange hues of the morning sky mingled with the retreating darkness of the night as Sir Frederick stood outside his tent and prayed to shining Damarra. With the new day, he hoped that the sun would reveal the enemies of the Crown and deliver them unto him.

Once he had greeted Mother Sun properly, the tall knight inspected Balmoor's riders while they prepared to resume their pursuit of the escaped prisoners and their powerful allies.

Sir Balmoor saluted his superior and reported, "My riders are ready whenever you are, my lord."

"Good. We ride shortly. Have them mount up."

Balmoor turned on his heels and left to carry out his orders.

Before he could make it to his replacement mount, Frederick spotted Sir Stogal and his riders galloping back into camp. The returning knight reigned in his steed and dismounted quickly.

Stogal said, "Good news and bad news, my lord."

"I'm not in the mood for a guessing game," Frederick replied, "so spit it out!"

"We spotted one of the wagons carrying several individuals. They're still on the road, but are a good distance ahead of us. Judging by the way they were running their horses, if they didn't camp last night, they'll have no wagon team today. There's no sign of the other wagon though."

"And the good news?"

"That was the good news, my lord."

"You disappoint me, Stogal. Next you will be telling me that they spotted you too."

"Now that you mention it, one of my men was spotted." Stogal recoiled under his superior's glare. "'Twas not me, my lord."

Sir Frederick's face reddened as he took two steps closer to the worried knight. Behind Stogal, his riders watched the situation unfold but remained silent. The senior knight's eyes narrowed as he watched the cavalrymen. He met each one's gaze and then returned his attention to Stogal.

Frederick did not hesitate in his command. The Knight of Damarra cast a sideways glance at Balmoor who looked on with much interest. Frederick could see the blood lust on his face.

Bloodthirsty fool, I will give him what he wants. And show them all what it means to fail me and, by extension, His Majesty.

"Excellent! I want you to personally execute the one that was spotted. Bring him before me and remove his head."

Forehead beaded in sweat, Stogal looked bewildered by his lord's command. The knight stood there for a moment, perhaps silently praying. If he was a Knight of Oparre worth his salt, he paid homage to Damarra daily. Finally, without a shaking hand, he pointed at two of his veteran riders and then to the recruit in between them.

Frederick watched them seize the younger man, no more than five-and-ten years of age. *Conscripts are getting younger and younger these days. Our wars of purification take their toll, but the resulting new world order will be worth it.*

The young rider searched the faces of the Knights of Oparre. Frederick kept his eyes forward. The other cavalrymen followed his dispassionate lead. Balmoor's anticipation for blood filled the air between them as he chuckled at the recruit's plight. Stogal drew his sword but hesitated. Frederick nodded curtly.

"My lord, I didn't--" the young man's words were cut short as Stogal's blade passed through his neck with deadly precision.

The falsely accused man's head toppled onto the sand. Mortified, Stogal watched as the body fell sideways. Sir Frederick averted his eyes by directing them at the newborn executioner. *The first one is always the hardest.* The reprieved man looked horrified but relieved. Frederick knew an innocent man, perhaps one with a family waiting for him to return home, had just died due to Stogal's cowardice and dishonesty. None of the men here would either forget it or forgive it.

"Put your eyes back in their sockets and mount up! We have fugitives to capture," Frederick ordered as he stalked away from the gruesome scene. "And thanks to someone, they'll be ready!"

ઉଓ୪ଓ୪ଡ଼

After a hot, merciless day of fruitless pursuit, a frustrated Sir Frederick sat behind a small folding table in his spacious yet sparsely furnished desert tent. He examined several maps of the Oparre-Panglov border. His index finger traced the route of the coastal road leading to Imputnim. Led by the murderous wizard, the prisoners had turned away from the main road to the coast.

Magically concealed tracks caused the pursuing cavalry to miss their detour initially. The mistake had cost them time and distance, possibly their prized quarry too. Frederick had no one to blame for the mistake, other than him. Thinking the wagons would be easily caught by a troop of horsemen, he had chosen to send their most reliable tracker back for wizardly assistance. Instead, his men and their horses, already exhausted from their first trek across the Sands of Sorrow, slowed by the day.

The tent flap stirred as a cool breeze filled the interior. The hair on the back of his neck stood on end as Aethyr energies crackled inside the confined space. He had come to recognize the telltale signs of magic over the years, especially since his sword and armor had been enchanted by King Orson's court wizard. The knight leapt to his feet and turned in time to see a luminous wizard's door open in midair.

As the portal expanded, his hand found the hilt of his sword. Frederick's grip tightened around the wire-wrapped handle of his weapon as Proleus's apprentice, Marduk, emerged from the shimmering doorway. His wooly hair and caramel skin mixed with steel eyes and a smattering of freckles. His features betrayed his mongrel heritage, common enough among the natives of Moor'Dru. This unproven ally of Oparre had an obsidian wand tucked into an ornate weapon belt that featured a sword and pair of daggers. The silvery metal contrasted his dark, somber attire.

Although Marduk was a wizard, he was also a Protectorate Mage. Sir Frederick knew the members of the Protectorate Order had been trained to weave magic while wearing armor and using martial weapons. Based on elven Wand Bearers, they were the elite defenders of Moor'Dru, whether the fight was on the ground or sea, or even in the air for that matter.

The Protectorate Magi rivaled the best Knights of Oparre; their most powerful could hold their own against the feared elven Wand Bearers. King Orson's decision to ally his kingdom with the mage armies of Moor'Dru pushed Oparre closer to the brink of total victory or to a resounding defeat, if Proleus and his followers had ulterior motives. Frederick didn't trust any wizard, especially one who'd betrayed and murdered Salaac.

The mage had scarcely crossed the plane of the magic doorway when he said, "How's punishment detail suiting you? Quiet, I hear."

"I'm in no mood for it today, Marduk."

"I understand you are chasing a wizard, the one from Eastgate I presume," the mage said after the portal vanished behind him.

"And elven prisoners as well. They split up. One group is following the road to Imputnim, but the others headed deep into the desert. We would have caught them, but the wizard and his cohorts were gone in a wink."

Marduk chuckled at the knight's comment. "A rather long wink I assume for overloaded wagons to outrun Oparre cavalry."

Frederick's face reddened with anger. As he advanced on the wizard, he gripped the hilt of his sword tighter.

"Watch your serpent's tongue, mage, or I'll cut it out. You and Proleus may have the King's trust, but you don't have mine. I don't trust any wizard, especially a Protectorate from Moor'Dru."

Marduk smiled and said, "Yet, here I am, by your command."

Sir Frederick replied, "One might use a mongoose to kill a cobra, but one doesn't turn a blind eye to either."

The mage chuckled at the knight's simple yet observant wisdom. Marduk walked past him to the table and looked down at the maps. Finally, Marduk asked, "Do you know of a reason why a renegade wizard or his allies would want to free the prisoners you were escorting? Or have you given it any thought?"

"All I know is that their attack came as a complete surprise. I did not expect it, nor did any of my men."

"Well, that is the definition of 'surprise'."

Despite his impulse to throttle the Protectorate Mage, Frederick continued to speak. "Motive concerns me less than recapturing them. When we catch them, we can ask them. But no one we talked to in town knew where they'd come from or where they were going. My best guess is the coast. But that's why I brought you here, to help me locate the prisoners and kill this wizard. I want his head on a platter to serve up to His Majesty."

"Speaking of King Orson, he will not be happy when he learns you lost the prisoners to a rogue mage and some hired mercenaries. After all, you did lose one of them twice, right?"

Frederick lowered his voice so that his men wouldn't overhear. Then he said, "You are here because I summoned you. If I didn't need you, I wouldn't have called you. I admit that. But let's get one thing straight, right here, right now. I already have to deal with this outfit of lazy, immoral bush knights and a bunch of herdsmen turned horsemen, so I don't need you berating me further. I enjoy jocularity as much as anyone, but this isn't a laughing matter."

Frederick's tone grew graver and his stare icier.

"This rogue wizard is dangerous enough to nearly wipe out one of the King's cities with a single weave, so you are here to help me bring him to justice. But if you continue to belittle me, I'll be forced to put your head on a pike and that's how you'll greet King Orson and Proleus when I return to Oparre with these fugitives in tow. Do I make myself clear?"

"As a polished mirror on a cloudless day."

❧

Frederick and Marduk stared at the maps of the region for a time without speaking. The mage drummed his fingers on the table. The annoyed knight shifted his eyes.

"Sorry. It's an old habit," Marduk said, returning the glare.

So is beheading wizards, but I can restrain myself. Barely.

Instead of saying what was on his mind, the knight said, "Perhaps you can put your nervous energy to use. Can you see into the future and tell me where they are headed?"

"If scrying was that easy, wouldn't everyone be doing it?" the wizard answered. "Besides, I'm a Protectorate Mage, not a Mediator."

"A mage is a mage to me," the knight retorted. "What you can and cannot do with magic matters little to me. I have no faith in magic-users, though they do make useful trinkets and tools." His hand drifted back to his enchanted sword. "This war was supposed to have ended after Proleus pledged the use of his mage armies, yet here we are on another front of a widening war."

He turned toward his squire when the retainer entered through the tent flap. Galil eyed the mage before saluting his superior.

"Your lordship, there is a man here requesting an audience with you. He claims to be from the wagon we are pursuing."

Frederick raised an eyebrow and glanced at Marduk.

"By all means, bring him in."

"This should be interesting," Marduk said.

Galil exited the tent but returned a moment later. Two chainmail-clad guards followed him. They escorted a shackled prisoner between them. Instead of addressing him, Sir Frederick examined the olive-skinned man for a long moment.

Though he stands on legs, this one is as spineless as an urchin. Should be no trouble getting this traitor to talk. But can we trust a thing he has to say when fear holds sway over him.

Marduk waved his hands and ordered, "Guards, I can handle this one. Leave us. He is no threat here."

The guards hesitated until Sir Frederick nodded in agreement.

When the senior knight addressed the captive, he said, "Give me one good reason not to kill you right here and now, and I will take that into consideration before rendering my verdict."

Sweat beaded on the prisoner's forehead as he stared up at Frederick. The captive's lips trembled but no sound escaped.

"Well, I'm waiting," the Knight of Oparre said. "When I wait, the King waits. You don't want to make the King wait, do you?"

The bound man shook his head vigorously and said, "I am Katar, and I am a mercenary hired by the group you seek. It was only a job for me. I didn't know what their plans were. I swear. I beg of you to spare my life."

Frederick listened to the man plead for his life. He looked at Marduk who merely shrugged. *This mage is about useless.*

"I can lead you to the others," Katar offered. "They tricked me. I didn't know they had hired a wizard. I just wanted to do the job, get paid, and make it out alive."

Lies. And more lies. Maybe he wants to lead us into a trap.

Frederick stared at the man for a brief minute before he placed his foot upon a chair. His fingers wrapped around the hilt of his sword once again. The gesture motivated Katar to continue. "I didn't know he was going to try to destroy the whole city, and I didn't know freeing elves was part of the plan. I don't even like elves! The wizard is crazy! He threatened me because I touched his precious chest. I didn't know it was--"

"Chest? What type of chest?" Marduk interjected.

Marduk leaned closer. Frederick eyed the mage with suspicion after he asked about the chest. Confused, Katar stared at the wizard. Tension bloomed in tent like flowers in spring.

"Type?" he asked. "It's a metal chest, like a strongbox. It had markings on the top of it, but they appear to have been melted. He's very protective of it. I never saw him without it either."

Marduk and Frederick exchanged glances. Judging by the mage's sudden curiosity, the knight wondered what was so special about the item in question. He reminded himself of why he didn't trust anyone who used magic, especially wizards.

"Describe this wizard for me," Marduk ordered.

"He wears dirty brown robes and sandals and carries a black staff that looked like it was plucked from a fire. His hair is wild, much like the look in his eyes."

"Do you happen to know his name?"

"Dor. Like a portal."

Marduk's eyes gleamed and a smile crept to his thin lips. He said, "Yes, very much like a portal."

Maybe this mouthy fool won't be useless after all. He did learn the name of the mage who tried to destroy Eastgate.

"Do you know this wizard?" Frederick asked Marduk.

"Oh yes. Quite well. He is one of Salaac's allies."

"Salaac? He's been dead for months. According to His Majesty's sources, most of his faction that survived the coup have scattered to the four corners, and knowing Proleus, probably in fear for their lives."

Marduk surprised the knight by laughing in his face "Ignorance must indeed be bliss." Turning back to Katar, he added, "I think you should allow this one to live."

"What reason do I have for allowing him to live?"

"He may be of use to us in the future. The chest he speaks of is more important than any wizard, any elf, or a million of either. In the right hands, its contents can reshape everything."

The Protectorate Mage pulled a handkerchief from his sleeve and offered it to him. As he did so, the iron cuffs which had bound Katar loosened and fell to the floor. His magic did little to impress Frederick but frightened their prisoner further. The rogue shook like a child with the palsy.

Offering his handkerchief to the captive, Marduk said, "I have pled for your life, and as long as you remain useful, you will be spared. Betray me, and you will join Kaladimus Dor and the others in a very slow and painful death."

Katar took the cloth from the mage. He wiped his forehead with it before looking back at the mage.

"Do we have an agreement then?" Marduk asked.

The prisoner nodded dumbly.

"Did Dor mention another wizard by chance, a Braigen?"

"Not to me," Katar said, "but I can ask him about it."

"That will not be necessary. If you mentioned his name, it would alert Dor. If he hasn't mentioned him, he may be dead. If so, that makes this renegade the last of Salaac's powerful associates. Return to your camp and secure that chest. Once you do that, raise an alarm in the camp. You will remain behind with our prize, while the others are flushed out like boars for the hunting. Do this for us and you will have provided a valuable service here."

"Thanks, I guess. Does that mean there's a reward?"

"You have our gratitude," Marduk said, "but do not abuse it."

Frederick said to Katar, "You are free to go back to your confederates. But remember, if you betray us, death will be your only reward."

Katar wasted no time before he exited the tent. The knight and the mage waited a moment before following him outside. They watched as the traitor disappeared into the darkness.

"See to it that he makes his way back to his own camp," Frederick ordered the guards waiting outside. "But don't let yourselves be seen. Our riders will be right behind you, and I'd hate to spoil the surprise."

"Not on your life, sir," the shorter guard retorted.

"Not mine. Yours," Frederick answered coolly.

And he meant it.

Chapter 13

The sandstorm howled around Breuxias and the others as they trekked between two towering dunes. Shifting sand filling the swale tried to swallow the wagon despite the horses' best efforts. The Brute walked behind the wagon to ensure that didn't happen. Thanks to the control provided by the magical girdle, he could lift one corner with ease without tipping it, but struggled to walk as the additional weight pushed him down into the sand.

"This is madness!" he shouted over the raging storm.

Leishan failed to hear him and continued to lead the horses onward. The elves, however, turned toward the sound of the bellowing mercenary. Judging by most of their expressions, they were not happy with the idea of travelling through the tempest.

One of the pointy-eared bastards did seem to be enjoying himself, however, which confirmed something Breuxias already knew. Much like Dor, the survival of Yax'Kaqix depended on the suffering of others. Even in his head that condemnation rang loudly but did not sound out of tune with the songs sung of the infamous Blue Macaw.

Was the Wand Bearer leading them to their doom as well? Would their funeral songs be overshadowed by those glorifying the ancient Lord of War? Only time, and bards, would tell.

"Sheer and complete to be sure," Yax answered. "But fun."

"For you maybe," the Brute said, "I'm being abraded alive here."

The elf shrugged and said, "Wear a shirt."

He chuckled at his friend's familiar, infuriating response.

Breuxias believed Yax to be a masochist of the highest order. The elf came alive, even thrived, as the stakes rose and the odds stacked against him and any of those unfortunate enough to ally themselves with him for long. The Brute wondered which wizard had inflicted more collateral damage on their travelling companions, Yax'Kaqix or Kaladimus Dor.

Breuxias considered Dor to be an albatross, but the calamitous mage meant no harm despite the trail of carnage left in his wake. He had a sense of duty to his master and his mission, whereas the elf's typical motivations, until recently, involved power or profit, usually both in healthy portions. As a result, his adventures with Yax had made them wealthy men. However, the blood on their hands could fill a sea.

What was different about these prisoners? Where was the profit motive? Where was the power play? Why risk everything for a promise to a dead man, a dead fool at that?

It made no sense to Breuxias. He was usually the more soft-hearted, often acting as Yax's conscience. The elf had gone a bit mad since the loss of his son, growing colder, quieter, and more distant. The Old Man was either becoming senile or sentimental as he progressed farther into his sixth century of life. Based on his past association with the elf, he'd bet on the latter before the former. Likely, Yax had a heart as big as his own but would never admit it to anyone. Anyone still among the living anyway.

Reaching an area that afforded a better windbreak than anywhere else they'd been since the storm hit, Breuxias made a command decision. Leveraging the hand underneath the wagon, he lifted one side, grabbed it with his other hand, and then flipped it over. The force of the flip bent but did not break the loop at the end of the wagon tongue. The startled horses tried to pull away, but Leishan held them by their lead. The Säj mercenary could ride before he could run, so he reined them in with ease. Horses stood about as much chance of harming the expert horseman as old age did of killing the elves around him.

"What in the Nine did you do that for?" Yax cried.

"Shelter. That's what sensible people do in a sandstorm. They take shelter."

The Wand Bearer sighed and said, "I'm too tired to argue."

"Then don't."

Yax shrugged his shoulders.

He must be exhausted. I've never won an argument with him this easily.

As the fierce storm continued unabated, they took cover under the wagon. Though no one liked the situation, the horses had to be left tethered outside. If the team didn't survive the storm, it'd be a long, grueling trek to the mountains on foot.

Breuxias and the others sat in near total darkness. Dull light filtered in through the slits between the wagon boards. Inhuman eyes provided the only other sources of light underneath their improvised shelter. The elves' almond-shaped orbs shined an intense shade of red, enough to cast a sinister pall on their faces.

Zoltana watched him as he washed sand from his head, neck, and face. Normally, he didn't mind a woman drinking him in with her eyes. In fact, Breuxias enjoyed it so much he'd made a spectacle of himself for the ladies time and again. However, the elven woman unnerved him; she stared with the intensity of a wolf. He met her eyes and saw something else, something pained, haunted even. She looked away.

Speaking a pidgin mix of Unen'ek, Winaq'che, and Draconic dialects, Zoltana asked Yax, "Your friend doesn't speak our trade tongue, does he?"

"No," he lied. "Only what Unen'ek he has learned from me."

"Good. I did not wish to wound his pride with my inquiry."

"Inquiry."

"His threat against your life, the life of a Wand Bearer. I see that you let it go unanswered."

Though he stared at Zoltana, Yax spoke to his friend. "Breuxias blusters. And he worries. His heart is as big as his head. Sometimes it's an asset. Other times it's a liability. I know why he blames me. It's my fault. Of all the times to swear an oath. Or be one of those rare warriors bound by honor."

Statements like that helped Breuxias recall why he'd been friends with the elf for so long. They thought alike, sometimes too much alike for their own good, especially when they chose to think with their hearts instead of their heads.

"You mentioned a promise," she reminded Yax. "To whom?

"A Knight of Oparre actually," Yax paused when Zoltana issued a series of curses and then continued. "Sir Caayl wasn't like most of them. He might have been a traitor to his country, but he was a hero to your people, our people. He and a few other Knights of Ishta'Kahl smuggled Lady Shy'Elle out of the king's palace at Grymsburg. After he told me that, I promised to help when the time came."

Zoltana cursed and then thanked Kümatz with the next breath.

"And how did you know," she clarified, "that it was time?"

"When I looked into your eyes, he spoke to me. He called to me out of the Aethyr, and I knew I couldn't just let you go to your fate."

Breuxias sighed and rolled over onto his side. The Brute felt angry with himself for having judged his friend so harshly. In fact, he empathized with Yax now that he better understood what had spurred his reckless actions in Eastgate. On its own, the plight of a damsel in distress might not have been enough for the Old Man to jeopardize the entire mission. But for someone who prided himself on his word, an unbreakable oath and an otherworldly reminder would do it every time.

ଔଓଔଓ

The panicked neighing of the horses dragged Breuxias from his slumber. The series of groans and moans that rose above them prevented him from returning to his alluring dreamscape. The Brute blinked sleep from his eyes as he sat up in the darkness. He banged his head against the floor of the wagon.

Sonuvabitch!

As he nursed the lump on his forehead, he noticed the red-eyed elves conversing in the pidgin trade tongue, and he could hear Leishan's low, throaty voice singing a prayer or mantra in the clipped, alien tongue of his people. But none of their voices sounded like the basal tones he'd heard over the horses.

Breuxias wondered if it could have been the wind playing tricks. Another groan seemed to confirm his initial assumption, until it was answered by a blast of sound that reminded him of the Rhinodon horns used by his ogre brethren to communicate over long distances. When the horses' whinnies rose above the other noises, Breuxias raised the lip of the wagon and peered out.

Through the blinding winds, he could barely discern three massive shapes burrowing their way through the desert valley toward the overturned wagon. Whatever the things under the sand were, they were moving fast. Preferring to meet them in the open,

Breuxias activated the Belt of Titan Strength and flipped the wagon onto its side with his free hand.

Plucking a spear from amongst their stockpile of weapons, he said, "Looks like we've got company." Charging toward the threat, he warned the others to "Run!"

Reaching the first burrowing mound, Breuxias leaped to the side and plunged his spear into the partially exposed creature. Its tip imbedded one of the thick, scaly plates on its long body. Using the spear as a pole vault, he tried to spring over the beast, but its handle snapped under the strain. He landed in wet, roiling sand that threatened to collapse beneath his feet.

Only then did he realize they'd camped on one of the slow moving sand flows that snaked through the Sands of Sorrow. Sand, dust, and grit from the sundered mountain range had blanketed southeastern Ny in the wake of the Cataclysm. Much of the material had found its way into lakes, rivers, and streams and clogged as many as it covered. Who knew how many of the ancient river systems still ebbed and flowed below the surface. These sand flows were easy enough to spot under most circumstances, but a sandstorm was not most circumstances.

Breuxias sprang backward and not a moment too soon.

The broad, flat snout of the beast broke the surface first, and its toothy maw opened wide. The scaly, long-bodied creature burst forth from the sand as it sought out the Brute. It resembled a larger, mutated version of a river gar with its blend of fish and reptilian features. The creature featured powerful paddle-like appendages that ended in wide, flat claws like those of a sea turtle.

The sand gar snapped at him but missed. As it did so, it dropped back into the muddy waters beneath the thick layer of sand and grit.

Using both hands, Yax made grand gestures in the direction of another burrowing mound of monster. A beam of shimmering Aethyr energy arced from his palms into its path. The second sand gar collided with it and stopped moving. Breuxias had seen the paralyzing effects of that weave before but never on such a large target. Judging by the look on Yax's face neither had he.

The third monster would not be denied its prize. Leishan managed to free one of the horses and ride it out of harm's way, but the second steed was not so fortunate. Zoltana worked to cut its tether with a small knife that she'd concealed in her robe, but the gar was faster. It burst forth and opened its jaws enough to envelope the horse.

When the sand gar's mandibles clamped shut on the animal's flanks, its spine snapped loudly enough to be heard over the whipping winds of the storm. The beast shook its broad snout, opened its jaws as wide as a serpent, and crunched down on the horse again. The horse's appendages snapped forward violently as the sand gar devoured its prey.

As Zoltana backed toward Breuxias, the sand gar swallowed all but the horse's head whole. The severed head bounced and landed upright, facing them. Its wide unblinking eyes watched them until it disappeared into the waters beneath the sand.

Well, I won't be sleeping for awhile now.

Shell Horse and Leishan leveled their recurved bows and fired arrow after arrow into the armored beast with a bloody snout. But it showed them little interest.

Leishan's mount drew its attention instead. The scaly monster penetrated the layer of sand and loose rock as easily as parchment and snapped at the rear legs of the horse. Nudged by the experienced equestrian riding it, the mount kicked at its pursuer.

Leishan spurred the horse to further action, and it galloped away from its attacker. The horseman extended his free hand toward the elf as he passed. Shell Horse grabbed his hand, sprang onto the horse's back, and rode away with the valiant horseman.

Breuxias realized he had to act fast or the entire battleground would become unsteady enough to plunge them into the sand flow. He knew how to handle this troublesome beast though. It was time to embrace his true power. Racing past Yax, he signaled the elf to be ready to back his play.

Before the paralyzed gar could recover, the Brute seized the beast by its snout. Using strength not governed by the magical belt, he hauled it free of the sand flow, until its rear flippers and flattened tail lay exposed on the sand. The monster stretched the length of two wagons and likely weighed several tons. Yet the exertion had not even caused him to break a sweat. One of the reasons he used the belt in circumstances where he might lose control. Though a gift from the gods, one in particular, his own strength scared him.

Long familiar with the hammer throw, one of many competitions enjoyed by Faltyr's growing ranks of mercenaries, he planted his feet and lifted the sand gar by its snout. Breuxias spun once, twice, and then flung the limp beast into the air.

Yax released the ball of Aethyr fire from between his palms. The fireball streaked toward its destination and exploded upon contact with the gar. The blast's force burst the beast and reduced it to fiery chunks of flesh and bone. The exertion caused by the draining war weave forced the Lord of War to take a knee.

Wailing over the wind, one of the remaining gars burst through the ground and destroyed the wagon in a furious rampage. Yellow Ant rushed the beast with a spear and drove its point through one of the gar's clawed front flippers. The wounded creature whipped its head around and latched onto the elf. The gar shook Yellow Ant back and forth violently and then cast him away into the storm.

Breuxias lost track of Yellow Ant as he fixated on the white hot tip of the arrow notched by Shell Horse. He fired the Aethyr-fueled arrow from his position on the side slope of the closest dune hill. The projectile found its mark as it sunk deep into the exposed eye of the sand gar that had mauled Yellow Ant.

Leishan raced by the gar on the bare back of his mount and fired another arrow. His missile struck the end of the elf's and drove them both into the beast's brain pan.

The monster moaned and bleated as it struggled to move, but by the time its head hit the sand, its fight, like its life, was gone. Collapsing under its own weight, the sand gar slid back into the black waters from whence it came.

"Where'd the other gar go?" Yax asked. "Do you see it?"

Breuxias looked around but didn't see any signs of the third attacker. Leishan and Shell Horse waited on the side of the far dune, but Yax and Zoltana edged closer to him. Zoltana tossed Breuxias one of two spears she'd salvaged from their scattered equipment.

"Do you think it's gone?" Zoltana inquired.

"Damn well better be," Breuxias said. "If it knows what's good for it."

Zoltana placed one bare palm on the ground and closed her eyes. She exhaled slowly and said, "It doesn't. It's still here."

The sand at their feet vibrated. As another groan arose below them, no one needed his command to run this time. The gar powered through the sand, hurling itself a dozen feet into the air.

Breuxias rolled away from the beast but came up fighting. He charged once more, stepping lightly across the soggy sand. The Brute jammed the spear into the gar's vulnerable belly before it sank back into the mix of sand, rock, and river water.

The wounded beast wallowed and wailed. As it thrashed around, its long wet tail slapped Breuxias hard enough to knock him onto his back. Using the flat claws at the end on its broad flippers, it scrambled after him. The sand gar wiggled its head side to side as it advanced so that it could keep one eye on its prey at all times.

Fortunately for the Brute, the creature's fixation did not last long. Yax ensured that with a series of golden missiles fired from Starkiller. The blasts scorched the gar's armored back and drew its ire the Wand Bearer's way.

As it turned its attention toward Yax, Zoltana literally leaped at the opportunity to attack the distracted beast. The Winaq'che ranger sprang onto its back with the easy grace of an acrobat and landed right behind its head. Leaning forward, she buried the broken end of a spear into the gar's right eye.

Vitreous humor and blood poured from the gaping wound as Zoltana stabbed it again. As the last beast collapsed onto the sand, Breuxias found newfound respect for the elven woman.

With her fighting by our side, we might succeed at Mok'Drular after all.

Chapter 14

Sir Frederick shifted in his saddle and waited anxiously for the signal from Katar. The coming morn threatened to dispel the shadows his men needed to cloak their position. He had no reason, other than fear, to trust the traitor, but he felt that it was enough to ensure his cooperation. After all, he had come to them, and the scouts reported no signs of an ambush or other trap.

To his right, Stogal rubbed his hairless chin while Balmoor readjusted his ponytail. On his left, Marduk sat upon a white steed. He cleaned his fingernails with the tip of a dagger.

"Those colors, so fascinating," Marduk said. Using his dagger, he gestured toward the shimmering aurora blanketing the predawn sky.

Looking skyward, Frederick replied, "I've heard tale it was caused by what my Gre forefathers called the Sundering."

"Quite right," Marduk confirmed. "Whether you call it that, The Cataclysm, or whatever, it was the end of the previous cycle of ages. Two powerful rulers, mage-kings, dueled to the death; their demise was so devastating that it was felt around the world. The central portion of the Meshkenet Mountains was obliterated and much of the original coastline sank into the sea. A lush and fertile area became a wasteland. This aurora has haunted the night sky over the Sands of Sorrow since."

"And everyone lived unhappily ever after. Sounds like we were told the same fanciful bedtime stories as children," the knight-in-shining-armor said with a shrug. He turned his gaze from the display in the heavens to glare at the wizard. Not bothering to disguise his bigotry or contempt, he added, "Another fine example of why I don't trust magic-users. When the Aethyr is wielded by those with more power than sense, all hope for humanity is lost. That's why I support

King Orson's decree to hunt them down. The only good magic-user is a dead one."

"Beyond that caveat, where do you stand on this war?" Marduk asked, sounding conversational rather than snide.

The worm seems to have learned his place. For now.

"I do as His Majesty orders. And I go where he tells me, even if it's a sandy shithole like this. As a Knight of Damarra sworn to uphold the laws of rulership and order, it is not my place to question his authority. Like the Ireti god-kings of old, Orson is Mother's Sun living representative on Faltyr. His word is my law. Beyond that, I leave the bureaucracy to the bureaucrats."

The knight took a long drink from his canteen as he formulated his next response. He swished some of the water around in his mouth. Once he returned the canteen to its holder on the saddle, he turned back to before spitting onto the ground.

"Personally, I think invading Ror was a mistake," Frederick said. If Marduk looked surprised by the knight's opinion, he did not show it. "After all," Frederick continued, "why would you want to usurp the rule of a sovereign whose distant relative rules the second largest army on the mainland? Much less invade and occupy the buffer state between you and that army. Those actions will guarantee reprisals from the Crimson Phoenix and its allies."

"The Crimson Phoenix can ill afford to appease Oparre," Marduk said. "Their western border has been flooded with elven refugees chased from their burning tree cities. Add to the equation their Gre relatives fleeing the conflict in Ror and the Crimson Phoenix must go to war, if only to prevent an uprising amongst its own peoples.

"Don't worry though, brave Knights of Oparre. Elven magic is no match for that of the Protectorate armies marching alongside your soldiers. Even with the Crimson Phoenix as their ally, the elves of Silent Brook will fall, even if their own ruler keeps slipping through your fingers like sand through an hourglass. What was it like having her and her mirror image as your consorts?"

"Do not speak to me of Lady Shy'Elle. Once King Orson is finished with her, she'll be given over to me. I will take care of her for the rest of her life. The ordeal she has been through already has been enough without her having to suffer further."

"I see," Marduk said, returning his dagger to its sheath. Blowing on his nails, he rubbed each fingertip with his thumb.

His dramatic pause drew a frown from Frederick. He did not like where this conversation was headed. The knight felt his hand tighten reflexively around the handle of his own blade.

Finally speaking again, the mage added, "You certainly have your eyes set on a prize, don't you? I like that about you, Frederick. Even after you chased Lady Shy'Elle and the traitorous Sir Ausic into the Crimson Phoenix and managed to get captured, you had the stones to demand she be released into your custody under King Orson's orders. You must have the heart of a dragon beating in your chest or even larger stones rattling around in your skull. I would have paid my weight in gold to see the look on their king's face when you made that ludicrous demand."

Frederick turned in his saddle to face Marduk. The knight fixed him with an icy stare meant to warn the wizard he had crossed a line. And it might cost him his life.

Clearing his throat, Frederick said, loud enough for Stogal and Balmoor to hear, "While it is true I claimed Lady Shy'Elle as my prize to spearhead this Blood War, I was following His Majesty's orders to bring her back, even if it meant my own death. Instead, it cost the lives of all the men who accompanied me. Their heads removed like those of chickens on a butcher's block before my very eyes, only I was spared. I saw the look of fear in those men's eyes as they were executed one by one, leaving me to return in disgrace to tell King Orson of my failure.

"But I was not to be denied my prize. I crept into the lair of my enemy and took her from under their noses. Only when I made the mistake of trusting these fools to guard her did I lose her again. We will find her or I will find a scenic place to bury these pathetic excuses for Knights of Oparre."

A smirk forming around the corners of his mouth, Marduk replied, "Lady Shy'Elle's beauty is unrivaled throughout the lands, so I can understand your obsession with her. Many men have been lured by the enchantments of elven women. Even your friend, the prince, fell under her sway, before you put him to death on the king's orders anyway. Convenient how that worked out for you, isn't it?"

Frederick glowered at the mage but didn't respond to the gibe. Instead, he grinned down this bear and reminded himself, *I must not kill him until we have the prisoners. Then he can meet with any number of fates on the way back to the capital. Like his headless corpse falling overboard and being eaten by razorfish.*

"The Queen of the Winaq'che would make a wonderful bride, a powerful bride indeed. And I must say, even I would like to have a night alone with her," Marduk chuckled. "But if you think Orson will ever let you rule an occupied Silent Brook with Shy'Elle as your bride, you are a bigger fool than I thought."

Frederick's vision darkened as rage filled him. The blood of his Gre ancestors boiled in his veins. He drew his sword and pointed it at the mage. Several nearby horsemen raised their repeater crossbows and pointed them at him too. The knight eased his horse closer to the mouthy mage.

"Another word from you, Marduk, and I will not wait for an order from my king. Out here you are on your own. No Proleus. No glorious mage armies. No magical doors back home. Just you, your mouth, and whatever you have to back it up. Remember that next time you speak. I would hate for the Sands of Sorrow to take on a literal meaning for you. Do you understand me?"

Flinching as if he had been struck, Marduk appeared stunned by the gravity of the vague but definite threat on his life. The offended knight kept his eyes fixed on the mage. Rage threatened to consume him. His squire and the other soldiers in camp kept their weapons at the ready, but none of them uttered a sound. Neither Stogal nor Balmoor had moved a muscle.

Many of them had angered their superior in the past, and none of them wanted his fury directed at them. It wasn't that Frederick liked being angry; it was that he was constantly surrounded by irritants and incompetents. The Blood War had taken its toll and most of the professional soldiery were either gone or scattered to the four corners. Orson would not have considered Proleus's armies a decade earlier, but the war's toll and Allwain McNair's growing influence had changed his mind. Sir Frederick hated to displease his king by failing him further, but if the pesky mage uttered one more insulting comment, the knight vowed to make sure one this desert contained one less irritant.

ଔଓଔଓ

"Wake up! Riders! We have to go now!"

Kaladimus Dor jolted upright when he heard Katar raise the alarm. Still groggy from the elixir and sore from his wound, Dor reacted clumsily and managed to stand. After a brief moment, his thoughts cleared and he realized what had happened. They had been found. It didn't occur to him that they'd been betrayed. Not then anyway.

Tameri leaped onto the wagon seat and seized the reigns. She yelled to the horses, "Come on, guys, you can do it! You have to!"

Yawning Deer climbed onto the seat beside her, while Dor remained standing in the back of the wagon. He heard the all too familiar sound of the whip cracking. The wagon lunged forward but, for once, he managed to maintain his balance.

"Where's Katar?" Tameri asked.

Crouching low, Dor helped pull Zarena into the moving wagon as her midwife pushed from behind. Grabbing Xotl by the front of her robe, he kept from slipping in the sand.

Once both of the elven women were safely aboard, he said, "He's not in the wagon."

"He's there!" Yawning Deer cried, but Dor was busy moving Zarena to the back of the speeding wagon and to safety.

The mage looked up in time to see one of the Knights of Oparre slash the fleeing rogue across the back. The impact sent his limp body crashing to the ground in front of the charging horse. Though Katar wasn't trampled, Dor could not tell if he was alive or dead.

"Get us out of here!" Dor yelled, making a command decision. "Now!"

Tameri whipped the horses as if a dragon chased after them.

A graying, round-bellied knight galloped alongside them. Before anyone could react he jabbed his sword into Yawning Deer's side. The minstrel yelped as the sword pierced him, his blood quickly stained his tunic. Dor glared at the cavalier.

While Xotl pulled the old elf into the back of the wagon, the Master-of-Disaster pulled the staff from his pouch. He stepped over Zarena nimbly and moved to the side with the horseman, shielding her with his body. The knight swung again, this time at Xotl's exposed back.

Dor blocked sword with staff, grimacing from the force of the impact. The Protectorate Mage glared across at the enemy knight and tapped his staff on a floorboard. Its knotted end crackled with visible Aethyr energy as it responded to his command.

Dor yelled, "Let's see you try that with me!"

The knight swung with all of his might. When he made contact with the glowing staff, an electrical discharge surged through the sword and into the attacker. Thunder split the air, and his opponent was blown out of his saddle. By the time the enemy hit the ground, the shocking weave had reduced him to a smoking carcass encased in blackened laminate armor.

Tameri shouted, "Don't do that again, you scared the horses!"

"Good, they need to go faster!" the mage replied and readied himself for more riders. He'd slain one of their officers, possibly their leader, but the pursuing cavalrymen were not dissuaded.

The closest rider leveled his crossbow and fired. The bolt passed between Dor's legs, pierced his robes, and lodged in the back of the wagon seat, right behind where Yawning Deer had been seated.

The Protectorate Mage retaliated by projecting shards of ice from his outstretched hand. The enemy's horse reared as the icy missiles pierced its hide, fell backward, and landed on its rider.

"Look," Xotl said as she pointed out horsemen closing from a crest on their flank. Somehow they were already ahead of them.

"No way are we going to outpace all of those riders."

"I know a trick," the midwife stated.

Xotl closed her eyes and chanted over a coil of rope in the bed of the wagon. After she finished the weave, she tossed the coil to the magician.

Dor said, "Knowing Yax, I might be familiar with this one."

As the horsemen closed the gap, Dor let the writhing rope trail behind the wagon. Xotl touched the length of hemp before the riders reached it and a burst of Aethyr energy zipped along its length. Ducking incoming crossbow bolts, they tossed the coil of rope in the direction of their pursuers.

The animated rope rose into the air as the riders thundered toward it. It snapped taut, tightened as if pulled by unseen forces.

After the screaming horsemen and their neighing mounts tumbled away in a cloud of sand and dust, Dor and Xotl shared a laugh at their expense. It might have been wrong of him, but a few dozen feet of hemp put to creative use had broken a headlong charge by Oparre's prized cavalry in dramatic, even comedic fashion. After losing Katar, Finders Keepers needed a win and, at this point, Kaladimus Dor would take any one they could get.

೧೫೧೫

A single runner returning to camp saved Marduk's life. Oblivious to the animosity between his superior and the wizard, the messenger said, "The turncoat has given the signal, my lord!"

Sir Frederick tugged at the reigns of the steed. He glanced at Marduk one last time, murder still on his mind. He raised his drawn blade into the air and then swung it downward to signal his troops. His cavalry mounted their steeds and galloped toward the encampment. The Knights of Oparre and the Protectorate Mage followed behind them.

His cavalry crested a series of low dunes before spotting the makeshift shelter and lone wagon. The fugitives were already in the wagon, but Katar remained far enough away to make his performance plausible.

The knight's keen eyes could see the elven Queen's face from here. And Shy'elle's swollen belly. Despite the heresy, he almost wished the child inside belonged to him.

On Frederick's command, Sir Balmoor and his riders led the charge, with Stogal and his men breaking off to flank the wagon. Marduk and Frederick remained behind with the main contingent. Normally, he'd relish a good chase, but he had to keep a close eye on the Protectorate Mage and his coveted item, the chest.

Brandishing his gleaming blade, Sir Balmoor rode through the camp without stopping. Katar chased after the wagon in vain, but the knight rapidly closed on him. He raised his sword and connected with a painful, yet nonlethal blow with the flat of his blade. Katar tumbled forward, like a toy tossed aside by an uninterested child, and landed face down in the sand. Balmoor and his men kept after the wagon.

As he approached the camp, Frederick slowed his horse and circled it around the unconscious man. He dismounted and rolled the traitorous mercenary onto his side with a swift kick in the ribs. Katar groaned.

"He'll live," Frederick stated and turned his attention to Galil. "Secure this camp, seize everything."

As his squire and the riders who'd remained behind carried out his orders, the senior knight loomed over Katar. Finally, the downed man opened his eyes. The traitor's mouth contorted with pain as he tried to form words but failed. He struggled to his knees and vomited onto the ground.

From Frederick's side, Marduk asked, "Where's the chest?"

Katar tried to stand but moved too slowly for Frederick's taste. He grabbed the traitor by the arm and jerked him to his feet. Katar winced in pain and cursed him. Frederick backhanded him.

"The mage asked you a question. Where's the chest?"

Between moans and groans, Katar pointed to a patch of scrub brush. Marduk riffled through the bushes and then returned holding a backpack that looked like a glorified basket with straps.

The mage's nervous, even fearful expression turned to one of pure ecstasy once he looked inside the container. Marduk grinned like a devil as he removed a metal chest from the pack.

Decorated with wild markings and carvings, the ominous strongbox spurred Frederick's curiosity. Its scorched lid seemed intact despite the extensive cosmetic damage. Frederick could not make out the circular glyph engraved into it, but it looked reminiscent of the Iron Circle of Moor'Dru emblazoned on Marduk's gear. Unfortunately, the damage obscured its details.

Marduk smiled even broader as held his prize. Frederick didn't return the gesture.

The mage said, "Our masters will be pleased."

Frederick quipped, "I have no master, wizard; I have a king. I choose to serve him; I'm not kept like some mad dog on a chain. Frankly, I don't see the importance of a bauble that looks as though someone plucked it from a house fire. It's worthless."

"So can I go?" Katar interrupted their exchange.

Frederick snapped his head toward the rogue. "As soon as you answer a few questions for me, I will set you free."

"Ask away," Katar said, "I'll tell you whatever you want."

"Where are your friends going?"

"To the coast, I think," Katar answered. "The mage sent a bird carrying a message to their ship. It's supposed to meet them on the coast."

Enthralled by the chest, Marduk didn't seem to hear the question. Instead, he caressed the sides of the metal chest.

Frederick returned his attention to Katar and asked, "What does this ship look like? And does she have a name?"

"You'll know her by her name. They call her the *Seadragon*."

"You have been most helpful," Frederick said with a curt smile.

"So I'm free to go?" Katar asked.

Sir Frederick drew his sword and sliced across Katar in one fluid motion and relished the look of surprise on the scoundrel's face.

Katar struggled to keep his entrails from falling out but failed. His guts hit the sand with a wet *plop* before he slid to his knees. The burning eyes of the King's Executioner remained locked on the dying man's face. A wicked grin spread across Frederick's own visage.

"Why?" Katar asked as he sputtered blood from his mouth.

"I told you I would set you free. Instead of living with the guilt of your betrayal and the knowledge that you have lived as a thief and a coward, you will have a chance to come back as something useful, something pleasant, like a gust of wind or a bit of rain."

With another swing of Frederick's blade, Katar's head joined his entrails on the sand. A pool of crimson and gore spread out around him. At last, he was free.

Chapter 15

Despite the ferocity of the storm, Yax'Kaqix and the others found their fallen comrade with relative ease. Yellow Ant showed no outward sign of injury but that did not change the fact that the elf was quite dead. Curiously enough, his blue blood trailed from every visible orifice, and changes in the body's pallor led Yax to believe that blood from massive internal injuries pooled beneath the skin. He'd been crushed to death by the gar's powerful maw.

As the survivors stacked wood from the ruined wagon on Yellow Ant's improvised pyre, they rehashed the skirmish with the sand gars and determined what had happened to their comrade. By the time they placed his body on the bed of combustibles, Yax could hardly walk, much less conjure flames from the Aethyr. But it was his sacred duty.

Raising his leaden arms, the former monk chanted in the holy dialect of the Priests of Kümatz, the sacred keepers of time. Though it took longer than normal for the Aethyr to respond, it answered. He felt the ambient energies of the universe flow through him. When they emerged from his open palms, they took the form of fire. Liquid flame jetted forth and ignited the bonfire. Finally, after a long moment, he closed himself off and lowered his smoking hands.

Placing one hand on his shoulder, Zoltana said, "Thank you. That must have taken quite an effort after today's trials."

"You have no idea. I wish I could've done more. I have to rest."

"Then get some rest. You've already done more than most."

"I wish I could have healed him, but it was too late."

"You can't blame yourself. Yellow Ant put too much faith in his magic. Skin as hard as steel might save you from a blade or bolt but not being crushed by the jaws of those things."

"We're all lucky to be alive," Breuxias interjected.

In the common tongue, Shell Horse said, "But without Yellow Ant we're lost. He was the only one of us who knew the exact way back into Mok'Drular."

"What do you mean exact way?" the scowling Brute asked.

"The mountain route we took could pass for a labyrinth, but he memorized it."

Flopping down beside his remaining gear, Yax said, "We'll worry about it when we get there. The mountains are still a day away, if not two. But I have to sleep."

"I'll take first watch then," Breuxias replied.

Too tired to respond, the elf waved one clawed hand and then rolled onto his side. He was asleep before his head hit the sand.

In the middle of the night, Yax awoke from an all-too-familiar dream, one that haunted him often in the wake of funerals. The grisly image of his wife's corpse blackening and then burning on her pyre caused him to shiver more than the bitter chill that characterized lonesome nights in a desert.

He sought warmth, but the fire was all but gone. As he peered into its remnants, he imagined that he could pick out bits of Yellow Ant amidst the hot coals and ash.

Yax cocked his head toward the sound of someone approaching from behind, someone with footfalls as light as the Aethyr. He reacted before he realized it. Demon Queller came free of the sheath, yet it remained cold as ice as he swung it around. The humming blade halted less than an inch from the slender neck of the lovely elven ranger.

Lowering his blade, he said, "I'm sorry. I didn't mean to."

"It's okay," Zoltana answered with a faint smile. "You don't have to apologize for being who you are. You're a Choj'Ahaw. Wand Bearers are born and bred for battle. It is your nature."

"And we can usually function on little to no sleep, except for here. This desert is unnatural, cursed."

"Sands of Sorrow indeed."

"Agreed," he said, sheathing his weapon. Even the feather light elven sword felt like a leaden shark weight in his hands.

"It'll only get worse as we get closer to Mok'Drular," Zoltana cautioned.

Changing the subject, Yax asked, "Tell me more about the Aethyr device you mentioned earlier?"

"They call it the Eye of Ra'Tallah. It magnifies the Sands of Sorrow's tendency to distort magic and drain anyone using it."

Back in the ravine, they had discussed the various security precautions taken by those who'd turned the megalithic ruins of the once great ogre city into a prison. As a veteran Choj'Ahaw, he had considerable experience with Aethyr devices, fields, shields, walls, and even bubbles. This particular device sounded like one of the Dragon Towers that had dotted the face of Ny in pre-Cataclysmic times. Only this one operated in reverse, dampening rather than boosting people's ability to tap into the Aethyr energies around them.

The simple yet majestic structures had served as an energy grid. They had enhanced the ability of Faltyr's peoples to tap into the invisible but omnipresent Aethyr and use it in various ways, though primarily for long-range communication and the rapid exchange of information, goods, and material. However, all of the Dragon Towers had fallen silent after the Cataclysm. Now, most of them were no longer standing, and the bulk of those were located in western Ny and its outlying islands.

"Ra'Tallah," Yax said and then spat. Even saying the bastard's name aloud was enough to cause gooseflesh to race down his pale arms. "What fiends would invoke the name of that Ireti devil? Much less risk his wrath."

"So you believe the stories then," Zoltana said. "That he's not dead. Only sleeping, waiting for the stars to usher in his return."

"I don't know what to believe; every sorcerer is full of tricks. One capable of raising an undead army, occupying most of the main continent, and dueling the most-powerful-wizard-to-ever-live to a draw makes cheating death sound like child's play."

"A draw? Didn't Artemis win?"

"They disintegrated themselves, two colossal armies, and most of a mountain range. I'd call it a draw."

"Now that you put it that way. But what about the device?"

Yax rubbed his throbbing forehead and said, "Somehow we'll have to disable or destroy it. But if we don't get there then no plan will help us. Wake the others. It's time to go."

"Sure you couldn't use more sleep? I know I could."

Shivering in the night air, he stifled a yawn before responding. "It's too cold to sleep," Yax said.

Zoltana smiled and stepped closer to him. Slipping her limbs around his waist, she asked, "How about if I keep you warm?"

The Wand Bearer smiled despite his fatigue and the frigid air.

Leaning into her warmth, he said, "I think I'd like that."

"Me too." She took his hand and said, "Come with me."

"Don't mind if I do," Yax replied with a toothy grin.

଺଻

Smoke from Yellow Ant's smoldering pyre rose over Zoltana's shoulder as the merciless sun crested the jagged horizon. The shattered remnants of the Meshkenet Mountains dominated the skyline to the north and east. The expansive dune sea at the heart of the Sands of Sorrow stretched across the barren expanse separating their dwindling party from the sundered mountains. Running water and refuge from the elements remained days away despite their brisk pace across the dunes.

For now, however, water was the least of their worries. Before leaving the sandy valley, Zoltana summoned enough water from the river snaking deep beneath it to fill their skins. The Ranger of the North preferred the lush forests and dales of her homeland, but her training and experience allowed her to survive in any climate or environment on the face of Faltyr.

When the Winaq'che forced their Choj'Ahaw to turn in their wands millennia ago, rangers arose to fill their place in the ranks of the military elite. They gained such fame as versatile survivalists and wilderness combatants that the Unen'ek and many human cultures adopted them over the centuries. But the Rangers of the North remained the originals.

Zoltana's extensive training had prepared her for many things but not the sudden, traumatic loss of her homeland. Her heart sank and her mind swam after witnessing the burning of its ancient tree cities and seeing the Tor'Binel, the Silent Brook itself, run blue-black with elven blood. Her mind still reeled from the horrors produced by the brutal campaign the Kingdom of Oparre and its allies waged against elves and other fae creatures.

Before she had managed to recover her wits, she led her family into an ambush laid by wizards recruited from Moor'Dru by King Orson. The brutal skirmish with members of the Mage Army resulted in her family being separated, captured, or killed. Zoltana and Zarena escaped thanks to the intervention of their adopted uncle, Chahak the Thunderer.

A former Choj'Ahaw and friend of *The* Blue Macaw, the old elf had abandoned his duty to the Eternal War and fled the South Isles for new life among the Winaq'che. And like most elves in Silent Brook, Lord Chahak had found peace until the men of Oparre pushed north of the Nargawald. Then he went to war. Now, the old Thunderer would die a prisoner at Mok'Drular, unless she and Yax rescued him first.

Her thoughts turned from her family to the infamous Choj'Ahaw, Yax'Kaqix. Zoltana recalled sitting on her uncle's knee and listening to the first stories her uncle told about his adventures in the South Isles. Of all the combatants, companions, and conquests mentioned in those wild tales, her favorite had been the former monk turned Choj'Ahaw named Blue Macaw, for it was Yax'Kaqix who'd restored weary Chahak's will to live and provided his excuse to exit the Eternal War.

For Zoltana, she sped across the dunes on the heels of a legend. And last night, she'd lain with him, though not in the way she'd hoped. Not yet anyway.

She had kissed him as they snuggled underneath his voluminous cloak, but memories of the men of Oparre and their rough use of her came flooding back. Zoltana felt filthy, like a temple defiled, unworthy of the attentions of an Eternal Warrior like the Blue Macaw. She intended her flirtations and innuendo in the most lascivious fashion possible; instead, she ended up teary-eyed and seeking solace in his strong arms.

As they had lain together under the shifting aurora of the night sky, they had discussed their various triumphs and traumas. Eventually, she told him about the fiery invasion of her homeland and the depredations of the soldiers upon her people. She tried but failed to go into the details of her own ordeals, but Yax understood.

He had seen the horrors of war first hand. When her voice hitched in her throat and tears filled her eyes, he pulled her tighter to him and rocked her to sleep.

Zoltana awakened that morning wrapped in his warmth. His arms encircled her, his lean, muscular body pressed against her own emaciated one. The sturdy cloak concealed their intimate embrace from the elements as well as the others. Reflexively, the elven woman snuggled closer to her savior, not wanting their moment together to end.

But end it did. Like all good things. For the sake of propriety and the Lord of Battle's reputation, Zoltana stole from his bed as the frigid night gave way to a rapidly warming morning. She kissed him on the forehead and whispered her thanks.

Even as they raced toward the mountains, she meditated on their night together. Part of her wished it had gone differently, but the rest of her felt rejuvenated by her experience. Refuge and respite had come to her in the form of the Blue Macaw. He had helped her find her center, her solace, and from there she drew strength. The Ranger of the North was ready to follow Yax into the mouth of the Nine Hells if that's what it took to rescue Chahak and the others from Mok'Drular.

Chapter 16

Sir Frederick and Galil surveyed the abandoned camp while they awaited the return of Balmoor and Stogal. The Knight of Damarra spotted Marduk beyond the secured perimeter. The mage sat cross-legged with his back turned to the sentries. Frederick could see the captured chest in the wizard's lap but not what he was doing with it.

What's that sneaky bastard up to now?

He sauntered closer to the distracted wizard and his sorcery. Much to his chagrin, his overzealous squire followed close at his spurs. The two stopped between a pair of wagons used to ferry supplies for the cavalry. Frederick and Galil peered around the side of a wagon canopy to observe Marduk's activities.

The mage didn't seem to notice the eavesdroppers as he placed a circular gold object atop the lid of the chest. He opened it like a clamshell to reveal a bright, polished mirror. The robed spellcaster spoke into the looking glass. When he did, its silvery surface glowed.

Frederick looked on, both curious and confused.

"What type of sorcery is that, my lord?" Galil asked.

Frederick replied by pressing a gloved finger to his lips. He smiled at his squire and then drew the digit across his neck.

In the distance, he heard Marduk say, "The chest is damaged but intact. All can now proceed as planned, Master Proleus."

Frederick removed a telescoping spyglass from his belt and peered through it. The image of a well-groomed, bearded man dominated the glowing mirror. The rich gold-embroidery on his robes signified his status as High Mage of Moor'Dru, a position Proleus seized following his coup against Salaac and Braigen, the other two members of the Council of Three.

Frederick preferred to think of him as Proleus the Usurper or The Slayer of Salaac. Though Marduk's master seemed eager enough to help them eradicate the Winaq'che and the fae, the Knight of Oparre didn't trust any man whose reputation was built on the usurpation of another's rule. He could not abide a traitor.

Frederick strained his eyes but failed to recognize the shadowy man lurking behind Proleus. The palm-sized mirror and poor lighting made it difficult to identify him. But the silhouette was familiar. He had seen it numerous times behind the screen in the confessional at the Cathedral of Mother Sun in the capital.

"You have managed to obtain that which has eluded us for quite some time. No ordinary men, including the knights accompanying you, have been able to secure the chest," Proleus praised his apprentice. However, he cautioned, "Bring it to Grymsburg immediately, before it corrupts you."

What in Mother Sun's name is in that chest? And what do they want with something that dangerous?

"And the Queen?" Proleus asked. "Were you able to recapture her?"

"No, Master, she continues to elude the useless troops under the ineffective command of the King's disgraced executioner. They are still in pursuit, but I have little faith we will catch them before they reach the coast. The cavalry must pace their already exhausted horses while Dor drives his to the point of death with his spells to stay ahead of us."

"You mean to tell me that Kaladimus Dor is still alive."

"Unfortunately, Dor escaped, along with the Queen. But with the chest in our possession, surely he poses no threat."

Proleus scowled for a second and then said, "Not a threat? Dor is far too dangerous to be left alive, you fool! He wants the chest as much as we do. You must remedy this oversight on your part at once, Marduk. Use whatever means necessary to kill him."

As his master's praise turned to criticism, Marduk recoiled from the mirror at the scathing comments.

"I understand, Master. He will be dealt with. What should I do about the Lady Shy'elle?

The man lurking in the shadows maneuvered around Proleus, allowing Sir Frederick to confirm his suspicions. The Knight of Damarra recognized the placid face of Allwain McNair. Always the manipulator, the towering Gre priest, clad in his customary white and gold-trimmed robes, loomed over Proleus. A purple sash, emblazoned with a golden orb with rays of light extending forth from it, signified his adherence to Damarra. His diamond-encrusted gold circlet marked him as the Holy Father, the head of the Reformed Church of the Holy Trinitas.

The Holy Father administered the approved state-run church bureaucracy, though many said that the modern church ran the state these days. After all, Allwain McNair had served as the personal spiritual advisor to three kings of Oparre in his lifetime. Three kings who had seen Oparre expand like the bladder of an airship, but at what cost? The kingdom had been in a perpetual state of war for over half a century now. It was really an empire.

The sun poked through the early morning clouds. Its rays blinded Frederick as they reflected off the surface of the looking glass. He shifted his position, careful not to alert Marduk to his presence. As he squinted for a better look, the dawn's light cast both men in the mirror as fiery, grinning devils for the briefest of moments. The horrific illusion faded in a literal blink of the eyes.

The Holy Father, not Proleus, answered Marduk's question. "Whatever you do, do not lose the chest. It is our priority, not some spastic mage or even the Queen of Silent Brook. The contents of that chest are vital to bringing about the completion of our plans, not her child."

"On this subject, we are agreed," Proleus interjected. "The infant heir to two powerful kingdoms would have made an ideal vessel, but any half-breed son of an elf bitch will do in a pinch. With rape as pervasive as war in Silent Brook, there are sure to be a surplus of them born in the coming months. If castle rumors are to be believed, Sir Frederick the Elf-Lover may be persuaded to impregnate one especially for us. He is a patriot after all."

Proleus added, "I stringently disagree on the fate of Kaladimus Dor though. I made the mistake of underestimating his power once before. Dor is not to be taken lightly. He may belong to my order, but his loyalty lies with Salaac's faction. Had it not been for him and Braigen, the young fool would have been dead many years ago. Dor owes them his life and would likely die to complete his mission out of respect to his late masters."

"Do not fear, either of you," Marduk said. "Sir Frederick and I will hunt the troublesome mage down and kill him. If we can recapture Shy'elle in the process, we'll bring her and the chest to Grymsburg."

Sir Frederick stayed his hand, but he shook with rage. He wanted to throttle Marduk as well as his master and the conniving Holy Father. He wondered if there were any honorable men left in Oparre, in all of Ny. Though many might consider him a villain for his acts, the Knight of Damarra did follow a code of honor and ethics; two of them actually, one laid out by Mother Sun, the other outlined by his king.

Infuriated to hear that someone was making plans for his prize, he squeezed the spyglass until the front lens cracked. He'd imagined it to be the narrow necks of the co-conspirators. Without a word, he slipped the broken spyglass to his squire.

Frederick didn't need it to see the treacherous wizard close the magic mirror and tuck it deep into the folds of his robe. Or watch as Marduk turned toward the riders returning to camp.

The senior knight and his squire emerged from their hiding place as Sir Stogal and other horsemen entered the camp. Frederick noted that there were fewer horses than men returning to camp than had left in pursuit.

In fact, many of returning men shared horses. Balmoor did not appear to be among them. Every trooper looked dirty, bruised and bloody. The fearful expression on Stogal's face foretold the story his superior did not want to hear. Sir Frederick recognized the look of failure. He'd seen it in mirror on multiple occasions.

Once he dismounted, Stogal averted his eyes. Instead of Frederick, he stared at the bonfire on the edge of camp and the smoldering corpse of Katar lying atop it. The look on Stogal's face turned to terror.

"You lost them didn't you?" Frederick asked.

Stogal gestured toward a blackened corpse thrown across the back of a mount and reported, "The wizard killed Balmoor. Cooked him in his own armor with a bolt of lightning from that black staff! He and that mongrel bitch broke my horse's neck with a rope they enchanted. I'm fortunate they didn't break mine in the process."

Sir Frederick examined the charred body of the slain knight before returning his attention to Stogal. He whispered orders to two of his personal guards. They grabbed Balmoor's corpse, dragged it from the horse, and tossed it onto the fire beside the burning body.

"I expected as much from you, Stogal. You reek of booze and failure. Like your dead friend here. Had it been your neck, you'd save me the effort now."

On the verge of a breakdown, Stogal cried, "We were unprepared and no match for a wagonload of magic-users! You have to believe me!"

Joining the quarrelsome cluster of soldiers, Marduk stepped between Sirs Frederick and Stogal. Scolding the knights like an angry nanny, the mage wagged a finger at both of them. Frederick's eyes narrowed as he suppressed the urge to stab the snake in the kidney.

"We have no time for this bickering!" Marduk yelled. "I tire of this infighting. You are soldiers, and you have an objective. Show some discipline. Kaladimus Dor must die! He is a very dangerous man and cannot be left alive."

"You're in no position to give orders, Marduk!" Frederick warned. "I'm in command here. Stogal is fortunate enough not to be on that bonfire alongside Balmoor. If you push me, you'll end up there too!"

"Then what are your orders, commander?" Marduk asked.

"I've tired of chasing them across this godsforsaken wasteland," Frederick said. "So we'll change tactics and head for the port of Imputnim. The *Hero's Welcome* and the *Regal* are docked there. They are two of Oparre's fastest warships and will be able to catch any vessel this ragtag band has at their disposal."

He placed a firm hand on Stogal's shoulder and smiled menacingly. The nervous knight flinched at his superior's touch. "Marduk and I will sail on the *Regal*," Frederick added. "You, Sir Stogal, shall lead the boarding party from the *Hero's Welcome*. You will bring me the head of the wizard so that I may present it to the King. I suggest you be prepared this time. If you fail me again, your head will serve as a conciliatory gesture to his highness for your ineptitude."

Either way, Frederick figured he would have the pleasure of watching the bumbling knight die on the high seas.

ઙ୭ઙ୭

Dor watched Tameri as she steered the wagon, eyes fixed forward, staring blankly at the desert road ahead of them. She seemed lost in thought and unaware of him seated next to her.

Inhaling deeply, she smiled and said, “We’re almost there. I smell salt from the sea.”

“I hope the *Seadragon* is waiting,” Dor replied.

“Don’t worry. Uncle Macz will be there. He won’t let us down.”

The confidence in her voice reassured the worrisome mage. Dor peered into the darkness behind them but saw no one in pursuit. They might make it to the coast safely after all.

Dor removed a small pouch from the inner pocket of his robe. He packed his briar wood pipe with a pungent blend of herbs then transmuted the chill in the air to emit a flame from the tip of his finger. The wild-haired mage touched the tiny torch to the herb and lit it. He sat back, propped his feet on the toe board, and puffed on the pipe. He savored the sweet smoking blend before exhaling slowly. When he did, his entire body relaxed. His worries melted away into the dying night.

Dor placed his free hand on Tameri’s arm to get her attention while he offered her the pipe with the other. The young woman’s soft skin felt warm in spite of the chill in the air. She exuded so much ambient Aethyr energies that he jerked away as if he had been shocked. He marveled at the mysterious, magical woman.

When she looked over at him, her attention drifted toward the smoldering pipe. The blue-grey smoke twisted and danced in the gentle coastal breeze. Dor watched her retreat further inward and wondered what ghosts haunted the Savior of Istara. He noticed her eyes followed the curling wisps of smoke. She seemed distracted by them as they rose into the air. Hoping to calm her troubling thoughts, Dor offered the pipe again and waited for her response. Tameri waved it away, a look of disgust on her face.

“I’ll have none of your herbs dulling my senses,” she said. “I need what little wit I have left to see us through this caper.”

"Suit yourself."

The mage shrugged his shoulders and took another pull on the pipe. He relished the relative quiet of a new day and allowed his thoughts to drift back to her, to her beauty and power. Glancing over, he smiled. She caught him staring, but returned his smile.

They continued to exchange furtive glances and awkward small talk until the vast blue waters of the Ireti Ocean came into view. As the wagon tracked toward the sandy shoals, they spotted the Hallowed Vessel anchored near the shore. Its shallow draft allowed the *Seadragon* to hug the coastline as closely as a vessel a fraction of its size.

Tameri snapped the reigns, causing the horses to gallop toward the shoreline. Dor stowed his pipe and held on to his seat to avoid falling overboard. Behind him, the elves jarred to sudden wakefulness.

"What's going on?" Zarena asked with alarm evident in her voice.

"Relax, our destination is near," Dor said.

Xotl hugged Zarena tightly and cried, "By the gods, we are saved!"

Yawning Deer managed a terse smile, but the old minstrel had lost a lot of blood before Xotl stopped the bleeding. He looked paler, thinner than normal.

"How're you holding up back there, songbird?" Dor asked. "Want a pull off this?"

The old elf smiled broader than before and said, "It'll take more than a jab from a pointy bit of steel to do me in. I'll pass on the pipeweed though. My side hurts enough already without coughing up a lung for a bit of pain relief."

Dor shrugged, "More for me then."

The mage puffed away happily as they neared the shoreline.

Dor heard those on deck shouting as others waded through the shallows to greet them. Watching them slog through the soggy sand, he pondered how they would get the heavy figurehead aboard the ship before King Orson's troops arrived.

The exhausted horses dragged the wagon across the wet sand to the edge of the sea. Macz stood paramount among those who had come to greet them. Stopping the wagon, Tameri leapt from her seat and hugged her uncle tightly.

Dor helped Zarena and Xotl from the wagon and then turned back toward the desert road. He scanned inland for troops and the coastline for other ships but saw neither.

Paranoia gripped him like a snug glove, but the herbs allowed him to function despite it. He could not let his guard down now, but he could not waste his time on improbable scenarios. He had to focus on realistic possibilities.

Those chasing them would soon discover where they had gone. They might change tactics but they would not stop. If they did not come by land, they would by sea. And the port of Imputnim remained too close for comfort.

Not sparing time for pleasantries, Dor took the first opportunity to interrupt the family reunion.

"We have to switch the figureheads now, Macz. No time to waste."

"Aye, Captain. Leave the heavy lifting to us."

The *Seadragon*'s crew worked feverishly to replace the faux figurehead. Once removed, the same ropes and pulleys were used to lower the real one onto the ship. Dor found his nerves tested as the men fought to maintain control of the cumbersome item.

One of the lines slipped and the figurehead pitched to the side wildly. It slammed into the railing on the bow with a resounding crunch. But neither it nor the ship suffered the slightest scratch.

"Be careful!" Dor exclaimed. "Or you'll be fishing it out of the drink."

Macz scowled at him but went back to work helping his crew members attempt to lower the artifact again. Seconds later, another rope snapped and caused the ornate sculpture to drop toward the large metal spar protruding from the ship's bow.

Dor wanted to cover his eyes; instead, he willed the figurehead toward the support spar but expected to it to topple into the sea. As if drawn by unseen forces, the relic landed on the protrusion and slid into place perfectly.

The fins on the *Seadragon's* newly acquired figurehead rippled and slithered along the bow of the vessel. The finger-like fins melded onto the side of the hull and became solid again. Another surge of Aethyr energies rippled through the entire ship. Dor gasped as the device welded itself into place, once again becoming a permanent fixture of the Hallowed Vessel.

Everyone that witnessed the phenomenon stared in awe or murmured in wonder as the energy surge bled away.

"Well, that was simple enough, right, Captain?" Macz gibed.

Tameri sidled closer to Dor and placed her hand on his arm. Though he stared at the figurehead, he focused on her warmth.

"My father and Yax will be waiting. Orders, Captain?" she asked.

"You're right." Dor smiled at Tameri before adding, "Set course for the Pelican Coast, Mr. Maczitalius. Our friends will need a ride."

"You got it, sir!" Macz said as turned back to the awestruck crew. "You heard the Captain, boys. Hoist the sails! We have people depending on us, and we'll not let 'em down!"

The crew set to work immediately. They raised its brass anchor and then unfurled its silk sails. As the winds shifted in response to the Hallowed Vessels' movements, the *Seadragon* cut through the water with ease as it tacked toward the open sea.

Chapter 17

As the sun rose in the east, Breuxias and the others trekked north, toward the merciful shadows cast by the Meshkenet Mountains. Jagged red peaks mixed with dull basal wrecks, the stunted ruins of volcanoes last active when they helped usher in the Cataclysm.

Time and space feel twisted in this cursed desert. Has another day slipped away already? If that's the case, how long until we reach the remnants of the sundered range?

He stopped alongside Yax and Zoltana at the top of a sandy rise. The elves peered into the distance and conversed in hushed tones. He lifted his half-depleted waterskin to his lips and took a few conservative sips before nosing into their conversation.

Sure, I'm nosey, but it pays to pay attention.

"What do you see?" he asked his friend. "I know that look."

"There." Yax gestured toward the horizon. "Do you see it?"

The blinding glare from where sunlight met sand made discerning details at this distance difficult. But he hazarded a guess.

"What are those? Standing stones?"

"No, bones," Zoltana said. "Really. Big. Bones."

Cupping his hands to shield his eyes from the sun, the Brute squinted to get a better look at the objects on the horizon. Bleached bones the size of columns used in the construction of ogre cities protruded from the sand. Judging by the size and configuration, they belonged to one of Faltyr's fiercest yet noblest creatures.

"I'll be damned," Breuxias muttered. "It's a dragon."

No one spoke as they approached the wyrm's remains. Impressive at a distance, the gargantuan bones jutting from the Sands of Sorrow humbled them all. They stopped a respectful distance from the dragon and surveyed its grave site.

Partially buried rib bones standing half the height of Caleb's tower cast welcoming shadows of cool darkness onto the sand. Its massive horned skull peeked through the desert floor where it surveyed them with its eyeless sockets.

Breuxias paced its length from the tip of its snout to where the spiny vertebrae of its tail disappeared beneath the sand. Returning to the others, he emitted a low whistle.

“Amazing,” he said, truly impressed. “Never seen a dragon this big, much less been this close to one.”

“This is an elder wyrm,” Zoltana commented as she ran one hand along a dragon rib. “You can tell by the striations on the bones.”

“Kind of like counting tree rings?” Breuxias asked.

“Something like that,” Zoltana replied with a smile.

The Brute didn’t know if he was being patronized or not by the elven woman. He chose to take her response in the best possible light and soldier onward. Patronizing or not, the ranger had a lot to teach.

“The bones of most creatures fuse when they reach the end of their growth cycle,” she added. “Dragons are no different in that regard. However, they go through a new growth cycle every time they molt. Their bones grow rapidly during this period and then fuse again at the end of their current cycle. Each time they fuse, the process creates a ring around the bone much like the growth ring on a tree.”

“And what classifies this one as an elder?” Breuxias asked.

“Density pattern of rings on the bones coupled with the length of the body and size of its horns lead me to believe it.”

“Wonder how long it’s been here.”

“No telling,” Yax said. “Maybe the sandstorm uncovered it.”

“It uncovered something else too,” Shell Horse interjected.

The elf fell to his knees beside the rib cage and worked to uncover something obscured by the sand. When Breuxias and Yax spotted a glint of metal, they joined him in his impromptu excavation. They uncovered a gold-accented claymore clutched in the bony hands of a large humanoid skeleton. Not a spot of rust tarnished its shiny blade.

“I guess we found out how it died,” Yax speculated.

“It’s definitely a dragonslayer,” Shell Horse added, “ogre-made and ogre-wielded. But I can’t make out the runes.”

The word “ogre” turned Breuxias’s curiosity to fixation.

He asked the elves, "Mind if I examine it?"

"Not at all," Shell Horse said. "Can you read their runes?"

"As well as you speak my tongue," Breuxias said. "I was raised by a tribe of ogres in the Broken Lands."

Shell Horse stared at the Brute for a long moment, as if he might be reassessing the human. Finally, as the elf moved out of the way, he asked, "What do you mean 'raised by them'?"

"For a while anyway," Breuxias said. "It's a long story."

"And a fascinating one," Yax interrupted, his wide blue eyes stared longingly at the enchanted sword, a rare find that predated the Cataclysm by untold centuries. "The first dozen times I heard it anyway. What does the blade say?"

"Patience, Old Man," Breuxias reminded Yax. "I'm a bit rusty. They're definitely pre-Cataclysmic runes, looks like the final dynasty of Mok'Drular. If I could see them all, I could be sure."

The Brute reached out to wipe sand from the runes. As his fingertips brushed the blade, a howling wind swirled around his party. Blinded by the sand and grit, he whipped his head around as a mournful roar rose around them. Though he could not see it, he heard the horse whiney, slip its reigns, and gallop away from them. He jerked his hand back as if bitten. The sandy assault and sorrowful moan ceased as soon as he broke contact with the dragonslayer.

"What was that?" Zoltana asked. "Every hair on my body is standing on end."

"Me too," Yax added. "Maybe you shouldn't do that again."

"Do what?" Breuxias inquired. "All I did was touch it."

"Exactly!" the elf said as he tapped his pinkie finger. "Haven't we covered why touching random magic items is bad?"

Breuxias had lost one of his own pinkie fingers to a cursed spider ring that they'd found in a goblin nest in western Ny. The reminder made him feel a bit sheepish; it angered him as well. The Old Man couldn't let anything go, whether one night or a thousand nights had passed since the incident occurred. Yax considered his elephantine memory to be an asset, but his friend often considered it an annoyance.

"So the sword did that?" Breuxias asked.

"No," Yax said. "The ghost did that."

"The ghost?!"

"The dragon's spirit to be exact," Yax explained. "It's still here, and it's not happy. So much for time healing all wounds."

ଓଓଓଓ

Zoltana watched her shadow grow short as the day grew long. Their shady respite at the base of the dragon skull would not last much longer. She had to find out why Yax'Kaqix intended on lingering beside a pile of haunted bones. Nothing good judging by the ritual paraphernalia he laid out on the unrolled animal hide. Her curiosity turned to concern as the sinister intent of his actions became clear.

"What in Kümatz's name do you think you're doing?"

"Making contact," Yax replied. Looking across the fire at her, he added, "Maybe even finding us a way to Mok'Drular."

Zoltana tried to hold the Blue Macaw's intense gaze but failed. Her eyes drifted along with her thoughts. She reflected on the night they'd spent together beside Yellow Ant's funeral pyre. Grief caused people to do funny things, sometimes with total strangers, but she'd idolized Yax since childhood. She'd felt safe and warm wrapped in the strong arms of the fiery Choj'Ahaw.

Uncle Chahak's stories had not prepared her for this side of Yax'Kaqix, a facet willing and able to make contact with the dead, a practice condemned by most civilized peoples since the time of the Cataclysm. The Nubari, along with other human and demihuman tribes huddled along the southern coast of Ny and its outlying islands, continued to utilize necromancy after the end of the last cycle of ages, but the Unen'ek no longer approved of it.

Was that why the Blue Macaw flew so far from home?

Zoltana's eyes drifted across his perfect musculature, a body hardened by a lifetime of wandering and warfare. Her gaze focused on his chiseled arms, big hands, and long fingers as he reached into his "possibles bag" and retrieved a corked clay vial. Her fears about what it might contain dampened her arousal at the breathtaking sight of the shirtless, tattooed elf glistening with sweat in the midday sun.

Warrior, wizard, monk, and now necromancer.

Somehow, Yax managed to conceal mystery after mystery behind eyes as clear and blue as the sea itself. She wondered what else they hid.

As he uncorked the container and poured a small measure of gray powder onto the ground, Zoltana asked, "Are you sure about this? A living breathing dragon is dangerous and unpredictable enough."

Instead of answering, Yax poured a few drops of water onto the mysterious substance and then started chanting in his dialect.

Breuxias crouched beside her and said, "Don't worry. I've seen him do this sort of thing before."

Zoltana eyed the human with incredulity. He suffered from overconfidence in his inborn talents and magical gifts, much like Yellow Ant. In her opinion, Breuxias was well on his way to becoming as reckless as his mentor, the errant Choj'Ahaw chanting over a few drams of dust piled on a mound of sand and bones.

Fixing her eyes on the human, she asked him a pointed question. "You've seen him do this with a murdered dragon's angry, possibly vengeful spirit?"

Shifting his gaze away from her, he muttered, "Not exactly."

"What do you mean 'not exactly'?"

"It was more like a goblin," Breuxias admitted.

"A goblin!" she cried. "Are you serious?"

"It's the same basic principle, metaphysically speaking."

"Metaphysically speaking, huh?"

"Hey!" Yax interjected. "I'm trying to concentrate on harnessing the forces of the universe here. I'm touched that you're concerned about my safety, but it's a lot more dangerous to interrupt or distract me. I know what I'm doing here." Lowering his voice, he added flatly, "Trust me."

Zoltana fumed silently but didn't complain further. As much as she hated to admit it, she did trust the Blue Macaw. After all, he'd saved her and her sister too. And now the stubborn elf risked his soul to bargain with the restless, tortured spirit of a long dead dragon. All of that to fulfill a promise to a dead man to save her people. If any man in her life deserved the benefit of the doubt, it was Yax'Kaqix.

In the absence of further interruption, Yax resumed chanting. He waved his hand over the discolored powder on the sand. As Yax did so, several dark purplish mushrooms budded and grew to full size.

"Why are you growing Stygian Shrooms?" Zoltana asked.

The ranger wondered if her endless stream of questions had annoyed him yet. Yax had remained calm and cordial when he'd redressed her earlier; he hadn't been cold or cruel. His explanation on this occasion proved no exception.

Yax smiled across the fire at her as he picked the purple caps. "I need these for the ceremony," he explained. "To approach a spirit properly, one must ingest a tea made with them to take one close to the boundary between the living and the dead."

The Blue Macaw paused long enough to place the magic mushrooms into a small pot of water. Holding out his palms, he increased the intensity of the fire until the water came to a boil. Satisfied with his efforts, he met her gaze once more. "Only at this crossroads can one be relatively safe from harm. It will make it hard for the dead to distinguish us from their own. And it should shield us from any attempts at possession."

As the foul taste of fear welled up inside her like sulfur springs, Zoltana felt her trust in him waver.

"Relatively safe? Should shield us? You don't sound sure."

Yax shrugged his shoulders and said, "There are no guarantees when dealing with the living. Why would there be with the dead?"

Zoltana sat in silence and meditated on his words. Her ambivalence prevailed, however, as her emotions warred over whether to be comforted or confounded by them. She was not the only one around the fire disconcerted by Yax's vague assurances and ghastly actions.

Leishan remained aloof and apart from their circle. Though she did not speak the language of the Säj, she read his body language as easily as that of any man or beast. And he appeared as close to full flight as the skittish horse on the lead in his hands.

Yax coaxed him into joining them eventually; but not until after the elf had poured the steaming mushroom tea into a cup and said a blessing over it.

"This will protect you," Yax told them. "A sip to be safe. Two sips to be sure. But be warned. Drink no more."

Without sipping it himself, he passed the cup to the right. Breuxias sipped twice and made a horrible face before handing it over to Shell Horse. The elf uttered a familiar prayer in Winaq'che and then drank from the cup. Leishan argued with Yax again but finally relented. The horseman not only drank from the cup but followed the elf's instructions to slather the horse's lips with the concoction.

Better safe than sorry.

She shuddered at the thought of a dragon possessing the body of a horse. Apparently, Yax knew the same legends about that being the way a Nightmare was born. They had enough obstacles ahead of them already without adding a fire-breathing flying horse to the list. When Zoltana took the cup from Leishan, she offered a prayer to Kümatz and then drank twice.

Zoltana handed the cup to Yax, who set it in front of him. He selected a small bone-handled knife from the array of ritual items and drew its razor sharp obsidian blade across his left palm. Blue blood oozed forth from the wound and dripped into the cup at his feet. Lifting the cup, he sipped once, twice, and then drained the rest of its contents.

Zoltana watched with growing unease when Yax placed his bloody hand into the flames and let his vital fluids drip onto the bed of coals. The fire flared brightly and shifted shades from red to blue before finally reaching an almost colorless white. He held his hand steady and continued chanting until the flames resumed their normal hue. The elf's stony expression didn't change throughout the ordeal.

Pulling his left one from the fire, Yax said, "Join hands!"

After some initial hesitation, Zoltana grabbed the proffered hand. Despite her fears, it wasn't any warmer to the touch than normal. Peeking at his palm as the others joined hands, she saw that the damage from the knife had been healed. No traces of his blood remained.

Once their circle of power had been completed, Yax said, "From here on out, no one else speaks. Let me do the talking. Do not speak to the spirit, even if it speaks to you. And no matter what happens, do not break contact with me before I break contact with you."

Zoltana nodded her assurances along with the others. She squeezed his hand to give him another form of assurance. Tilting his head in her direction, he smiled before returning her gesture.

When he spoke again, Yax used Dragonese, one of the oldest tongues on the face of Faltyr, a guttural language full of glottal stops, punctuated by occasional hissing. Though the Nubari and even lizardmen like the Sobeki used a form of it, only elves and other fae retained the ability to communicate with dragons in their own tongue. As a Ranger of the North, Zoltana knew it as fluently as Winaq'che.

"Son of Kümatz, Lord of Dragons," Yax cried, "I call to you across the Veil. Hear my cry! Join us here and now!"

Wind and sand whipped across the dunes and through their circle, battering and blinding the participants. An inhuman roar built over the sound of the wind and rose to a crescendo as the fire flared again. The fire burned brighter than before and seemed to take on a life of its own as a being of spirit sheathed in flame rose from its heart. Each of the dragon spirit's fiery eyes shined with the intensity of a sun.

The gravelly voice of the disembodied dragon asked, "Who trespasses on my prison in the sands? Who wakes me from uneasy slumber speaking the Old Tongue?"

"I do! Blue Macaw, Son of the Lords of the South Isles, Chief of Battle, Servant of the Aethyreal Flame!"

The dragon spirit sped toward the elf like a shooting star, only to be stopped mere inches from Yax's face by a field of Aethyr energy. Denied an easy vessel, the angry spirit howled madly and raced around and around the circle.

The ghost swirled about each of them, including Zoltana. She focused on Yax's eyes across the fire and ignored the raging being.

Unable to possess any of them, the dragon spirit dove back into the fire to sulk. Its burning eyes bored into the Blue Macaw.

"I am no fool!" Yax said. "You won't find any vessels here, willing or unwilling."

"A clever one," the dragon spirit replied. Its sinister staccato laughter lingered like rolling thunder in a summer storm. The sound raised gooseflesh on the elf's extremities.

The otherworldly presence asked Yax, "What if I told you I could smash your pathetic barrier and take any vessel I desire?"

Releasing Zoltana's hand, Yax drew Starkiller and pointed it at the dragon's skull. The Golden Wedge on the end of the wand shined as intensely as the eyes of the disembodied dragon.

"You'd best be quick. Otherwise, I'll blast your bones to bits. How'd you like to wander the wastes as a cloud of ash?"

"No fool indeed," the ghost said with another throaty laugh. "What do you want from me, little elf? I grow weary of these games."

"Directions."

"You summoned me from the Aethyr and risked your lives, your very souls, for directions? Maybe you are a fool."

As the bemused expression on the spirit's countenance turned to one of annoyance, Zoltana realized that it might be right.

Chapter 18

Reaching the bottom of the stairs, Tameri exited the shaded companion way and entered the artificially lit deckhouse of the *Seadragon*. Aethyr-powered torches, ensconced in brass rings along the cherrywood paneling, provided the ship's interior lighting. She paused to let her eyes adjust to the dimmer conditions. Soon, she could see as clearly as if it were daylight.

Tameri followed the railing around the rectangular opening in the middle of the cabin to the interior stairwell. The broad staircase wound downward into the bowels of the Hallowed Vessel. Leaning over the rail, she counted a dozen decks below her before the rest faded into darkness. The marvelous Aethyr ship contained more space than a wizard's tower inside a hull half the size of a war galleon.

For the sake of convenience, everyone had been given private accommodations on the expansive second level. It contained a galley, a saloon, and even a flush latrine and hot bath. Her quarters on the *Seadragon* were more opulent than any she'd ever known. Another reason she'd hated the idea of surrendering them to take up residence in a moldy old tower.

After reaching the second deck, Tameri passed by her father's door on the way to her cabin. She brushed her fingertips lightly across its surface. Wherever he was at the moment, she hoped he was safe. The worried young woman whispered a prayer for him as she rounded the corner of the corridor.

She approached Xotl's and Zarena's quarters. The elven women had chosen to room together, citing the pregnant woman's condition. They had selected a room at the end of the hallway. As fate would have it, it was directly across from her own room. So Tameri could not help but notice that their door was ajar.

Her natural tendency to snoop pulled her toward their door instead of hers. Careful not to be heard, she crept close enough to overhear their conversation. She pressed her body against the wall to sink into the shadows at the end of the corridor and then leaned her head closer to the crack in the door.

"You must not fret, Your Majesty," Xotl said in a hushed tone. "We are safe now. We are among friends."

"I admire your optimism," Zarena replied.

Tameri found herself confused by the midwife's comment.

"Neither of us have the luxury to think any other way, My Queen," Xotl added. "We must remind ourselves that we will return home soon enough to vanquish the enemy and secure the throne for your child."

Tameri's heart thumped in her chest. Her thoughts raced with unanswered questions. *Queen? Could this be the coveted Lady Shy'elle? If so, how could that be? The Queen of Silver Brook was freed from Castle Grymsburg. There was no mention of her being recaptured. Curious.*

She eased closer to the door. The occupants inside the bed chamber failed to notice Tameri as she peered inside. Her father had always been proud of her ability to sneak. Over the years, she perfected the technique taught to her by Yax'Kaqix. She graduated from her training after she managed to surprise him.

"Our voyage home is far from over." The pregnant woman said, rubbing her engorged belly, "And there is little time before the child comes. I can feel the changes taking place inside me."

"Rest, milady; you need to take it easy," Xotl suggested and motioned to the bunk.

The queen seated herself on the edge of the bed and said, "I would but the swaying of this ship is making me sick."

"Perhaps some bread will help settle your stomach."

The elven leader blanched as she looked at the plate of food on the table beside the bed. The sight of it seemed to revolt her.

Using a knife on the serving tray, Xotl sliced a piece of bread and handed it to her regent. Reluctantly, the pregnant woman took it, thanking her. As Xotl curtsied, Tameri shifted her weight to see get a clearer view while remaining unnoticed.

"Perhaps the Prince will be born at sea," Xotl said as she selected a wedge of cheese.

A heavy silence filled the air while the queen chewed on her bread and Xotl nibbled on her cheese. Tameri held her breath and pulled away from the door. Sweat ran down the side of her forehead. Her heart raced when their conversation resumed. She edged back toward her vantage point, risking discovery once more.

The human woman heard Xotl say, "Let's get you ready for bed, milady. I'll prepare you a proper bath in the morning."

Tameri peered through the crack in the door in time to see the midwife help the pregnant queen into a fresh gown, one of her own on loan to the elven women. The curious young woman did not divert her eyes as Xotl wiped the pretty queen's exposed skin with a damp cloth before buttoning the garment. When warmth filled parts of Tameri no desert sun could heat, her breath hitched in her throat.

Xotl shifted her gaze toward the door. Her eyes met those of the eavesdropper. Tameri suppressed the urge to flee as the fierce midwife snatched the knife from the table and stepped in front of the queen.

"Curious ears and eyes can make for dangerous enemies. Show yourself fully," Xotl demanded, "or I'll have your throat cut before you can scream."

Tameri pushed the door open and stepped inside. Xotl closed and locked it behind her. The human focused on the sharp kitchen knife clutched in the half-elf's hands as they circled each other.

"My apologies," Tameri said. "I didn't mean to listen in on your conversation. Your secret is safe with me. I promise."

The human woman lowered her eyes and knelt before Queen of Silent Brook. She put her life in the Lady Shy'elle's hands.

"Tameri, correct?" Zarena/Shy'elle asked.

Without looking up, Tameri replied, "Yes. I am the daughter of Breuxias, milady."

"That is a lovely name, one known to us, revered by us. You are the Savior of Istara. And I am Lady Shy'elle, Queen of Silent Brook. I'm trying to save my people too. Can I trust you?"

"Of that I can assure you, Your Highness. And I beg your apologies again." Tameri explained, "I came to make sure you had everything you needed. I had no idea as to your true identity. I was merely worried about you and your child."

Lady Shy'Elle reached out and touched Tameri's hand.

"Do not avert your eyes. You have no need to be ashamed, child. We would not harm one who would risk so much to liberate her people."

With the queen's permission, Tameri looked into her wide eyes. They shared a brief, friendly smile. The elf squeezed her hand.

Shy'elle said, "There is yet a question lingering on your lips."

"How did you find yourself in chains? The last I had heard you'd been freed and sought refuge in the Crimson Phoenix."

"That is too long, too trying a tale to be told tonight," the queen said with a faraway look in her eye. After a moment, she added, "Sufficed to say, Tameri, you must not let anyone know I am aboard. The King's Executioner seeks me on behalf of his masters in Oparre, but their true purpose is darker than acquiring me.

"A corrupted priest of Damarra, known as Allwain McNair, wants my child for the dark magic he has planned. Their insidious plan, if successful, would cast our turbulent world into a fresh new hell, one that it may not recover from this time. My heir must serve as a symbol of hope for a brighter future, not help usher in the next cataclysm."

"Your secret is safe with me, milady. No harm shall come to you as long as I draw a breath. I swear to protect you and the blessing the gods have bestowed upon you," Tameri promised.

Xotl eyed Tameri with great suspicion but she ignored her.

Lady Shy'elle said, "Though it was unnecessary, I thank you for your oath."

The pregnant woman's face contorted with pain and her hands dropped to her swollen belly. Tameri moved to help her lay back on the bed, but the overprotective midwife forced the younger woman away.

"Are you okay, my queen?" Xotl asked.

"Yes, but you're right," the prostrate queen said, "I need rest."

"These pains will become more frequent as the time of his birth approaches. You should know this by now." Xotl grabbed the damp cloth from the table, dipped it into a water basin on the table, and wiped the sweat from the queen's forehead.

"Is there anything I can do?" Tameri asked.

"There is one thing you can do, girl. You can take your leave, so I can attend to the queen," Xotl commanded but was ignored.

Lady Shy'Elle grimaced in pain again and clutched her stomach. Xotl maneuvered the queen into a sitting position and then unbuttoned her gown. The pregnant woman's swollen breasts dribbled milk, and a dark blue spot stained the mattress between her legs. All three fell silent as their eyes tracked from the blood-stained bed to the lady's weeping nether region.

"My gods!" Tameri exclaimed.

Xotl cried, "Your majesty, you're bleeding!"

"Should I get Dor?" Tameri asked as she wrung her hands. "My dad says he's not good for much but he's an expert with medicinal herbs."

"So am I," the midwife responded. "That's why I had him bring this down earlier in the day." Xotl grabbed a small leather pouch from a nearby table and opened it. She removed a handful of cottony bandages and several small jars of dried herbs.

Lady Shy'elle took several labored breaths while Xotl pulped and mixed the herbs in a saucer using the back of a spoon. The queen smiled through gritted teeth at the nervous, overprotective women hovering over her. Her eyes rolled back as she grimaced again, her tiny hands clutched to her stretched belly.

"Are you sure?" Tameri asked. "I could--"

She stopped herself midsentence. She'd healed the injured and soothed the sick countless times during the siege of her home city but that was before she'd learned that her Aethyr investiture derived from Eresh, Lady Death Herself. The last time she'd laid hands on a child, it had been the dead body of her childhood friend. That catalyst led to her being branded Savior of Istara.

Some savior.

"Go now," Lady Shy'elle managed, "keep our secret safe. The life of my unborn child depends on it. All our lives depend on it."

The midwife turned to Tameri and glared at her. "You heard her, leave us," Xotl ordered.

Tameri didn't argue this time. She looked back once before leaving the room. She saw the queen writhing in pain as Xotl prepared a tea, or perhaps a poultice, from the herbs. She prayed for them, prayed that Eresh would stay far from Shy'elle and her child.

ᲝᲜᲝᲔᲝ

Dor loitered on the mahogany planked deck of the *Seadragon.* Enjoying the moonlight, he leaned wearily on his staff and stared skyward. The stars twinkled and shimmered above but thick, ominous clouds lingered on the horizon. He turned his attention to pale Ishta'Kahl's distorted reflection on the rolling surface of the sea, but his thoughts remained fixed on the coming storm.

They were safe for the moment, but the rogue Protectorate Mage doubted their pursuers would give up the chase. He had become accustomed to being hunted by one party or another since recovering the contents of the chest in his possession. So maybe it was just paranoia. Dor turned to face Tameri when she joined him on the poop deck. Her beauty seemed to shine even brighter under Ishta'Kahl's silvery light. He admired her for a moment before taking her hand in his. She squeezed it gently, and a single tear rolled down her cheek.

"Don't worry, Tameri, your father will be okay," Dor said softly.

"It's not that, it's…" She trailed off, turning her eyes seaward.

"What is it?" Dor asked. "You can tell me."

Turning to face him fully, she smiled, albeit reluctantly. He returned the gesture. As he did so, he wiped away her tear.

Tameri's smile grew wider as they stared into each other's eyes. She ran her fingers through his tangled hair. Her gentle touch brushed away the cobwebs of doubt, worry, and fear cluttering his anxious mind.

Dor recalled his first kiss with Keera. As the physical and emotional distance between them vanished, warmth had flooded him from nose to toes. The energy between them had electrified him in a way that no lightning strike ever could. Now, he felt those same feelings welling to the surface, only this time for Breuxias's daughter.

Feelings can be so confusing. And distracting. Seems like I'm not the only one who's distracted though.

"If it's not about your father, then what is it? You look as if you've encountered a ghost," Dor told her.

"I'm fine, just a little tired."

The lonesome mage relished the idea of falling asleep with the beautiful Savior of Istara pressed against him. He did not dare say it, so he said nothing instead. Silence filled the space between them. Fighting the urge to do something rash, he sighed and leaned on his staff once more.

"Speaking of tired," she said, "you look exhausted."

"I am. It's been quite an adventure so far, hasn't it?" Dor asked as he shifted position. *Something else is bothering her, but I hate to press the matter.* He tried to smile but yawned.

"Understatement of the year, that's what I call it," Tameri responded. "Why don't you go below and get some sleep while you have the chance? The others can handle the ship without you for a while."

"I'll be sure to keep them in line, Captain," she added, complete with a mock salute.

"Maybe you're right," Dor said as he stared into her eyes.

Before he could react, Tameri leaned forward and kissed him on the lips. He was shocked but managed to return her kiss.

Dor broke from her embrace when he heard footsteps approaching from the direction of the port stairs. Macz grinned when he discovered them huddled together as he emerged onto the poop deck. Tameri averted her eyes but didn't pull away from Dor's embrace. But that didn't stop the inexperienced, overwhelmed magician from pulling a disappearing act on her.

"I'm going below for a bit of rest," Dor said as he blushed.

He headed for the starboard stairs as her uncle drew close. The mage nodded toward the older man but shifted his eyes toward the narrow staircase. When he glanced over his shoulder, Tameri stared after him. Dor left her and her uncle to command the *Seadragon* and went below. The exhausted mage was almost to his room when he spotted Xotl. She stood in the hallway holding a bundle of bed linen. Instead of acknowledging him, the midwife slipped into her chamber and shut the door behind her. The lock clicked into place, echoing in the corridor.

Guess I'm not the only one lacking social graces.

He shrugged his narrow shoulders and entered his private cabin at the other end of the hall. A loaf of fresh bread and some cheese sat on the table next to a glass bottle filled with water. He joined them at the table. As he sat and ate his simple meal, standard cabin fare, his eyes focused on the porthole across the room. He could see nothing but blackness beyond the glass.

Soon enough I'll be seeing nothing but the back of my eyelids.

The mage removed his pipe and herb bag from his almost bottomless pouch and then packed the briar bowl. A simple snap of his fingers produced enough of a flame to light the pipe.

Dor puffed on his handpicked blend of herbs and felt their relaxing effects envelope him. As he exhaled rings of blue-gray smoke, his eyelids grew heavy. Before long, he yearned for his bed.

He welcomed the downy padding of his mattress. It beat the hardwood of a wagon bed any day or night. But he struggled to get comfortable, grimacing at the residual soreness from his wound. Finally settling into position, he took one last look around the room of the *Seadragon's* spacious cabin. His tired eyes passed across the basket backpack in the corner, but he pushed any thoughts of the troublesome burden from his mind.

Dor doused the lamps with a simple clap of his hands. He allowed the darkness to envelop him and the mattress to comfort him. Closing his eyes, he surrendered to the gentle swaying of the ship and let it rock him to sleep. And without the contents of the chest to haunt his dreams, the mage slept soundly for the first time since his first trip into the Sands of Sorrow.

Chapter 19

While the others observed his exchange with the dragon spirit, Yax'Kaqix transmuted his own fears as he would any other Aethyr energy. He turned his terror into bravado as he leveled Starkiller at the horned skull of the beast, charged its Golden Wedge, and hoped for the best, even as he prepared for the worst.

"I've been many things in life," Yax said. "Right now I'm trying to be the savior of many souls. Can you help me? Can you help them?"

"That depends."

"Depends on what exactly?"

The floating phantom's lipless mouth curled into a wicked smile. "On whether or not you can help me."

"Alright then," Yax answered. He lowered the wand but kept it pointed at the dragon's remains. "Let's make a deal."

Beside him, Zoltana's eyes bored into him with an intensity rivaling that of the flaming serpent in their midst. Did he know what he was doing? Not really. But he also knew that with risk came reward. And those who ventured nothing gained nothing.

To find Mok'Drular and infiltrate the camp, much less extricate that many prisoners would be a feat of epic proportions. Without powerful allies, it would most likely become a failure of epic proportions. He could think of few allies more powerful than a dragon.

"If I am to traffic with spirits," Yax added, "I must know who I'm doing business with. For all I know, you could be Ra'Tallah himself who was said to return in the wake of a great storm."

The dragon spirit hovered in the space over the fire without responding. Its gaze proved so intense that Yax nearly lost his nerve. Fearing the worst, the Wand Bearer prepared to blast the bones.

Finally, the roiling, burning apparition of smoke and fire spoke.

"My memory like my mind is scattered to the four quarters. I was old when the Long Road was young, so I am known by many names to the peoples of Faltyr. To my recollection, Ra'Tallah is not one of them. Among your people, I am called Kak'nah'Kan, Great Fire Serpent. I tire of this place. I am sure we can come to some sort of agreement. Like my mate, I am an honorable soul."

Yax bowed his head at the mention of Kak'nah'Kan, but he did not avert his eyes from the spirit in the fire. The dragon claimed to be the very embodiment of one of the chief saints recognized by the high priests of Kümatz. Great Fire Serpent served as his patron as well. Either the dragon spirit knew what lies to tell to gain the elf's trust or fate had led them to the gravesite of a legendary hero of the elves.

Could this be the spirit of the dragon who came to the rescue of an elven city on the mainland besieged by an army of ogres? If so, can it be trusted? After all, Kak'nah'Kan paid the ultimate sacrifice to help my people long before the sundering of the Jade Throne. If not, I'm being manipulated.

"What is it you require in return?" the Wand Bearer asked.

"I have lain within view of my home for Kümatz knows how long. It is torture to be within sight of it but never quite able to reach it. Take me with you and I will be your guide."

"How do you propose I do that?"

"Bind my spirit into one of my bones and carry it as the beacon to light your way."

"That simple, huh?"

"One condition," the dragon spirit said. "A simple request."

"Here it goes," Yax responded. "There's always a catch."

The Wand Bearer raised Starkiller as if conducting a symphony rather than a necromantic negotiation. Everyone around the circle reacted by drawing away from the fire, but no one broke contact. He was no longer physically connected to Breuxias or Zoltana, but he'd anchored the circle of power through them when he'd taken their hands earlier. The shield of Aethyr energy should protect them if the spirit survived to attack in the wake of its bones being destroyed.

"Wait!" The dragon spirit cried, its gravelly roar giving way to panic. Clearly, it did not know any more than Yax about its final destination in the afterlife, and it had no desire to find out. "It's a simple enough matter, a sign of good faith so to speak. I want you to return the dragonslayer to my mate so that it will no longer be a threat to dragonkind."

Yax lowered the wand and allowed the energies stored in its golden tip to dissipate. He said, "That's a reasonable request, one I will honor. How can I be sure your mate will honor our pact?"

"A dragonslayer is a powerful tool for negotiating with my kind. If she does not think enough of my memory to agree to our covenant, slay her with it. Strike her down, if you can, little elf."

"You don't sound very worried."

"I'm not. As I said, my mate is an honorable soul. If she yet lives, she will help."

"Then we have a deal."

As Yax returned the wand to his belt, the iridescent flames sheathing the spiritual essence of the dragon shifted slightly and took on a softer hue. The elf wondered if he'd made a mistake by trusting the restless spirit of a murdered dragon. The decision seemed foolish, if not fatal. In the end, it would turn out to be a bit of both.

With Great Fire Serpent's permission, Yax used Starkiller to remove one of the oversized teeth from its skull. He selected a small specimen, one about the size of his outstretched hand, and cut it free of the mandible. The sand did not stir; the wind did not whip; but the dragon spirit let out a sorrowful cry as a part of its anchor to the world of the living was separated from its remains. The mournful sound rose to a frantic cry as Yax chanted aloud another incantation.

While his weave drew in Aethyr energies to him, the Wand Bearer piled an assortment of dried herbs onto the fire. The flames rose higher as thick, pungent smoke filled the air around him. He inhaled the vapors and looked to the heavens, only to have his view obscured by the colorful aurora dancing in the skies over the Sands of Sorrow.

Yax had the vague sensation that the ritual had bent time around them, distorting their perception of its passage, and the appearance of the aurora confirmed that it had taken all day and part of the night. In his opinion, the delay had been worth it. With its spirit bound into the tooth, Great Fire Serpent would lead them to the lair of its mate. Hopefully, she would agree to take them to Mok'Drular from there.

One way or the other, Yax swore to himself as they broke camp and set out to traverse the dark dunes of the Sands of Sorrow with naught but a ghost as their guide. Like his ancestors had done when they'd first arrived on this world, he would trust a dragon to lead them. He hoped it ended better for his party than for the elves of Faltyr. But if ever times called for desperate measures, it was now.

ఆ໑ఌ

Dragonslayer strapped across his broad back, Breuxias ran up one dune and down another. The desire for water dominated his thoughts, yet they had too many people in their party and too little water. *Water discipline must be maintained despite my parched tongue.* Though he would not drink until they stopped to rest, he could not prevent his mind from torturing him in the interim. He imagined himself walking on water but being unable to drink a drop. He ascended the slope of one mighty wave and then plunging into the slack between the next in a seemingly endless series of rolling slopes and troughs.

As he raced along behind the others, Breuxias cast his eyes skyward to dispel the palpable illusion of the sea. Not because he feared the images of the rolling, crashing waves or the beasts that could lurk beneath them. Thoughts of the sea made him think of Tameri. Thinking about his daring daughter made him worry for her safety. He had not always been a good father, yet he loved her with everything his grizzled heart had left to offer.

Tears moistening his cheek, he did something that he didn't very often. But tonight was a night for magic, for rituals, for deals. So he offered his own prayer. And though he looked skyward, he prayed to the only god or goddess that he knew to exist. Breuxias observed the effects of Death everyday in some way or another. She touched all their lives, but his more than most on Faltyr.

O' Death, O' Eresh, Lady of the Nine Hells, if you must reap one of us in this quest, I beseech you. Let it be me. If an exchange must be made, I offer myself freely and without reservation. I am but a grain of sand in the hourglass of creation. My death, like my life, is in your hands. I ask this not for myself but for my daughter, Tameri. My sins are beyond counting and my best years are behind me. She has her whole life ahead of her. Grant me this one request, Lady Eresh, and I am your man, your servant.

The magic in the mushrooms coursed through his veins. When he stared at the night sky in his ecstatic state, the pronounced aurora over the Sands of Sorrow exploded with color. Vivid greens, reds, and purples swam together in phantasmagorical fashion. He could see every strand and string, every loop and whirl of Aethyr energy composing the ever-changing field of energy.

The dizzying display caused him to stumble and almost tumble to the bottom of the slack. Instead, the Brute slid to a stop in the loose sand and giggled at his own foolishness. He didn't stop laughing until he'd regained his footing on the shifting slope. Glancing about in the darkness, he caught sight of Yax leading the others over the crest of the next dune. *Only the Old Man isn't leading us anymore*, Breuxias reminded himself. The dragon spirit, currently bound into the tooth clenched in his friend's outstretched hand, served as their guide.

If our guide truly guides us true, his mind babbled. *After all, it wouldn't be the first time a vengeful spirit tried leading us to our doom*, he reminded himself. He trusted Yax's judgment most of the time, but his altered state caused him to recall something he'd overheard Dor mutter on their way into Frolov Keep.

Who is the real fool? One who runs headlong into danger or the idiot who follows him?

Since he'd played both roles countless times in his lifetime, Breuxias reckoned he was a fool regardless. As he slogged to the top of the next sandy mount, his mushroom-addled brain wandered from thoughts of trust to texture. The sand in his boots ground between the leather and his exposed flesh. The pain and irritation of bulbous blisters that had burst and bled as they traversed mile after mile of the dune sea bore into his brain.

His poisoned thoughts latched onto the idea that the sand mingled with the mangled flesh of his feet to become part of him. He pondered the possibility that everything the sand had once been now resided in him. Not only the particulate remnants of the sundered mountains but everyone and everything that had lived in their shadow. Every breath he took filled him with more of the shattered remnants of the past.

Instead of panicking at this realization, he stilled himself. He breathed in the air and then exhaled his fears, anxieties, and regrets. He understood that the Sands of Sorrow was the largest tomb on the face of Faltyr, the site of the greatest destruction wrought in millennia. And no one could pass through it without it becoming a part of them.

The residue of incalculable loss and unfathomable tragedy hung in the air, making it toxic to mind, body, and soul. Anyone crossing this desert could not help but inhale it, absorb it, and have it sink into every fiber of their being. He could understand why so few survived the trek across this blighted waste. Its brutal, sterile conditions combined with an unnatural malaise and melancholy to make it a fertile reaping ground for Eresh.

Death walks here with open arms.

As he drank in the night air, he accepted the forces at work around him for what they were and thanked them for the epiphany as well as the warning. With fresh eyes, he surveyed the series of parallel dunes and then glanced behind him. The pattern became clear to him as the mushrooms brought it all together. He imagined the dunes as concentric circles, rings to be precise, radiating outward from a source, an epicenter. Breuxias could see it in his mind's eye, the impact crater left behind when Artemis and Ra'Tallah crashed into the nearby mountain range at the end of the last cycle of ages. Their cometary fall from the heavens triggered a series of volcanoes and earthquakes that darkened the skies and cooled the seas for centuries to come.

When the smoke cleared, the center of the range had been blown away, like a castle of sand caught in a hurricane, while the land around it would never be the same. Spires of rock rose from the once fertile plains north of the old Meshkenet range. Clouds of sand and ash blanketed everything between the shattered mountains and the Ireti coast to the far south where the waters of the angry sea drank the home islands of the Nubari and the western islands of Moor'Dru.

He wept again when he thought of the untold millions of souls lost that fateful day. *Had Eresh been prepared for such a deluge of souls? Had Death been able to reap them all? If so, was there a place in the Nine Hells reserved for those lost in the Cataclysm? If not, where had their souls gone?*

Breuxias's eyes tracked toward the heavens but focused on the shifting aurora instead. And then he knew. Eresh blessed him with yet another epiphany. As he watched, face after face, of both man and beast, swam into focus before fading back into the swirling field of colorful energy.

Sands of Sorrow indeed.

Chapter 20

Sir Frederick, Marduk, and company rode through the dimly lit streets of Imputnim. Its antiquated gas lampposts provided meager light compared to the Aethyr lanterns used in the capital. The crumbling concrete streets of the old city housed a handful of unsavory individuals including harlots, drunkards, and others who lurked in the shadows.

Those they passed pretended not to notice the knight and his companions as they made their way toward the port district. Anyone who had been conversing fell silent as the retinue passed. No one spoke to them, not even the harlots. No one dared make eye contact with the King's Executioner or anyone in his troop for that matter.

Sir Frederick carried the most infamous coat-of-arms in the kingdom, a headless serpent in the maw of a rampant lion adorned with a crown. Below the grisly scene, a blood red banner read: Death to the enemy. Galil bore the standard openly now. Had it been deployed before their arrival at Eastgate, Frederick wondered if the wizard and his allies would have dared attack their convoy. Fear of reprisals might have made them think twice.

At least, it's proving to be an effective tool here to deter any unsavory elements. Some of its gangs have been around as long as Imputnim. Last thing we need is another setback or delay. Winning is about making fewer mistakes than your enemy. Right now, I'm surrounded by losers. And I cannot lose Shy'elle again.

In an effort to calm his agitated mind, Frederick surveyed the ancient buildings lining the avenue leading to the waterfront. He could do little more until they reached the warships, so he might as well enjoy the scenery, one of the few perks of traveling.

The pockmarked buildings lining the avenues of the newer neighborhoods resembled badly eroded rocks in the desert, as if they had been abused by sand, wind, and time. Made of coquina blocks, cobbled together from a mixture that included seashells and concrete, the solid structures had stood for untold centuries and would likely stand centuries more. The closer he and his men drew to the seaport, the older the buildings along the roadside.

The well-travelled nobleman noted the transition from Baax to Ireti architecture. One tradition had been built upon the other, much like the city itself, but the differences could be seen around the lintels, staircases, and the caps and bases of the various pillars and columns. Baax pillars were constructed of stacked marble cylinders adorning coquina structures, usually those decorated with a mortar facing to give them the smooth appearance of the older Ireti buildings. The Ireti had constructed the originals from quarried marble, granite, or similar materials centuries before the Cataclysm. Even in their various states of disrepair, the Ireti buildings looked like handmade works of art, whereas the Baax were merely polished, manufactured imitations.

Churches and shrines built in antiquity, dedicated to the major and minor gods of Faltyr, had once lined these streets, which explained the grandiose structures. With the completion of a newer temple district across town, most of these buildings been converted into shops and homes for the merchants, shipbuilders, dockworkers, and various other inhabitants of the old city.

After prominent families moved across town to be closer to their newer, more exclusive churches, the area had become a slum of considerable infamy in the intervening centuries. However, some of the temples and shrines continued to operate, even in the heart of the city's ghetto. Frederick would like to think that most of them did it out of the goodness of their hearts, but in his experience, most of those churches probably extorted more coin from the poor than any gang in the city.

"I remember my father speaking of Imputnim," Frederick said. Though he rarely spoke of his family, the city and sea air made him feel nostalgic. "He told me it was once a primary hub for trade on the Long Road. All the peoples of Ny passed through here. You could hear a hundred languages as you passed through its streets and meet members of a score or more races. Now it stinks of fish and filth, while it slowly sinks into the sea."

"Seems to be the case in more and more places as this cycle of ages draws to a close," Marduk said. "Perhaps we can ensure that the next cycle is one of prosperity rather than rot and decay."

Frederick's father had brought him here when he was a boy. He recalled passing by decaying fountains, most no longer functioning and others in desperate need of repair. His father had explained to him that the city had once known opulence and splendor, like the rest of Ny, in the gilded age before the Cataclysm. But now Imputnim, like most of the eastern portion of the continent, was being slowly choked to death by the unrelenting hand of time.

Despite Marduk's platitude, the Knight of Oparre shared his late father's mindset. Time killed everything. Even those the Executioner had slain had merely run out of their own personal time. At least that's what he told himself, what he had to believe to sleep at night. The abrupt clatter of metal ringing upon metal drew the attention of the introspective knight. He snapped his head toward the shadowy alley to his left and spotted a blind man holding a tin cup. As the white-haired beggar shook the cup, a few coins clanked around inside. Though the man had no eyes, he stared straight at the knight.

Bringing his horse to a halt, Frederick dismounted in front of the old man, drawing low growls from the three mangy dogs curled up around the beggar. The imagery of the squalid scene affected the Knight of Damarra in some fundamental, even primordial way. Every hair stood on end as the knight approached the blind man with the three dogs. A dirty sash that had once been white wrapped the swarthy man's head. Though it covered much of the beggar's face, Frederick could see the sunken pockets of the empty eye sockets. He had seen enough traumas on the battlefield, and inflicted as many in torture chambers beneath Grymsburg, to recognize this particular disfiguration.

Ignoring the threat posed by the dogs, the curious knight lifted the cloth and blanched at the extent of the disfiguration. Acid had eaten away the beggar's eyes and left his scarred face looking more like the wax of a poorly-made candle than the flesh of a man.

"My lord, be careful of disease," Galil warned from behind. "He may be poxy or have the dropsy. Who knows with that layer of filth?"

"I'm not diseased, boy!" The blind man called, shifting his gaze toward the squire. Looking back toward Frederick, he added, "As for you, my lord, I know begging is forbidden, but I haven't eaten in three days. Please forgive a starving blind man for trying to survive."

"Before I pardon you, tell me how you came to have these wounds?"

"I used to be an adventurer," the beggar began. "When I came to Imputnim, I was a brash young man seeking my fortune. A company of mercenaries took me under their wing and taught me how to fight, plot, and plunder. After a lucrative venture into the sunken city of Laeg, we returned along the Dead Road with a wagon overloaded with treasures." The blind man coughed wetly and then spat a bloody clump onto the ground. He wiped his mouth with a crusty sleeve before continuing. "The rough road combined with the weight of the wagon caused one of the wheels to break, leaving us stranded with a king's ransom. After filling our packs and pockets, we buried the remainder of our treasure along the Dead Road and set out on horseback toward the city."

Frederick and the others listened intently as the man told his story. They gathered around him and his slumbering hounds.

"My company made camp just a day away from the city," the blind man said, edging his cup closer to his audience. "Shortly before dawn, a party of Sobeki attacked us. They killed everyone else, but I managed to kill three of the lizardmen before they overpowered me. One spit its acid into my eyes and onto my face," the beggar's voice wavered as he spoke of the attack, "blinding me, disfiguring me. Then they beat me until I passed out. When I awoke in their camp, their king forced me into hard labor. I don't know how long I toiled away."

"How did you manage to get free?" Frederick asked.

"By the grace of the gods, I suppose," the beggar stated. "Their village was overrun by a group of soldiers sent by the king. They slaughtered every Sobeki man, woman, and child and then set all who had been enslaved free. I was accompanied by an older man who helped me back to the city. Now, here I am, rich beyond measure but not the eyesight to find my fortune." The beggar added with a bitter laugh, "Leave it to a bitch god like fate to keep fortune from a blind man."

Frederick chuckled at the old man's attempt at humor. In similar dire straits, the knight wasn't sure that he'd be able to see any mirth in such madness. He admired the poor man's resilience. Though he said nothing to the beggar, he signaled his squire. Galil dropped a small but hefty coin purse into the cup. Frederick's father had taught him other lessons as well, charity chief among them. And as a young man, he had dedicated himself to his country and Damarra to help those in need.

Nowadays, it seemed a swift death was the only mercy Sir Frederick could offer most of those who crossed his path. On the rare occasions that he could still help someone in other ways, he tended to overcompensate. In this case, the nobleman had given the man more than most soldiers would see in a year of service to the crown. The blind man smiled a mostly toothless grin when he felt the weight of the cup. The coin purse had come from the other direction, but the beggar nodded toward Frederick.

The Knight of Damarra turned away from the uncomfortable, eyeless stare of the old man. His gaze fell on Marduk and Stogal, causing him to scowl at the misers. Though some of the troopers had contributed coinage after hearing the beggar's tale, the mage and the other knight had refrained from offering assistance. He hoped that they'd receive a similar cold shoulder from passersby if they ever found themselves living on the streets.

"You have your pardon and a more than a pittance. Find shelter, food, and perhaps a bath. Don't waste this on wine or women," Frederick instructed aloud. Then he whispered, "Just remember, wine and women are rarely a waste."

"Thank you and bless you, kind sir," the beggar exclaimed. "May the light of the All-Father and his burning bride enlighten you, protect you, and keep you safe in the sea of darkness around you. Remember that you are the light you bring to this world."

The blind man made the sign of Kahl, a world tree drawn in the air, and then touched the knight on the forehead. Sensation surged through him as gooseflesh raced down his limbs. Stogal and the other soldiers reached for the handles of their swords, but their superior stayed their hands with an upraised fist.

"He's harmless, leave him be," Frederick ordered. "Mount up. We have some real criminals to catch."

Even as he rode away, the Knight of Damarra kept glancing back at the blind man and his three dogs until his retinue rounded a bend in the avenue. He felt as if something about the scene escaped him. It was familiar yet foreign. He'd donated money to a thousand beggars in a thousand cities and towns across Faltyr. What about this one haunted him so much?

Sir Frederick felt Marduk's eyes on him, judging him. And he didn't like it one damn bit.

"Do you have something to say, snake?" the knight asked.

"That was very noble of you. A complete waste of gold on an indigent, but a touching gesture nonetheless. I didn't realize the King's Executioner had a heart beating under his icy exterior, much less one full of warmth and kindness," Marduk taunted.

Frederick did not respond. He refused to engage with the mage. He had grown tired of the squabbling and would no longer give into it. Instead, he spurred his horse toward the docks.

As he continued along the narrowing streets, the knight relished the smell of sea salt filling his nostrils as much as the murderous thoughts of drowning the mouthy magician filling his head. The vista changed from decaying structures to shallow sea as they rounded a corner dominated by squat warehouses. Moonlight danced on the murky water as it gently lapped at the sides of stony piers. From here, Frederick could see ships of all types and sizes moored alongside the docks.

When he spotted a pair of tall masts in the harbor, illuminated by the passing beam of Imputnim's lighthouse, he maneuvered them toward the pier closest to the bulky shadows of two warships anchored offshore. The royal galleons *Regal* and *Hero's Welcome* could approach no further into the shallow port without risk of sticking or capsizing. Their launches would likely be waiting at the end of the dock. As Frederick spurred his horse toward the pier, an old gypsy woman slipped from the shadows of an alleyway between two decrepit warehouses. Three black cats trailed after her. Her loose, flowing dress and shawl whipped about her in the breeze rolling in from the sea. She waited in the road as the horsemen drew closer.

The mystery woman laughed madly as she danced widdershins while her cats circled about her clockwise. Her dry cackle sent shivers down Sir Frederick's spine as he approached. Whereas the blind man had soothed the knight, the gypsy aroused in him a fear he'd not faced when charging any foe. The Knight of Oparre was about ready to strike her head from her withered body when she pointed a gnarled finger in Marduk's direction.

"You turned a blind eye to a blind man," the crone said, loud enough to draw the attention of passersby and dockworkers alike. "You judged him by his outer appearance, even though he spoke the truth. Your soul is almost beyond redemption. Unless it can be cleansed by the dragon's fire, you will burn in the worst of the Nine for an eternity."

Spittle flew from her mouth and found its way to Marduk's cheek. He was stunned at the sudden assault. The mage was either too horrified or surprised by her actions to react. Stogal drew his sword and moved to intervene, but the old gypsy stopped him by raising her hand, for his whinnying steed refused to budge an inch closer to her.

"You're no different," she cried. "The hand of Eresh will reap your wicked soul as well. Mark my words, Knight of Oparre."

Sir Frederick's hand dropped to his sword. The crone looked at him and smiled through withered lips. If she raised her hands to cast a weave, he would have to cut her down in the street, regardless of how entertained he was by the gypsy's commentary regarding his companions.

"I am sorry, good knight, but I have no use for your companions," she said, using the exact word he had used in his mind to describe them. "Their hearts are as black as the Abyss on a moonless night. But I still have hope for you."

As Marduk wiped spittle from his eyes, the gypsy curtsied in her moth-eaten gown and, dancing madly, disappeared into the shadowy alley from whence she came. One by one, the cats darted into the darkness behind her.

Saddle leather creaked as Stogal and Galil moved to dismount and give pursuit.

"Stay in your saddles," Frederick ordered. "The crone was just speaking her mind. Doing that is still allowed in Oparre."

"That will have to change," the mage said. "If you do not silence dissidents, they will sow the seeds of revolution."

"The only one I saw silenced here was you, Marduk."

And I enjoyed it. Best part of the trip so far. Until I kill that mage and reclaim my prize, my love. And perhaps my child.

Chapter 21

Zoltana's tired eyes lingered on the jagged line of mountains until Yax drew her attention back to a thin, but distinct, patch of green across the deep divide. The rush of energy provided by the mushrooms had faded with the new day, but their psychedelic effects lingered. In that time, their party had crossed the expanse of dunes, passed across a barren wasteland of vitrified sand and stone, and then descended into the wide arroyo at the base of the mountains.

Even in her exhausted state, she knew that green in a desert meant water. Water meant life. But in this foreboding place, it also meant danger. In an area as desolate and remote as this desert, she considered their chances of stumbling across an unguarded, untainted source of fresh water to be slim.

She hefted her spear and advanced toward the tree line with the others. The sound of running water drew her through the copse of trees. Emerging from the tangled mess of foliage, they located the oasis, a series of mountain springs feeding a pool of clear water. A bubbling stream, following a narrow channel cutting through the rocks, provided a natural drain for the tiny body of water.

They also found clear evidence that something guarded the oasis. As Zoltana advanced into the charred expanse between them and the waterline, her thin shoes crunched on the ground. She had a veteran mercenary on either side of her and two more armed men behind her but still felt unsafe in the shadow of the remnants of the ruined mountains. In all probability, unseen predators observed their party from the caverns, canyons, and crevasses in the heights above them. She wondered if one of them was the living, fire-breathing mate of the dragon spirit.

The Ranger of the North could not deny that the possibility of communing with one of the Children of Kümatz appealed to her, almost as much as the possibility of being consumed by one terrified her. After refilling their waterskins, Zoltana and the others took turns washing the layers of dust and sand from their hair, clothes, and bodies. Her dip in the pool proved so rejuvenating that she dozed off in the shade while waiting for the boys to finish.

They didn't linger long, deciding to move on without camping in the area. The men of Finders Keepers judged the oasis as too exposed for their taste. Leishan caused their sole delay when he argued with Yax and Breuxias about keeping the horse with them as they moved into the mountains. Though it wasn't her business, the ranger intervened on the horse's behalf. After all, she did speak the language common to all beasts.

Unfortunately, her linguistic gifts did not apply to human tongues. However, her powers of persuasion managed to overcome the language barrier between her and Leishan. She convinced him it was in the horse's best interest to remain in an area with plenty of food, water, and shade.

The path into the mountains would be treacherous enough already. One misstep could send any of them plummeting to their doom. The horse would fair far worse than them in that terrain.

To strengthen her argument, Zoltana added, "I'm not convinced arriving in a dragon's lair smelling of horse is a good idea anyway." Even the horse agreed with that statement.

As the sun sank in the far west, it set ablaze the sea of dunes that stretched toward the horizon. The Sands of Sorrow shimmered in the dying light, a discolored mirror of the aurora dancing in the sky over it. From their camp site high in the hills above the sprawling desert, she could finally appreciate its awful beauty.

Sleep claimed her not long after sunset. When she awoke, the gray light of day colored the sky. Despite the coolness of the morning mountain air, the Blue Macaw's cloak kept them both warm. She shifted slightly, not wanting to disturb his slumber. If anyone on this trek needed some extra sleep, Yax certainly qualified.

Zoltana studied the features of the sleeping Wand Bearer. Her eyes trailed from his pronounced widow's peak, high forehead, and arched eyebrows to his small nose, thin blue-tinged lips, and rounded chin. Coupled with his majestic ring-laden ears and wild blue-black hair, Yax'Kaqix made one handsome elf in her opinion. His appearance embodied the classic features attributed to the first Jade

Emperor, who'd led them across the stars to join the Eternal War against the minions of Chichu'äm over thirty thousand years ago.

What could she hope to offer someone as long-lived and highly accomplished as the Blue Macaw? The blood of royalty may flow in her veins, but her sister became the elder, and the heir, by a span of minutes. Those few minutes had relegated Zoltana to a different path, a path that had led her to roam the forests of Silent Brook for most of her adult life rather than sitting alongside precious Zarena in court.

Until their imprisonment together at Mok'Drular, Zoltana hadn't been allowed to call her sister by her birth name openly in decades. Not until after Zoltana sacrificed her chance at freedom by playing decoy and riding south with a traitorous Knight of Oparre. In the end, the ranger's sacrifice had been for naught. Both sisters had been captured separately and then imprisoned at Mok'Drular. Their reunion had been painful, for many reasons.

Even though she was pregnant with a half-breed already, the obsessed knight would have taken Zarena nightly. Instead, Zoltana had pretended to be her sister and underwent the ordeal on her behalf. She'd given up her freedom for her ungrateful twin and now her chastity, purity, and pride. She'd even pretended to love him and every awful minute of it, all to keep Sir Frederick's foul paws away from her sister and her unborn child. As the months passed and her twin's belly grew larger, she feared their ruse would be discovered. But the delusional knight saw himself as a gentleman. So his requests for her visitations had waned as her pregnancy waxed. Zoltana figured he had enough female prisoners to keep his perverse passions satiated for now.

Zoltana didn't know if she'd done it out of love for her sister or duty to her people. She'd likely die not knowing and she could live with that. Regardless, the deed was done. Zarena had survived; and with her, their best hope for ultimate victory against mighty Oparre.

The heir to two thrones grew in her twin's womb, but it would not be old enough to affect the war directly for years to come. By then, Tor'Binel would be an ashy wasteland, while the Winaq'che would be little more than a broken people scattered to the four corners of Ny. Smiling at the elven Wand Bearer snoozing beside her, she wondered if hope for a swifter victory might be close at hand.

Thoughts about the Blue Macaw and how he'd literally leapt into their lives at the right place at the right time nagged her as Mother Sun rose higher in the sky. The burning orb appeared to parallel their progress as they scrambled to the top of the treacherous slope of razor sharp scree. Bloody and bruised, they reached the next destination on their dangerous trail to the dragon's den before midday.

A winding megalithic roadway snaked its way through the eastern range of the Meshkenet Mountains. Ogre highways served as a testament to the skill of their ancient engineers and masons, not to mention the raw strength of their laborers. Dressed, fitted granite blocks composed the stepped system that seemed more staircase than roadway to Zoltana. Each step reached her waistline and few of them had cracked despite the destruction of the western range by Artemis and Ra'Tallah.

Zoltana wondered how many of the Winaq'che's feats of engineering and architecture would survive the fires of the Blood War. *Few, if any*, she reckoned. Unlike ogres and even the Unen'ek, her people preferred wood to stone as a medium.

Unless the Elves of Silver Brook found a way to turn the tide of the war against their invaders, nothing would be left of Tor'Binel or the Winaq'che but ash and cinder. Perhaps they could fight the fires of the Blood War with dragonfire. Turning her attention back to the matter of the dragons, Zoltana noticed Yax whispering to the spirit bound into the dragon tooth. She watched the Wand Bearer as he pointed to the blasted remnants of a volcano cone to the north. Her eyes lingered on the blunted dome as she uttered a silent prayer to Kümatz.

Zoltana hoped the living dragon would honor the word of her fallen mate. If the female dragon violated it, none of them would likely live to see Mok'Drular. She trusted Yax. After meeting the elf responsible for the legend of the Blue Macaw, she even believed in him. But she didn't see a way to liberate her people without their aid.

While the sun sank in the distance, her group rested in the shadow of the volcano. The cavernous opening of a lava tube exited upslope from the ogre highway. The highway itself continued north.

After an animated conversation with the spirit of Great Fire Serpent, Yax stuffed the wyrm's tooth back under his robe. Without so much as a word to the living members of the party, the Wand Bearer ascended the slope and headed toward the lava tube. Breuxias and Leishan climbed after him. With a shrug to Zoltana, Shell Horse followed the two humans as they climbed the short distance to the expansive opening into the volcano.

She cast one look back over her shoulder as the sun crept toward the western horizon. Its rays set fire to the sparse clouds around it and caused them to flare with hues of red, pink, and orange. The fiery hues reminded her of the blaze spreading through Silent Brook while its best defenders and their noble kin languished and died in bondage within the confines of Mok'Drular.

Zoltana vowed to Mother Sun that she would help Yax and the others free her people. The noble ranger would rather not lay eyes on the setting sun again than fail in her mission. If the fates were on her side, the gods would answer her prayer.

ꕥꕥ

Yax meandered along the route of the lava tube as it snaked through the soft basalt while the others trailed behind him. The smooth, rounded sides of the corridor showed no signs of modification by magical or mundane means. But that didn't mean this path was devoid of danger.

The mammoth remnant of a lava flow from eons ago could easily support one ogre standing on the shoulders of another, but Yax could see no way for it to accommodate a dragon the size of Kak'nah'Kan. The elf's insatiable curiosity burned to know the answer to this conundrum. After his last conversation with the cantankerous, half-mad spirit bound into the tooth dangling around his neck, he tabled the question for now.

Though he and the other elves could see well in these conditions, he used Starkiller to light the way for the humans in their party. Any side flows could have produced smaller tubes in the walls or floor that might prove treacherous to those traversing the main path of the flow.

The Great Fire Serpent bound into the tooth had indicated that this tube would lead them into the lair complex beneath the dormant volcano. He had not elaborated on the distance through it or provided details beyond it. Yax had probed him for more information, but the spirit grew surlier the longer it remained trapped in a fragment of its body. They needed to reunite the dragon spirit with its next-of-kin before it attempted to possess one of them again.

"Stop here," Yax cautioned. "The lava tube drops into the heart of the volcano. It curves, so I can't see the bottom. No telling how far down it goes."

"Good thing we didn't keep the horse with us," Breuxias said. "We'll barely make it down that slide without a broken neck or leg. No chance for that critter."

"Too bad," Shell Horse interjected. "We could have used the horse as an anchor for a rope rig and then rappelled to the bottom."

"If we have enough rope to make it to the bottom," Breuxias said as he stared into the darkness beyond the wand's light.

Zoltana asked, "How would we anchor the rope anyway?"

"Easy," Yax replied. "We're not going to use rope at all."

"What're we going to do then?" she inquired.

"Luckily," Yax said with a mischievous grin, "I have a little something for handling sticky situations like these."

"Did you just make a pun?" Breuxias asked. "I'm about to stare down an elder wyrm, the cranky old lady version of one at that, face possible incineration, and the last joke I hear is a pun."

Leishan gibbered in his native tongue and then laughed.

"What's so funny?" the Brute asked as he turned on the Säj.

Yax stopped chuckling long enough to explain, "Leishan said, 'would you rather it was a knock-knock joke?'"

Everyone shared a laugh at Breuxias's expense, including him.

While the others were distracted, Yax removed his spider ring from the pouch under his armor. He eyed the powerful, parasitic item warily before slipping it onto his ring finger. The elf bit down on the end of his tongue as the chimerical spider settled into place and took its proverbial pound of flesh, a measure of his blue blood in this case.

Without explaining himself, Yax commanded the ring to emit a ribbon of webbing which he anchored to the lip of the sloping tube.

Trusting the ring's properties to keep him from sliding to his demise, the elf stalked down the slope into the darkness. The silvery line trailed behind him like an astral cord stretching out behind a dreamer.

Relying on his natural eyesight proved trickier than he'd imagined as he descended the incline into the depths of the volcano. Most lightless abysses didn't present a challenge to elven dark vision; then again most subterranean passages didn't lead to a dragon's den. The acoustics of the lava tube made stealth impossible, so Yax moved with caution instead. The elf worried less about his descent than that of the human clambering down the sticky line of webbing. Should his friend lose his balance and tumble toward him, the Wand Bearer knew he'd have to be ready to leap out of the way. He had no intention of being skewered by the ogre blade strapped to the Brute's back.

The faint raw egg odor in the tubes became more noticeable. As they went deeper into the volcano, its stench grew more pungent as the distinct smell of rotting meat mixed with the lingering sulfur. After a modest climb, the lava tube leveled out but, without the aid of his dark vision, Yax could not be sure if it sloped again. He drew Starkiller from his belt and summoned a ball of Aethyr light.

The sphere of glowing energy atop the wand illumed the black confines of the natural corridor like a torch. Yax concealed his disappointment and buried his fears as his companion joined him. The two guildsmen exchanged quizzical expressions.

Breuxias asked, "What do you see up ahead?"

"Nothing."

"Nothing?"

"Absolutely nothing," Yax said emphatically. "That's what has me worried. It's pitch black up ahead."

"I thought you could see in the dark, even without the wand?"

"Ideally, but dealing with dragons is never ideal."

"What do we do?"

"Proceed with caution."

"Caution?"

Yax looked around. "Is there an echo in here?"

"Apparently," Breuxias said with a grin. "Lead the way."

Yax moved less than a dozen paces into the unnatural darkness before his left greave collided with something solid and unmoving. The elf stumbled yet remained upright. He took another step then stopped. His boot rested on unsteady ground, if it was indeed ground at all. The substance beneath his sole felt more like a sponge than stone.

A low moan arose in the tube as a sudden breeze sucked past the Wand Bearer. As the wind direction shifted, he caught a whiff of something familiar yet elusive. Yax sniffed at the air and then froze. The realization hit him with the weight of a millstone.

"Well," Breuxias asked, "what are you waiting for?"

"My knees to stop shaking."

"What in the Nine do you mean?"

"I think I'm standing on something."

"What kind of something?"

The Wand Bearer lowered Starkiller until its faint light revealed a broad section of wet pink musculature blanketing the tube.

"Um, a tongue," Yax said, "I think."

The mercenaries cursed their luck as the wind changed direction again. A newborn spark caught fire in the darkness and blossomed into a raging inferno. Flames spewed forth from the hellish mouth of one of Kümatz's scaly children. Dragonfire washed over the elf and his unfortunate friend, engulfing them.

Chapter 22

Breuxias awoke to the flickering light cast by the dying puddles of liquid fire scattered around his smoking form. *Has Eresh claimed me at long last? If so, which of the Nine Hells is this? What fresh nightmares does she have in store for me here that could compete with being roasted alive by a dragon?* The familiar groan of his elven companion broke the illusion of death's release.

When Breuxias turned his head, he spied Yax'Kaqix lying in a pool of fire. Yax marveled at the dancing flames even as he patted his body to extinguish them. The Brute scowled as he watched the awestruck pyromaniac wallow the rest of the blaze to extinction.

The damn fool elf played in dragon's fire like a child in a puddle while he did his best not to panic or piss himself. The extensive scars covering his body served as a testament to his past exposure to a fiend's flames that had sought to send him screaming into the Underworld. He had undergone months of alchemical treatments at the hands of the sage Metron Illbringer to repair most of the physical damage, but the mental trauma had never fully healed. Despite his association with Yax and the fireball-slinging Master-of-Disaster, he hated fire almost as much as he feared it.

His hatred for most things fiery and fire-breathing spurred him to action. Breuxias didn't know how or why they'd survived the wyrm's assault, but he didn't intend on giving the beast a chance to rectify its mistake. As he rose to his feet, he reached for the handle of the dragonslayer. He left the belt inactivated. The Brute would need every ounce of strength to deal with a wyrm.

The dragon moved in the dimness beyond the firelight, a wall of shadow passing through a sea of night. The tube ballooned in size here like a carafe of wine at the end of its tapered neck, a perfect spot for the dragon to ambush prey. Raising its head far above him, the wyrm snorted fire and then belched a ball of flame.

Firelight flooded the lava tube, illuminating their enraged adversary. Though by no means the size of an ancient wyrm like Kak'nah'Kan, the horned skull of the dragon marked it as an adult. The red wyrm's bulk filled only a portion of the expansive chamber, presumably so that it had room to maneuver. Fortunately, the ceiling was low enough to prevent the beast from using its wings.

The fireball struck the sloping tube beyond them and exploded. The intensity of the sound and heat roaring around them caused Breuxias to stagger backward. Sweat coated his flesh and then boiled away in an instant as the rain of fire enveloped them but did not harm them. He watched in a mixture of marvel and terror as the rain of fire dripped from his muscular form. Unfortunately, the smoke and fire made it difficult to breathe in the confines of the lava tube. He felt faint already.

Perhaps Eresh would not have me. Have I sent so many devils to the Nine Hells that I'm no longer welcome there?

"How in the gods' names are we surviving this onslaught?"

Glowing wand in hand, Yax replied, "We haven't survived yet." With his free hand, the elven Wand Bearer reached for the dragon tooth hanging from the leather cord around his neck.

Breuxias didn't know what Yax had in mind, but he hoped the elf hurried. Fire served as one of the weapons in a dragon's deadly arsenal; the mercenary had no desire to face impalement on its claws or feel the force of its bite. Depending on its age and upbringing, the wyrm could have a command of Aethyr magic that would leave all but the most powerful wizards looking like a common street magician.

The dragon's face contorted from a look of confusion to one of rage. Flames curled from its nostrils and its agape mouth. Its head snapped forward, and teeth the length of daggers clacked together.

"Fire may not harm you," the wyrm bellowed in the Common tongue, "but let's see if you're immune to digestion!"

Breuxias raised the dragonslayer and stood his ground with Yax. But the Wand Bearer drew no steel. Instead, the elf held the dragon tooth aloft in his right hand.

The remnant of Kak'nah'Kan blossomed into existence as a specter sheathed in flames. Yax and the living dragon both cried aloud, one in pain, the other in surprise. The dragon spirit hovered in between them like a shifting, shimmering rainbow in the dark.

Great Fire Serpent boomed, "Who dares trespass in my domain? For millennia, I have called this mountain my home."

Hissing like a bonfire extinguished by a sudden deluge, the living dragon slinked back into the shadowy recesses of the lava tube.

When the red wyrm finally responded, it said, "This is not your home, foul spirit. It belongs to me, Mighty Mizgeroth. My mother and I rule these mountains."

The dragon spirit's fiery avatar dimmed visibly and deflated like the buoyancy bladder of a gnomish airship. Its expression softened. The Great Fire Serpent glided toward Mizgeroth, as if inspecting the living dragon more closely.

"Aerabeth is your mother?" The spirit chuckled. "Well, I'll be. I can see the resemblance now. Better you took after her, I guess. She was a beauty, for a beast."

Blinking his amber eyes, Mizgeroth asked, "You know Mother?"

Kak'nah'Kan laughed again, this time a throaty, rolling chortle that echoed off the walls of the natural stone corridor.

"Of course, I do. I'm your Father."

"Father, is that really you?" The son stared in disbelief. He turned to the two men in the lava tube and snapped, "Is this some trick of the mind? Or some feat of elven magic to manipulate me, to lure me into a trap? I warn you. If you cross me, I will peel you like a fig, debone you like a fish, and then devour your still beating hearts."

The Great Fire Serpent intervened on their behalf.

"Fear not, my son; these questing fools are no danger to you. As for me, the long dead wyrm you would know as Uberoth, I was ambushed on a hunt and killed by a murderous ogre wielding an outlawed blade. I waited in the dark, in the hollows beneath the central range of the mountains, until those mountains were no more. As fate would have it," Uberoth continued, "I exchanged one prison for another. The sundered mountains rained down from the sky, covering my bones in a blanket of sand and ash. I wandered the wastes but feared to go far from my earthly remains. I kept waiting, hoping, and even praying that one day my love would find me and carry me home.

"Instead, these crusaders stumbled across me and my old bones and agreed to ferry me home. In exchange, they seek an audience with your mother to ask a favor of our clan. As my heir, I ask that you honor this pact as you would honor your dear, departed father."

Mizgeroth did not reply. Instead, he circled the spirit and sniffed at its shifting form. A single teardrop ran from one of the dragon's massive eyes. It turned to steam so quickly that Breuxias wondered if he'd imagined it. But the dragon's noisy, wet sniffles cemented the reality of the touching scene. Father and son--shade and serpent--entwined in an embrace across the Veil, an embrace that had waited a cycle of ages.

ભ્રૂભ્ર

As he watched a son reunite with his long-dead father, Breuxias could not help but feel a pang of jealousy. The Brute had spent the better part of his life trying to track down his father. In that time, he'd tracked his lineage to Moor'Dru, only to have Kaladimus Dor sink the *Nightsfall* out from under him before their arrival on the island.

Now, strife and civil war divided Moor'Dru. Proleus and his faction tried to consolidate their hold in the wake of the bloody coup that toppled Salaac and the Council. The usurper's alliance with Oparre provided him with badly needed, battle-hardened troops to quell the popular uprisings. After recovering the *Seadragon* from beneath Frolov Keep, Breuxias, Yax, and Dor had made landfall on Moor'Dru only to be chased away by a small army of mages loyal to the Proleus Faction.

At this rate of risk versus reward, the Brute figured he would die before ever learning the identity of his father. He hoped and prayed the gods would be merciful enough to provide him the answers he sought, if not in this life, then in the afterlife.

Eager to reunite his family and converse at length with his own father, Mizgeroth led them through a series of natural passages toward the heart of the dormant volcano. The wyrm moved at a rapid pace as it took one abrupt turn and then the next, so Breuxias gave the beast a wide berth, as did Leishan, but the elves followed close at its heels.

In the wake of the aborted skirmish in the lava tube, the horseman of the Säj had made the treacherous descent alongside Zoltana and Shell Horse. They had marveled at the dark majesty of the red wyrm. The awestruck Ranger of the North had even bowed and offered a greeting in the hoary old language of dragonkind.

Breuxias, on the other hand, remained wary and alert to any sign of attack. He did not trust their kind. In his experience, beings with such immense power usually valued the lives of others on a sliding scale. Were they worth more alive than dead to the dragons? Only time would tell. And by the time they discovered the answer to that question, it would likely be too late to do anything about it.

Mizgeroth slowed his advance as the lava tube tapered into a narrower channel that sloped downward again. As Breuxias drew closer to Yax and Zoltana, he observed them exchanging coy grins. The Brute swore that if his friend winked at the elven woman he'd never let Yax hear the end of it. Breuxias had endured enough jokes over the years about his lothario nature, his multiple wives and kids strewn across three nations. Turnabout was fair play.

"You have to be more careful," Zoltana said as she chided Yax, "We almost lost you back there."

"I'm still not sure what happened," Breuxias interjected. "Was it the dragon spirit that spared us?"

"Partly," Yax answered. "The bearer of its spirit is all but immune to it and its kind."

The Brute asked, "What about me then?"

"A dragonslayer has powers beyond your ken. Like a Choj'Ahaw, it slays, but it also protects."

"I'll keep that in mind," Breuxias said. He eyed the powerful weapon with newfound appreciation.

A few twists and turns later, Mizgeroth led them to a dead end. Up ahead, the lava tube narrowed until it became a dark circular opening in the stone wall. Scarcely a meter wide, the hole seemed too small for any of them, much less the sizeable serpent.

Tired of treading in the wake of dragons, Breuxias asked, "Are you lost? Or merely mad? A child couldn't fit through there, much less a dragon."

Mizgeroth snaked his horned head around in the corridor and locked eyes with the human. As he stared into the dragon's eyes, Breuxias realized that they were smaller than before. In fact, the entire wyrm had shrunk to accommodate the reduction in the size of the lava tube. The dragon seemed no larger, no longer than the troublesome wyvern they had dispatched not once but twice.

Mizgeroth snorted and flames shot from his nostrils, "Has anyone ever told you that it isn't wise to provoke a dragon?"

When confronted with fear and fatalism, Breuxias responded with humor. Even the threat of a dragon could not suppress his natural tendency. Instead of quivering in his boots, he smiled easily and said, "I've heard the same about women. That might explain a few of my divorces."

"I like you, human," the dragon said with a throaty laugh. "You're funny. That's why I'm not going to eat you today. But I beg you, tread lightly with Mother. She has a foul temper when stirred from slumber." Mizgeroth snapped his teeth. "And she's liable to be hungry."

Without waiting for a response, the miniaturized wyrm shrank once more. Its eyes changed from their customary orange glow to beady, black buttons on the face of a mouse the color of smoke. With nary a squeak, the sleek vermin scaled the basalt and then disappeared into the darkness beyond the opening in the rock face.

Breuxias exchanged puzzled looks with Leishan and the elves. Yax merely shrugged his shoulders and tilted his head toward the hole. After a long moment, a sharp mechanical click reverberated through the basalt. The entire wall shuddered and then rolled aside like a wheel, revealing it to be part of a circular portal concealing the ancestral lair of the dragon clan, one of the hidden wonders beneath the surface of Faltyr.

Besides the faces of his own children, Breuxias considered it to be the grandest, greatest thing he would ever see in this life.

And he was right.

Chapter 23

Dor awakened to the sound of men shouting and scrambling in the hallway outside his cabin. Sunlight streamed in through the portholes, forcing him to blink sleep from his eyes. Clambering out of bed, he plucked his robe from a nearby hook. He dressed hastily as he headed for the door. But the half-conscious mage stopped abruptly when he felt his stomach turn.

Nausea welled up inside him once he realized he was alone. No shadowy presence lingered at the edge of his consciousness. He could recall no nightmares. In fact, he'd slept quite soundly, without a single fitful dream, something he had happened since his first journey into the Sands of Sorrow.

Dor grabbed his backpack and tossed it onto the bed. He flung the lid open and cursed at the sight of a rectangular chunk of stone. The chest was gone, and Katar was the most likely suspect. Had the rogue switched out the backpacks and then been killed before he could reap the reward of his ill-gotten gains? If so, the cursed desert had reclaimed the Book of the Underworld once more. Either way, he could not rest until he recovered it.

"Hells' bells!"

The calamitous mage of Myth bolted from his cabin. He charged up the companion way, nearly knocking a sailor down when he passed. Emerging on deck, Dor winced at the bright light of the day. Once his eyes adjusted, he clambered up the aft castle stairs toward Macz and the ship's helm.

"Turn this ship around! We have to go back!"

Macz stared at the young mage as if he had lost his mind. "That would be suicide!" he exclaimed, gesturing toward the stern of the ship. "We've had two warships tailing us ever since we passed the port of Imputnim. They're both flying the purple cross, so those belong to King Orson himself!"

Dor summoned the ship's spyglass from its position in the luminous control console. Taking the Aethyr device in hand, he peered in the direction of the two enemy ships on the horizon. The spyglass brought each ship and their crews into sharp detail.

Each war galleon was twice the length of the *Seadragon*, if not longer, although the lead ship, the *Hero's Welcome*, was slightly wider. Large shuttered portholes ran alongside their hulls midway to the waterline. From what he knew of their navy, Dor wagered those would house either ballista or smaller chain-driven repeating crossbows called *polybolos*. Sour-faced royal marines equipped with shoulder-fired repeaters assembled on the main decks as well as the fore and aft castles of the crowded warships.

The expansive sails of the galleons billowed outward in an unnatural fashion for such a calm day; likely the work of a sea witch, air elementalist, or other Aethyr user. Dor searched the ranks of those onboard to see if he could spot the spellcaster. The mage's breath hitched in his throat at his spied a familiar face aboard the *Regal*.

Marduk. What's that snaky sonuvabitch doing aboard?

Without realizing it, Dor had ordered the enchanted spyglass to reveal something hidden, so it obeyed the best it could. The device zoomed in on the backpack worn by the traitorous mage before revealing the melted chest inside it. But even the spyglass stopped shy of penetrating the strongbox's unusual alloy.

His panic subsided as anger replaced it; he was angry with himself for having failed his mission. Instead of delivering the chest and its contents into the right hands, the Master-of-Disaster had managed to fumble it into the waiting hands of the enemy.

"Don't you see?! They have my chest and now they want me! They will not give up until I'm dead; they'll kill you, her, and the entire crew," Dor warned as he drew his staff and pointed it in the direction of the pursuing ships. "We have to turn and fight."

"We can't beat two royal galleons!" Macz replied. "Even if we pitched you overboard, they'd still kill us. So we run."

"But they have my chest! With it in the wrong hands, we are all destined to suffer. You don't understand the full extent of the power contained inside it. We can't leave it with the enemy."

"I don't much give a damn, Mr. Dor! Others lives are depending on ours, your friends and my family." Macz reminded the irate young man. The sternness in the older man's voice came second only to his passion. He stood firm in his position on the situation. So did Dor. Storm clouds formed in the distance to match the magician's demeanor. Thunder rolled and lighting flashed on the horizon. Even the wind started the blow in gusts.

Tameri interceded by placing her hand on the agitated wizard's arm. "Macz is right," she said. "All of our sticks are in this fire, even those not aboard now. Yax and my father are depending on us." Tameri turned to her uncle and added, "But Dor is right too. He's the captain. If he says we run, we run. If he says we fight, we fight till the end. Either way, we follow the captain's orders."

Macz asked, "So, what are your orders, Captain?"

Dor steeled his nerves as the extreme weight of command landed on his narrow shoulders. The lives of his friends depended on him, and he could not let them down. But the likelihood of outrunning the galleons with Marduk forcing wind into their sails remained slim.

"There's only one thing to do if we hope to outrun them. They are using a mage to force wind into their sails. But the weather is too risky for me to do the same," Dor said and pointed to the dark clouds in the distance. "So we have to put him out of commission."

"Does that mean you want to turn and attack?"

Dor barely heard Macz's question. He was weighing the fate of Faltyr against the bonds of friendship. In the end, the young mage realized he had to succeed in his mission. Nothing could stop him from his achieving his objective, even if it meant his own death or the death of those close to him.

"Turn us about! We'll make a hit-and-run attack, take out that mage, and perhaps steal back the chest in the process."

"That's suicide, but you're the captain, Capt'n," Macz said.

Ignoring the older man, Dor addressed the crew.

"The enemy may be coming after me, but they mean to kill every last one of us! I can't speak for you, but I'm not up for dying today! So prepare for a fight!"

The mage raised his charred staff high above his head and awaited thunderous applause. Instead, the crew stared at him in silence.

Macz whispered, “Hope you fight better than you speechify.”

Dor sighed and turned toward the ship’s obstinate mate. Macz’s long life of plundering and adventure showed in every wrinkle and scar on his face. His body had the lean, cut look of one who’d worked hard for a living. In Dor’s experience, people like Max always resented working for someone younger and softer.

Despite Breuxias’s assurances, the man had done little other than undermine Dor’s position since he’d come aboard. And now was not the time to have to deal with the possibility of a mutiny. If he hadn’t been Tameri’s uncle, the irate mage would have likely shocked him senseless as an example to the crew.

Instead, the wily wizard relied on a simple trick of Aethyr-fueled hypnosis to bring Max around to his way of thinking. It was cheap, even immoral, but time was of the essence. The mage had no time to argue.

“If you can do any better,” Dor said, “you’re welcome to try.”

As he spoke each word, he waved the spyglass back and forth. The shiny brass cylinder glinted unnaturally bright in the midday sun.

Betraying his own opinion, Macz found himself addressing the crew. In his mesmerized state, he shouted with gusto, “Hear this, boys! Our captain says we turn and fight! Personally, I agree with him. If you aren’t with him, then you’re against me! Now, who is with me and Captain Dor ‘ere!”

Though some were bewildered by the second mate’s sudden change of heart, most of the crew reacted by cheering in unison. They drew their various weapons and raised them high into the air. Here was the enthusiasm their captain had failed to stir.

Macz stared dumbly at Dor. His wide eyes testified to his befuddled state. Slowly, the older man blinked away the veil of confusion cast over his mind. Instead of being angry with the mage, he drew away, frightened that his own tongue could be stolen away so easily.

Tameri winked at the mage and whispered, “Could you teach me that trick sometime? I might actually be able to win an argument with my father using that one.”

They shared a laugh at her uncle’s expense, while Macz returned to the ship’s wheel. Without further comment, he turned them toward the pursuing warships. Dor tightened his grip on the railing of the command deck as the *Seadragon* banked hard to starboard.

As those on the main deck readied for the coming conflict, their untested captain prepared his mind and body for another bloody fight, his first in command of the Hallowed Vessel and its crew, the men and women of Finders Keepers.

ଔଓଔଓ

From the aft castle of the royal war galleon *Regal*, Sir Frederick observed the *Seadragon* through Captain Wroisethorn's spyglass. He smiled broader with each passing minute as the distance between the warships and the fleeing vessel diminished. Soon enough, Shy'elle would back where she belonged. With him.

Marduk and his allies had their priorities, but the knight had his own goal: to recover the woman who had haunted his dreams since the time they'd spent together locked inside a room in Castle Grymsburg. After the Crown Prince had become enamored with her, King Orson had trusted his icy executioner to guard the confined queen. He had failed His Majesty there too. Not only had he fallen for her affections, he'd fallen asleep after a night of unrivaled passion, on his part anyway. Apparently, for her, it had been part of the plan all along. Seduce and neutralize him while her allies in the castle planned her escape.

Focusing on the coming battle rather than past betrayals, Frederick watched as Marduk concentrated the Aethyr into providing a steady stream of air to propel the galleons at swifter speeds. The mage released the spell as they closed within ballista range of the *Seadragon*, but the gusty winds did not cease. The storm front had moved closer while they'd focused on the enemy.

"All hands, prepare for boarding!" Frederick ordered. "Kill their crew, but the elven prisoners are to be captured alive. Repeat alive! No one is to harm the elves."

The ship's aging commander sidled closer to the Knight of Oparre. Captain Wroisethorn puffed out his chest in preparation to speak. Row after row of polished medals gleamed as he leaned in close to Frederick and said, "These are His Majesty's galleons, and they are under my command. Don't you think I should be giving the orders here?"

Sir Frederick pulled an ovular golden pendant, emblazoned with a purple amethyst cross, from within his armor. He let the heavy device, a Royal Seal of Oparre, his badge of office, dangle from its sturdy steel chain. Then he said to the peacock, "I am the Royal Executioner in pursuit of my duties on behalf of His Majesty. If I do not return with these prisoners, it will be one of our heads on the chopping block. I assure you, it won't be mine."

"I'll signal the *Hero's Welcome* to lead the attack."

"Now, that's the spirit, Wroisethorn."

Within a few moments, the *Regal's* captain passed along the plan of attack to a yeoman who carried it to a flagman on the forecastle. The flagman signaled across to the other galleon and then awaited a response. When it came, he repeated the decoded cipher to the yeoman who returned to his captain. The yeoman whispered to him as if the message's contents were a state secret.

After Marduk joined them, Wroisethorn said to Frederick, "The *Hero's Welcome* signals ready to attack. We're waiting your orders, sir."

Noting the crispness of the captain's reply, the Protectorate Mage commented, "Making fast friends here too, I see. I hope you're ready for a real fight, Frederick. You won't be able to order your way out of this coming storm."

The knight allowed himself a moment to gloat. After all, Marduk had boasted and prodded Frederick since he'd arrived. Frederick said, "I hope you're prepared to witness His Majesty's Royal Navy at their finest. That ship doesn't stand a chance in the Nine Hells."

"Cap'n, they're coming about!" the helmsman cried.

Both Sir Frederick and Wroisethorn snapped their heads in the direction of the *Seadragon*. A smirk crossed the knight's face as the enemy ship turned toward them. His grin slipped, however, when he noticed how quickly the smaller, junk-rigged vessel maneuvered into the wind.

"A real fight indeed," Frederick stated under his breath.

Men scurried about the deck as the *Seadragon* closed the distance. While the heavy galleons slowed, caught in the swirling crosswinds of the storm, the smaller ship gained speed. Its battened sails allowed it to sail into the wind at an extreme angle of attack, so it approached from their starboard side, negating the larger ships' advantage of having the weather gage.

The *Regal* stayed its course, but the *Hero's Welcome* turned to intercept them. The senior knight watched as the boarding party on the *Hero's Welcome* prepared their attack. Sailors waited with wicked hooks and barbed poles held fast in their grip. Royal marines assembled behind them; they leveled their bows and crossbows at the *Seadragon.*

This mage has caused me enough grief.

Frederick shouted, "We end it here; we end it today! Prepare the ballista! Marines, bows and repeaters at the ready!"

"For the King!" Wroisethorn shouted.

The *Regal*'s crew erupted in cheer and sprang into action.

Shutters on the ballista ports popped open along the sides of the galleon's hull. Each port concealed a siege engine designed for naval warfare. The ballista crews loaded their weapons with three-feet-long wooden missiles and then cranked them into firing position. On deck, the bow and stern crews fitted wooden box magazines onto the tops of their swivel-mounted polybolos. Though inaccurate beyond a short distance, the repeating crossbows fired iron-tipped quarrels that proved effective in raking the deck of enemy vessels.

Sir Frederick turned toward Marduk and gestured proudly at the engine of destruction in motion around them. The knight risked a smile. Surprisingly, the mage returned the gesture in his sour, tightlipped fashion.

"Buck up, Marduk," Frederick said, slapping the other man on the back. "That ship doesn't stand a chance. Each galleon is twice its size and breadth, and we outnumber them ten to one."

"Don't forget. They have a Protectorate Mage on board," Marduk reminded the knight. "Don't underestimate Kaladimus Dor. Braigen called him the Master-of-Disaster for a reason. You saw why in Eastgate."

Frederick placed a strong hand upon the shorter man's shoulder and squeezed. He looked down into his eyes and reminded him, "We do as well."

The mage nodded dumbly, but the knight could tell that something about Dor had him spooked. Frederick hoped it didn't cause Marduk to hesitate in dealing with the renegade. Any hesitation in a fight could get them killed, especially when tangling with a wizard.

"Captain, the ship isn't changing course!" the helmsman reported.

The *Seadragon* sailed straight for the *Regal*, but the *Hero's Welcome* maneuvered to block them. At this rate, the bulk of the lead galleon would prevent the smaller ship from reaching them.

"And neither shall we!" Frederick responded.

"Attacking them head on is not a method I would recommend," Wroisethorn warned. "Ramming a ship that size head on could sink it. We need to be able to board them if you want the elven prisoners alive."

"We'll board them, even if we have to ram them first. Unless Stogal beats us to it. Either way, the crew of that ship is going to die today. Lives may be lost, but then again, we are at war."

Wroisethorn did not respond, but the older man's withering gaze lingered on the obsessed knight. Frederick didn't much care what the preening nobleman thought. A royal captain, like his ship, was another tool of war to be used to achieve King Orson's objectives. If that allowed Frederick to recover his prize, Lady Shy'elle, in the process, so be it.

As the *Seadragon* passed close to the bow of the *Hero's Welcome*, the galleon tacked hard to starboard to avoid a direct collision. The enemy's gambit allowed them to slide around the portside of the bulky ship-of-the-line without altering their course. However, the enemy exposed itself to a broadside from the galleon.

From his position on the *Regal*, the knight watched as a hail of missiles filled the narrow space between the *Hero's Welcome* and the *Seadragon*. Arrows and bolts fell among the enemy crew, creating fewer casualties than expected, while the timbers from the ballista either splintered against the hull of their ship or fell intact into the sea. The crew of the *Seadragon* returned fire with flaming arrows.

The enemy altered its course as more missiles filled the air between the passing ships. Tacking to port, it forced the *Hero's Welcome* to turn in the same direction to stay alongside it. As the ships spun in a slow deadly circle, the bow of the *Seadragon* nosed toward the *Regal* once again.

"Stay our course, Wroisethorn!" Frederick cried above the din. *Nothing will stop me from victory, from recovering Shy'elle.*

The Knight of Oparre knew the *Regal* could sink the enemy ship with its ram. Worst case scenario, he told himself, they'd fish their prisoners out of the sea. Coming from a land called Silent Brook, he wagered that the elven queen could swim. If not, with a belly swollen with child, she should be able to float long enough to be recovered by the sailors onboard the royal galleons.

"Aye," Captain Wroisethorn answered with little enthusiasm.

The *Hero's Welcome* turned slower than the *Seadragon,* causing its crews' gaff hooks to miss on their first attempt. But it provided the ballista crews a clearer shot on the shorter vessel. Unable to penetrate its hull, the artillerists aimed a bit higher and shot holes in the *Seadragon*'s sails with their torsion-powered projectiles.

More arrows filled the air as the archers and crossbowmen on the *Regal* opened fire on the speeding ship. Frederick smirked as the exposed crew of the *Seadragon* scrambled to avoid the incoming missiles. He moved closer to the bow of the ship to get a better view of the faces of the wounded and dying aboard the enemy vessel. He wanted to watch as Kaladimus Dor, who had become quite the thorn under his skin, died a painful death.

From his position near Sir Frederick's side, Galil yelled, "Get away from the front of the ship, my lord! You could be knocked overboard when we ram them!" His words fell on deaf ears though. The overeager knight heard but did not register them.

As they watched from the bow of the *Regal*, the sailors on the *Hero's Welcome* braved flaming arrows to try the gaff hooks once more. Several sturdy hooks bit into the portside railing of the *Seadragon* before it could slip by the lead galleon. The heavier ship acted as an anchor, slowing the smaller vessel's forward momentum.

"What the in the Hells are they doing?" Frederick asked.

"It appears Sir Stogal's crew will be the first on the scene after all," Marduk said. "Let's hope he has better luck this time."

The taller ship continued to tack toward the smaller one. The crew of the *Hero's Welcome* worked feverishly to lock the two ships together in order to board the *Seadragon*. But the galleon could not seem to reel in its catch. The enemy cut the lines almost as fast as they were secured.

In frustration, sailors and marines leaped onto the open deck of the smaller ship. A few foolhardy souls missed their mark and plunged into the treacherous waters between the two dueling vessels. However, Sir Stogal and many others landed on the opposing ship successfully. Weapons drawn, they attacked.

Sniffing, Frederick asked, "Do you smell that, Marduk?" Without awaiting a reply, he added, "That's the smell of victory!"

Chapter 24

The shining splendor and ancient majesty of the dragons' lair overwhelmed Yax'Kaqix. Normally blasé, the elf felt humbled by the scale and grandeur of what his wide eyes beheld from his position on the other side of the ogre door, a hidden opening in the northwest corner of the mammoth cave. The kidney-shaped cavern was the remnant of a lava chamber, likely emptied in eons past when the volcano had blown its top and vaporized most of its cone.

The familiar glow of the aurora over the Sands of Sorrow streamed down from the irregular skylights in the roof of the volcano. Its sickly green light illuminated the ruins of a subterranean city, one constructed in antiquity to serve the needs of the dragon clan, their acolytes, and servants. A million points of light glowed, shimmered, and shined throughout the chamber. To the keen eyes of the elf, each one represented untold treasures lurking in the shadows.

Four parallel lava vents of irregular lengths provided the only other source of lighting. Cut into the floor of the cavern, they ran northeast of the small rise overlooking the city. Having resumed his form, Mizgeroth waited at the base of the rise on a set of dragon-sized steps overlooking the longest of the lava vents.

"Welcome to our humble abode," the dragon chuckled. "You're the first living humans and elves to set foot in this place in a cycle of ages, if not two. History's not my strongest subject. I prefer to burn things."

As Yax and the others followed him down the winding set of stone stairs, Mizgeroth warned, "Do step lively. Wouldn't want anyone to fall and break a neck. Not yet anyway."

Carved into the gray-green basalt walls north of the lava vents, a series of ogre-sized cliff-dwellings juxtaposed row after row of smaller residences located to the southeast. The structures lay on either side of a set of granite doors inset into an elaborate steel-reinforced framework in the east wall. A pillar of carved basalt taller than Caleb's tower had been laid across them, barring them from being opened without the aid of multiple dragons.

Judging by the thick layer of moss and algae on the doors, no one had opened them in millennia. Even if someone could open them, who knew if the passage beyond remained accessible after the Cataclysm sundered the mountains. The heart of the dormant volcano had remained intact, but how much damage had been done to the cone and the network of lava tubes and carved corridors used by the dragon clan?

In all likelihood, Yax would never know. And it pained him. Curiosity burned inside him. Anything that he could not know, that defied description or comprehension, nagged at him. On some nights, it made sleep impossible. Thankfully, the myriad wonders of the dragons' lair would suffice to quell his nagging curiosity for now.

Breuxias and Shell Horse looked to be indulging their natural curiosities as well. Both men stared into one of the vents dug into the stone floor. They pointed and conversed in excited tones.

Breuxias remarked, "There are breastplates from Oparre stacked on top of Ireti and Baax helms and shields."

"I saw a spear point from before the Splintering of the Jade Throne," Shell Horse said. "Now that's what I call old."

"Damn right," the Brute replied. "How old is this place?"

"I'm guessing it predates the Cataclysm by a few millennia," Yax answered.

The Wand Bearer could not help but be drawn to the flames. The liquid fires and molten material of the inner world flowed far below but their warmth welcomed him. He gazed into the lava. It took several moments, perhaps even minutes, before he wrenched his attention away from it. His eyes darted along the irregular sides of the crevasse leading down to the lava flow. He understood Mizgeroth's compulsion to burn things all too well.

Discarded items from a dozen races and a score or more cultures littered the sides of these massive trash pits, the ultimate way for the dragons and their followers to dispose of unwanted items or individuals over the ages.

Spying modern debris scattered alongside the older material, Yax turned back to Mizgeroth and said, "You told us we were the first humans and elves here since the previous cycle of ages, but Oparre is a post-Cataclysmic kingdom. How do you explain their arms and armor among your refuse?"

The dragon's lips twisted into a malevolent grin. Yax had seen many things in his lifetime, but he had never seen a dragon smile. He'd rather have seen it sneer; it would have been less intimidating.

"I said you were the first *living* ones brought here since then. We have been here since before the Warring Wizards sundered the mountains, before the dawn of Mok'Drular, I think. You'd have to ask Mother. I spend most of my time stalking and killing these little steel clad buggers for food and fun. Much easier prey than one finds in the Underworld. Plus, human roasts nicely inside of a breastplate."

"Oh," Yax said, vocalizing part of what he was thinking.

"Shit," Breuxias added, finishing his friend's thought.

"Any other questions, comments, or criticisms?" Mizgeroth asked. The unsettling leer plastered across his scaly face gave the elf pause.

Yax stared at the mortified expressions on the faces of his companions. He tried to reassure Zoltana with his customary cocky grin, but the Wand Bearer could not summon it. They were in it deep. Should the dragons not honor their agreement, dragonslayer or no dragonslayer, they'd be meat for the beasts, savory meals seared to perfection by fire-breathing monsters.

If their hosts' intentions proved to be less than hospitable, Yax didn't intend on getting eaten without a fight. Resting one hand on Starkiller, he said, "No, please lead on."

As the party turned south, they encountered a low broad wall that bordered an extensive rectangular plaza. Elaborate friezes, painted on the crumbling plaster facing the wall, detailed numerous races paying tribute and worshipping at the feet of ancient dragon lords. Yax observed dressed granite blocks through the cracks and holes in the plaster. The megalithic blocks used in the wall had been stacked and then fused together by the intense heat of dragonfire.

Another low, broad staircase led to a raised avenue running due south. As Yax reached the top of the stairs, he stopped and marveled at the breathtaking sight before him, one he'd never forget. Stepped pyramid temples dotted the plaza. The temples had been constructed from the same vein of granite as the wall bordering the plaza complex. The spectral lights filtering down through the skylights in the roof of the cavern cast the pyramids in an eerie pall.

Though Yax could not discern their configuration from his present position, he knew it to be symbolic, even sacred in nature. After all, the cities of the Unen'ek were based on those of their former master--The Cosmic Dragon--and his descendants. He wondered if this place dated to their arrival on Faltyr. If so, this subterranean city could have been the first beachhead established here at the outset of the eons old conflict that would come to be known as the Eternal War.

Despite its similarity in form and function to an elven city, the subterranean refuge of Mizgeroth's clan of dragons differed in one major detail. No city ever built by the Unen'ek had been so littered, much less littered with treasure.

As they advanced along the raised avenue, Yax saw gold, silver, steel, copper, and even platinum coins minted in various times and places. Untold fortunes lay scattered along the side streets and courtyards or piled against the wide bases of the pyramids. A colorful sea of gems and semiprecious stones glittered and sparkled on the floor of the plaza and the steps of the temples, enough to create the illusion that a million pairs of eyes winked invitingly at the elven adventurer.

Yax crossed his arms to restrain himself from any temptations that might arise as they passed enough wealth to build and maintain an empire for untold generations. He forced his eyes forward as he fought the burning desire to loot the myriad treasures in the plaza. But he did not dare raise the ire of the dragon leading them through its home. Breuxias and he might make it out alive, richer men for the gamble, but the others would be doomed to either dragon fire or digestion, perhaps both if they were particularly unfortunate souls.

As if sensing the elf's intentions, Mizgeroth paused and stared. With a sly grin, the emotive dragon padded over to pile of coins and gemstones and scooped up a handful of treasure. The dragon stared down at the shiny mix of metal and minerals with the same lustful expression that Yax imagined he'd had fixed on his own face moments ago.

"It's a shame you have to see the place in such a poor state. Hardly any servants anymore, other than the elder things lurking in the temples and the shadows; debris from the roof that rained down during the Cataclysm laying everywhere; and this shiny stuff undigested."

Mizgeroth popped a king's ransom into his maw and chewed loudly. The broad, flat teeth positioned in the back of his mandibles ground the precious metals and stones to powder as Yax gawked at the wyrm. The elf stared as the dragon wandered to an impoundment of dark water beyond the western wall and drank its fill from the pool.

"But times changed long before I was born," Mizgeroth said, wiping the water from his lower jaw with the back of his paw. "People used to travel here from the other side of Ny to bring us tribute, to show us their love and adoration. In those times, most of the races of the Overworld provided us with unswerving loyalty and dedicated service in our campaign against the Lords of the Underworld.

"In exchange, we provided them with gifts, treasures, knowledge, and power. Unfortunately, we corrupted them in the process. Some grew spoiled, lazy, entitled. Others grew grasping, greedy, and sought the power of the Aethyr. Eventually, they turned against us, against the Eternal War, and now we are scattered and few, a dying breed.

"Like you elves, our resources dwindle but not as fast as our numbers. I eat a lot; but, as you can see, I could graze on coins and gemstones for a lifetime and not deplete the clan's reserves. And at her advanced age, Mother doesn't have much of an appetite for anything but sleep. She should have left this world ages ago, but she would not go without Father. Perhaps now that he is back, he can convince Mother that her time nears its end."

That would be one less dragon between us and a big enough fortune to bring the Kingdom of Oparre to its knees.

With some effort, he pushed the plot from his mind, ashamed to have conjured it at all after hearing Mizgeroth's story about the decline and fall of his kind, another tragic victim of the Eternal War.

As a former monk who'd served in the Temple of Kümatz back home, the elf had heard the story before but never straight from the dragon's mouth.

"Why does her time grow short here?" Yax asked.

"See for yourself," Mizgeroth said as he led them onward.

As they passed through a smaller plaza in the middle of the avenue, Yax and the other elves gave its centerpiece a wide berth. He cursed in his native tongue, spat at the base of the basalt pillar, and made a sign of protection. At the apex of the pillar, an obsidian egg sat on an elaborate perch of gold and platinum. A crack split the egg and the Ultimate Horror, sculpted from stone, overlaid with metal, and encrusted with gems, emerged from center of the obsidian centerpiece.

This symbolism was not lost on him. Yax'Kaqix was familiar with Chichu'äm, for he had fought against the Queen of the Underworld's minions for centuries. If one believed the dogma, this dark deity, often referred to as the Mother of Darconius, slumbered at the heart of this hollow world. Her eight spidery appendages represented her corrupting influences and grasping desire for power. Her four wings spread out to cover the four quarters of Faltyr. She was the grasping, greedy enemy of all life.

Beyond the monument to the enemy at the heart of the Eternal War, He observed three larger pyramid temples to the southeast and two rows of columns, pillars similar to those seen earlier. Judging by the symbols and glyphs inscribed on the columns, they had been used as a hatchery or perhaps even an incubator for dragon eggs. Of the thirteen pillars, not one of them had an intact egg resting on its apex.

Pulling his attention from the forlorn site of the empty hatchery, Yax's gaze settled on something anomalous among the pile of wealth on which they now walked. He spied the tip of a great red tail at the base of the pyramid situated at the far end of the plaza. As his eyes followed the dragon's tail, the elf noticed that it wrapped around the temple. Then the scene before him gelled in his mind.

Mizgeroth's elderly mother coiled around the entire pyramid temple. He realized he'd only seen two pyramids on this end of the plaza. The mound in between the structures turned out to be the peaked but hornless head of the female dragon. The clan matron dwarfed the bones of her lover they'd discovered in the Sands of Sorrow.

Flickering light from a lava vent running along the far wall of the cavern created a hard silhouette, separating the rough molting skin of the dragon from the ornately hewn pillar cascading down the wall from an opening in the roof of the volcano. The soft stone had been carved into the shape of the World Tree, supposedly located at the center of the universe. The lava vent illuminated the gold, silver, and crystals or diamond that had been used to decorate it. Symbolically, this World Tree, another hidden wonder of the ancient world, stretched from the fiery depths of the Underworld to the open expanse of the Heavens.

Breuxias whistled his apparent appreciation. Yax thought the Brute had been ogling the sculpture along the wall of the cavern until his friend said, "Correction. This is the biggest dragon I've ever seen. Astounding."

Approaching her gingerly, Mizgeroth nudged the larger dragon with his nose and said, "Mother, You have visitors."

"Fine, dear. I'll eat them later." Aerabeth smacked her dry lips together and then licked at them with a forked tongue as long as a sand gar. Her pointed teeth dwarfed those of her adult son. Finally, the old dragon yawned. "Now, be a good boy and let Mommy sleep."

"Not dinner, Mother," Mizgeroth said with a dry chuckle. "Visitors. They bring word from Father." He turned to them and explained, "She gets a bit confused nowadays. I blame the molting. It's such an ordeal at her age."

Breuxias nudged Yax in the ribs with his elbow. The Brute whispered, "Are you sure this is a good idea?"

The elf shrugged and asked, "Do you have another idea for how we break a couple of thousand people out of a prison in a box canyon?"

Without breaking eye contact, the Brute returned the shrug.

"Damned if we do, damned if we don't, right?"

"Always," Yax answered. He wouldn't have it another way.

"Father?" Aerabeth asked, craning her head in their direction. She sniffed at them with nostrils the size of millstones. "Is that you, Father?"

"Not your father," Mizgeroth said. "My father!"

"Uberoth!" the old dragon cried. Her booming voice echoed off the bare stone walls like thunder. "My Uberoth!"

The dragon spirit responded instantly. The tooth flared so hotly in Yax's other hand that he fumbled it, but he caught it before it hit the ground. The fetish seared his flesh as the Great Fire Serpent, known to his clan as Uberoth, manifested itself once more. Its fiery eyes fell on Aerabeth.

"I am here, my queen!" Uberoth roared. "My love for you burns like a star in the heavens, fueling me long past the point of bodily death. Though I am only a spirit, I have longed to embrace you and warm you on cold nights. If you would still have me."

His tone sounded like a triumphant hero returning home from a recent conquest, not a disembodied shade left to wander the sandy wastes for the better part of two cycles of ages.

Aerabeth raised one paw from her bed of coins, gems, semiprecious stones, and other valuables. With a lopsided grin, she crooked a single clawed finger to beckon her mate.

"Know that I welcome your embrace, lover, if only the shadow of it," Aerabeth said. With a throaty purr, the old wyrm added, "Come, my beloved, and tell me of your death."

"I hate to interrupt this touching reunion, but there'll be time for sentimentality later. We've done our part as I promised, Uberoth. It's time for you to do yours."

As the ballsy but not particularly brainy Wand Bearer called the dragon spirit by its true name, he held its tooth aloft. Aerabeth snarled in his face, opening her mouth wide enough to block out everything but her gaping maw and its array of saber-length teeth. Though terrified, Yax stood his ground. After all, his options were limited. His knees shook so badly that he doubted he could run far enough, fast enough. He summoned the courage to stare down the dragon and steeled his nerves.

"And what were you promised for ferrying a lost soul home?" Aerabeth asked, snapping her jaws together with enough force to rattle the elf's bones at a score or more paces. "Gold! Magic! Ultimate power! You dare barge into my home, awaken me, and make demands!"

The angry dragon tossed fistfuls of coins and other items from her horde. Yax and the others dodged the barrage of treasure as it rained down around them. As a marble bust shattered at Yax's feet, the younger dragon intervened.

"No, Mother, stop it!" Mizgeroth roared, flames shooting from his nostrils. "It's not like that. They need our help."

Aerabeth stopped snorting and throwing treasure. But she did not settle back down on the mountain of wealth piled around the pyramid. Instead, the towering dragon leaned forward on her front legs and stared at the party of interlopers. Mizgeroth had roused her curiosity.

Yax recognized the familiar glint in her amber eyes. Why? Because the elf saw it every time he looked in a mirror. Curiosity.

Aerabeth asked, "What sort of help?"

Chapter 25

Zoltana and the others followed Mizgeroth as the transformed dragon led them through the winding network of subterranean passageways spider-webbing the remnants of the Meshkenet Mountains. Time meant nothing in the dark corridors, remnants of the Low Road, the system of transit used by the Ogres of Ny and their allies in cycles of ages past. Night and day came and went without the ranger knowing or eventually caring.

Her primary concerns remained the fate of her sister, her sister's unborn child, and her people. To a lesser extent, her concern grew for Yax and her Uncle Chahak. Fighting men like them, the brave Brute, and the burly horseman accompanying Yax would suffer the worst in the coming storm. Zoltana prayed her and the Blue Macaw would weather it well. She looked forward to finding out if there was more between them than furtive glances and kisses stolen in the night beneath Yax's cloak.

Behind her, Breuxias and Leishan shared the light of an Aethyr lantern, a relic of The Golden Age. The grateful dragon spirit had presented it to them for shepherding him home. The device would light their way whenever its circular brass hood was raised. To prevent interfering with the elves' dark vision, the humans kept a slower pace as they guarded the rear while Mizgeroth took point. Despite the dragon's assurances, Zoltana remained watchful of the Low Road, a well-patrolled avenue in antiquity but a subject of many tales of terror in the savage modern age. Some of those stories originated in the prison camp at Mok'Drular.

When they'd first arrived in the dead city, guards and prisoners had resided within the walls of the intact ogre structures at the far end of the box canyon. But humans, elves, and even some of their fae brethren had disappeared on a regular basis during the cold nights at Mok'Drular. Now, most of the prisoners and guards lived in temporary tent cities or new buildings constructed from materials scavenged from the original structures at the site.

Her eyes settled on the back of the breastplate strapped around the transformed dragon's torso. The suit of armor had been taken from one of his recent victims, an officer at the prison. With growing horror, Zoltana realized that his nocturnal activities accounted for a healthy portion of the missing. But she doubted Mizgeroth was the only creature prowling the Low Road in search of tasty morsels.

The dragon clucked his tongue against the roof of his mouth loud enough for the sound to echo off the high, arched ceilings.

Glancing at Zoltana, Mizgeroth said, "Two things I've learned this week. Old age and death make people awfully sentimental. Good thing for you lot. If you'd come begging for aid with empty hands in the days of my father's father or even his father, the Old World-Shaker himself, you'd have been an afternoon snack."

Though the eyes of the elves glowed in the darkness, those of the dragon burned like binary stars. His human guise, the fair image of an ancient Gre king taken from a marble bust in the dragon's lair, did little to diminish the fire in Mizgeroth's eyes. If anything, their reddish glow cast a sinister pall on the pale countenance of the dragon and caused his coppery coif to shine like the halo of a fallen angel.

In the end, will this dragon prove to be the lesser evil? Or have we made a terrible mistake, a deal with a devil?

Forcing air through her constricted throat, the ranger asked, "Are you saying that you'd have eaten us rather than helping us? If so, why should we trust you to carry out the wishes of your parents?"

Mizgeroth shrugged, "Trust me or don't trust me. Doesn't matter to me. Either way, I'm a growing boy, so I'll need to eat someone soon. If it ends up being the people perpetrating this Blood War, it works out for all of us, doesn't it? After all, what's that old saying: the enemy of my enemy makes a good meal?"

Zoltana said, "I don't think--"

Yax interjected, "That's it exactly. Your parents will be proud of you for embracing the old ways, the honorable ways, of your people."

"Thanks," Mizgeroth said, flashing a cocky grin. "I wouldn't have eaten you guys anyway. You're too good for my ego."

The party of reluctant allies bonded over a shared laugh as they neared the end of their journey, the ruins of once great Mok'Drular. Though Zoltana had not used the Low Road before, she did recognize the city glyph inscribed over the archway of a staircase at the end of the corridor. A stylized pick axe overlaid the image of an unsleeping eye so that the curved blade of the pick formed the eyebrow.

Before reaching the stairs, Mizgeroth paused at an intersection about midway down the avenue leading to the ruinous city. When he gestured to the passageway running westward, Zoltana noticed that it also bore the Mok'Drular insignia at the apex of its archway. She didn't recognize the meaning of the flying creature in other glyph.

"The west corridor leads to the floor of the canyon containing Mok'Drular," the dragon explained. "It will be the best avenue of escape, since it connects to the eastward route to the sea here. You should leave the lantern here for now. You'll need it to guide you to the coast."

Of course, the glyph's a pelican! For the Pelican Gulf.

After Leishan hung the lantern on a hook beside the east arch, Mizgeroth said, "The staircase at the end of the lane will take us to the cliffside tombs. They'll make the perfect vantage point to plot our attack."

"Keep in mind this is a rescue operation," Yax reminded him.

"Exactly," Zoltana said. "My people's lives are at stake."

The dragon chuckled and headed for the staircase. He commented, "Steak. Now that's something that I haven't had in a long time. The key is finding a Rhinodon big enough to cut filets from its flanks."

As he mounted the stairs, he turned back toward them and held up the back of one freckled hand, "You wouldn't guess it by looking at these paltry paws, but my claws are sharp enough to slice a steak straight off the hoof and leave the poor mutilated bastard standing in a field. Waste not, want not, Mother always says."

The assembly of humans and elves exchanged nervous glances by lantern light while the dragon rambled onward. Zoltana observed that even the Blue Macaw look worried. She hadn't been afraid, much less fearful of failure, until that very moment. What had Yax gotten them into by striking a deal with dragons? And what would it cost them in the end?

They ascended a steep staircase composed of several flights of steps carved from the living rock, ruddy ferrous sandstone. The stairs had been crafted by ogre hands and scaled to the same size as the stepped highway through the mountains, so the climb would be arduous. The muscles in Zoltana's legs burned by the time they exited the staircase onto the mausoleum level. Vaults cut into the face of the cliffs lined the eastern wall of the canyon containing Mok'Drular. From the dragon's statements, she figured she was in one of them.

Mizgeroth confirmed her suspicions soon enough. He led them through the back of the dimly lit tomb, past a stone sarcophagus taller than Breuxias and longer than a wagon and team of horses.

"Let's hope there are no blood demons lurking in there," Yax commented. "We'd hate to have a repeat of Frolov Keep."

"Can we not discuss the possibility of vampiric ogres roaming a dead city on the edge of a haunted desert?" Breuxias said. The Brute shuddered at the terrifying thought and moved faster toward the light cast by the open door.

They stopped in the deep shadows along the edge of the doorframe. The breathtaking remains of Mok'Drular, the heart of a long dead empire that had once united the ogre tribes in eastern Ny, lay beyond the open archway of the tomb. Zoltana let the others sightsee, plot, and then plan, offering any information required without looking at the blasted city. Despite its natural beauty, Mok'Drular held nothing but pain for her.

ꕥ

In Yax's opinion, modern ogre settlements, although situated in similar isolated locales, paled in comparison to the cities constructed by their ancestors. As he looked down on the ruins of one of their grandest, the elf mapped them in his head. Before he could develop a sound strategy, if one existed for a rescue operation conducted in broad daylight against overwhelming odds, the veteran Choj'Ahaw had to survey the future battlefield.

Most of the original structures had been carved from the ferrous sandstone of the box canyon. The domed citadel on the far north end of the city and the council house that overlooked the amphitheater served as notable exceptions. Granite blocks similar to those seen in the lair of the dragon clan had been used in their construction. Much of the granite appeared to be waxen or even glasslike, probably vitrified by dragonfire or another magical calamity in the distant past.

Originally used for moots, plays, and other gatherings, the amphitheater dominated the eastern lobe of the kidney-shaped canyon. Thirteen tiers high and open to the west, it faced the cliffside dwellings across the city. Built in traditional fashion, their doors opened in the direction of the rising sun. They also looked toward the tombs of their ancestors built into the east wall of the canyon. In between the houses of the living and the dead, a twisted spire of wrought iron, in the form of a double helix, protruded from a large, circular hole dug in the center of the stage. Four guide ropes as thick as Breuxias's biceps steadied the structure. A giant teardrop-shaped quartz crystal adorned the top of the tower.

Vibrant Aethyr energies pulsated inside the magical stone, the ominous Eye of Ra'Tallah. According to Zoltana, the Eye magnified the natural tendencies of the Sands of Sorrow to leech energy from Aethyr users. Her assessment had been no exaggeration. Even at this distance, Yax found it difficult to draw the energies required to use his most passive abilities. Mizgeroth had maintained his human form, so the device had its limits.

The Eye of Ra'Tallah made the tent city of prisoners possible. Without their abilities and far from their besieged homelands, the demoralized elves, refugees from Silent Brook and Nargawald, huddled together under tattered canopies made from horse hide. Thousands of them waited for the scraps and gruel that constituted their midday meal. Many appeared thankful to have food on their plates and shelter over their heads.

The guards lived in slightly better conditions. The lowliest of soldiers shared newer versions of the slave tents while senior enlisted men slept in barracks constructed from material scavenged from ogre structures. Their officers enjoyed the run of the citadel, and they used the council house to observe and administrate day-today operations at the prison camp. Hundreds of crossbowmen, many armed with repeaters, kept watch over the floor of the canyon.

"Listen carefully," Yax said, his tone that of a born leader. "We don't have much time to get this organized before everyone goes back to work. Elven prisoners aren't allowed to wander the grounds unescorted, so Breuxias and Mizgeroth will accompany us into the camp. After we've infiltrated it, Mizgeroth will depart to set up for the main event. While we spread word among the prisoners to prepare for the escape attempt, Breuxias will report for guard duty and bide his time until time for afternoon labor detail. His goal will be to get as close to the armory as possible. I'll intercept him there, start a scuffle, and that'll draw the guards from the armory door."

Turning to the dragon, Yax added, "Make sure you attack on our signal. Once the fight on the ground starts, it'll draw the attention of every crossbowman in the canyon. If you don't take them out in time, we'll all end up shot to pieces before this starts. Once Mizgeroth has their attention, Breuxias will try to take a set of keys from one of the guards posted at the doors. If he fails, it becomes each of our priority in turn. We have to get those keys. The doors are booby-trapped, so we cannot force them. It won't be much of a fight without weapons. Do you understand me?"

Everyone nodded their assent, even absent-minded Mizgeroth.

"Leishan," Yax said, and then relayed a stream of orders in the horseman's native tongue. The Choj'Ahaw repeated them in the Common tongue for the benefit of the group, "You'll remain here as a lookout and provide cover when the show starts. Take aim at enemy officers and any spellcasters or other targets of opportunity that might sew more chaos on the battlefield. If they get organized or end up with their backs to a wall, whether it is one of stone or fire, we're doomed. After we have the key, we rise like a tide. With enough momentum, even a small wave can become powerful enough to sweep away the mightiest of armies. With the element of surprise on our side, we will flow and then we'll crash, suddenly and without mercy, until we are free, free as birds or free as the dead. Is the initial plan of attack clear enough for everyone?"

Everyone but the dragon nodded this time. Perched like a vulture, he stared at the camp as if torn between two emotions.

"Did you hear me, Mizgeroth?"

"Don't worry about me," the dragon replied as he stepped away from the door. He fanned one hand in front of his face. "I can barely stand the offal smell from here, a disgusting mix of elf and human. Makes me want to vomit. You may taste great, but you smell like dung. The sooner all of you are gone from this place the better. You're really starting to bring down the whole neighborhood."

Yax couldn't help but chuckle at the dragon's effete mannerisms. With a broad grin on his face, the elf said, "Stick to the plan and things will go smoothly," he reiterated. "Watch the armory. When we draw the guards away from it, disperse the crossbowmen and provide air support, so we have a chance to pass out the arms inside. Once we have those, we'll be able to execute a fighting withdrawal while you launch your attack on the spire."

As soon as Yax mentioned the device, Zoltana interjected, "The Eye of Ra'Tallah is all that stands between my people and freedom. It must be destroyed. Don't let us down, dragon. Your magic may work here, but we're powerless until then."

Mizgeroth bowed his head and said, "You have my word."

"Even if that is true," Yax said, "it's still going to be one helluva fight."

"Aye," Breuxias added, "Arms and magic will level the board to a certain extent, but you're still talking about a disorganized band of half-starved prisoners-of-war against professional soldiers."

"You know as well as I do," Yax reminded him, "surprise, fire, and panic will turn soldiers to sprinters nine times out of ten. The key is to drive them toward the mouth of the canyon while we get the bulk of the prisoners out through the catacombs."

"Leave it to me," Mizgeroth said. "It'll be my pleasure."

Chapter 26

Dor stood on the aft castle of the *Seadragon* with charred staff in hand. The mage's fierce determination propelled the Hallowed Vessel through the water as it accelerated toward the enemy warships. Storm clouds lingered in the sky around them, likely attracted by his presence, but he had to take the risk.

At his side, Macz steadied the wheel while Tameri readied her bow. Her uncle reported, "The lead ship is moving to block the target, Captain!"

"Ram them!" Dor ordered.

"No!" Tameri shouted when she heard the exchange. "Just because this ship will survive doesn't mean we will."

Dor ripped his attention from the enemy and fixed her with a puzzled look. He hadn't thought of the effect the force of impact might have on those on deck or in the hold of the ship. But it was too late now, their course was set.

"Hold on!" Macz said as they careened toward the galleon.

"Damn fool wizard!" Tameri grumbled as she braced for impact. "Why did I even open my mouth?"

The galleon veered away to avoid being rammed directly. It turned slowly but maneuvered quicker than Dor realized.

As it came alongside the *Seadragon*, the enemy captain ordered his men to fire. Dor reciprocated by issuing a similar command. A hail of arrows and crossbow bolts filled the narrow gap between the two ships, striking down crewmembers on both sides. Large ballista bolts tore through the *Seadragon*'s sails but bounced off of its deck and sides without doing any visible damage. Screams filled the air as another onslaught of missiles wounded more crewmembers. Captain Dor looked on with grim determination. If he didn't do something soon, he wouldn't have a crew left.

The innovative mage tapped the black staff on the deck and left it standing upright. He summoned a protective Aethyr shield and centered it on his staff. The iridescent sphere would protect anyone in the area of effect from projectiles but would do little good if boarded. Unfortunately, he could not extend it far beyond the aft castle of the *Seadragon*. As a result, most of the crew fell back to fighting positions near the stern of the ship.

Beside him, Tameri strung her bow and then pulled a couple of arrows from her quiver. The Savior of Istara dipped their tips into a bucket of tar before igniting and firing them in rapid succession at the rear galleon. Both arrows fell short of their distant targets, the troublesome knight and the traitorous mage.

"So much for that!" she said and reached for more arrows.

"Worry about them later!" Dor shouted. "Prepare for boarders!"

As the lead warship turned back toward the *Seadragon*, it passed within meters of their portside. Royal marines fired bolt after bolt from repeating crossbows while sailors with boarding poles and grappling hooks latched onto the side of their ship. Impatient marines leaped from the taller ship and spilled onto their deck.

"Cut the lines! Don't let them get closer!" Dor ordered.

As the members of Finders Keepers met the marines with cold steel, Tameri dropped her bow and drew her sword. Macz released the wheel and joined her. Dor took the helm while he assessed the battle.

While the chaos on deck unfolded, the control panel bleeped and flashed madly. Dor turned to check the flashing panel, but the blade of a broadsword dissuaded him. The mage looked down the weapon.

"Hands off, mage!" The boarder ordered, brandishing his shiny sword. "I'm not sure what in the Nine that bleedin' device does, but you'll not be touchin' it as long as I draw breath."

Falling back on his training as a Protectorate Mage, Dor spun on his left foot and planted his right squarely in the man's chest. The roundhouse kick staggered the marine, but he remained on his feet. The enemy lunged forward, but the mage leaped backward and seized his staff.

"You'll have to do better than that, boy!"

The mage feigned with his staff, and the marine lashed out at him with tremendous force. Dor sidestepped the overhand swing.

The blade crashed into the flashing panel. The tip of the sword snapped cleanly as it made contact with the unknown alloy. Both men stared in shock at the abruptly ended blade.

Dor broke the stalemate by trying to sweep the marine's legs with his staff, but the skilled swordsman blocked the blow and then went on the attack. He hammered at the magician with the broken blade. The beleaguered mage deflected blow after blow with his staff while scrambling around the ship's wheel. With his onslaught, the marine pushed Dor perilously close to the railing.

The boarder said, "You got no place left to go but the Abyss."

"I've been to the dark heart of the Abyss and spoken to its denizens," Dor said, lying to buy himself time. "They know me well." As he finished the weave, he added, "So be sure to tell them I sent you!"

The marine swung for the wizard's neck. The mage ducked under the blade and then jabbed upward with the speed of a viper. As his staff slammed into the boarder's exposed jaw, an electric discharge blew the marine from the aft castle of the *Seadragon.* His lifeless corpse slammed into the side of the galleon and plummeted into the sea.

An unseen foe surprised the dangerous wizard by grabbing him from behind. Dor let the black staff slip from his hands and seized the attacker by his wrist. Using his weight and momentum, he rolled forward and flipped the attacker over his shoulder and onto the deck. Before this marine had time to react, the Protectorate Mage drew one of the many daggers concealed within his robes. Raising the blade high above his head, Dor dropped to his knees beside the downed man. He steadied himself for the killing blow.

"You weak-tit bastard, you don't have the stones," the marine taunted as he struggled to reach the handle of his own knife. But he never made it.

"I may be a lot of things, but I'm not weak!"

Dor plunged the dagger deep into the man's exposed chest with all the force he could muster. He stabbed the downed marine repeatedly. Gore covered his face and hands by the time he regained his composure. When he stared across the corpse strewn aft castle, his bloodshot eyes met those of Tameri. Her face displayed a range of mixed emotions, notably shock and disbelief.

Rising to his feet, Dor tried to wipe the sticky blood from his face and hands but only smeared it. His lungs burned from the fierce exertion required by combat, and his heart pounded in his ears. The mage grasped the nearby control panel to maintain his balance as he caught his breath.

As he looked around for his staff, thunder rumbled and rolled. Afraid that he was the nexus of another impending disaster, he searched around for the source of the sound. Lightning played across the bow of the *Seadragon*, but the figurehead deflected it into the seawater below. The surge of electricity in the air coursed through the magician. Every hair on his body responded by standing on end. As the bolt dissipated, Dor stared across the open sea at the spell's caster.

From the deck of the rapidly approaching *Regal*, Marduk prepared another spell as Royal Marine archers, spurred onward by a Knight of Oparre, plucked their bowstrings. As the enemy's arrows flew through the air, the captain of the *Seadragon* responded with his own missiles.

Calling out to the Aethyr, Dor raised an open palm and fired a volley of blue-green magical arrows toward the mage and the archers. The beams of energy lanced out and struck with deadly precision. Only those close to Marduk survived the onslaught. Instead of summoning another lightning bolt, the mage had chosen wisely to create an Aethyr shield too.

Going on the offensive again, Marduk slapped his hands together. A loud crack of thunder split the sky again, and a series of fiery, meteorite-like orbs streaked forth from the mage's cupped hands. As the flaming spheres arced through the air toward the *Seadragon*, Dor called for his staff, and it flew to his waiting hand.

At his command, a burst of tiny fireballs erupted from the staff's tip and streaked toward the incoming missiles. Each fireball slammed into one of the chunks of fiery stone. When the magical projectiles collided, they detonated over the prow of the *Seadragon*, raining shrapnel onto the deck. Taking advantage of the chaos and confusion caused by the pyrotechnics, fresh boarders rushed the portside stairs leading to the aft castle. Tameri skewered one and Macz tussled with another, but three slipped past them to storm Dor's position.

As they topped the stairs, Dor prepared to defend the wheel with his life. The *Seadragon* belonged to him now, and he'd die before letting it be taken. He blocked the first attacker with his staff. The other two moved to flank him as he tried and failed to disarm his opponent. Realizing his mistake, he jumped backward. The enemy's flashing blade missed his face by a span of inches.

Seeking to press his perceived advantage, the boarder lunged forward. This time, Dor swept his staff around the blade in a tight circle and flipped it from his attacker's grasp. He snapped the far end of the staff upward and connected with the man's exposed head. Putting his hips into the backswing, he knocked the dazed marine overboard.

The two marines remaining on the aft castle charged the grinning wizard with reckless abandon. They hoped to drag him to the deck and deal with him there. It proved to be a fatal mistake. Like any magician worth his salt, Dor always had another trick up his sleeve.

If they want me dead, they'll have to try harder than that.

In the blink of an eye, the mage disappeared but left his staff behind. The marines approached the murderous Aethyr device, rumored to have been created in the Underworld, as it levitated in place inches above the deck. But they never reached it.

Letting the invisibility weave slip, Dor winked into existence behind them. He clutched a dagger in each hand. The mage struck deadly, devious wounds as he buried the blades deep into their exposed backs. The marines sank to the deck without realizing their prey had become the predator.

଄ଓ଄ଓ

Tameri and Macz fought alongside the ferocious crew of the Hallowed Vessel. Composed of guildsmen and experienced sailors trusted by Caleb or Breuxias, the *Seadragon*'s personnel consisted solely of fighting men and women. Even the wounded cook stood toe-to-toe with the full fledged members of Finders Keepers and held his ground against the tide of boarders, until things started exploding in the sky above them.

A series of thunderous blasts forced Tameri to turn toward the bow of the ship. Sporadic clouds of black smoke hung in the air above the figurehead. The force of the blast had showered them with shrapnel and blown several crewmembers and enemy marines to the deck. The heat and pressure of the blasts had been intense, even at this distance.

Distracted by the explosions, the cook, who fought on Tameri's other flank, failed to see a mariner board with his repeater. He fell dead with a quarrel through his thick neck. Blood spurted from the wound onto her face. As the marine ratcheted another bolt into his crossbow, Tameri flung the dagger in her offhand, striking him just below his collarbone.

"Dor, if you have another plan, now would be the time to implement it!" she shouted as more men reinforced the crossbowman. One glance back at the mage revealed that he had troubles of his own. A familiar Knight of Oparre and several marines fought their way toward the stairs to the aft castle.

Macz moved to block them from making it to Dor's position on the command deck. But the knight disarmed her uncle in one swift motion. Denying Eresh another of her kin, Tameri intervened. Her thrust caught the enemy's downward stroke. She couldn't hope to stop the blow, but she blocked it long enough for Macz to roll out of the way.

"Out of my way, girlie!" the knight commanded.

Their blades remained crossed as they faced one another. The orders of a foreign knight failed to sway the Brute's daughter from her path. Instead, she attacked her opponent with all the ferocity in her being. Apparently amused by her onslaught, he blocked and parried but did not attempt to strike a fatal blow.

"You're wasting my time," the Knight of Oparre said with a huff. "Now, get out of my way!" he roared as he launched into an all-out offensive.

He battered her slender sword aside with his broadsword. With her weapon turned aside, he caught her with the flat of his blade on the backswing. Its impact jarred her ribs and rattled her teeth. As she gasped for air, he backhanded her across the mouth with a gauntleted fist.

As Tameri spun to the deck, her head bounced against the railing with a dull thud. Everything blurred around her. Time seemed to slow. Fresh pain exploded in her hand as he stomped down on it with his boot.

"Pick on someone your own size, you bloody bastard!" Macz cried.

Her uncle fought the knight to the best of his ability, but his opponent was a trained duelist. The broadsword bit deeply into Macz's fleshy thigh. The aging sailor cried out in pain, but the steel blade did not stop until it hit bone.

Macz sank to his knees, blood flowing from his wound. The Knight of Oparre lashed outward with one spurred boot and kicked her uncle in the chest. He fell backwards onto the deck. The enemy positioned himself to conduct a coup de grace with the broadsword.

Tameri pulled herself to her feet as the flat coppery taste of her own blood filled her mouth. Her tongue flicked across molars that felt loose enough to pull free. While she leaned on the railing, the world spun out of control around her. The battle before her seemed surreal; madness, murder, and mayhem surrounded her. When she saw her uncle's mortal peril, her will to fight returned before her senses. Or her sense of restraint.

In that moment, she gave into her dark investiture. She embraced her heritage, her power, and called upon the Aethyr.

Screeching, Tameri rebounded from the railing and sprang at the marine between her and the knight. Her attack took him by surprise, and he parried too late to change his fate. The first slice opened his belly, spilling his entrails; the second removed his head from his shoulders.

She bent and grabbed the severed head by its greasy hair. She tossed it with all her might at the knight. It bounced off him, showering him with the blood of his countryman. As he turned to face his persistent opponent, his gaze latched onto the severed head at his feet. He hesitated and it cost him.

Fueled by anger and rage, she issued a blood curdling scream as she charged the stunned knight. She vowed to end her opponent's life regardless of whether or not her uncle was dead. He'd pursued them long enough. If he wished, he could continue his pursuit from the Underworld.

Sparks flew as their swords clashed.

Tameri fought fiercely utilizing a chaotic combination of techniques taught to her by the three men in her life, her uncle, her father, and Yax. Though she kept her opponent on the defensive, he refused to give any ground to the lighter combatant.

The knight teased, "A woman who fights like a man! Tell me, do you fuck like one?"

"You needn't worry about how I fuck, tyrant's tool," Tameri cautioned. "You'll die a thousand deaths a day impaled on a demon's dick where I'm sending you."

"Such ugly words coming from such a pretty little girl."

The talkative knight lunged forward, finally going on the offensive. She parried his swings and dodged his repeated thrusts as he drove her back across the deck. He towered over her but that did not sway her. In fact, it gave her an idea. She ducked low to avoid his blade, executed a tight shoulder roll, and raked her sword across the back of his leg. He was dressed desert fashion still, so her blade found flesh not covered by armor. He roared in pain as blood flowed from his hamstring.

The Knight of Oparre recovered faster than she expected and advanced on her with his blade raised high. Standing, Tameri blocked the heavy blow before his sword could cleave through her skull. Sidestepping him, she redirected the momentum of his attack and forced him off balance. Once again, she ducked, rolled, and struck the other leg, drawing more blood. He stumbled but did not fall.

Roaring like a Gre berserk, her enraged opponent hammered away at her blade, swinging wildly with all his remaining strength. Tameri was barely able to defend herself from the flurry of blows as she crouched on the rolling deck of the *Seadragon*. His strength outmatched hers.

He battered her sword away and then punched her in the mouth with a mailed fist. Her world spun again as she tumbled backward into the railing. Screaming with renewed vigor, Tameri used the railing to launch herself at the knight once more.

The chainmail clad warrior smirked as his sword found its mark. It pierced Tameri's chest just below her right breast. The force of their combined momentum skewered her on the blade. She dropped her sword. He grabbed a handful of her hair and pulled her to him.

The Knight of Oparre did not speak until he was hilt deep inside the mortally wounded woman. Then he said, "You're as good a fighter as any man; unfortunately, it's your soul that'll be suffering in the Nine before mine."

"Is that so?" she managed, blood dribbling from her lips.

Tameri seized him by his throat.

"If you're trying to squeeze the life outta me, you'll have to try harder than that."

"No...," she whispered, "...just your soul."

Even before she realized that she'd cried out to Eresh, Lady Death had answered her call. The knight screamed his last as her grip sucked the life force from him. His face shriveled, his skin grew ashen and gray, and his eyes sunk into his skull. As she released him, the towering corpse tumbled over the railing. She watched him sink into the darkness; the hollow recesses of his sunken eye sockets stared back.

Tameri yanked the enemy's blade free, grimacing as it sliced back through her ruined ribcage, and tossed it away. As the bloody sword clattered down the stairs, her mortal wound ceased to flow, scabbed over, and closed before her eyes. The terrible power of the Goddess of Death flowed through the Savior of Istara, the Hand of Eresh Herself, again. Confusion competed with elation as every bruise and cut on her body healed as well. She stared at her hands, seeing death there, and fell to her knees. Tameri thanked the Dark Mother for the awful power that had saved her life. That had once upon a time saved Istara.

The marines who'd witnessed the knight's death stopped short of the dark woman. They stared in awe and fear at her blatant manifestation of necromancy. She imagined that she appeared the very image of Death Herself. And perhaps, at that moment, she was. Either way, none of them dared advance, instead choosing to turn and bolt into the wild melee against her fellow crewmembers.

Tameri searched for her uncle. He was alive but battered and bloodied. While keeping an eye on the skirmish, she helped him to sit upright. He smiled a toothy grin at her and laughed like a wild man. Judging by his reaction, he'd missed his niece draining the life from the knight. She reckoned the less he knew the better.

Tameri spied her captain on the aft castle. Dor dispatched two marines with daggers and then scrambled for the control panel before reinforcements could reach his perilous position. When he reached the glowing console, the tide of the battle changed abruptly as the enemy met with more unexpected resistance. This time from the Hallowed Vessel itself.

Chapter 27

Zoltana and Shell Horse led the infiltrators through the back of one of the recently constructed stables to avoid drawing attention. Their party had exited the Low Road through the ogre door near the back of box canyon and then made their way through a series of interconnected but unoccupied rooms carved into the canyon wall. This stable and its pens full of noisy and smelly livestock screened their insertion into the camp from the crossbowmen stationed on the opposite wall of Mok'Drular.

As the infiltrators slipped through an unguarded door, two guards crouched in the hay strewn in an empty stall at the far end of the structure. One tossed a set of bone dice causing the other to grumble. Coins changed hands along with the dice. If the guards noticed them, they didn't indicate it. Their dice-rolling and belly-aching continued as the insurgents walked past them.

Disguised as slaves and guards respectively, the party emerged from the stable and hoped for the best. No one shot them down in their tracks or raised an alarm, so they kept walking toward the cluster of tents used to shelter the prisoners. Cook fires worked to prepare what little food was available for their midday meal.

King Orson and his faction of human supremacists wanted the elves and their fae relatives wiped from the face of Faltyr; however, they didn't want it to occur before they had a chance to pry every secret, steal every treasure, and leech every bit of power from the fae races. The current prisoners served as slave labor to build grander, more secure facilities to house the steady influx of new prisoners captured and sent east to Mok'Drular.

Specialists such as Shell Horse had been bribed, intimidated, tortured, and even mutilated to surrender the secrets of their craft. For his stubborn refusals, Shell Horse had been chosen to serve as an example. Fortunately for him, Yax and the other members of Finders

Keepers had rescued him along with Zoltana and her sister. Instead of going to face certain death in Grymsburg, the ranger and the weaponsmith had a chance to free their people from a similar fate.

Zoltana nodded in the direction of the armory as they neared it. The theater house on the western side of the amphitheater had been converted to store arms and armor for the troops guarding Mok'Drular. The armory's forge consisted of a squat building composed of stacked granite blocks stolen from nearby structures. For now, no smoke curled from its twin stovepipes. Due to the extreme daytime temperatures, the forge ran at night, which meant the set of bronze doors leading to the armory were locked from sunrise to sunset.

Each of the swarthy, muscular guards on duty at the facility wore a key on a chain around their thick necks. Though of mixed ancestry, Breuxias shared the same Nubari lineage as many of the conscripts from southern Oparre stationed at the camp. Zoltana hoped that the scarred, tattooed Brute would blend in with the rest of the soldiery. It would make getting a key that much easier.

As Zoltana and the others headed toward the guards stationed around the perimeter of the elven tent city, she said, "Luckily, these new recruits aren't accustomed to the desert heat yet. The midday break will give us a chance to contact the elders."

"While you do that," Mizgeroth said, "I'll have a look around. I feel like a shark in a school of mullet; so many tasty morsels and no way to devour them all before they escape."

The transformed dragon split from the group and walked toward the officer barracks at the north end of the canyon. Yax hissed to get his attention, but Mizgeroth waved his hand in a dismissive fashion. When he hissed again, he attracted the attention of the perimeter guards.

Breuxias shoved Yax toward the camp and cried, "Get a move on, blueblood! You're cutting into my lunch hour."

When the Wand Bearer wheeled around to glare at him, Breuxias tapped the hilt of the sword hanging from his belt. The action looked all-too-familiar. Yax shifted his gaze from Demon Queller to his friend. A grin touched the corner of the elf's mouth as he raised his hands in mock surrender. Breuxias marched the elves past the perimeter guards without raising a challenge. The shorter men took one look up at the Brute and then tipped their helmets. He saluted and then followed Zoltana toward a group of elves clustered around one of the cook fires.

She bumped into a ragged, dirty figure and blanched when she felt him caress her bosom. The Ranger of the North grabbed the grubby man by the front of his dingy robe and shook him. As they locked eyes, she recognized the man as a half-breed poacher she'd had trouble with in the Queen's forests. More than a thousand leagues east of the Silent Brook and she'd crossed paths with the same pervert. He averted his eyes and blurted out a hurried apology.

Before Yax could intercede, a heavily tattooed Winaq'che warrior stepped between them. Zoltana recognized the senior Eagle Knight as one of her sister's bodyguards, a reliable, loyal soul known as Shield Bear.

"Break it up," he cautioned, "or the guards will get involved."

Zoltana released the ragged half-elf. Shield Bear let go of both of them as Breuxias rounded the side of a tent. The imposing sight of the Brute seemed to cause the elf to rethink his role as peacemaker. On the other hand, the site of the advancing guard caused the poacher to flee into the crowd of elves packed into the camp.

"Too late," the Eagle Knight lamented.

"It's okay," Zoltana said. "He's with us."

"Who's this 'us'? And what's that to me?"

"Forgotten me already," Zoltana said, unveiling her face.

"Lady Zoltana? Is it really you? But Zarena and you were taken away in chains. What happened? Is she safe?"

"Still you heart, Bear. Your charge lived when last we parted. She should be safe and sound by now. As to what happened, it's too long and sordid a tale for a public forum. Come. Freedom is at hand."

ଔଓଔଓ

Yax waited for Zoltana and Shell Horse to enter the tent before proceeding. The Eagle Knight remained outside with Breuxias while Lord Chahak and the other honored elders were informed. The Wand Bearer hazarded one mournful look back at his right arm, his constant companion, and the friend who wore the enchanted blade on his belt like a prize.

Should something dreadful happen to either of them in the coming conflict, the elf wasn't sure if he would ever recover. Demon Queller, a parting gift from Lord Chahak himself, had been with him longer, but the Brute had been like a son to him, especially after the loss of Kan.

Is a promise to a dead man, or the liberation of thousands of my distant kin, worth the risk of losing them? I just don't know anymore, but I guess it's a bit late to worry about it now. We're all-in. And it's all my doing. One way or the other, we'll make it out of here. I'll make sure of it.

The familiar weight of Starkiller tucked into his belt, under the grubby prison garb, reassured the Wand Bearer. The Aethyr amplification device might be useless as long as the Eye of Ra'Tallah kept watch over the camp, but it remained a potent status symbol. The presence of a single Choj'Ahaw was often enough to turn the tide of a battle. Now, there were two here.

Lord Chahak, known to Yax'Kaqix and the elves of the South Isles as The Thunderer, sat around a fire waiting for stew to boil. Venerable, even by elven standards, his drooping earlobes and wrinkled face denoted him as an elf who'd survived more than one cycle of ages. The former Wand Bearer looked more like a kindly grandfather putting on a kettle than one of the most feared, revered Choj'Ahaw in a dozen generations.

"Reliving previous victories or past conquests, honored elder?"

Pulled out of his reverie, Lord Chahak saw them for the first time. He blinked at them sleepily before speaking, "Why is it that the Lady Zoltana always knows how to make an old elf smile?"

"I am a Ranger of the North. The ability to soothe a savage beast is but one of the job requirements."

Chahak discarded the stick and stood with surprising ease. It pleased Yax to see that all of the fire had not yet gone out in the old Wand Bearer's furnace. Following their last encounter, the senior Choj'Ahaw had cast off his headdress, tossed his wand down a spider hole, and fled their homeland for the Silent Brook. His new life had revitalized him and extended his life longer than he would have lived as a Choj'Ahaw. Perhaps, The Thunderer would still be of use to them.

"And I am relieved to see you yet live. It does my heart good to see a single ray of sun in the stormiest of skies. But what of your sister? What of the hope of our people?"

"Worry not, Honored Elder; if all went as planned, Zarena awaits us on board a ship of legend on the other side of the mountains. The one from the prophesy helped free her and shepherded her to safety."

"How did you know it was the one?"

"The unsung song of the Dweller in the Dark follows the individual everywhere. The Underworld's seductive melody has tainted both heart and mind. If it escapes their lips, I fear for all of us."

Yax's mind reeled at the sinister implications of their discussion. It sounded as if Zoltana and Chahak discussed one of the same dire prophesies Caleb had related to them back in Fraustmauth.

"How did you come to be free?" Chahak asked Zoltana, "And why did you return to this charnel house?"

"Funny story actually," she replied, forcing a laugh. "I ran into an old friend of yours in town. Of course, you know…"

Yax removed the wrap covering his face and grinned toothily.

"This one needs no introduction," Chahak boomed, the expression on his face one of mock shock and horror. Had Yax not known The Thunderer for several centuries, he might have been convinced by the old elf's performance. "The Blue Macaw and his actions are known to me and my house. How does this rascally, opportunistic mercenary come to find himself in the Lady's company?"

Yax decided to give Zoltana and the other elves unfamiliar with the ranks of the Choj'Ahaw a good scare. He stepped forward, placed his face mere inches from his former superior, and asked, "How does a bloated old blowhard with a vain, self-applied nickname come to find himself in such a lowly, dishonored position as a slave to humans?"

"What's the meaning of this?" Zoltana sounded confused and even offended by her uncle's behavior. She stared at both men as if they were on the verge of killing each other. But she chose to defend her savior. "Yax and his friends saved us. We'd be on a ship halfway to Kingsport by now were it not for them."

"Did he charge for his services, like the whore he is?"

"Whore?" Yax said with a laugh. "I've bedded a tenth the women as you, you syphilitic old goat. Then again that did include your mother. She paid handsomely for my services too."

Laughing heartily, Lord Chahak grabbed the younger Choj'Ahaw by his slave garb and drew him into a bear hug. Zoltana looked confused but laughed along with the two mad elves. Yax enjoyed the revelry and camaraderie. He'd missed sharing that with The Thunderer. And though he didn't know it at the time, it would be his last occasion for mirth for a long time.

ଔଷ୍ଠଔ

Even with the Eye of Ra'Tallah operational, the elf and fae prisoners at Mok'Drular managed to work a kind of magic. News of Zoltana's return and her powerful allies spread through the camp like the wildfires about to engulf the ogre city. The lack of adequate translators worked against the guards as plans circulated right before their eyes. The noise introduced in the original message as it passed from one elf to the next worked to their advantage. By the time the tale returned to her, Zoltana had been replaced by her twin. The Queen of Silent Brook had returned and commanded a secret army beneath the sundered mountains. She prepared to lay waste to their tormentors, but the prisoners had to do their part. And they were ready, ready to fight for freedom or an honorable death alongside their queen.

Those trained to fight would form a line of battle to screen the guards from the noncombatants. Once the riot started and the dragon launched its attack, Zoltana would lead those in the rear to the hidden ogre door and the passage under the mountain. As the sun sank toward the wall of cliff-dwellings on the far side of the canyon, the plan went into motion, quietly and without notice.

Or so Zoltana thought, until the half-elf poacher emerged from the guardhouse near the armory. A retinue of guards accompanied him. She tried to hide her face, but the traitor pointed her out to them. Yax, Chahak, and Shield Bear gathered around her as she reached for the dagger under her robe. The other prisoners followed suit. Several of the perimeter guards joined those encroaching upon the elven labor detail, but they found it difficult to move through the crowd of prisoners. They allowed only one to move through them with ease, their ally, the towering guard with a dragonslayer strapped to his back.

Breuxias demanded, "What's going on here?"

The half-elf cried, "That's her! I'm sure of it."

"Yes," the Brute said, ignoring the guards and prisoners surrounding him. "It's the woman you assaulted earlier."

"No, I mean, yes," the traitor responded, "You don't understand. I know her. That's the queen's sister. She's one of those rangers."

Zoltana locked eyes with Yax and nodded. He looked hurt to be left out of the loop, but it had been for his own protection. He had risked enough for them already without worrying about the fate of the queen. She mouthed an apology even as one of the other guards reached for her. The Wand Bearer surprised her with an apology of his own. But he was a man of action, not words.

Yax intercepted the guard, grabbed him by the wrist, and smashed a closed fist into his elbow hard enough to break the man's arm. With a single devastating blow, the Battle of Mok'Drular had begun; like all conflicts, it didn't go as planned.

The guard captain of the armory, the closest officer to the chaotic scene unfolding in the canyon, ordered, "Seize them too, else we'll have a full blown riot!"

Breuxias reacted to the orders by seizing Yax and punching him in the side of the head. Everyone who could see the blow flinched. Zoltana felt fortunate she'd never angered the Brute.

The dazed Wand Bearer asked, "What are you doing?"

Breuxias snatched the elf to his feet by the front of his robes. As he pulled his friend close, he grinned and said, "Improvising."

The Brute punched Yax again before tossing him over his hip onto the sand. Guards and prisoners cleared out of the way as the elf sprang to his feet and charged the taller, broader human. For the moment, they avoided a full-scale riot by providing a brutal piece of theater for the crowd of spectators. Zoltana hoped that Mizgeroth would intervene before they killed each other. She didn't know what Breuxias meant by improvising, and playing gladiator didn't seem like it would get them closer to a key for the armory. If anything, it would draw more guards to reinforce those on the floor of the canyon.

The fight had attracted at least two more soldiers in as many blows. But the gamblers from the stable were betting on the outcome instead of getting involved in its resolution.

"Stop this!" The guard captain shouted. "Stop this at once!"

Apparently, Zoltana wasn't the only one to disapprove of their bloody sport.

"Stop?" Breuxias boomed. "We're just getting started."

Everyone watched in awe as the Brute jerked Yax from the ground, pulled him close enough to head butt, and then tossed him like a sack of dry goods over the captain and his retinue. The elf sailed through the air, twisted like a cat, and hit the sand rolling. He slid to a stop between the armory guards.

Yax leaped to his feet with Demon Queller in hand. Zoltana had been so engrossed by their theatrics that she'd missed the wily elf drawing his blade from the scabbard on Breuxias's belt during their last pass. The captain lost his head in one precise cut, and the Wand Bearer caught the armory key by its chain before it hit the ground.

Pivoting on the ball of one foot, Yax spun in a tight circle. He killed or maimed the guards accompanying the captain before they could raise their pikes. But their screams were lost in the battle cry that went up from the prisoners as they cheered him.

The ululation of the elves signaled their unseen ally, their air support. Zoltana had not known the wyrm was overhead until he dropped his camouflage. As the spell faded, mighty Mizgeroth became visible to all those within the confines of Mok'Drular.

A panicked cry split the sky over the city; it consisted of one terrifying word: *Dragon!*

Chapter 28

Dor's hand hovered over the control panel of the *Seadragon*. He waited until the enemy ship reached pointblank range before touching a gem carved into the shape of a chess knight. The stone glowed red, and the eyes of the figurehead took on the same luminous hue. Thick, black smoke belched from the nostrils as its mouth opened. As the figurehead twisted in the direction of the enemy, a surge of magical energy rippled throughout the ship.

"What the…" Dor said before being interrupted by hellfire.

The animated figurehead spewed forth a jet of intense heat and flame. The liquid fire washed across the deck and sails of the *Hero's Welcome*. The only grapple lines left after the fiery assault snapped as the *Seadragon* accelerated away from its blazing opponent.

The fire on the warship burned out of control. The majority of the deck crew on the side of the attack was obliterated instantly by the intense heat. Their flesh melted from their bones, and their bones turned to ash, only to be carried away on the wind.

Survivors leapt overboard in an attempt to douse the sticky fire that coated their bodies as others scrambled to release the life boats on the opposite side of the ship. It was too late to save their ship. So they opted for their lives.

But Dor's fury had not yet abated. He instructed the Hallowed Vessel to do its worst. The panes of the odd-numbered portholes on the side of the ship facing the enemy retracted into the hull. Guided by the ill will of their captain, phantom hands slipped coppery barrels through the open portholes and fixed their elevation. The whine and hiss of a hundred boiling teakettles rent the sky, only to be replaced a moment later by the dull thumps of the steam-driven cannons. Half dozen conical projectiles cleared the space between the warring vessels in the time it took for Dor to take a breath. The cannon shot penetrated the hull of the burning galleon above the waterline but hit with enough force to knock the bottom out of it as they exited.

Within a span of heartbeats, the *Hero's Welcome* listed to starboard as it took on water as a dangerous rate. Everyone aboard the *Seadragon's* deck watched its fate unfold. Screams and cries filled the air as desperate men threw themselves overboard, only to keep burning once they hit the water. A column of smoke rose into the sky as the galleon sank into the sea. The hiss of steam lingered long after the doomed ship disappeared beneath the waves.

The marines remaining aboard found themselves trapped between the mercenaries of Finders Keepers and the sea. Tameri, Macz, and the rest of the crew pushed the enemy to the edge of the railing.

"Hope you can swim back to Oparre," Tameri said, raising her sword. "Of course, you can always take your chances against us."

One of the marines sheathed his weapon, bowed politely, and replied, "If you will excuse us, madam." Like lemmings, the marines plunged overboard one by one into the sea. A cry of victory rose from the ranks of the victorious crew as the enemy swam for the *Regal*.

Dor and Tameri locked eyes across the smoky deck of the *Seadragon*. She smiled despite looking exhausted. He returned it. The remaining galleon tacked hard to starboard to avoid the same fate as its sister ship. Though no one manned the wheel, the *Seadragon* moved to block the escape of the *Regal*. By activating its combat controls, Dor had ensured the ship would operate solely on his mental commands.

Tameri retrieved her bow and joined some of the crew as they fired arrows at the enemy ship. They hooped and howled with glee as their missiles crossed the expanse between the two ships. Despite taking a number of casualties, crew morale had shifted with his utilization of the *Seadragon's* offensive capabilities.

Maybe I can captain a ship after all.

Dor raised his staff to the sky and commanded the winds to fill the sails. They responded to his call but so did the clouds around them. Thunder rumbled overhead as the rains came too late to save the *Hero's Welcome*. The *Seadragon* gained speed but not as much as its captain wanted. The enemy's missiles had taken their toll on the mundane sails. One out of three battens had sustained enough damage to be practically useless. The bulk of the others had sustained light damage, but the gusting wind threatened to rip and tear them beyond repair.

"Get us closer!" Dor ordered.

Macz limped up the stairs to the aft castle and joined him at the helm. The wounded sailor attempted to wrestle control of the wheel, but an unseen force opposed him. The ship had locked its heading on what appeared to be a collision course for the *Regal*.

"I don't have control!" Macz shouted above the wind and weather. "The ship is doing everything! It's possessed!"

Captain Dor replied, "I was speaking to the ship, not you."

Dor spotted Marduk on the prow of the *Regal* and extended his staff toward his rival. The other Protectorate Mage worked rapidly to finish a weave, so the *Seadragon's* captain took no chances. The Hallowed Vessel's figurehead spat a ball of fire at the enemy vessel.

The spritsails and sails of the fore-mast burst into flames as the fireball exploded over the bow of the galleon. The blast consumed the polybolos crews manning the heavy repeating crossbows mounted on swivels there. Fiery chunks of them rained onto the decks, while other pieces plunged into the sea.

Marduk conjured a protective bubble before the entire bow of the *Regal* was engulfed in liquid fire. The mage's shimmering sphere brightened before it burst under the extreme heat produced by the *Seadragon*'s breath weapon. His agonizing screams played like music to the ears of Kaladimus Dor. He considered incineration an appropriate fate for Salaac's betrayer.

❧❧

Composite bow in hand, Tameri joined the wild haired young mage at the wheel. Lightning flashed overhead as the rains increased. It gave the Protectorate Mage a sinister appearance as light and shadow played across him. She'd never seen him like this before. He crackled with power as Aethyr energies ran between him and the Hallowed Vessel.

Dor stood on the quarterdeck with his hands extended to the warring heavens. His eyes blazed like the fires of the Nine Hells as he funneled wind into the ragged sails. The unnatural winds rose and fell in gusts as he split his concentration between the sails and the smoking galleon.

Having witnessed the fate of their sister ship, the fire crews on the *Regal* had been ready. They pitched glass fire grenades onto the flames and passed buckets filled with a fire retardant solution. The galleon continued to make a wide turn to clear the battlefield. Dor shifted the wind direction to offer pursuit. As the galleon turned, the square-rigged sails of its four remaining masts caught the wind current.

The ballista crews of the tall ship ensured their widening lead by firing a broadside at the charging ship. They aimed high and launched a volley of missiles into the wind. The three foot long projectiles sailed toward the bow of the *Seadragon*. By the time Dor aimed his staff at the ballista bolts, it was too late. They tore through sails on all three masts as they passed from bow to stern. One of the shorter shots bounced off the quarterdeck and splashed into the sea, forcing Tameri to tackle Dor to the deck.

"Are you trying to get yourself killed?" She yelled at him, even as she helped him to his feet. "They're fleeing! Let them go before we sail into their reinforcements."

Dor weathered her storm but did not flinch, much less respond.

"I've had enough of this nonsense." Turning to her uncle, she said, "Set course for the Pelican."

"Belay that order!" Dor cried. "Marduk is no more and their ship is aflame. We strike while the iron is hot."

Tameri stepped in front of him as he moved toward the helm.

"My father is depending on us! He's depending on you!" She yelled, dressing him down in front of the entire crew. "Risking an attack on that ship would be foolish. They outnumber us at least thirty to one. Let them flee and let the few of us who remain live to fight another day. We won this battle, but at what cost? Taking on the crew of that ship after the losses we've sustained is worse than suicide. It's murder. You might as well sentence most of us to death now."

Dor acted oblivious to her presence as he brushed by her.

"She's right, Captain! The hull may be sound, but our sails are holier than a bishop on All-Father's Day. Everyone but the ship's cat is dead or wounded. Another exchange like that, and we'll be dead or dead in the water," Macz said, becoming another voice of reason in the ear of the obsessed magician. Tameri welcomed her uncle's assistance with the pig-headed wizard.

Dor turned back toward Macz and said, "It's a risk I am willing to take. They have my chest aboard, and I will have it back. It cannot fall into the wrong hands!"

Tameri grabbed Dor by the collar of his robe and jerked him toward the stern of the ship. She stared into his wide eyes. She fancied that she saw his determination give way to fear, fear that she might throw him overboard. But she knew it to be the reflection of her own emotions. They were her strength as well as her weakness, something they had in common. So she appealed to something she knew they shared: guilt.

"Your chest is the reason we're in this mess now, Kaladimus Dor! How many innocent people have to die because of you and that damned box? How much blood do you have to wade through to complete this so-called mission? I thought I had blood on my hands, but surely Eresh holds you in higher esteem than me. After all, you've sent her enough souls to earn yourself a place by her side in the Underworld."

The wizard blinked back sudden tears. Now she had him. Tameri thought her father unduly harsh when he'd warned her about the young wizard. Thankfully, in the process of telling her about him, he'd provided her with the emotional battering ram necessary to break down Dor's walls.

The mage shook as much as his voice when he said, "You speak from a position of ignorance and irrationality. You don't understand the importance of that chest, and I'm not at liberty to tell you anything about it. You're aboard *my* vessel; you're a part of *my* crew! Question my command again, and I'll remove you from both at the earliest opportunity. Do you understand?"

The storm had increased in intensity with Dor's fury. The wild-eyed mage shook her hand loose from his arm. As he did so, electricity crackled between them and popped her like a whip across the hand. The static buildup between them had become dangerous, but she braved the risk of electrocution to win this battle.

Again, Tameri stepped in front of him and blocked his path. His intense eyes bore into hers. She would not be ignored, much less defeated. Like any masterful chess player, she had saved her best piece for her final gambit.

She deployed it like poison in his ear. "The queen is aboard," she whispered. "As is her unborn child."

Dor stared at her quizzically. He asked in a hushed tone, "What do you mean the queen is aboard? What queen?"

Tameri looked around before offering an explanation. Most of the crew had scattered; Macz and a few others lingered nearby. Probably taking bets on whether or not she'd throw the wizard overboard. Her uncle had an unfair advantage in that wager. He'd seen her do it to a customs official who'd gotten too friendly with her. If anyone was listening, the snapping of the sails and crashing of the waves would prevent anyone from overhearing their conversation.

"The Queen of Silent Brook. Zarena is really Lady Shy'elle. You see, I too have been sworn to secrecy, yet I have broken my promise to save lives. What about you, Mr. Master-of-Disaster? Risking the life of an unborn for a stupid box seems a bit extreme, don't you think?"

Dor looked flummoxed. While he remained unable to respond, she continued her tirade, "After her escape from Grymsburg, the queen travelled under her birth name and used her twin sister for cover. She was recaptured by a knight named Sir Frederick. For some reason, your buddy Proleus and his allies in Oparre want her baby. And not just because he's the heir to two kingdoms." Wagging her finger in the mage's face, she added, "I think you know why, but I won't pry into your business. Obviously, it's more important than your friendships. But mark my words, if any harm befalls to her child, his blood will be on your hands. And your blood might end up on mine."

Dor remained quiet after Tameri berated him. He seemed to be absorbing the deluge of information slower than his robe absorbed the rain. When he shifted his gaze toward the smoldering galleon on the horizon, she thought she'd lost him. She could see his eagerness to reclaim his stolen property. A conflict raged inside him, evidenced by his perplexed expression.

"Turn us around, Macz!" Dor said, finally relenting. "The helm's yours." Turning to Tameri, he added quietly, "I think it's about time I met Her Highness."

Always save the Queen for your last gambit. Checkmate.

ఆణ్ఆణ

Dor rejoined Tameri and Macz on the quarterdeck of the *Seadragon* as it sailed into the mouth of Pelican Gulf. He returned from his umpteenth visit to the quarters of the crown of Silent Brook and her newborn son, heir to the bulk of eastern Ny.

Though he loathed admitting it, Tameri had been right about turning away from the fight with the *Regal*. The queen's son had been born within hours of losing sight of the fleeing galleon. The little prince's birth had been difficult and bloody, requiring the assistance of both Dor and Tameri. Had they been engaged in battle at the time, the queen as well as her son would have surely perished. In traditional elven fashion, the newborn prince would not be named until the first new moon after his birth. Until then, they'd taken to calling him: His Adorableness. A fitting name indeed, Dor decided as he climbed the stairs of the aft castle.

He considered the half-elven prince to be as cute as the flying snakeheads leaping and splashing alongside the hull were hideous. The serpent like fish frequently trailed sailing ships, awaiting any scraps dumped overboard. Though not normally dangerous, they had been known to attack swimmers and fishermen in the shallows near shore.

Reminds me of me, mostly harmless until murderous.

His gaze drifted west, along with his thoughts, toward the chest. The desert coastline transitioned to piney hills after they passed Minotas, the island nation located a few leagues north of the Panglov. Beyond the placid waters of the Pelican, the eastern terminus of the Meshkenet Mountains dominated the horizon to the northwest, blocking his view of the evil land beyond them.

Even now, he knew he'd have to go there, to the rotten heart of Oparre, and take back the chest. Dor puffed on his pipe and exhaled through his nostrils. He tried to relax for now. Until they located

Breuxias and Yax, nothing further could be done to retrieve the strongbox and its contents.

Tameri slipped an arm around his waist and leaned against him. Her warmth felt good in the crisp breeze. The unlikely pair embraced in silence, absorbing the peacefulness of the scenery around them. After a while, Tameri squeezed him a bit tighter and then released him. She smiled up at the dopey magician.

"My father would have been proud of you back there," she said.

"For what? What did I do? I lost the chest, failed at the one job I had to perform, and Marduk may have gotten away as well! Not sure if that slippery bastard lived or died. But I'd put my gold pieces on the latter. He has more lives than a cat."

"I remember you mentioning him. I take it you have a past."

"He's the sniveling coward who killed Salaac while members of the Proleus faction sacrificed themselves to make it possible."

No amount of his favorite herb would relax the agitated mage at this point, so he dumped the contents of his pipe overboard and pocketed it. The smoldering herbs never hit the water. One of the pursuing serpent-fish snatched it out of the air and then disappeared into the sea.

Hope the pipe weed calms him better than me.

Turning to Tameri, Dor said, "He may be a hero to Proleus, but he's a traitor to Moor'Dru. If the Cult of Darconius ends up with that chest because of him, he'll be a traitor to all of Faltyr."

Take a step back from him, Tameri stared into his eyes and said, "Get over it! It's gone, Dor. About three weeks back that way." She gestured southwest with a slender thumb. "It's not the end of the world, is it?"

He shifted his gaze toward the direction she'd gestured.

"It's not is it? That's not what I was told," he quipped.

"Dor, what are you talking about? I'm sure the contents of that chest were valuable, even powerful and dangerous, but…"

Someone shouting from the prow of the ship interrupted her.

"Contact front! Multiple! Damn near a dozen ships, Captain!"

Dor hurried to the control panel and removed the spyglass. He ran down the stairs, past the midship cabin, to the bow of the *Seadragon*. By the time Tameri joined him, he was surveying the flotilla of ships.

The magical spyglass brought the distant warships into brilliant focus. He focused on the lead ship and the array of men crowding its deck. The mage spied someone staring back at him with a silvery spyglass. Shifting his attention from the other voyeur, Dor focused on the flag flown at the top of the mizzenmast. A black flag emblazoned with a red phoenix flapped in the wind. In each of its talons, the crimson bird clutched a flaming arrow crossway across its breast.

A sigh of relief escaped him. Tension eased from his shoulders.

"Stand down!" Dor ordered. Closing the spyglass, he added to Tameri, "They're friend, not foe, for they fly the Crimson Phoenix. Looks like good old Caleb got my message. Good idea suggesting I send him a bird. Finding them along this coast will be hard enough, much less transporting all those people. This remarkable little vessel may hold a few hundred of them, but I doubt it'll hold thousands."

Tameri asked, "Do you have any idea where to start looking?"

"No clue beyond the mountainous coastline that joins Panglov and Oparre. But I'm sure one of those captains will know where to start. Perhaps they've spotted remnants of ogre settlements along the coast. If so we should start searching there."

Tameri prodded the stormy mage, "Always the optimist, huh?"

"Always."

Sarcasm colored his response. Dread filled his tone. But he laughed anyway. Dor laughed to spite the nagging thoughts that his failure to secure the chest's contents had doomed them all. After all, what would the lives of these prisoners-of-war, much less the life of their sovereign and her heir, matter if his actions ushered in the cataclysmic end of this cycle of ages?

Calamity's Door indeed.

Chapter 29

The warning came too late for the poor bastards garrisoned near the mouth of the box canyon containing Mok'Drular. Breuxias and his allies cheered as Mizgeroth spat a stream of fire into the open windows of the building being used as the officers' barracks. A number of soldiers fled the burning structure, only to be caught in the open. Turning his head, the dragon rained hot death on them.

Dozens of crossbowmen, those patrolling the terraced walls and open avenues in front of the cliff-dwellings along the canyon's northwest rim, took aim at Mizgeroth, but few survived long enough to fire a single bolt. The red wyrm's breath weapon engulfed them, burning many to pillars of ash in their tracks.

In Breuxias's opinion, those were the lucky ones. Others suffered slower, more gruesome fates as they staggered around coated in the sticky liquid flames. A few threw themselves from the walls, preferring the quick death at the abrupt end of their plunge to the prolonged agony of death by incineration. Those who remained, stalwart fools fighting alongside battle-hardened veterans, returned fire with their repeaters, but Mizgeroth flapped his powerful wings and shot upward into the sky.

As the dragon shrank from sight, Breuxias turned his full attention to their next objective, securing the armory. He joined Zoltana, Shell Horse, and both Wand Bearers in a fighting withdrawal toward the armory. Activating his belt, the Brute drew the dragonslayer and swung it in a wide arc around him. He cleaved two guards at the waist with the devastating weapon. Yax, Zoltana, and Shell Horse gave him a wide berth as they fought their way toward the same location.

Lord Chahak and Shield Bear shouted orders to the mixed array of Eagle Knights, Jaguar Knights, rangers, warriors, monks, mages, and other militant patriots who stood between the noncombatants and the armed guards. The defenders formed a thin line that stretched from the armory to the tent city. Any guards caught among the rioting prisoners found themselves torn apart or pummeled to death with fists, rocks, or stolen weapons.

Chahak disarmed a charging guard and then bashed the man's brains out with his own weapon. He raised the bloody mace and thundered above the din of combat, "Strong hearts to the front! Arm yourselves! Tonight we drink as free elves or dine with our ancestors!"

Behind them, Yax and Shell Horse dispatched the remaining soldiers guarding the door and then put the key to use. As soon as they opened the reinforced bronze doors, they armed Zoltana and several others and sent them to filter noncombatants into the hidden passage to the Low Road hidden behind the stable. With one last glance at the weaponsmith, Yax left Shell Horse to handle distributing the weapons while he made his way to the ragged front line.

The riot became a brawl soon enough as reinforcements poured into gaping holes in the line. Breuxias chopped, slashed, cut, or stabbed any other human who crossed his path on the floor of the canyon. On either side of him, a Choj'Ahaw fought with the spirit and tenacity of a demon. To his right, Yax spun, ducked, rolled, and dived as he maneuvered around his own people to reach a fresh victim. And on his left flank, Lord Chahak laughed with delight as he crumpled another soldier's helmet with the stolen mace.

"You were right," The Thunderer called across to Yax'Kaqix.

Yax hacked the sword arm from a guard and said, "Which time?"

Laughing again, Chahak replied, "About missing this!" He emphasized his point by slamming the mace into an advancing guard's face so hard that blood shot out of the man's ears.

"Glad you're enjoying the reunion," Yax said as he drove the Demon Queller's blade into the throat of the disarmed guard.

"He's not the only one," Breuxias interjected. The Brute glanced skyward and added, "Any idea when that blasted dragon is going to take out the Eye?"

Mizgeroth dove low over the floor of the canyon and sprayed fire onto the charging reinforcements. The dragon pulled out of the dive and roared over the heads of the elves, eliciting as many whoops as screams. Crossbow bolts lodged in his scales and pierced pinholes in his wings, but he took no notice. His fore claws plucked guards from the skirmish; as the wyrm climbed back into the sky, he popped them into his mouth and chewed.

"Soon I hope," Yax responded as he beat back a surge by a pair of guards. "Otherwise, there may not be anyone left to escape."

The elf dove beneath their pikes and then cut across one of the ash poles. He snatched the head of the pike from the air, threw it as he rolled forward, and stabbed the man on the left. The sharp tip of the thrown pike pierced the other guard's heart, killing him instantly.

Casualties mounted on both sides as Breuxias and the elves fought against the growing number of soldiers. Mizgeroth had attacked them from behind, setting aflame the only visible exit to the canyon, so the enemy advanced toward the elven incursion rather than risk the flames. The dragon enjoyed the orgy of destruction so much that it had either forgotten the plan or altered it to suit his own dark designs.

Breuxias couldn't help but wonder if Mizgeroth had played Yax for a fool. Though he couldn't fathom the dragon working with the men of Oparre, he couldn't comprehend why the wyrm would honor an agreement made with an elf by his dead father and sleeping mother. The Brute's suspicions grew when cries of alarm went up from the rear guard.

Breuxias glanced in the direction of continuing evacuation. The fleeing prisoners bunched up as they filtered through and around the stable into the concealed passageway secreted in one of the cliffside tombs behind the building. Sounds of panic and conflict arose from that direction, but he had his own fight to worry about surviving.

Leaving his overrun position at the armory door, Shell Horse joined them and cried, "They're attacking the rear! We're trapped!"

"I know," Yax said. "Don't panic! We'll get there as soon as we can." The Wand Bearer cut down his current opponent, turned toward Breuxias and Chahak, and asked, "Can you hold the line as we evacuate?"

Chahak answered, "We will or we won't. No way to tell."

Breuxias provided a more resolute response. "Go! We'll stand like a stone wall until the others are evacuated or die trying. Provided we live, we'll meet you at the archway beyond the stable."

With a nod to his friends, Yax sprinted toward the rear. Shell Horse chased after him, but the Choj'Ahaw proved much fleeter of foot.

"Frankly, I prefer the former," the Thunderer said.

"Be a lot easier if that damn dragon would cooperate!" Breuxias yelled with the hope that Mizgeroth would take the hint.

Lord Chahak brained one of the soldiers, hurled the gore-covered mace into the path of another trooper, and then plucked a discarded sword from the ground. After stabbing the trooper tripped by the mace, he said, "There's an ancient elf saying about trusting dragons."

Breuxias continued to create a path of carnage around him. He cleaved a mustachioed guard's head from his shoulders and then hacked the legs out from under a portlier one. The Eagle and Jaguar Knights around him inflicted similar damage on the enemy, but they were the exceptions, not the rule. Despite the unpredictable dragon, the men of Oparre still had the weight of sheer numbers on their side.

Breuxias finally managed to ask Chahak, "What's that?"

The Thunderer cut down an opponent, fixed his new human ally with a wry grin, and said, "Don't."

The Brute realized why Yax held the disgraced Wand Bearer in such high esteem, even after Chahak threw down his wand and left his life as a Choj'Ahaw behind to live on the mainland with the Winaq'che. The old elf kept him in stitches. In the midst of the carnage around him, the Thunderer never failed to find humor in the situation. Breuxias, however, tired of the dragon's game; he filled his lungs like a blacksmith's bellows and shouted, "MIZ-GE-ROTH!"

He could hardly hear himself over the clatter of steel on steel and the cries of the wounded and dying all around him. But the dragon snapped his head around toward the man wielding the dragonslayer. Using the blade, Breuxias gestured toward the spire and the crackling Aethyr device affixed to the top of it.

"The Eye, you damn fool dragon," he called, "pluck out the Eye!"

Mizgeroth disengaged from his harassment of the crossbowmen trying to organize behind the wall of desperate guards and soldiers fighting with swords, maces, and pole arms. The dragon gained enough altitude in a single beat of its massive wings to dive toward the Eye of Ra'Tallah. As he passed over the spire, he seized the Eye in his powerful rear claws and tried to fly away with it.

As the device separated from the tower, the discharge of Aethyr energy flashed brightly enough to illuminate the entire canyon. For a brief moment, the harsh light expelled the heavy shadows cast by Mother Sun as she set over the rim of the sandstone walls. The explosive discharge caused Mizgeroth to wail like a harpooned whale as the Aethyr energies shocked him.

The red wyrm fell toward the unforgiving stone; the luminous stone clutched in his claws. From his position, Breuxias wondered if he'd managed to slay the dragon by merely pointing the dragonslayer and commanding it. If so, the Brute pledged to pen that epic tale with his own hands.

If I survive to write it, he reminded himself.

ꕥ

The Aethyr discharge rippled through the canyon causing Yax'Kaqix to whirl about before he reached the glut of prisoners trying to move through and around the stable. He watched in awe as the dragon tumbled toward the stony floor of the amphitheater. Mizgeroth released the Eye of Ra'Tallah, and the device shattered against the ground. Spreading his wings, he rode the unleashed Aethyr energies as an eagle would a thermal.

The secondary explosion proved more pyrotechnic than the first. The destruction of the Eye brought down its spire onto the top of the armory. The forge's smokestacks toppled to the ground, crushing troops on their way to reinforce the guards. The red wyrm sailed over the scene of destruction it caused and roared in appreciation of its handiwork.

With the prisoners' connection to the Aethyr restored, spells flew from all quarters and shifted the momentum of the fight. Despite the devastation wrought by the weaves, crossbowmen peppered the riotous prisoners with quarrels from behind a wall of shields and pikes.

As the hail of lethal bolts struck the rioting prisoners, Yax's own mentor became one of their victims. Even at the end though, the old Thunderer lived up to his name. Chahak waved his hands and the projectiles in his torso reversed their trajectory. The iron quarrels became bolts of lightning and struck dead the men who'd fired them. Raw electricity chained outward through the ranks and stunned, injured, or killed scores of troopers and guards. A final clap of thunder signaled the Wand Bearer's passing from this world to the next.

Poetic, couldn't ask for better when my time comes.

The left flank collapsed while the center turned into a chaotic brawl. But as Yax watched, Breuxias stood like the stonewall he promised. The gem in his belt gleamed in the twilight. The Brute sliced or scattered a half dozen or more men with each swing of the dragonslayer's oversized blade. Yax fought every impulse to rush to the aid of the man who'd been his friend and surrogate son for the past decadus. Ultimately, the frightened expressions on the faces of the fleeing prisoners made the decision for him. So the elf did the only thing that he could for his friend: he sent him reinforcements.

Targeting bales of hay on the south side of the corral attached to the stable, the Wand Bearer called upon the Aethyr. The hay burst into flames. Panic spread amongst the horses and dromedaries used as mounts and beasts of burden by the men of Oparre.

Drawing Starkiller from beneath his robe, Yax blasted the corral's gate from its hinges. He fired a couple of weak bolts of Aethyr energy into the backsides of several horses, prompting them to lead the charge against the men breaking through on the left. The Wand Bearer whooped loudly as the animals crashed into the press of guards, troops, and overwhelmed defenders.

Peddling backward through the stable doors, he hoped that the stampede would buy Breuxias and the others enough time to fall back in the direction of the hidden entryway to the Low Road. The press of elves packed into the stable parted to give the Wand Bearer access to the rear set of double doors. Peeking around the doorframe, Yax saw why they'd stopped crossing the avenue between the structure and the tombs carved into the cliffs.

The ground itself betrayed them by behaving as quicksand rather than the native sandstone. Several elves had sunk into the mixture, not deep enough to suffocate them but sufficient to trap them. Across the avenue, a dozen or more crossbowmen, secreted behind the columns of the colonnade leading into the row of tombs, shot down the prisoners stuck in the sand trap.

The elves who'd avoided the treacherous ground hid behind piles of coal and slag south of the armory to keep from being cut down by a crossbow bolts. Yax knew they wouldn't last long out there. The Wand Bearer scanned the row of columns to find the one responsible for weaving the quicksand spell. Due to the steady stream of orders being relayed by the enemy, Yax spotted the officer-in-charge, but the thickly built human did not appear to be the culprit. The sorcerer remained cloaked in the shadows beyond the colonnade.

Focusing his attention across the way, Yax watched as the troops along the colonnade clashed with Zoltana, Leishan, and several other armed elves defending the entrance to the Low Road. The ranger and the horseman fought in a desperate hand-to-hand battle with a larger knight and his subordinates. Both Zoltana and Leishan appeared to be wounded. With no time to waste, Yax decided to draw out the wizard, so he glanced across the doorway to Shell Horse. He pointed at the officer and said, "He's the one giving orders; put him out of commission."

The weaponsmith nodded and brought a purloined short bow to his shoulder. He wheeled around the side of the thick post used as part of the doorframe and fired. His arrow shattered on the column beside his target but achieved the desired effect as the enemy fired on them.

A bearded human in a dun-colored turban emerged from the shadows. His cupped hands spun in front of him, and a vortex built between his palms. The wizard slapped his palms together, and the spinning ball of force shot forward, quickly growing into a dust devil. The miniature tornado raced across the quicksand, scattering trapped elves in its wake, and then slammed into the narrow end of the stable.

Yax dove over the wall of a stall and onto a pile of shit-stained hay. Wooden shrapnel filled the air around him, cutting, piercing, or bruising him in a dozen or more places. Bloody and bewildered, the elf struggled to his feet. Both barn doors had been blown away, along with a section of wall and roof. Larger pieces of shrapnel and debris had doomed a few of the prisoners seeking refuge inside the barn, Shell Horse among them. Bits of straw floated in the blood pooling around his prone form. Yax could see the weaponsmith's lower extremities protruding from beneath one of the collapsed roof supports, but the debris obscured the rest of the gory scene.

Yax cast as many quick offensive and defensive weaves as he could safely concentrate on at one time. With his brand of Aethyr magic, he did not believe it was the amount of energy one channeled and transmuted that was dangerous; the hazard for him, a combat caster who often stacked spells, was the energies of the different weaves intertwining and then collapsing or exploding outward. But if he was careful, he could ensure that his skin would have the resiliency of steel, his body would move with the speed of a jaguar, and his feet would step with the lightness of a feather upon on eggshell. With those spells active, he might make it across the avenue alive.

If I don't, I'll prepare better in the next life.

Chapter 30

Drawing Starkiller and Demon Queller, Yax'Kaqix rounded the doorframe and charged across the courtyard. The jade wand started the symphony of destruction as its Golden Wedge emitted blast after blast of deadly energy. Crossbowmen fell dead in their tracks, their repeating crossbows clattering to the stone floor of the colonnade.

As the survivors returned fire, Yax flung the enchanted sword away from him and it spun through the air as if possessed. Demon Queller sought out the incoming projectiles and cut them from the air. Once it completed its second spin around his body, the elf caught it. Sheathing Demon Queller on the run, Yax flung his other hand outward toward the row of columns and crossbowmen. Instead of using the wand, thick streams of grey webbing spewed forth from the spider ring and coated the side of the colonnade. The enemy fought against the sticky bonds, but the webs held most of them tightly. The sorcerer and his superior remained free unfortunately.

Slippery as an eel, I see. I'll sink my fangs into you yet.

Yax fired several more blasts as he ran toward the row of columns. He sprang forward, rolled, and took cover behind one of the thick stone pillars supporting the roof. One pinpoint blast after another, he used Starkiller to clear out the troops in the tomb fighting the elves guarding the entrance to the Low Road.

However, he appeared to be too late to help Leishan and Zoltana. Both lay unmoving on the floor of the tomb. Rage took him then. The Choj'Ahaw used his anger on a regular basis but rarely did he give into it. Of the two mercenaries, Breuxias powered himself with rage, anger, and other hot-blooded emotions. Yax, on the other hand, prided himself on being a cold, calculated killer.

Yax stepped from behind the column and reached out with the Aethyr. He felt for the connection between him and all beings and then searched for the connection between him and one being in particular, the man who'd ordered the slaughter of his friends. As the officer relayed his final orders, the Wand Bearer seized the strand of energy between them and plucked the man from his feet as if he weighed no more than his sword.

The bewildered man screamed "Fire!" as he flew toward the elf's outstretched hand. Yax caught him in a vice-like grip and sunk his clawed fingers into the man's fat neck. The officer died by his own orders as the crossbowmen's quarrels flew toward their intended target but struck him instead.

Yax smiled as life fled from the man's eyes.

"Fire, huh? You want it, you got it!"

Chanting loudly in the tongue of his people, Yax called upon the Aethyr once more. Still using the dead officer's body as a shield, the enraged Choj'Ahaw jammed the Golden Wedge into his mouth with enough force to punch through the back of the human's skull. A jet of liquid fire shot forth from the end of the bloody wand and engulfed everyone trapped in the colonnade, including the troublesome sorcerer.

Drained by his exertions, Yax dropped the heavier human, along with most of his offensive weaves, and stuck the gory wand into his belt. Bleeding from a number of superficial wounds and suffering from a splitting headache, he staggered over to check on his friends. A ring of dead soldiers served as testament to Leishan's ferocity and martial prowess, but the horseman had succumbed to his numerous wounds during the fighting.

Zoltana fared little better in the rearguard action. Hot tears coursed down Yax's cheeks as he held her close to him. He prayed and petitioned and worked as much magic as he could muster. But it wouldn't be enough. He could tell from her wet, hacking cough, irregular heartbeat, and rate of blood loss. During centuries of fighting on battlefields across and even underneath Faltyr, the Wand Bearer had seen countless people die in myriad ways, so he read death signs as easily as he read the movements of the stars in the sky.

Yax tried to summon a healing weave powerful enough to make her whole, but Zoltana stopped him. "Save your strength," she said, "you'll need it for what's to come."

"But I have to save you," Yax said, tears choking his voice.

"You did. You kept your promise. You freed us. Freed me."

With her last breath, Zoltana was finally free. Yax kissed her on the lips and then cradled her lifeless body against him. He did not register the passage of time, much less the steady stream of prisoners rushing past him. This loss overshadowed any feeling of win in this situation, no matter how many escaped at this point.

"We have to go, brother," Shield Bear said, placing a comforting hand on Yax's shoulder. "Reinforcements are on the way. We have to go. It's now or never."

"Agreed. But these bastards are gonna hound us all the way to the coast. We've gotta find a way to stop them." The voice came from a familiar shadow darkening the massive doorframe of the tomb. Breuxias stood with the bloody dragonslayer laid over one shoulder. He shook his head when he saw the lady's corpse.

Standing with Zoltana in his arms, Yax surveyed the interior of the chamber as well as the row of columns beyond it. He shook his head and said, "The only way to do that would be to collapse the colonnade."

"No problem," Breuxias responded. He unbuckled the magic belt and tossed it to Yax. "I'll need every bit of strength for this feat. If I survive, I want my belt back."

The Brute took a half step and swung the broad blade. The enchanted blade sliced through a granite column supporting the archway leading from the tomb to the colonnade. When the cut piece fell toward him, a column section the size of a trunk on an oak tree, he caught it with one hand and pushed it over effortlessly. The severed pillar shattered into pieces, scattering the floor with debris. The remaining noncombatants escaping through the area stopped and stared in awe at Breuxias's destructive display, a few of them even cheered.

"What're you doing?" Yax exclaimed. "That's madness!"

"No way to collapse it safely from inside. Might bring the whole thing down on top of everyone."

"I'm not sacrificing you too! I can't lose you like I lost Kan."

"Your son made his choice. As am I."

Breuxias cut through the other column supporting the archway. Flashing his customary cocky grin, he said, "Now go! If you see my daughter before I do, tell her I love her very much."

The sound of countless tons of stone shifting above them sounded like thunder rolling through the room. Breuxias backed away from the row of cracking, collapsing columns. The initial collapse rained rock and debris onto the row of stone sarcophagi and nearly buried the lingering elves along with them.

Prompted to action, the Wand Bearer and Shield Bear retreated toward the tunnel leading to the Low Road. Yax glanced back at his friend, but the passage was blocked. He could only murmur a soft prayer and hope to see the Brute again.

ઉ§ઈ၀રુ§ઈ

A cloud of dust arose from the crumbling mass of stone as it buried the entrance to the escape route. Hot breath burning in his lungs, Breuxias paused long enough to admire his handiwork. His muscles ached when he turned to face the mass of troops swarming toward the stables across the floor of the canyon.

Breuxias retrieved a discarded shield, raised it, and charged.

With a final battle cry on their lips, the elves that'd remained behind to screen the prison break joined his suicidal attack on the oncoming horde. The panicked line of troops found themselves trapped between hellfire and opponents who fought like hellcats. But the weight of sheer numbers was on their side. Though Breuxias and his allies inflicted heavy casualties, one by one they fell as assuredly as Damarra at the end of each day.

The flames dancing on the walls and floor of the ruined city illuminated the scene as the sun disappeared over the rim of the canyon. The shadowy forms of the elves fighting alongside him fell one by one under a lethal volley of crossbow bolts fired by the advancing troops. Fresh agonies fueled his rage as several of the projectiles made it past the shield and sunk into his torso.

Breuxias staggered back a few steps but found he had nowhere left to go; he'd cut off his only route of escape to save the elves. Now, a mountain of debris separated him from the best father he'd ever known and the daughter he'd never truly known. He stood all but alone facing the remnants of the detachment of troops assigned to Mok'Drular.

As his sole remaining ally circled high above him, Breuxias saw only one way to come out the victor, even if a pyrrhic victor. And even then, that fiery path could lead straight to the Nine Hells. The sheer number of soldiers charging toward the Brute made the decision for him. Breuxias chopped the dragonslayer downward across his body. Its enchanted blade cut through the bolts protruding from his chest.

Choking back the blood welling up in throat, he cried to the heavens, "*MIZ-GE-ROTH*, do your worst!"

Breuxias swung his sword and cut through the neck of the first soldier to reach him. The flat of the blade caught two more on the backswing and sent them flying. He sliced, chopped, and hacked at the enemy, but scores more surged forward. The Brute could only sever so many spears before one of their tips found a vital organ.

A shadow fell across the firelight on the far wall of the canyon, plunging Mok'Drular into near darkness. Spared the vicissitudes of the crossbowmen, Breuxias fought for his life with renewed vigor, even as Death's winged steed came for him out of the growing night. When the light at the end of the tunnel appeared to him, it was the fiery breath of a dragon once again.

At first, Mizgeroth's fire hit him like a warm embrace. It enveloped the Brute and the mass of bodies pinning him against the collapsed colonnade. But as the flaming soldiers writhed against him in their anguished final moments, the feeling of peace and purification turned to hell and heartache. Fear flooded him as he realized that something had gone terribly wrong.

Before his eyes boiled in their sockets, Breuxias turned his head in time to see the spear tip embedded in his wrist. The dragonslayer slipped from his grasp as he slipped into the grasp of Death Herself.

He died being unable to distinguish his own screams from those of the dying men of Oparre. Though he had no eyes, he could see as Eresh reached out for him through the dragon's flames. If her black eyes judged him, the Brute could not tell, nor did he care. He felt safe. He felt at peace. And he would feel at home in the welcoming arms of his mother.

The ebony goddess floated before his mind's eye, a dark shadow in a sea of flame. She reached toward him with outstretched arms, the mother who'd called to him often from the land of dreams, a face without a name until now. Eresh, Lady Death, came to guide her swarthy son home to the land beyond the Veil.

What Hell would he go to? Did he deserve the rewards of Elysium, purification in Erinya, or punishment in Tartarus? Would he see his father there? Or did his father still wander the land of the living?

Land of the living, Breuxias lamented. *Dead for a span of moments and already talking like one of them.* Had he eyes he would have wept. Instead, he rose from his charred remains and into the waiting arms of his otherworldly mother.

ᨀ

With the storied Blue Macaw leading them, elf after ragged elf emerged from a cyclopean portal cut into the cliffside above a rocky beach on the coast of the Pelican Gulf. Still garbed in the robes of a slave, Yax ascended from the dark corridors of the Low Road into the light of day. He cradled Zoltana's corpse close to him, like he had once ferried his wife to her pyre.

The fugitives from Mok'Drular gathered along the stepped stone highway, built by ogres in a previous cycle of ages to aid overland travel along the rugged coastline. While they rested, Yax prepared the elven woman's body for her final resting place. He laid her body atop a low stone bench placed along the roadside for weary travelers.

Yax whispered soothing words over Zoltana, prayers in the dialect of the Priests of Kümatz, the sacred keepers of time and recorders of births and deaths. As prisoners crowded around him, the former monk became aware that his private eulogy would not suffice. He climbed on top of the bench, stood over her body, and addressed the assembly.

"For those who do not know me or have not heard of me, I am the Blue Macaw. Lord Chahak was my friend, my mentor. Though we have lost hundreds of good men and women today, we have time to eulogize but one. I only knew Lady Zoltana for a short time, but I held her close to my heart. She seemed a kindred spirit, an elf willing to fight against tyranny and oppression wherever she found it. And she was willing to die so that you could live to fight another day.

"So let today be a lesson to you, my new friends. This is just the beginning of your fight. If you follow me on the long road to victory, the worst the enemy can do is to kill you and free you from this place, from this Eternal War. If you continue to run, you will be chased to the ends of this world and into the gates of the Nine Hells.

"The choice is yours. This valiant Ranger of the North chose to stand and confront the evil men of Oparre, and I stand with her even now. To the end or our end."

Shield Bear shouted, "To the end or our end!" The rest of the elves repeated it and then chanted the impromptu battle cry.

Yax looked down at Zoltana. He felt powerless to do anything now but send her on her journey. Though he could heal many injuries, he had not been able to save her. She'd suffered too much blood loss before he'd reached her.

If only he possessed the power to return her soul to her body. But he didn't. And likely never would. Though a powerful necromancer in his own right, Yax realized the power to raise the dead tended to be limited to soulless animated corpses. The power of true resurrection was the rarest, greatest, and most coveted among necromancers.

Summoning the Aethyreal flames once more, the exhausted Wand Bearer coaxed them to engulf the elven woman's form. Aethyr fire poured from his hands until he was satisfied that she'd burn to ash.

Zoltana's fiery aurora burning atop a slab of stone mirrored Rayne's passing too much for Yax's comfort, so he averted his eyes. Instead of the pyre, he focused on the countless ships traversing the blue-green waters of the Pelican. Though he couldn't locate the *Seadragon*, he felt its unique energies swirling out there on the horizon. And he knew that they would find them.

As her final act, Zoltana had ensured it by lighting their way.

Chapter 31

Sir Frederick examined the chest that sat on the desk in Marduk's cabin. Covered in glyphs, it had been cast by an expert metalworker. Though he could not read them, he wagered they were magical in nature. Behind him, the disfigured mage lay on the narrow bunk. The majority of Marduk's body had been encased in gauzy cotton bandages, giving him the appearance of an Ireti mummy. The *Regal*'s chirurgeon worked with precision and care to change the dressing wrapped around the injured man's head without causing his patient too much discomfort.

Frederick's morbid curiosity got the better of him and he leaned over the edge of the bed. He stared at the gruesome visage of the mage. The grizzled knight had seen worse but rarely on a man who'd lived. The skin on Marduk's face had largely been burned away, revealing the musculature beneath the missing flesh. What remained was blistered and blackened from the intense heat of the figurehead's attack. One eye had turned a sickly gray in its socket. All that remained of his left ear was a blackened hole on the side of his head.

"Can you speak now?" Frederick asked.

Marduk opened his mouth causing painful creases to develop at the corners of his mouth. "How long before we reach Kingsport?" The mage struggled, his voice raspy and strained.

"Moons to go yet," the knight responded. His eyes lingered on the mage's ruined face as the healer removed the last piece of cloth. Frederick hid his disgust at the grisly sight as the healer gently rubbed a sulfurous smelling salve on the exposed skin. Marduk winced in pain from the chirurgeon's touch. Pieces of charred flesh flaked off in the process, causing the knight to grimace.

"I'll ensure King Orson knows you saved the *Regal* and its crew," Frederick said. "I don't know where that ship came from, but we'd be burnt to the waterline had you not made such a sacrifice. I hate to say it, but you have my gratitude. I only wish I could have repaid you by skewering that villain Kaladimus Dor."

"We have the chest. We'll get another chance to put Dor's head on a pike," Marduk forced between coughs. "Its contents will draw him like a moth to a flame," he added, his laugh accompanied by painful sounding coughs.

"What do you know of that ship, the one that attacked us?" Frederick queried.

Marduk coughed again and took a drink of greenish yellow liquid offered to him by the healer. "I know it is a powerful ship, I only know of its legend, but I didn't think it still existed," he said, speaking easier this time.

"Where did it come from and how did Dor come to have it?"

"A long time ago, a secret council of the Protectorate Mages met and elected to construct an experimental Aethyr ship. They made this Hallowed Vessel so powerful it could take on an armada of warships by itself," Marduk said between labored breaths.

Frederick waited until the healer had helped the burnt shell of a man swallow another sip drink of the alchemical fluid.

Marduk laid his head back on his pillow and continued, "It was not designed to be a warship, though it had the capability. It was designed to be an exploratory ship, to sail the seas and skies of Faltyr. The High Council heard of its powers and decided to scrap the ship before it fell into the wrong hands."

"It didn't look scrapped to me, it appeared to be intact and quite functional," Frederick noted.

"Aye, it may look complete, but it can't be," Marduk replied. "Had it been, we would be at the bottom of the sea regardless of the protection weaves I summoned. The magical parts were removed and scattered throughout the world. How Dor came to be in possession of it is beyond me."

Marduk closed his eyes as the chirurgeon coated the burns on his face with a brownish salve. Though Frederick had more questions, he allowed the man to continue his ministrations. The healer removed a fresh set of bandages from his bag and then rewrapped the mage's head. The aged healer snapped shut his black bag and turned his attention to the looming Knight of Oparre. The chirurgeon said, "His wounds are more severe than I first thought. Perhaps you can continue your line of questioning some other time. Right now he needs rest."

"I'll make them quick then," Frederick responded. He didn't intend on leaving Marduk's cabin without answers regarding the chest. "We'll be discussing a state secret, so I suggest you leave before I remove your tongue to ensure that what you've heard here is kept safe."

The old man's eyes widened at the knight's threat. The King's Executioner was known to be a man of his word, so the healer relented. Averting his gaze, the chirurgeon stepped past Sir Frederick and exited the room without further commentary. The knight folded his arms behind him to avoid the temptation to touch the chest. He crouched before the damaged item. He wondered what had caused such damage to its lid.

"What's in this that's so important?" Frederick asked.

Marduk said, "It holds the fate of all Faltyr inside. It also contains death and destruction for all who would see it destroyed."

"Explain," Frederick demanded. "No more secrets."

"That chest holds the key to mankind's victory over the elves. It will grant your king tremendous power, so much that he could claim Faltyr as his own if used properly. A powerful magic resides inside, more powerful than me or that damned Dor, or any single mage for that matter, could ever hope to control."

"And what does it have to do with Shy'elle?"

"Forget about the Queen of Silent Brook," the mage said. "We have the real prize. And fear not, my blueblood-loving comrade, there will be a host of elven whores paraded before you once we reach Castle Grymsburg with the chest."

Marduk tried to laugh but succumbed to a coughing fit instead. The knight stood by as the mage suffered through the agony. The simplest remedy Frederick knew for his pain involved a sharp blade drawn across an exposed neck. At this point, however, that would be a kindness.

When the burned man spoke again, he explained, "It's not her that we need anyway. It is her child. But if it cannot be procured, any half-breed babe can be found before the stars have aligned into their proper sequence. Time is yet on our side."

"What would you do with this child?" Frederick asked. "What foul plot would involve the infant heir to the throne of two nations?"

"Do I detect a hint of chivalry, Frederick? Compassion can be a weakness."

Frederick leaned over the mangled mage and stared directly into his eyes. He saw the fervent gleam common in fanatics and fools. The knight saw something else there too. Fear. It made him smile.

Sir Frederick stated, "No harm will come to the queen or her child, I can promise you that."

"Your loyalty is to your king who is allied with my master. So you make empty promises," Marduk said but didn't sound convinced.

Frustration and anger threatened to overwhelm the knight's good sense once more. The damnable Protectorate Mage frustrated him, at least as much as the fugitive Kaladimus Dor, if not more. Sir Frederick walked over to the porthole and let the soothing view of the open ocean wash away his murderous thoughts. As he watched the rising and falling of the sea, he listened to the labored breathing of the spell weaver.

I could end Marduk's life and no one would be the wiser.

But the knight did not like secrets; in fact, he abhorred them. He considered those who dealt in deception and intrigues to be as vile as any villain. Frederick preferred a cut-and-dry approach which made him an ideal executioner but a lousy courtier. He swallowed his hatred for the odious mage and forced his hand from his sword hilt. He decided a tactical withdrawal would be best, before he did something he'd regret.

Before taking his leave, Sir Frederick said, "I'll take my leave of you, for now. The best of my personal guard are keeping watch at your door. After we reach Kingsport, a royal transport will carry us up the river to Grymsburg. Your precious chest will be safe once it's inside the walls of the castle. Whatever it contains, whatever secrets you may be hiding, had better be worth it in the end."

"Don't worry. It will be. I can promise you that much."

As the Knight of the Oparre reached for the door handle, he said, "I've lost a lot of men for this paltry prize. Good men, in some cases, and I'm not convinced they didn't die in vain. That displeases me.

Your answers displease me further. Perhaps King Orson will have better answers for me. If not, I'll find someone who does."

"Perhaps when the time is right," Marduk quipped, "the gods themselves will enlighten you as to the true nature of our affairs."

Frederick's posture stiffened at the wizard's response. Instead of turning and slitting the burned man's throat, the dutiful knight turned the door knob and stepped into the hallway.

Two guards saluted and then moved aside to let him pass.

Shaking with rage, the troubled knight emerged onto the deck of the *Regal*. Damarra sank into the waters on the western horizon, taking the day with her. As her amber light faded, Frederick meditated on what had become of his life and his homeland. And then he did something that he hadn't done in a long time. He prayed. One way or the other, he would have his answers. Even if required seeking them from Mother Sun.

ଔଷ୍ଠଔଷ୍ଠ

The *Seadragon* patrolled the western coast of the Pelican Gulf, its crew searching the rocky coastline. For days now, her captain, Kaladimus Dor, had chased any tendril of smoke or sign of fire in hopes of locating the party that had set out for Mok'Drular. He would search for weeks or months more if that's what it took to find them or, at the very least, word of their fates. For once, time had become their ally. The chest might have fallen into the hands of the Proleus Faction and the smiling devils behind the reformations that had so corrupted the modern Churches of the Holy Trinitas, but Caleb and Braigen had taken precautions should such an event arise.

The object inside could not be moved without the specially constructed container to shield anyone in close proximity from its corrupting energies. And the chest itself had been enchanted to prevent it being teleported, levitated, or moved through other magical means. It would be months before the strongbox and its sinister contents reached Castle Grymsburg. All was not yet lost.

If Dor could recover his friends and gain thousands of elven allies with a grudge against the crown of Oparre in the process, he might be able to leverage a mission that would stab at the heart of the upstart kingdom, perhaps even cut the heads from the serpents behind its throne. If he could catch Proleus away from his vast resources in Moor'Dru, the young mage might very well kill or capture the usurper.

A strike at Castle Grymsburg would be an ambitious gambit but not an impossible one with the Hallowed Vessel at his command. For now, Dor had to focus on the task at hand: finding his friends. The flotilla of ships grew as they sailed north toward the coast of Ror and word of their mission spread to vessels far and wide. Either the elves of Faltyr had more allies than they would have ever believed possible or Oparre had made that many enemies with its Blood War. Regardless of their motivations, dozens of captains had postponed their business to search for any sign of elven refugees on the coast.

Another day passed before the keen eyes of a fisherman's son spotted smoke, spiraling upward toward the heavens, on the steep slopes that formed the eastern terminus of the Meshkenet Mountains. Judging by the number of individuals reported by the fishing trawler, the venture at Mok'Drular had been a success. But one could not tell by the look of the ragged creatures Dor spotted through the spyglass.

Hundreds and hundreds of half-starved elves, gnomes, and assorted fae filtered down from the slopes and cliffs to the narrow rocky beach. The *Seadragon* and scores of other watercraft sent launches or rowed into position to assist the fugitives in the last leg of their escape. Dor observed few dry eyes among the crews and families aboard the boats that assisted in the rescue operation. Strangers welcomed strangers with open arms, baskets of food from their ships' stores, and casks of ale, wine, or water.

What the errant Mage of Moor'Dru witnessed warmed his heart and moistened his cheeks. He realized that hope, much like the Blood War, had not been lost. If they thwarted the machinations of a dark god and won the war in the process, Dor knew it would be this day of mercy and fraternity that ensured it, a day when peoples sailing under countless flags banded together to save those whose banner had been burned along with their tree cities and sacred groves.

Tameri joined Dor at the port railing of the *Seadragon*. As the launches returned, he watched expectantly for any sign of his fellow guildsmen. Among the humans, he failed to spy the bald, brown pate of the Brute or the almond eyes and yellow skin of the rider of the Säj.

She asked, "Any sign of my father yet?"

Dor lowered the spyglass and shook his head. When he turned to her, he realized that they stood less than a pace apart. He tried to reassure her with a smile, but he faltered as he stared into the big brown eyes of the Savior of Istara. The mage saw so much pain and loss there already. She had saved her city but lost so much in the process.

Could Tameri deal with losing her father? Would I be able to help her through it if she does? Would she even want my help?

He tested the waters by slipping a free hand into hers. She squeezed it and smiled. This time he had no problem smiling at Tameri. Damarra dipped toward the wall of rocky slopes lining the western bank of the gulf before the last of the *Seadragon*'s launches returned. Though he did not spy any of the human guildsmen, Dor found a familiar face, the devil in the flesh likely responsible for liberating the poor souls at Mok'Drular.

Yax'Kaqix stood in the bow of the boat with one foot propped on its starboard side. He wore his customary armor below the remnants of a tattered robe. Dor lowered the spyglass once he noticed that his friend had tears on his cheeks. Obviously, Yax mourned someone special. Dor wondered who.

The Wand Bearer had barely cleared the railing of the *Seadragon* when Tameri asked, "My father? Is he on one of the other launches?"

Lowering his head, Yax held out Breuxias's belt, the Brute's prized possession. Tameri gripped Dor's hand tighter as she glared at the elf. Her lips trembled as tears filled her inky orbs. The Wand Bearer refused to meet her gaze but looked up when asked a similar question by a familiar voice.

Lady Shy'elle, the Queen of Tor'Binel, waited at the top of the stairs. She cradled her newborn child, the rightful heir to the Kingdom of Oparre and the Silent Brook. When Yax laid eyes upon the mirror image of the dead ranger, he wept fresh tears. They served as his response to the sister he had been able to save, the same elven queen saved by the slain knight to whom he'd made a promise. Fate was indeed a bitch, at least to Yax.

Before Dor could process the loss of Zoltana and his friends, Macz cried, "There on the horizon. It's a dragon!"

Cries of "Dragon" split the morose stillness of the scene as men and women on the deck of the *Seadragon* sprang into action. Its captain raised the spyglass to his eye and observed the red wyrm glide over the tops of the mountains toward the sea, toward their position.

"Let me see," Yax commanded as he snatched the glass away. The Wand Bearer peered into the distance for several moments before returning the telescope to the flabbergasted magician.

Returning the spyglass, Yax said, "Pray this isn't trouble. For now, signal any armed craft in this ragtag armada to stand down. If anyone attacks that dragon, he'll burn them to the waterline."

"If we don't attack," Dor replied, "we'll be a floating feast."

"Trust me," the elf said, "Mizgeroth may not be our friend, but he is not our enemy yet. Let's try to keep it that way."

The horned red dragon circled the flotilla before approaching the Hallowed Vessel. Smoke and fire steamed from its mouth and nostrils, partially obscuring the wyrm from view. Despite the smokescreen, Dor saw that it carried something in its claws, a bundle of some sort.

As he descended toward the deck of the *Seadragon*, Mizgeroth disappeared from view for a brief moment. When he emerged from the cloud of smoke, the dragon had transformed into an angelic being. Red scaly wings protruded from the back of a tall, pale humanoid. He clutched the sizeable hide-bound bundle to him as if it contained precious cargo. By the time he landed on the ship, he appeared human.

Dor had never stood this close to a dragon before, much less one who appeared the spitting image of Kobin Firehair, the long dead Gre conqueror responsible for sacking both the Baax and Ireti Empires. The mage recalled the detailed busts of Kobin and other barbarian kings of Ny located in the Hall of History back home in Myth.

Yax broke the silence when he said, "Breuxias?"

Mizgeroth nodded and then kneeled before them. He laid the bundle containing the remains of the fallen warrior on the deck.

"I brought him back to you, as you did for my father."

Yax wiped a tear from his eye and said, "His remains belong to his family, to his daughter." The elf squeezed Tameri's shoulder.

Rising to his feet, the transformed dragon said, "Your father died as he lived, a hero. Without his sacrifice, none of this would be possible. Now, the elves are free and the men at Mok'Drular are dead. I'm sorry that Breuxias ended up as one of them. It wasn't my choice."

Dor and Yax exchanged quizzical glances.

Tameri knelt beside the bundle containing her father and asked, "Choice? What do you mean 'choice'?"

As she unwrapped layers of hide borrowed from army tents, the dragon explained, "Between the collapsed corridor at his back and the press of soldiers rushing at him. The men of Oparre had your father trapped in a killing box, but I had them. So he told me to do it, to bathe them all in fire. We both thought he'd be safe. He had the dragonslayer, but it slipped from his grasp in the final melee. When the flames cleared, I realized what had happened. But it was too late."

As the wrap came away from the Brute's face, charred skin went with it. Though Dor gagged at the sight of the eyeless face of his friend, Tameri stared unblinking and unmoving. He thought she might be catatonic until she leaned down and kissed Breuxias's lipless mouth. She hummed an alien tune as she exposed the rest of her father's badly burned body to the spectators on deck. He lay with his hands folded across his broad chest. The dragonslayer in his grip gleamed brightly.

Tameri stared at her reflection in the blade.

"So," she said, "You're the one who killed my father."

"Believe me," Mizgeroth replied, "if I could give my life to save a hero such as this, I would do it in a heartbeat."

Running her fingers along the handle of the oversized sword, she said, "Pretty words but do you mean them?"

"I do," the dragon answered.

"Then what if I told you," Tameri said, "it's never too late."

Dor realized what she intended but not why. Why. Such a small word to cause paralysis, but it did in the Protectorate Mage's mind that day. It cost them all greatly, but it cost the dragon his life.

Displaying surprising strength, Tameri drew the dragonslayer and swung it in a skillful arc at the exposed neck of her father's killer. Mizgeroth's head flew from his body and bounced against the railing. The surprised look on the decapitated dragon's face competed with the befuddled expressions on the faces of the crew of the *Seadragon*. Before his body could change shape, she kicked it overboard into the sea.

The dragonslayer hit the deck with a clatter. Tameri cast her black eyes back at the others. She seemed to look through Dor rather than at him. The Savior of Istara raised her voice and a hymn to Eresh she'd only dared hum before now.

Yax grabbed her by the arm, but Tameri shot him a look that forced him to reconsider his rash action. When he released her, she retrieved the dragon's head. She tilted Breuxias's head, until the blood of the dead wyrm ran down his throat. As Dor watched in mute horror, she commanded her father to rise.

And he did.

Chapter 32

Breuxias joined the sea of sparks rising from the conflagration on the canyon floor. From here, Mok'Drular appeared to be bathed in dragon fire. Though he no longer had a nose, he imagined how his corpse smelled as it cooked along with hundreds, if not thousands, of others. After all, he was no stranger to the sickeningly sweet aroma of burning corpses. He had no ears either, but he could not shut out the agonizing screams rising from the depths of the raging inferno. He still felt the fire's heat, but there was no longer any pain. It had been replaced by a sense of growing peace and acceptance at his new state of being.

Perhaps it was the waiting arms of Eresh, his mother, as she floated above the field of the dead and dying. Coupled with her outstretched arms, her understanding smile called him home. Perfect white teeth stood out in sharp contrast to her skin, for it was as dark and shiny as polished obsidian. Her writhing tresses of inky curls cascaded down her bare shoulders, trailing all the way past the neckline of her bone white gown. Death looked like his own daughter, give or take a few decades, for Eresh's face was mature, but ageless.

As she pulled him close, Breuxias, his voice choked with tears, could only murmur, "Mother." He had wandered Faltyr for more than forty winters and never found such comfort in anyone's embrace. He was home.

"Yes, my son."

"Is this the end?"

"No, my sweet child, this is only the beginning."

Through watery eyes, Breuxias watched as countless versions of his blood mother descended on and embraced the drifting souls of those killed at Mok'Drular. Once she had gathered them in her multitude of arms, Lady Death and her myriad incarnations flew north at a speed that would make dragons jealous.

Helpless to do anything but watch the scenery as they passed, Breuxias surveyed the continent of Ny one last time. Like his life, it passed too swiftly to recall everything but the highs and lows. Fraustmauth passed in a wink, but the forest fires in Tor'Binel and the Nargawald lingered too long. Souls of the freshly dead joined them when they crossed this war torn region.

He had not considered himself a part of the Blood War until recently, and though it had cost him his life, he considered his sacrifice worthy. He'd saved those he could and died defending people persecuted by a genocidal tyrant. It was the best any noble-hearted warrior could ask for in this life. Though he had not lived to see the war's end, he hoped Tameri, Yax, and Dor would survive long enough to see peace in their time.

Thoughts of family filled his mind again as they sailed over the jagged peaks and steep, deep river valleys of the Broken Lands, his adopted homeland as a child. Though he could not spot Bak'Dramna at these breakneck speeds, he remembered his time at the ogre city with fondness. His foster family had raised him within their rough-and-tumble culture. He had learned to fight like he would debate, with ferocity and finality.

The blood of gods flowed in his veins, ensuring him from permanent harm during their horseplay. It also guaranteed he could deliver a blow that would clobber a fully grown ogre. To keep him from harming his friends, Breuxias's foster father had forged the belt he'd worn since childhood. It had restricted his strength to ogre power. Now, like his body, the indispensible belt was gone.

Soon enough, the Broken Lands went with it, transitioning to sporadic ice-covered islands dotting the frigid sea north of Ny, far beyond the reaches of Breuxias's earthly travels. The flock of souls thickened as they reached the top of the world, spiraling clockwise, the opposite direction of the monstrous vortex forming in the sea.

Whispering calming words, Eresh hugged him tighter and dove into the eye of the maelstrom. Cold, black seas surrounded him for what seemed like an age, before Death dragged him into one of the rivers of the dead flowing through the heart of the world. Finally, firelight appeared in the blackness, and the subterranean waterway transitioned to one of molten rock. Souls flowed along the river of magma, until it poured into the Underworld through a gilded opening in a wall of volcanic stone. The magma emptied into a lake of fire at the bottom of the cavernous chamber.

Despite the absence of the sun, Breuxias could see, presumably thanks to the flickering firefall. Eresh's Reaper incarnations passed the souls they'd escorted into the arms of spectral Judges. The Judges weighed their litany of sins, crimes, and vices and sorted them for entry into one of the Nine Hells. His mother, however, continued to hold him close.

Death did not release him until they lighted atop a watchtower of a monstrous stone-and-bone castle. The harrowing structure sat atop a spire of rock that rose from the fiery lake. The skeletal faces of countless races decorated the keep's exterior; skulls had been inserted into precisely cut cubbies in the castle's black walls. Its exterior housed a million toothy grins and at least twice as many blazing red eyes. His mother's estate, known in myths and legends as Ereshkegal, ended at the far wall of the chamber, where a geometrical arrangement of nine gates awaited the souls of the dead.

Eresh took a step back to appraise her child; her eyes judged him, but still held love for him. Since she had spent his entire life communicating with him solely through dreams, his eyes weighed her too. Mother and son stared for a time, happy to be reunited, yet hating the circumstances. Breuxias could not help but think that was the way of the world. As they aged, families tended to see less and less of each other, often only at births and funerals, one a joyous occasion and the other tragic. Then why wasn't he sad? He regretted many things in life and missed the years he would not have with Tameri, Yax, or even Dor for that matter, but he was filled with elation at reuniting with his mother.

Behind her, never-ending streams of sorted souls entered the hellgates, presumably never to be seen again. The spray of colors as the souls were processed reminded him of the unnatural aurora over the Sands of Sorrow, likely the last place he'd see Tameri, until she passed into the Underworld. As her father, he hoped their reunion would come later rather than sooner. When Breuxias did speak, he asked about Tameri's fate, not his own, for he thought his story had been written, all save his eulogy.

"What are your intentions toward my daughter?"

"Always blunt as a hammer," Eresh replied, with a sly grin, "and about as sharp. So unlike your father in that regard."

"I wouldn't know. Like you, he abandoned me to the wilds of Faltyr."

"I see you're every bit as dramatic as your father."

"Stop trying to distract me. I want the truth. You owe me that much!"

"Owe you? I owe you nothing! Other than a reaping and fair, balanced judgment upon your death. Who do you think you are?"

"I thought I was your son. But I see I mean as little to you as I did my father. Can we just get on with this? Banish me to whatever hell you will; I'll suffer it as I've suffered life."

His mother laughed then. It was a haunting sound that welled from inside her. The voices of countless souls chuckled, cackled, and crowed. Had Breuxias skin, it would have crawled. Her eyes held him in their gaze; though dark as a starless night in the blackest hell, they were not cold. He remembered the familiar warmth of her embrace. It was then he realized which parent was responsible for his stubborn defensiveness and gallows humor.

"I don't want to fight. I have fought all my life. I have no desire to start my death on the same sorry note. Especially with my own mother."

"The wise fool knows to end on a high note. Your fiery last stand at Mok'Drular was an epic one. Bards will sing of it for ages to come, if there are ages to come."

"Is that your way of paying me a compliment?"

"I am the first to admit that my parenting skills need work."

Breuxias could not help but laugh then. "Makes two of us. Looks like I might have taken more after you than you think."

Eresh stepped toward him then; a pearly smile fixed on her face once more. The Goddess looked wilder and older up-close. Stress lines around her eyes and mouth revealed a being that spent as much time worrying as reaping, as much time lamenting past mistakes as living to fulfill her divine mandate. Smiling did not come natural to her, which told Breuxias that Eresh took her job seriously enough to feel compassion for those she reaped.

But does this smirking she-devil have sympathy for the living?

"Yes, my son." Eresh said, answering his unspoken question with another question. "Why do you think I have aged so much during these troubling times? I worry about all those poor souls, living and suffering through painful, ultimately pointless physical existences. I worry about those I love even more. I worried about you, and my granddaughter, just as I worried for your father before he joined me in Ereshkegal."

"My father! He's here?"

"Yes, my child. Why do you think he never contacted you? It was not his choice. The constant intrigues of the Blood War, and his untimely murder by those who initiated it, took that opportunity from him. The greatest diviner of his age, and when confronted with the certainty of his own death, did he shirk his duty? Betray his nature? No. Like father, like son, he fought until his fiery end at the hands of agents of Darconius, the people who started the Blood War, the same people who have my book."

"Greatest diviner of his age? Surely you do not speak of Salaac the Seducer."

"I do indeed. And I will have you know the man lives up to his reputation. Even without a physical body, he still has the passion and drive of a school boy. Complete with the raging hormones."

Had she not been the color of coal, Breuxias believed his mother would have blushed when describing his father. He could not help but grin at seeing Death smile like a smitten maiden, but his joy did not last. Though he had no brain, his mind ached when he considered his father's true identity and its implications.

Salaac had been the head of the Council of Three, the highest ruling body in Moor'Dru, before being murdered by the Proleus Faction during its recent coup. Breuxias had been on his way to Moor'Dru to pursue a lead about the identity of his birth father. Had he not encountered Kaladimus Dor, while Dor was returning from a mission for Salaac, Breuxias would have made it to Moor'Dru in time to ask the wrong questions about the wrong man. Yax and he would have likely been imprisoned or worse, so Dor had saved them inadvertently when he'd sunk the *Nightsfall*.

The Master of Disaster's fate had become entangled with his own from that day until now. He was dead, and Dor had lost the book. Did that mean Dor was dead too? Had Tameri died alongside him? And what did that mean for the fate of Faltyr, its living and its dead?

Breuxias took a handful of reflexive breaths before he realized its futility. The dead experienced fear and even anxiety, but had little need of the histrionic mannerisms of the living. He found some measure of peace in this epiphany. But newfound terror clawed at his essence. Powerless to divine the answer to these questions, much less affect the fates of his friends and loved ones, he almost drowned in the wave of sorrow that washed over him. Instead, his inner fire reignited like a phoenix rising from its own conflagrant demise.

Anger and then rage fortified him against becoming one of the dispassionate dead or mournful spirits he had sent howling back to the Underworld on more than one occasion. He would not become some wandering shade, seeking to evade Death's judgment. He rooted himself there in Ereshkegal, his mother's kingdom where she ruled over the Nine.

Forcing himself forward, the son approached his mother, his reaper. To say that his feelings toward her were conflicted would be an epic understatement. Like all abandoned children, he felt entitled to an explanation, if nothing else. He met her midnight gaze once more, but his anger faltered like a moth faced with an extinguished flame. He saw so much of himself reflected there. He could no more deny his mother than he could his own existence. And he could not fault her for failings they shared.

Breuxias embraced his mother. He held her tightly, and she returned his hug. This time both wept bittersweet tears. Eresh hummed a soft haunting tune to her son. He recalled it readily, for it was one familiar to him as a child. He would often hum it, usually after waking from a dream about the black-eyed goddess. On a number of occasions, he had hummed it over his sleeping children. Tameri sang it to this day.

"Do not fear for the safety of my granddaughter," Eresh said, whispering soothingly, "I will look after her and the others. They are my chosen after all. Your job is done. You have drawn them together and cemented their bond in blood, your blood, my son."

"But what about the book? What happened to it?"

"Like any piece on the board, it has been moved by one of the players. And though it has moved, it is not yet taken. Only Death can master the true power of the *Liber Inferum*; any fool who tries to do so deserves their fate. Still, it does not stop Darconius from returning in the spring or his minions from trying to resurrect his avatar while the light of the False Sun shines on Faltyr. It has happened every cycle of ages since my book was stolen. Only when returned to my castle in Ereshkegal can that cataclysmic cycle be broken."

"Maybe you could have communicated this better than through riddles and prophecies. Or gotten off your ass and recovered your own damn book!" Breuxias felt his anger rising. He hated that the people of Faltyr suffered because of its gods and their petty feuds. He loathed being powerless to stop it even more. "Beats involving me and my daughter in this foolishness. I highly doubt her story will end with 'happily ever after' if you're involved, Mother. Mine sure in the Nine didn't!"

Adopting one of his tactics, Eresh struck him hard across the mouth. Pain shot through his soul like lightning. It hurt to his core. Huffing and puffing again, Breuxias fought to calm himself. It would do him little good to fly off the handle. He might stand a chance against any other god, but what son stands a chance against the back of his mother's hand.

"Watch your tongue, petulant boy! I will only endure so much disrespect. I may be your mother, but first and foremost, I am a goddess. Like mortals, we must live by certain guidelines or face the consequences. I am as ill-prepared to face my father's wrath as you are to face mine. Believe me. On both accounts. Now, come with me quietly. It is long past time for you to meet your father. We have been watching over you since his rather premature arrival."

Eresh did not wait for his response. She turned and descended the interior staircase of the watchtower. Breuxias had been teleported by magical means before, and its effects on the body were pronounced. Tingling, residual numbness, nausea, and headaches were not uncommon. This instance had been as simple as blinking his eyes. One moment he had been outside in Ereshkegal; the next, he was standing on a winding set of stairs inside his mother's Palace of the Dead.

Life was wondrous, but death might be interesting too.

Following her down the winding stone steps, Breuxias asked, "What was premature about Old Salaac's arrival? He was a damn near two-century-old diviner. Couldn't he forecast his demise?"

"Irony at its finest. The Fates sup on it as you would venison. Your father could foresee the Blood War, forecast the return of Darconius, and even predict the arrival of Kaladimus Dor, that divine fool, but not his own betrayal and murder."

"I can see why the Fates are called the Bitch Gods."

"That they are, my son. Among the worst of my kin."

"So they are children of the All-Father too?"

"No. They are something else. Something smelt from the same cosmic forge, but wholly different."

"I can see there is much for me to learn."

"Indeed, my child, but you have an open lease on time now. Unless your father is wrong again, my chosen fail, and Darconius looses all the dead onto the surface of Faltyr. Then you will roam with the rest. Roam and feed until the domain of the living is as empty as the Nine Hells under the False Sun's reign."

Breuxias touched her ebony shoulder. Eresh paused before turning the knob on the door at the base of the stairs.

"Is that to be the fate of Faltyr? Consumed by the dead?"

Opening the door, his mother said, "Who knows? Like I said, I am Death, not the Fates. If you want to know more about futures and fortunes, I suggest you ask your father."

Eresh ushered her son into a vast library. The room was as tall as the watchtower and deep as the building was tall. The effect of the cylindrical room proved dizzying. Countless books, tomes, and scrolls filled the shelves lining the curved walls. Spirits in countless forms floated from shelf to shelf organizing, replacing, or pulling volumes. Pieces were taken to and from an impressively cluttered desk on an expanse of floor hovering in the room's center. Eresh glided toward the person seated at the desk. Breuxias paused at the edge of the doorframe before taking a tentative step into midair. Empty space proved as solid as anything here, so he eased his way to the floating platform.

Eresh stood beside the chair, but the white-haired man in it still faced away from them both, presumably consumed with his research. She smiled broader, warmer than ever. Perhaps for the first time since his birth, the three of them would share a moment together. Breuxias felt himself become lighter, happier, as a smile crossed his face too.

His mother laid a hand on the high back of the chair. She had no more than nudged it into motion when Breuxias caught fire. The pain he'd experienced at his death assaulted him again. He doubled over, screamed, and clawed at his eyes. By the time Eresh rushed to his aid, her son was gone, pulled back across the borderlands separating the living from the dead.

Chapter 33

Tameri recalled the incantation precisely; even the tune required was familiar to her. She had seen the ritual in the church copy of the *Liber Inferum* she'd discovered in the catacombs under Istara. Her eidetic mind, developed through years of working as both scrivener and scribe, had recorded it in precise detail. While copies did not contain the powers of the complete text, or the trapped essence of Ra'Tallah for that matter, the copy used by the Priests of Eresh included spells of immense power, even ones to raise the dead. But true resurrection, the reunification of animus with organics, was strictly forbidden without Eresh's blessing. Being her granddaughter, Tameri assumed she was entitled to it to revive her slain father, Death's own son.

Assumption is a powerful, often foolish, force in the universe. It has changed people's fates for the better, led them to ruin, and, in some rare cases, transformed whole civilizations. It can be a creative force or destructive, especially in a case where an assumption is dead wrong.

At first, Tameri feared the spell had not worked at all. A strange jolt of energy had jarred her sword arm, forcing her to drop the dragonslayer after its deadly cut. The dragon's blood spattered Breuxias's torso and face, but gave no indication that it had somehow aided in the sanguine ritual.

Until a low, mournful moan escaped from his blistered lips. The burned brute coughed painfully, choking on the remaining blood in his throat. Tameri cradled his head and turned it gently. He tried to spit the sticky fluid onto the ship's deck, but it ran from his lipless mouth. Red-stained teeth stood out in stark contrast against blackened gums and charred jaw muscles.

Though he had no eyes, Breuxias looked toward his daughter and managed one word, "Water."

"Gods be damned, girl," Yax said, leaning over them, "you did it. You actually did it." The elf smiled for the first time since coming aboard with the elven refugees.

Dor rushed to their side, bringing with him a waterskin. He knelt beside Breuxias and trickled water into his parched throat.

"I've--"

"Don't speak, dad," Tameri said. "You're too weak. Yax, there has to be something we can do to help him. I don't know what went wrong; the spell should have restored him completely. I did everything right."

"Except the whole trying to raise the dead thing," Dor whispered. Unamused, Tameri glared at him, and he fell silent.

Breuxias wriggled on the deck of the *Seadragon*. Hellish pain racked his ruined body. Even the salty sea air tortured him. He tried to speak but his well-meaning daughter interrupted him.

"Yax," Tameri shouted, "did you hear me? We have to do something or he'll die from shock like this."

The elf set into motion. He summoned Xotl to his side and conversed with her in sharp, clipped tones, in the Winaq'che dialect. When the midwife shook her head, he gripped her shoulder and whispered to her. After finally nodding, she joined him at Breuxias's side. They placed their open palms over different parts of the burned man, palms that glowed with healing white light as they chanted in the language of the First Elves.

The effects of their Aethyr magic were small at first, but increased in pace. Charred, fused muscles and destroyed skin vanished, replaced by rapidly growing replacements. However, they were limited in the scope of their work. Yax concentrated on regenerating Breuxias's head and neck, while Xotl tried to cleanse and restore his badly damaged lungs and torso.

Tameri ignored the gathering of onlookers, crew members and refugees, but she spotted her uncle Macz standing close, his eyes focused on his former brother-in-law. Breuxias and he had not gotten along when they were younger, but Tameri knew that they'd become friends over the years. Since they had both trained her in sailing and skill-at-arms, she felt like she'd been the focal point for that friendship. Fighting back tears, her uncle smiled and placed a reassuring hand on her shoulder. Strengthened by his support, she forced herself to look back at her father.

Wiping tears from her cheeks, she asked, “How’s that?”

When Breuxias attempted to speak again, Tameri could hear him better, but he still spoke in a raspy whisper. “Better. Some.”

“That’s great, dad. You’re going to be fine. Yax and Xotl will stabilize you, and Caleb will be able to restore you fully.” Turning to Dor, she added, “If we ever get underway, that is.”

Dor tore his gaze from the fire-ravaged form of his friend. When his eyes met Tameri, he calmed visibly. He nodded, handed her the waterskin, and stood to address the crew.

“You heard the lady. Peel your eyes away and put your asses in motion. The quicker we reach Fraustmauth, the more likely we’ll save Breuxias’s life.”

A few crewmembers responded immediately. Most of them, however, were spellbound or in a state of shock at the miraculous, if grisly, magics being worked before their eyes.

Dor wrested their attentions quickly enough. He slammed the smooth end of his gnarled staff onto the deck, and thunder rolled in the distance. The wind responded to the powerful scion and filled the ship’s sails. Ropes and wood creaked and groaned as the *Seadragon* responded to his command faster than its crew.

“If you won’t obey,” Dor said, “we don’t need you. I can do this myself, if I so choose. Get to work or start swimming.”

Not a soul on the ship’s roster failed to respond, and some of the elven and fae refugees pitched in to help. Macz took over grilling the crew in place of their captain. Dor returned to Breuxias’s side and took Tameri’s hand. When their eyes met this time, hers beheld him with something new, respect.

“Never make it. No time. She’ll be here for me soon.” Breuxias spoke easier this time, but the exertion took his breath.

“Who’s coming for him?” Dor asked.

“Mother.” Breuxias practically spat the word. A series of coughs racked his partially restored chest.

“What do you mean?” Dor shouted, sounding flummoxed and agitated. “You’re not in the Underworld anymore. You’re the only soul she summoned. Right, Tameri?”

“Don’t push him.” She cautioned him. “He needs to rest.”

"You don't understand," Yax said. "You're not the sole scion in the world." The elf spoke with considerable effort. Sweat poured down his face, and blue blood dripped from one nostril. He crackled with energy. "Not the only one on this ship either."

"Yax is right," Tameri said. "Father's mother is Death Herself. I'm afraid what he means is Eresh is coming for him. Maybe us too after what I've done."

The color drained from Dor's face. "What do we do?"

Yax said through gritted teeth. "Prepare to die."

As if on cue, the winds shifted, assaulting them from the north. The *Seadragon*'s forward progression slowed to a crawl. The waters around the flotilla became choppy, frothy, and then boiled. Panicked cries arose from every ship around them. Fish, dolphins, sharks, and countless other forms of marine life died agonizing deaths and floated to the roiling surface of the sea. Above them, the skies clouded as if Kaladimus Dor commanded them. But judging by the bewildered expression on his face, the calamitous mage did not steer this storm front. Freezing rain, coin-sized hail, and finally half-frozen birds rained from the sky, prompting those on deck to take cover.

Dor activated the protective Aethyr shield built into the ship's magical countermeasures, but not before he and several others were pelted by hailstones or struck by a dying gull. Yax and Xotl had to disrupt their weaves because of the icy onslaught. Both bled from their gums and noses already, not from being struck by falling objects, but from the energy they'd channeled.

Using his body to shield Tameri and her father, Dor asked, "Would it be too cliché to describe this as 'all Hells breaking loose?' Providing we live through it."

"Probably," Tameri replied. She smiled despite the severity of the situation. Dor had developed a habit of putting a smile on her face, often at the direst of times. It was one of the things she had come to love about him.

"Too late." He tried to smile but faltered. Instead, the mage's expression turned to one of pure terror.

Had she slipped and admitted her fledgling love for him aloud, Tameri wondered. No, as she turned, she realized that it was not love Dor feared. Like most men, it was Death Herself.

Eresh manifested out of the Aethyr mere paces from the burned body of her son. Tameri recognized the ebony woman from dreams and visions, but she had never seen her grandmother in the flesh. Eresh had provided her with the knowledge and power to raise an army of soulless dead to save Istara, but for some reason, she did not approve of Tameri's decision to resurrect her father. If looks could kill, her grandmother's could and would.

Why can't she just let me have my father? She helped me save mother and an entire city of people who'd forgotten her. Why not her own son?

As if reading her thoughts, Eresh clapped her hands and every living person within sight of them--save Tameri, Breuxias, Dor, and Yax--dropped dead. They fell where they stood, like puppets with cut strings. Their souls clung to this world, hovering above their bodies as luminous spheres of energy, akin to will-o-wisps.

"Selfish girl." Eresh said, sounding as disappointed as a grandmother can manage. "Would you continue to deprive me of my son? You who took him for granted from the day you slithered out from between your mother's legs. Breuxias did the best he could as a father, to provide for you, to shelter you; he not only protected you but taught you how to protect yourself. You were too busy criticizing his faults to recognize his splendor, ignoring him for your pathetic storybooks.

"You grew up the son of a demigod, one of the most good-hearted to ever walk the surface of this blighted sphere, but you wasted your entire life too absorbed by fantasies to notice. It wasn't until you woke up to the true nature of reality deep in the heart of my necropolis that you began to appreciate him, much less the gifts I bestowed on you through him. Savior of Istara, some savior you are. Were it not for my help and my blood in your veins, you would have died a slave. Or worse.

"Now, you want to deny me my child. The mother who bore him and then had to give him up, so his father could find a safe place for him in a world full of my enemies, full of foolish men who fear me for their fragile natures, for their ultimate fates. Outside of the realm of dreams, I had not held him since he was weaned from my bosom, until the day he died. And on the eve of our first family gathering, at the moment I was to reunite my son with his father, you abuse the powers you've inherited to steal my child away from me. To bring him here again, where we are doomed to be apart until I am forced to reap him once more!

"Were you not born of my blood and vital to our plans, plans that will alleviate the suffering of so many and slow the tide of souls clogging the gates to the Nine, I would strike you dead right now. Instead, I offer you a deal. One chance to save yourself, your friends, and all the other souls I would reap in my son's place. And I suggest you take it.

"Release my boy to me. Now! Or be responsible for the deaths of everyone here." Eresh's tone broadcasted her offer's finality.

"Listen to her," Breuxias said. Tasking himself further, he added, "I'm not worth the lives of one person. Definitely not so many. Let me go. I love you, Tameri. Will miss you too, but this is not my home anymore. I belong with my mother and Salaac."

The exertion proved too much for him. Spasms of coughing and cramps in the newly regenerated muscle tissues wracked his weakened form. Tameri could see that her father was in agony. Every moment of his life, every breath that he took, would be torture, until Caleb mended him, if the sage could ever do it fully. She could not force him to endure it; nor did she have it in her heart to abet her grandmother's mass murder to keep him here.

Fortunately, the reckless Protectorate Mage bought her the time to hold her father close one last time. Having regained his composure, Dor rose from his dying friend's side and gripped the black staff tightly. When he stepped forward, Eresh backed away a step. Her eyes shifted from her son to Dor's staff.

"Careful, Scion of Taranis," Eresh said. "You don't know the power you hold in your hands, even absent my book."

"Forget the book." Dor said, daring to take another step, repeating their slow dance across the deck. "And forget this staff. Apparently, we both know it can banish otherworldly beings. What I wonder is if Faltyr's gods and goddesses qualify. I also wonder what this staff's original owner has to do with you and Breuxias. What's Salaac's part in this? He's the fool who started all of this mess with the chest. I have the right to know."

"As usual, your clouded mind has as much wrong as you do right, my little thunderbird." Eresh chuckled, halting her slow retreat. Tameri imagined it sounded like a thousand suffocating souls gasping for air. "As you already know, Salaac of Moor'Dru, my son's birth father, is not only perceptive but prophetic and quite persuasive. As a result, we agreed to use each other for a period of time to steer the events at the end of the current cycle of ages. If it works out, if you--Death's Chosen--fail to disappoint, Darconius will shine his unholy light on Faltyr one final time."

"You propose that we usher in the Last Cataclysm. Well, I tell you now, I will have no role in the dead walking this world."

"At last, Yax'Kaqix summons the energy to speak," Eresh said. "Or is it the courage, Old Man, you who fear death more than any of My Chosen. Why? Because you have sent more souls to me than Hungani Fever? Because you fear the Priest of Kümatz are correct, that elves have one incarnation, one chance at life? Nay, I say it is because you have fought me and lost, like my daughter will do, if she chooses to resist me further. The hand does not command the body, not even the Hand of Eresh. Nor do I take orders from My Chosen, like you, Blue Macaw, Servant of the Aethyreal Flame. Even if you fire the pyre, I do the reaping."

"What do you expect from us?" Tameri asked. "Other than my father's soul? If we are to do your bidding, beloved grandmother, he would be more useful to us here than to you. You have waited to be with him this long; surely you can wait a few decades longer. What is a decade to one who is immortal?"

"Save your pitiful charms for the boy mage. They are lost on me, beloved granddaughter," Eresh purred, less like a cat and more like a murderous lioness. "I will be sure to ask you when your soul is roasting in the Nine, awaiting your burgeoning beloved."

With her sardonic, sanguine wit, Tameri was unsure if her grandmother was being sarcastic or not. Either way, she'd broadcasted Tameri's feelings for Dor to the entire crew, the four of them who were still breathing anyway.

"Make no mistake," her grandmother added, "I will have his soul. And I will have my way. Not because I am haughty and prideful. Not because the dead are my domain. I will have my way because it is the only way to recover my book and end the cycle of suffering and unnatural death Darconius and I started so long ago. Though I have never been a willing participant, my would-be usurper and I have played out this game at the end of each cycle of ages, ever since his allies stole my book. Despite cataclysm after cataclysm, my book has yet to be returned. When it finds its way into the wrong hands again, Darconius reappears to try and gain control of this world. Each cycle grows shorter, each cataclysm worse, and each recovery period slower and more incomplete than the last attempt to rebuild a global civilization.

"I am the reaper of many races, but I am no monster. I am as natural as light and shadow, night and day. I do not require dominion over all souls at once, simply at their appointed time, give or take a few extreme cases. Darconius, on the other hand, would unleash every soul in the Nine to consume the living, to create his version of paradise, a realm of the undead, who will serve him for all eternity. So you can either follow the course Salaac and I have charted for you, and in the process possibly save the world, or you can deny your roles as our reluctant champions and watch the world crumble to ruin. Probably for the last time, I fear, now that you've handed my book to the enemy."

"That's my mother, Goddess of Death, Mistress of Guilt Trips," Breuxias laughed, the dry, wry sound broke the tension but felt so bizarre to Tameri, like it would be the last time she heard his laugh. She stared at her dying father, and instead of crying, she laughed too. The look of him trying to grin without lips was gruesome but also comical, like an animated skull chortling at her.

Not everyone was in the mood to laugh, but even Eresh and the half-drained elf smiled. Tameri had never understood why her grandmother's priests had always considered death a moment for rejoicing until now. Seeing her father like this, she knew that he would never be the same, but he would always be the same. Instead of walking by her side as he'd done in the Sands of Sorrow, he would walk alongside his parents for the first time. Her grandmother had been right. She had not appreciated her time with her father, not until it was too late. Now she could not bring herself to rob him of eternity with his father and mother.

"Are you sure you're okay with this," Tameri asked him.

"I'll miss you and your siblings, but it'll be good to be home. Maybe I can finally get some rest."

"If anyone's earned a rest," Yax said, tears flowing from the corners of his wide blue eyes, "it's you, my friend. Fiercest fighting, hardest working human I've ever known."

"Racist." Breuxias replied, laughing again.

"Polygamist."

"Guess neither one of us is perfect," Breuxias reassured him.

"That's why there's Nine Hells," Yax said. "To make sure you end up that way one day. I'm an elf. I get one shot at it. Who knows? If we stop Darconius and his minions, maybe that will start to make up for some of my imperfections."

"Good luck, Old Man."

"Good luck, old friend."

Yax kissed Breuxias on the forehead and started to stand. The brute lashed out with surprising strength and grabbed the elf by an elbow. Drawing him close a final time, he said, "Keep an eye on my daughter. Especially around Calamity's Door here. Hope you hear me too, you damn fool wizard. I don't need eyes to see you eyeing my daughter. Do right by her or leave her be."

"Anything for you," Yax said, gripping his friend's hand.

"Yes, anything," Dor echoed. "You have my word."

Tameri cherished the banter and jocularity among the three friends. She would miss listening to them bicker. Though he would never admit it, she knew Yax would miss it too. She didn't have to wonder about Dor. He embraced them all, hugging them tightly. In the midst of the group embrace, Tameri felt like she was home for the first time since the events in Istara.

And she loved it.

ઉઇ෴ઉઇ

Breuxias was outside of his body before he realized it. Standing beside his mother, he watched as Tameri and the others discovered that he'd gone quietly in their loving arms. Despite their mournful tears and broken hearts, he had never experienced more love, not in half a dozen failed marriages, and not even in the arms of his own mother. He beamed like the sun now shining on the deck of the Hallowed Vessel.

The winds gusted from the south and the ship's sails filled with air, causing its ropes to creak. The familiar noise reminded him of his first trip aboard the *Seadragon.* The waters of the Pelican Gulf grew calm and quiet as his being. The birds recovered, as did the sea life. Humans, elves, and fae alike awoke from the sleep of death to behold an adopted family mourning their fallen patriarch, the Son of Death.

Watching the scene unfold before him, Breuxias slipped one hand into Eresh's. She smiled then, and he could see his mother's love and devotion shining in her inhuman eyes. He could not have been more at peace than if he'd lived longer than any elf, dragon, or god who'd ever set foot on faraway Faltyr.

About the Authors

Jeremy Hicks spent several years as an archaeologist before teaming up with **Barry Hayes**, his long-time friend and co-author, to realize a creative dream to turn their nightmares into fiction. The writing team of Hicks & Hayes created a dark, edgy fantasy environment known as **Faltyr**; wrote a screenplay (***The Cycle of Ages Saga: Finders Keepers***) to introduce it; and then adapted it into this novelization.

As co-owners of **Broke Guys Productions**, they have written three other screenplays, including the script for *Sands of Sorrow*. Jeremy has several short stories in **Dark Oak Press** anthologies, and a ***Tales from Faraway Faltyr*** digital short series in the works with **Pro Se Productions**. Look for it online in Fall/Winter 2015.

This is their second novel.

☙❧

For more information about the Cycle of Ages Saga, check out the official website here: **www.cycleofagessaga.com**

Don't forget where it all started.

Finders Keepers

Book 1 in the Cycle of Ages Saga

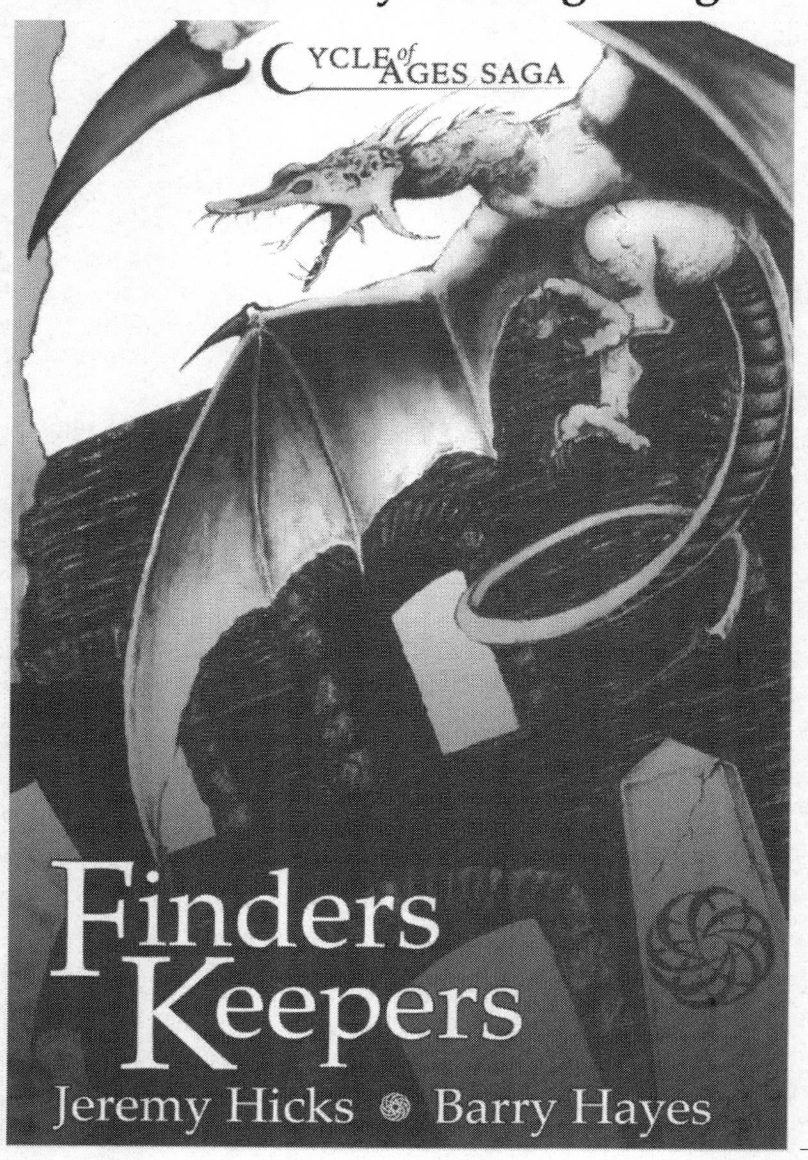

Made in the USA
Charleston, SC
23 October 2015